A DADDY
FOR HER SONS

BY
RAYE MORGAN

Raye Morgan has been a nursery school teacher, a travel agent, a clerk and a business editor, but her best job ever has been writing romances—and fostering romance in her own family at the same time. Current score: two boys married, two more to go. Raye has published more than seventy romance novels and claims to have many more waiting in the wings. She lives in Southern California, with her husband and whichever son happens to be staying at home at the moment.

This is dedicated to Lauri, for everything wonderful
that comes out of her oven!

CHAPTER ONE

A NIGHTMARE. That was what this had to be. She must be dreaming. But what had she expected from a blind date?

Jill Darling was no shy innocent, but her face was blazing. She could feel it. The man was trying to… Ugh, it was just too creepy to even try to name what he was doing. She couldn't really be sure unless she took a look under the table. And that would cause a scene. She couldn't do that. She knew people in this restaurant.

But…was that really his foot sliding up and down her leg?

He was leaning close, talking on and on, his breath hot on her neck. Okay, maybe that was all in the game. But what the heck was that foot doing?

She tried to move away, but she was trapped, huddled right up against the edge of the planter that sat right beside their table, tickling her nose with its palm fronds. They were eating in the restaurant of the nicest hotel in this part of town. It had Irish linen tablecloths, real sterling silverware and a small combo playing for dancers on a tiny dance floor to the side.

She took a long drink from her water glass, then

looked over at him. She tried to smile, but she knew it was wobbly and pretty darn unconvincing if he should happen to actually notice it.

Karl Attkins was his name. Her friend's brother. He was good looking enough, but somehow cold, as though she could have been anyone with an "available female" label stamped on her forehead. Should she ask him about the foot? And maybe warn him not to lose sight of his shoe. It wouldn't be easy to replace that here in this crowded restaurant.

Oh, Lord, he was using his toes now. She was going to have to say something. If she didn't, her nice steak dinner just might come back up. And all that wine she drank, trying to keep busy. This just wasn't cool. She took a deep breath and tried to think of a way to say it without being insulting.

But then he gave her the out she needed.

"Would you like to dance?" he asked, cocking an eyebrow as though he knew she must consider him quite debonair.

Dance. No, not at all. But she steeled herself to the effort. Dancing ought to give him a reason to put his shoe back on, and if so, it would all be worth it.

"Sure," she said breathlessly. "Why not?"

Well, the fact that they were playing a tango at that very moment might have been a reason to sit this one out. But it hardly mattered. At least the man was shod once more. She tried to keep the electric smile painted on her face as he led her to the proper position. And then she glanced at her watch and wondered how much longer she was going to have to endure this torture. She had to put in a good chunk of time or the friends who'd got her into this wouldn't believe she'd really tried.

Oh, Mary Ellen, she groaned silently as Karl pushed her to and fro dramatically across the dancing floor, leaving her to lunge about like a puppet with its strings cut. *I love you dearly, but this is just too high a price to pay for your friendship.*

"But, Jill," all her friends had counseled solemnly, "you've got to do it. You've got to get back into the swim of things. It's been over a year since Brad...well, since you've been alone." The timing had helped make her receptive. Changes were making her feel vulnerable. Her sister was probably moving away, and her younger half-sister had recently died. Loneliness was looming large in her life. "Time is streaking by," another friend lectured. "Don't let it leave you behind. Don't be a coward. Get out there and fight!"

Fight? For what?

"A man, of course," said Mary Ellen. "Once you hit your age, they don't come a dime a dozen any more. You've got competition."

"But, what if I...?"

"No! You can't give up!" her friend Crystal had chimed in. "Your kids need a father figure in the home."

Mary Ellen had fixed her with a steely stare. "And you want to show old Brad, don't you?"

Show old Brad. The need to do just that surged in her. Of course she wanted to show old Brad. Sure. She would date. If he could do it, so could she. Stand back. She was ready for the challenge.

But where would she find someone to date? Mary Ellen knew just the man for her.

"My brother Karl is a real player," she said airily. "He'll get you back into the swing of things in no time. He has so many friends. You'll be dating like crazy before you know it."

Dating. She remembered dating. The way your heart raced as you waited for him to come to the door, the shy pauses, the way your eyes met his and then looked quickly away. Would he kiss you on the doorstep? Were you really going to let him?

Fun!

But that was then. This was a completely different thing, seemingly from a galaxy far, far away. She was older now. She'd been married and she had two kids. She knew how things worked. She could handle it. Or so she thought.

No. This was a nightmare.

At least her dress was pretty, and she didn't get many chances to wear something like this anymore. A sleek shift dress in teal-blue, it was covered with sequins and glistened as she walked, making her feel sexy and pretty and nice. Too bad she was wasting that on a man who spent more time looking at himself in the mirror than she did.

The tango was over. She turned back toward the table in relief, but Karl grabbed her free hand and twirled her around to face him. The band was playing a cha cha. He grinned. "Hey mambo!" he cried out and began to sway. He seemed to consider himself quite the ballroom dancer, even if he couldn't tell one Latin dance from another.

Jill had a decision to make. Would she rather dance, or go back to playing footsie? She wasn't sure she knew how to cha cha. But she knew she didn't want to feel that foot on her leg again.

What the hell.

"Everybody loves to cha-cha-cha," she murmured as she let him twirl her again.

And then she looked up and saw Connor McNair staring at her in horror.

Her blood ran cold. She was still moving, but no one could accuse her of dancing at this point. The music didn't mean a thing.

Connor. Oh, no.

First, it appalled her to think that anyone she knew might see her here like this. But close on that thought came the shock question—was Brad with him?

No. She glanced around quickly and didn't see any sign of her ex-husband at all. Thank heaven for small blessings. Connor must have come to town and was staying here at the hotel—alone. But still, it was Connor, Brad's best friend, the one person most likely to report to him. She could hardly stand it.

He was mouthing something to her. She squinted, trying to make it out. What was he trying to say?

She couldn't tell, but he was coming out onto the dance floor. Why? She looked around, feeling wild, wanting to run. What was he going to do?

"May I cut in?" he asked Karl.

He was polite, but unsmiling, and Karl didn't seem to be in a friendly mood.

"What? No. Go get your own girl," Karl told him, frowning fiercely. And just to prove his point, he grabbed Jill and pulled her close.

She looked over his shoulder at Connor. He offered a safe harbor of sorts, but there was danger there, too. She didn't want to talk to Connor. She didn't want to have anyone close to Brad anywhere near. The pain of Brad's desertion still ached inside her like an open wound and she didn't want anyone from his side of the rift to see her like this—much less talk to her.

So she glared at Connor. Let him know she didn't need him or his rescue. She was doing fine. She was here enjoying herself. Sort of.

She got back to dancing, swaying her hips, making her sequins sparkle, and trying hard to smile at Karl. Let Connor see that she was having the time of her life. Let him take that bit of news back to Brad, if that was what he was after.

"Mambo!" she cried out, echoing Karl. Why the heck not?

Connor gave her a look of disbelief as he stepped back to the sidelines, but he didn't leave. The next dance was a simple two-step, but that meant Karl's arms around her again, and she couldn't disguise the shudder that gave her.

And there was Connor, taking in every nuance. She glowered at him. He was very handsome in his crisp white shirt with the dark slacks that looked tailor-made. But that was beside the point. Didn't he have a table to go to? What gave him the right to stand there and watch her? Biting her lip, she tried to keep him out of her line of vision and blot him out of her head.

But then he was back, right at Karl's elbow again, stopping them in their tracks.

"Excuse me," he said, looking very serious. "Listen, do you have a silver BMW in the parking lot?"

Karl blinked. His eyes narrowed suspiciously, but he couldn't resist the question. "Why, yes I do. What about it?"

Connor's brows came together in a look of sorrow. "I'm afraid your car's on fire."

Karl dropped Jill like a hot potato and whirled to face Connor. "What?" he cried, anguish contorting his face.

Connor was all sympathy. "I think they've called the fire department, but you might want to get out there and…"

No more words were necessary. He was already gone.

Connor took Jill by the arm, looking annoyed when she balked and tried to pull away.

"Come on," he said impatiently. "I know a back way out."

Jill shook her head, not sure what he thought he was doing here. "But…I can't just leave."

Connor looked down at her and suddenly grinned, startling her. She'd forgotten how endearing he could be and she stared up at him. It was like finding a beloved forgotten toy in the attic. Affection for him trembled on the edge of her mood, but she batted it back.

"Why not?" he said. "Do you want to spend the next two hours with the guy?"

She tried to appear stern. She wanted to deny what he was implying. How could she go? What would she say to her friends? What would she tell Mary Ellen?

But in the end, his familiar grin did her in. "I'd rather eat dirt," she admitted, crumbling before him.

"There you go." He led her gently across the dance floor, only hesitating while she scooped up her sparkly little purse. They headed for the exit and he winked at a waiter who was holding the door for them, obviously primed to help with the escape. He paused only long enough to hand the man some folded money and then they were out the door.

"But what about his car?" Jill asked, worrying a bit. She knew the sense of guilt would linger long after the evening was gone. "He loves that car."

"Don't give it a second thought," he advised, steering her toward his own souped-up, twenty-year-old Camaro, a car she remembered from the past, and pulling open the passenger door.

"His car isn't really on fire, is it?" she asked as she plunked down into the leather seat.

"No." He sank into the driver's seat and grinned at her again. "Look, I'll do a lot for an old friend, but setting a guy's car on fire…no, that's a step too far."

She watched him start the engine and turn toward the back exit.

"But you will lie to him about it," she noted.

"Oh, yeah."

She sighed and settled back into the seat. All in all,

at least she didn't have a naked foot exploring her leg at the moment. That alone was worth its weight in gold.

"Rickey's on the Bay?" he asked in the shorthand they both remembered from earlier years.

"Of course," she responded without thinking. That was where everyone always went when the night was still young enough to make the last ferry to the island. She turned and looked at the lights of Seattle in the distance. If only you could go back in time as easily as you could go back to the places where you hung out in your youth.

"I can't believe I'm letting you do this," she said with a sigh.

"I can't believe you needed me to do it."

She laughed. "Touché," she muttered. So much for the great date that was supposed to bring her out of her shell and into the social whirl.

She pulled her cell phone out of her purse and checked it.

"What are you doing?" Connor asked with just a hint of suspicion in his tone.

She glanced up at him and smiled impishly. "Waiting for Karl to call. I've got to explain this to him somehow."

He shuddered. "Is Karl the mambo king?" he asked.

She gave him a baleful look.

"Don't worry. I gave the waiter a little money to tell old Karl what the score was."

She raised an eyebrow. "And just what is the score, pray tell?"

He hesitated, then shrugged. "I told him to tell Karl I

was a made guy from the mob and we didn't take kindly
to outsiders poaching on our women."

"What?"

He looked a little embarrassed. "Yeah, I know. Definitely corny. But it was the best I could think of on the
spur of the moment."

She had to hold back her laughter. He didn't deserve
it.

"I didn't even know you were Italian."

"There are a lot of things you don't know about me."
He gave her a mocking wink. "A lot of things you don't
want to know."

"Obviously."

She frowned, thinking the situation over. "So now
you've single-handedly destroyed my chances of dating
anyone ever again in this town. Thanks a lot."

"I'm just looking out for you, sweetheart."

She rolled her eyes, but she was biting back a grin.

Rickey's was as flamboyant as a fifties retro diner
should be, with bright turquoise upholstery and juke-
boxes at every table. They walked in as though they
ought to see a lot of old friends there, but no one looked
the least bit familiar.

"We're old," he whispered in her ear as he led her
to a booth along the side with windows on the marina.
"Everyone we used to hang out with is gone."

"So why are we still here?" she asked, a bit grumpy
about it. This was where so much of her life had played
out in the old days. And now, the waitresses didn't know
her and the faces all looked unfamiliar.

"Lost souls, searching for the meaning of life," he said, smiling at her across the linoleum-covered table. His smile looked wistful this time, unlike the cheerful grin from before.

"The meaning of life is clear enough," she protested. After all, hadn't everyone been lecturing her on it for months? "Get on with things. Make the world a better place. Face reality and deal with it. Or something along those lines."

He shrugged. "Sounds nice, until you start analyzing definitions. What exactly does 'better' mean? Better for whom? How do you get the whole world involved, anyway?"

She made a face at him. "You always were the great contrarian," she said accusingly. "And now I've let you kidnap me. Someone should call the police."

The waitress, a pretty young girl in a poodle skirt who'd just arrived at their table blanched and took a step backward.

"No, no," Jill told her quickly. "I'm only joking. Please don't take me seriously. Ever."

The waitress blinked rapidly, but risked a step closer in to take their order. She didn't hang around to chat, however.

"You scared her," Connor suggested as she hurried away.

"I scare everyone lately," Jill admitted. "What do you think? Am I too intense? Are my eyes a little wild?"

He looked at her uncertainly, not sure if the truth would be accepted in the spirit he would mean it. His gaze skimmed over her pretty face. She had new lines between the brows, a new hint of worry in her eyes. Her hands were clenched around her water glass, as though she were holding on to a life preserver. Tense was hardly a strong enough word. His heart broke just a little bit. What had happened to his carefree girl?

But that was just it. She wasn't "his," never had been.

He knew she'd been through a lot since Brad had left her. She had a right to a few ragged edges. But when you came right down to it, she was as beautiful as she'd ever been. Her golden hair sprang into curls in an untamed mass all around her head. Her dark eyes were still warm, her lips were still full and sexy. Still gorgeous after all these years.

And looking at her still sent him over the moon. It happened every time. She was like a substance he had to be careful he didn't mess with, knowing it would be too dangerous to overdose.

But he could see a difference in her and silently he swore at himself. Why had he stayed away so long? She probably could have used a friend. She'd lost her young girl sparkle and he regretted it. He loved that sparkle.

But now he frowned, studying her face as though he was worried about what he found there. "How are you doing, Jill?" he asked her quietly. "I mean really. How've you been?"

She sat back and really looked at him for the first time, a quiver of fear in her heart. This was what she really wanted to avoid. Silly banter was so much safer than going for truth.

She studied his handsome face, his crystal-blue eyes sparking diamond-like radiant light from between those inky black eyelashes that seemed too impossibly long. It had been over a year since she'd seen him last and he didn't seem quite so much like a kid living in a frat house anymore.

He'd always been such a contrast to Brad, like a younger brother who didn't want to grow up. Brad was the serious one, the ambitious one, the idea man who had the drive to follow through. Connor was more likely to be trying to make a flight to catch a party in Malibu or volunteering to crew on a sailing trip to Tahiti. Brad was a man you could count on. Connor—not so much.

Only that had turned out to be a lie, hadn't it? It was hard to trust anything much anymore once the man you'd considered your rock had melted away and wasn't there for you anymore.

She closed her eyes for a moment, then gave him a dazzling smile. "I've been great," she said breezily. "Life is good. The twins are healthy and my business is actually starting to make a profit, so we're good."

He didn't believe her. He'd known her too long to accept the changed woman she'd become. She'd always been careful—the responsible sort—but she'd also had a sense of fun, of carefree abandon. Instead, her eyes, her tone, her nervous movements, all displayed a wary tension, as though she was always looking over her shoulder to see what disaster might be gaining on her now.

"So good that you felt it was time to venture out into the dating world again, huh?" he noted, being careful to smile as he said it.

"Why not? I need to move on. I need to…to…" She couldn't remember exactly what the argument was, though she'd heard it enough from her friends lately. Something about broadening her horizons. Something about reigniting her womanly instincts. She looked at Connor as though she might read the words in his eyes, but they just weren't there.

"So who talked you into that fiasco tonight?" he asked her.

She frowned at him. "It was a blind date."

"No kidding. Even *you* wouldn't be nutty enough to go out with that guy voluntarily."

"Even me?" His words stung. What did he think of her, anyway? Her eyes flashed. "Just how nutty am I, Connor?"

He reached out and grabbed her hand, gazing at her earnestly. "Will you stop? Please?"

She glanced back, her bottom lip trembling. Deep breaths. That was what she needed. And no matter what, she wasn't going to cry.

"So where have you been all this time?" she asked, wishing it didn't sound quite so petulant.

"All what time?" he said evasively.

"The year and a half since I last saw you."

Her gaze met his and skittered away again. She knew he was thinking about exactly what she was thinking about—that last time had been the day Brad left her. Neither one of them wanted to remember that day, much less talk about it. She grimaced and played with her spoon. The waitress brought their order so it was a moment or two before they spoke again.

"So you said your business is doing okay?" he noted as he spread his napkin on his lap.

"Yes." She stared down at the small dish of ice cream she'd ordered and realized she wasn't going to be able to eat any of it. Her throat felt raw and tight. Too bad. It looked creamy and delicious.

He nodded, reaching for a fork. It was pretty clear he wasn't going to have any problem at all. "What business?"

She blinked at him. "Didn't you know? Didn't Brad tell you?"

He shook his head and avoided saying anything about Brad.

She waited a moment, then sighed. "Okay. When Brad left, he took the electronics business we had developed together. And told me I might as well go out and get a job once the babies were born."

He cringed. That was enough to set your teeth on edge, no matter who you were.

She met his gaze with a touch of defiance in her own. "But I gave birth to two little boys and looked at them and knew there was no way I was handing them over to someone else to raise for me. So I racked my brain, trying to find something I could do at home and still take care of them."

He nodded. That seemed the resourceful thing to do. Good for her. "So what did you decide on?"

She shrugged. "The only thing I was ever really good at. I started a Bundt Cake Bakery."

He nodded, waiting. There had to be more. Who could make a living baking Bundt cakes? "And?"

"And that's what I'm doing."

"Oh." He frowned, puzzled. "Great."

"It *is* great," she said defensively. She could hear the skepticism in his voice. "It was touch and go for a long time, but now I think I'm finally hitting my stride."

He nodded again, wishing he could rustle up some enthusiasm, but failing on all fronts. "Okay."

The product Jill and Brad had developed together had been a bit different from baked goods and he was having a hard time understanding the connection. Jill had done the bookkeeping and the marketing for the business. Brad had been the electronic genius. And Connor had done some work with them, too. They'd been successful from the first.

With that kind of background, he couldn't imagine how the profits from cakes could compare to what they'd made on the GPS device for hikers to be used as a map App. It had been new and fresh and sold very well. He wasn't sure what he could say.

He looked up across the restaurant, caught sight of someone coming in the door and he sighed. "You know how legend has it that everyone stops in at Rickey's on a Saturday night?"

Her eyes widened warily. "Sure."

"I guess it's true." He made a gesture with his head. "Look who just walked in. Mr. Mambo himself."

She gasped and whirled in her seat. Sure enough, there was Karl starting in their direction. He was coming through the restaurant as though he thought he owned the place, giving all the girls the eye. He caught sight of her and his eyes lit up.

Her heart fell. "Oh, no!"

CHAPTER TWO

AND THEN, KARL'S jaunty gaze fell on Connor and he stopped dead, visibly paling. Shaking his head, he raised his hands and he seemed to be muttering, "no, no," over and over again, as though to tell Connor he really didn't mean it. Turning on his heel, he left so quickly, Jill could almost believe she'd been imagining things.

"Wow." She turned back slowly and looked at Connor accusingly. "I guess he believed your cockeyed story." She put a hand to her forehead as though tragedy had struck. "Once he spreads the word, my dating days are done."

"Good," Connor said, beginning to attack his huge piece of cherry pie à la mode. "No point wasting your time on losers like that."

She made a face and leaned toward him sadly. "Are they all like that? Is it really hopeless?"

"Yes." He smiled at her. "Erase all thoughts of other men. I'm here. You don't need anybody else."

"Right." She rolled her eyes, knowing he was teasing. "You'd think I would have learned my lesson with Brad, wouldn't you?"

There was a catch in her voice as she said it. He looked up quickly and she knew he was afraid she might cry. But she didn't cry about that anymore. She was all cried out long ago on that subject.

Did he remember what a fool she'd been? How even with all the evidence piling up in her daily life, she'd never seen it coming. At the time she was almost eight months pregnant with the twins and having a hard time even walking, much less with thinking straight. And Connor had come to tell her that Brad was leaving her.

Brad had sent him, of course. The jerk couldn't even manage to face her and tell her himself.

That made her think twice. Here was Connor, back again. What was Brad afraid to tell her now?

She watched him, frowning, studying his blue eyes. Did she really want to know? All those months, all the heartbreak. Still, if it was something she needed to deal with, better get it over with. She took a deep breath and tried to sound strong and cool.

"So what does he want this time?"

Connor's head jerked back as though what she was asking was out of line. He waved his fork at her. "Do you think we could first go through some of the niceties our society has set up for situations like this?" he asked her.

She searched his face to see if he was mocking her, but he really wasn't. He was just uncomfortable.

"How about, 'How have you been?' or 'What have you been up to lately?' Why not give me some of the details of your life these days. Do we have to jump right into contentious things so quickly?"

So it wasn't good. She should have known. "You're the messenger, not me."

His handsome face winced. It almost seemed as though this pained him more than it was going to pain her. Fat chance.

"We're friends, aren't we?" he asked her.

Were they? She used to think so. "Sure. We always have been."

"So…"

He looked relieved, as though that made it all okay. But it wasn't okay. Whatever it was, it was going to hurt. She knew that instinctively. She leaned forward and glared at him.

"But you're on his side. Don't deny it."

He shook his head, denying it anyway. "What makes you say that?"

She shrugged. "That day, the one that ended life as I knew it, you came over to deliver the fatal blow. You set me straight as to how things really were." Her voice hardened. "You were the one who explained Brad to me at the time. You broke my heart and then you left me lying there in the dirt and you never came back."

"You were not lying in the dirt." He seemed outraged at the concept.

She closed her eyes and then opened them again. "It's a metaphor, silly."

"I don't care what it is. I did not leave you lying in the dirt or even in the sand, or on the couch, or anything. You were standing straight and tall and making jokes, just like always."

Taking a deep breath, he forced himself to relax a bit. "You seemed calm and collected and fine with it. Like you'd known it was coming. Like you were prepared. Sad, but okay." He shook his head, willing her to believe what he was saying. "Or else I never would have left you alone."

She shrugged carelessly. How could he have gotten it all so wrong? "And you think you know me."

He pushed away the pie, searching her eyes, looking truly distressed. "Sara was with you. Your sister. I thought…"

He looked away, frowning fiercely. He remembered what he'd thought. He'd seen the pain in her face and it had taken everything in him not to reach out and gather her in his arms and kiss her until she realized…until she knew… No, he'd had to get out of there before he did something stupid. And that was why he left her. He had his own private hell to tend to.

"You thought I was okay? Wow." She struck a pose and put on an accent. "The corpse was bleeding profusely, but I assumed it would stop on its own. She seemed to be coping quite well with her murder."

He grimaced, shaking his head.

"I hated you for a while," she admitted. "It was easier than hating Brad. What Brad had done to me was just too confusing. What you did was common, everyday cowardice."

He stared at her, aghast. "Oh, thanks."

"And to make it worse, you never did come back. Did you?"

He shook his head as though he really couldn't understand why she was angry. He hadn't done anything to make her that way. He'd just lived his life like he always did, following the latest impulse that moved him. Didn't she know that?

"I was gone. I left the country. I...I had a friend starting up a business in Singapore, so I went to help him out."

She looked skeptical and deep, deep down, she looked hurt. "All this time?"

"Yeah." He nodded, feeling a bit defensive. "I've been out of the country all this time."

Funny, but that made her feel a lot better. At least he hadn't been coming up here to Seattle and never contacting her.

"So you haven't been to see Brad?"

He hesitated. He couldn't lie to her. "I stopped in to see Brad in Portland last week," he admitted.

She threw up her hands. "See? You're on his side."

He wanted to growl at her. "I'm not on anybody's side. I've been friends with both of you since that first week of college, when we all three camped out in Brad's car together."

The corners of Jill's mouth quirked into a reluctant smile as she remembered. "What a night that was," she said lightly. "They'd lost my housing forms and you hadn't been admitted yet. We had no place to sleep."

"So Brad offered his car."

"And stayed out with us."

"We talked and laughed the whole night."

She nodded, remembering. "And that cemented it. We were best buds from that night on."

Connor smiled, but looked away. He remembered meeting Jill in the administration office while they both tried to fight the bureaucracy. He'd thought she was the cutest coed on campus, right from the start. And then Brad showed up and swept her off her feet.

"We fought the law and the law won," he noted cynically.

"Right." She laughed softly, still remembering. "You with that crazy book of rules you were always studying on how to make professors fall in love with you so they'd give you good grades."

He sighed. "That never worked. And it should have, darn it all."

Her eyes narrowed as she looked back into the past a little deeper. "And all those insane jobs you took, trying to pay off your fees. I never understood when you had time to study."

"I slept with a tape recorder going," he said with a casual shrug. "Subliminal learning. Without it, I would have flunked out early on."

She stared at him, willing him to smile and admit he'd made that up, but he stuck to his guns.

"No, really. I learned French that way."

She gave him an incredulous look. *"Parlez-vous francais?"*

"Uh…whatever." He looked uncomfortable. "I didn't say I retained any of it beyond test day."

"Right." She laughed at him and he grinned back.

But she knew they were ignoring the elephant in the room. Brad. Brad who had been with them both all through college. Brad who had decided she was his from the start. And what Brad wanted, Brad usually got. She'd been flattered by his attention, then thrilled with it. And soon, she'd fallen hard. She was so in love with him, she knew he was her destiny. She let him take over her life. She didn't realize he would toss it aside when he got tired of it.

"So what are you doing here?" she asked again. "Surely you didn't come to see me."

"Jill, I always want to see you."

"No kidding. That's why you've been gone for a year and a half. You've never even met the twins."

He looked at her with a half smile. Funny. She'd been pregnant the last time he'd seen her, but that wasn't the way he'd thought of her all these months. And to tell the truth, Brad had never mentioned those babies. "That's right. I forgot. You've got a couple of cookie crunchers now, don't you?"

"I do. The little lights of my life, so to speak."

"Boys."

"Boys." She nodded.

He wanted to ask how they got along with Brad, but he wasn't brave enough to do it. Besides, it was getting late. She had a pair of baby boys at home. She looked at her watch, then looked at him.

"I've got to get home. If you can just drop me at the dock, the last ferry goes at midnight and…"

He waved away her suggestion. "You will not walk home from the ferry landing. It's too late and too far."

She made a face. "I'll be fine. I've done it a thousand times."

"I'll drive you."

She gave him a mock glare. "Well, then we'd better get going or you won't make the last ferry back."

"You let me worry about that."

Let him worry—let him manage—leave it to him. Something inside her yearned to be able to do that. It had been so long since she'd had anyone else to rely on. But life had taught her a hard lesson. If you relied on others, they could really hurt you. Best to rely on nobody but yourself.

The ferry ride across the bay to the island was always fun. He pulled the car into the proper space on the ferry and they both got out to enjoy the trip. Standing side by side as the ferry started off, they watched the inky-black water part to let them through.

Jill pulled her arms in close, fending off the ocean coolness, and he reached out and put an arm around her, keeping her warm. She rested her head on his shoulder. He had to resist the urge to draw her closer.

"Hey, I'm looking forward to meeting those two little boys of yours," he said.

"Hopefully you won't meet them tonight," she said, laughing. "I've got a nice older lady looking after them. They should be sound asleep right now."

"It's amazing to think of you with children," he said.

She nodded. "I know. You're not the only one stunned by the transformation." She smiled, thinking of how they really had changed her life. If only Brad…

No, she wasn't going to start going back over those old saws again. That way lay madness.

"It's also amazing to think of how long we've known each other," she added brightly instead.

"We all three got close in our freshman year," he agreed, "and that lasted all through college."

She nodded. "It seemed, those first couple of years, we did everything together."

"I remember it well." He sighed and glanced down at her. All he could see was that mop of crazy, curly blond hair. It always made him smile. "You were sighing over Brad," he added to the memory trail. "And I was wishing you would look my way instead."

She looked up and made a face at him. "Be serious. You had no time for stodgy, conventional girls like I was. You were always after the high flyers."

He stared at her, offended despite the fact that there was some truth in what she said. "I was not," he protested anyway.

"Sure you were." She was teasing him now. "You liked bad girls. Edgy girls. The ones who ran off with the band."

His faint smile admitted the truth. "Only when I was in the band."

"And that was most of the time." She pulled back and looked at him. "Did you ever actually get a degree?"

"Of course I got a degree."

She giggled. "In what? Multicultural dating?"

He bit back the sharp retort that surfaced in his throat. She really didn't know. But why should she?

He had to admit he'd spent years working hard at seeming to be a slacker.

"Something like that," he muttered, thinking with a touch of annoyance about his engineering degree with a magna cum laude attached. No one had been closer friends to him than Brad and Jill. And they didn't even realize he was smarter than he seemed.

It was his own fault of course. He'd worked on that easygoing image. Still, it stung a bit.

And it made him do a bit of "what if?" thinking. What if he'd been more aggressive making his own case? What if he'd challenged Brad's place in Jill's heart at the time? What if he'd competed instead of accepting their romance as an established fact? Would things have been different?

The spray from the water splashed across his face, jerking him awake from his dream. Turning toward the island, he could see her house up the drive a block from the landing. He'd been there a hundred times before, but not for quite a while. Not since the twins were born and Brad decided he wasn't fatherhood material. Connor had listened to what Brad had to say and it had caused a major conflict for him. He thought Brad's reasons were hateful and he deplored them, but at the same time, he'd seen them together for too long to have any illusions. They didn't belong together. Getting a divorce was probably the best thing Brad could do for Jill. So he'd gone with his message, he'd done his part and hated it and then he'd headed for Singapore.

He turned to look at her, to watch the way the wind blew her hair over her eyes, and that old familiar pull began somewhere in the middle of his chest. It started slow and then began to build, as though it was slowly finding its way through his bloodstream. He wanted her, wanted to hold her and kiss her and tell her.... He gritted his teeth and turned away. He had to fight that feeling. Funny. He never got it with any other girl. It only happened with her. Damn.

A flash of panic shivered through him. What the hell was he doing here, anyway? He'd thought he was prepared for this. Hardened. Toughened and ready to avoid the tender trap that was always Jill. But his defenses were fading fast. He had to get out of here.

He needed a plan. Obviously playing this by ear wasn't going to work. The first thing he had to do was to get her home, safe and sound. That should be easy. Then he had to avoid getting out of the car. Under no circumstances should he go into the house, especially not to take a peek at the babies. That would tie him up in a web of sentiment and leave him raw and vulnerable to his feelings. He couldn't afford to do that. At all costs, he had to stay strong and leave right away.

He could come back and talk to her in the morning. If he hung around, disaster was inevitable. He couldn't let that happen.

"You know what?" he said, trying to sound light and casual. "I think you really had the right idea about this. I need to get back to the hotel. I think I'll take the ferry right on back and let you walk up the hill on your own. It's super safe here, isn't it? I mean…"

He felt bad about it, but it had to be done. He couldn't

go home with her. Wouldn't be prudent, as someone once had famously said.

But he realized she wasn't listening to him. She was staring, mouth open, over his shoulder at the island they were fast approaching.

"What in the world is going on? My house is lit up like a Christmas tree."

He turned. She was right. Every window was ablaze with light. It was almost midnight. Somehow, this didn't seem right.

And then a strange thing happened. As they watched, something came flying out of the upstairs window, sailed through the air and landed on the roof next door.

Jill gasped, rigid with shock. "Was that the cat?" she cried. "Oh, my God!"

She tried to pull away from him as though she was about to jump into the water and swim for shore, but he yanked her back. "Come on," he said urgently, pulling her toward the Camaro. "We'll get there faster in the car."

CHAPTER THREE

JILL'S HEART WAS racing. She couldn't think. She could hardly breathe. Adrenaline surged and she almost blacked out with it.

"Oh, please," she muttered over and over as they raced toward the house. "Oh, please, oh, please!"

He swung the car into the driveway and she jumped out before he even came to a stop, running for the door.

"Timmy?" she called out. "Tanner?"

Connor was right behind her as she threw open the front door and raced inside.

"Mrs. Mulberry?" she called out as she ran. "Mrs. Mulberry!"

A slight, gray-haired woman appeared on the stairway from the second floor with a look close to terror on her face. "Oh, thank God you're finally here! I tried to call you but my hands were shaking so hard, I couldn't use the cell phone."

"What is it?" Jill grabbed her by the shoulders, staring down into her face. "What's happened? Where are the boys?"

"I tried, I really tried, but…but…"

"Mrs. Mulberry! What?"

Her face crumpled and she wailed, "They locked me out. I couldn't get to them. I didn't know what to do…."

"What do you mean they've locked you out? Where? When?"

"They got out of their cribs and locked the door. I couldn't…"

Jill started up the stairs, but Connor took them two at a time and beat her to the landing and then the door. He yanked at the handle but it didn't budge.

"Timmy? Tanner? Are you okay?" Jill's voice quavered as she pressed her ear to the door. There was no response.

"There's a key," she said, turning wildly, trying to remember where she'd put it. "I know there's a key."

Connor pushed her aside. "No time," he said, giving the door a wicked kick right next to where the lever sat. There was a crunch of wood breaking and the door flew open.

A scene of chaos and destruction was revealed. A lamp was upside down on the floor, along with pillows and books and a tumbled table and chair set. Toys were everywhere, most of them covered with baby powder that someone had been squirting out of the container. And on the other side of the room were two little blond boys, crowding into a window they could barely reach. They saw the adults coming for them, looked at each other and shrieked—and then they very quickly shoved one fat fluffy pillow and then one large plastic game of Hungry Hungry Hippos over the sill. The hippos could be heard hitting the bricks of the patio below.

"What are you doing?" Jill cried, dashing in as one child reached for a small music toy. She grabbed him, swung him up in her arms and held him close.

"You are such a bad boy!" she said, but she was laughing with relief at the same time. They seemed to be okay. No broken bones. No blood. No dead cat.

Connor pulled up the other boy with one arm while he slammed the window shut with the other. He looked at Jill and shook his head. "Wow," was all he could say. Then he thought of something else. "Oh. Sorry about the door. I thought…"

"You thought right," she said, flashing him a look of pure relief and happiness. Her babies were safe and right now that was all that mattered to her. "I would have had a heart attack if I'd had to wait any longer."

Mrs. Mulberry was blubbering behind them and they both turned, each carrying a child, to stare at her.

"I'm so sorry," she was saying tearfully. "But when they locked me out…"

"Okay, start at the beginning," Jill told her, trying to keep her temper in check and hush her baby, who was saying, "Mamamama" over and over in her ear. "What exactly happened?"

The older woman sniffled and put a handkerchief to her nose. "I…I don't really know. It all began so well. They were perfect angels."

She smiled at them tearfully and they grinned back at her. Jill shook her head. It was as though they knew exactly what they'd done and were ready to do it again if they got the chance.

"They were so good," Mrs. Mulberry was saying,

"I'm afraid I let them stay up longer than I should have. Finally I put them to bed and went downstairs." She shook her head as though she still couldn't believe what happened next. "I was reading a magazine on the couch when something just went plummeting by the bay window. I thought it was my imagination at first. Then something else went shooting past and I got up and went outside to look at what was going on. And there were toys and bits of bedding just lying there in the grass. I looked up but I couldn't see anything. It was very eerie. Almost scary. I couldn't figure out what on earth was happening."

"Oh, sweetie boys," Jill muttered, holding one closely to her. "You must be good for the babysitter. Remember?"

"When I started to go back in the house," the older lady went on, "one of these very same adorable children was at the front door. As I started to come closer, he grinned at me and he…" She had to stop to take a shaky breath. "He just smiled. I realized what might happen and I called out. I said, 'No! Wait!' But just as I reached the door, he slammed it shut. It was locked. He locked me out of the house!"

Jill was frowning. "What are you talking about? Who locked you out of the house?"

She pointed at Timmy who was cuddled close in Jill's arms. "He did."

Jill shook her head as though to clear it. He's only eighteen months old. "That's impossible. He doesn't know how to lock doors."

Mrs. Mulberry drew herself up. "Oh, yes he does," she insisted.

Jill looked into Timmy's innocent face. Could her baby have done that? He smiled and said, "Mama-mama." No way.

"I couldn't get in," Mrs Mulberry went on. "I was panicking. I didn't know what I was going to do." Tears filled her eyes again.

Jill stared at her in disbelief and Connor stepped forward, putting a comforting hand on her shoulder. "We believe you, Mrs. Mulberry," he said calmly. "Just finish your story. We want to know it all."

She tried to give him a grateful smile and went on. "I was racing around, trying all the doors, getting more and more insane with fear. Finally I got the idea to look for a key. I must have turned over twenty flower pots before I found it. Once I got back into the house, I realized they were up here in the bedroom, but when I called to them, they locked the bedroom door."

She sighed heavily, her head falling forward on her chest. "I thought I would go out of my mind. I tried to call you but I couldn't do it. I thought I ought to call the police, but I was shaking so badly..." She shuddered, remembering. "And then you finally came home."

Jill met Connor's gaze and bit her lip, turning to lay Timmy down in his crib. He was giving her a warning glance, as if to say, "No major damage here. Give her a break."

For some reason, instead of letting it annoy her, she felt a surge of relief. Yes, give her a break. Dear soul, she didn't mean any harm, and since nothing had really happened, there was no reason to make things worse. In fact, both boys were already drifting off to sleep. And why not? They'd had a busy night so far.

Turning, she smiled at the older woman. "Thank goodness I got back when I did," she said as lightly as she could manage. "Well, everything's alright now. If you'll wait downstairs, I'll just put these two down and..."

Connor gave her a grin and a wink and put down the already sleeping Tanner into his crib as though he knew what he was doing, which surprised her. But her mind was on her babies, and she looked down lovingly at them as they slept. For just a moment, she'd been so scared....

What would she do if anything happened to either one of them? She couldn't let herself think about that. That was a place she didn't want to go.

Connor watched her. He was pretty sure he knew what she was thinking about. Anything happening to her kids would just about destroy her. He'd seen her face when she first realized she was losing Brad. He remembered that pain almost as if it had been his own. And losing these little ones would be ten times worse.

He drove Mrs. Mulberry home and when he got back, all was quiet. The lights that had blazed out across the landscape were doused and a more muted atmosphere prevailed. The house seemed to be at peace.

Except for one thing—the sound of sniffles coming from the kitchen where Jill was sitting at the table with her hands wrapped around a cup of coffee.

"Hey," he said, sliding in beside her on the bench seat. "You okay?"

She turned her huge, dark, tragic eyes toward him.

"I leave the house for just a few hours—leave the boys for more than ten minutes—the first time in a year. And chaos takes over." She searched his gaze for answers. "Is that really not allowed? Am I chained to this place, this life, forever? Do I not dare leave...ever?"

He stared down at her. He wanted to make a joke, make her smile, get her out of this mood, but he saw real desperation in her eyes and he couldn't make light of that.

"Hey." He brushed her cheek with the backs of his fingers. "It's not forever. Things change quickly for kids. Don't let it get you down. In a month, it will be different."

She stared up at him. How could he possibly know that? And yet, somehow, she saw the wisdom in what he'd said. She shook her head and smiled. "Connor, why didn't you come back sooner? I love your smile."

He gave her another one, but deep down, he groaned. This was exactly why he had to get out of here as soon as he could. He slumped down lower in the seat and tried to think of something else reassuring to say, but his mind wouldn't let go of what she'd just said to him.

I love your smile.

Pretty pathetic to grasp at such a slender reed, but that was just about all he had, wasn't it?

Jill was back on the subject at hand, thinking about the babysitter. "Here I hired her because I thought an older woman would be calmer with a steadier hand."

She rolled her eyes. "A teenage girl would have been better."

"Come on, that's not really fair. She got a lot thrown at her at once and she wasn't prepared for it. It could have happened to anyone."

She shook her head as though she just couldn't accept that. "I'm lucky I've got my sister close by for emergencies. But she's getting more and more caught up in her career, and it's a pretty demanding one. I really can't count on her for too much longer." She sighed. "She had to be at a business dinner in Seattle tonight, or she would have been here to take care of the boys."

"Family can be convenient." He frowned. "Don't you have a younger sister? I thought I met her once."

Instead of answering, she moaned softly and closed her eyes. "Kelly. Yes. She was our half sister." She looked at him, new tragedy clouding her gaze. "Funny you should remember her tonight. She was killed in a car crash last week."

"Oh, my God. Oh, Jill, I'm so sorry."

She nodded. "It's sad and tragic and brings on a lot of guilty feelings for Sara and me."

He shook his head, not understanding. "What did you have to do with it?"

"The accident? Oh, nothing. It happened in Virginia where I guess she was living lately. The guilt comes from not even knowing exactly where she was and frankly, not thinking about her much. We should have paid more attention and worked a little harder on being real sisters to her."

There was more. He could tell. But he waited, letting her take her time to unravel the story.

"She was a lot younger, of course. Our mother died when we were pretty young, and our father remarried soon after. Too soon for us, of course. After losing our mother, we couldn't bear to share our beloved father with anyone. We resented the new woman, and when she had a baby, we pretty much resented her, too." She shook her head. "It was so unfair. Poor little girl."

"Didn't you get closer as she got older?"

"Not really. You see, the marriage was a disaster from the start and it ended by the time Kelly was about five years old. We only saw her occasionally after that, for a few hours at a time. And then our father died by the time she was fifteen and we didn't see either one of them much at all after that."

"That's too bad."

She nodded. "Yes. I'm really sorry about it now." She sighed. "She was something of a wild child, at least according to my father's tales of woe. Getting into trouble even in high school. The sort of girl who wants to test the boundaries and explore the edge."

"I know your father died a few years ago. What about your stepmother?"

"She died when I was about twenty-three. She had cancer."

"Poor lady."

"Yes. Just tragic, isn't it? Lives snuffed out so casually." She shook her head. "I just feel so bad about Kelly. It's so sad that we never got to know her better."

"Just goes to show. Carpe diem. Seize the day. Don't let your opportunities slip by."

"Yes." She gave him a look. "When did you become such a philosopher?"

"I've always been considered wise among my peers," he told her in a snooty voice that made her laugh.

A foghorn sounded its mournful call and she looked up at a clock. "And now here you are, stuck. The last ferry's gone. You're going to have to stay here."

He smiled at her. "Unless I hijack a boat."

"You can sleep on the couch." She shrugged. "Or sleep in the master bedroom if you want. Nobody else does."

The bitter tone was loud and clear, and it surprised him.

"Where do you sleep?" he asked her.

"In the guest room." Her smile was bittersweet. "That's why you can't use it."

He remembered glancing in at the master bedroom when he was upstairs. It looked like it had always looked. She and Brad had shared that bed. He looked back at her and didn't say a word.

She didn't offer an explanation, but he knew what it was. She couldn't sleep in that bed now that Brad had abandoned it.

He nodded. "I'll take the couch."

She hesitated. "The only problem with that is, I'll be getting up about four in the morning. I'll probably wake you."

"Four in the morning? Planning a rendezvous with the milkman?"

"No, silly. I've got to start warming the ovens and mixing my batter." She yawned, reminding him of a sleepy kitten. "I've got a day full of large orders to fill tomorrow. One of my busiest days ever." She smiled again. "And hopefully, a sign of success. I sure need it."

"Great."

"Wait here a second. I think I've got something you can use."

She left the room and was back in moments, carrying a set of dark blue men's pajamas.

He recoiled at the sight. "Brad's?" he said.

"Not really." She threw them down in his lap. "I bought them for Brad but he never even saw them. That was just days before he sent you to tell me we were through."

"Oh." That was okay, then. He looked at them, setting aside the top and reserving the pants for when he was ready for bed. Meanwhile, she was rummaging through a linen closet and bringing out a sheet and a light blanket. That made her look domestic in ways he hadn't remembered. He thought about how she'd looked with Timmy in her arms.

"Hey," he said gently. "That's a pair of great little boys you've got there."

She melted immediately. "Aren't they adorable? But so bad!"

"I'll bet they keep you busy every hour of the day."

She nodded. "It's not easy running a business from home when I've got those two getting more and more mischievous." She sighed and sat back down. "Can you believe they were locking doors? I had no idea they knew what a lock was."

"Time to dismantle some and add extra keys for others," he suggested.

"Yes. And keep my eyes on them every minute."

"Can't you hire a daytime babysitter?"

"Yeah, hiring a babysitter really works out well, doesn't it?" She shook her head. "Actually Trini, my bakery assistant, helps a lot. She doubles as a babysitter when I need her to, and does everything else the rest of the time. And then, Sara comes by and helps when she has a free moment or two." She gave him a tremulous smile. "We manage."

He resisted the impulse to reach out and brush back the lock of hair that was bouncing over her eyebrow. The gesture seemed a little too intimate as they sat here, alone in the dim light so late at night.

But Jill didn't seem to have the same reservations he harbored. She reached out and took his hand in hers, startling him. Then she gazed deep into his eyes for a moment before she spoke. His pulse began to quicken. He wasn't sure what she wanted from him, but he knew he couldn't deny her much.

"Well?" she said softly.

He could barely breathe. His fingers curled around hers and he looked at her full, soft lips, her warm mouth, and he wanted to kiss her so badly his whole body ached with it. The longing for her seared his soul. What would she do if he just…?

"Well?" she said again. "Out with it."

"What?" His brain was fuzzy. He couldn't connect what she was saying to what he was feeling.

"Come on. Say it."

He shook his head. What was she talking about? Her brows drew together and her gaze was more penetrating.

"My dear Connor," she said, pulling at his hand as though to make him say what she wanted to hear. "It is time for you to come clean."

"Come clean?"

He swallowed hard. Did she know? Could she read the desire in his eyes? Did she see how he felt about her in his face? Hear it in his voice? Had he really let his guard down too far?

"On what?" he added, his voice gruff with suppressed emotion.

"On why you're here." She was looking so intense. "On why Brad sent you." She searched his eyes again. "Come on, Connor. What exactly does he want this time?"

Brad. His heart sank, and then he had to laugh at himself. Of course that was what she was thinking about. And why not? What right did he have to want anything different? What he wanted didn't mean a thing. This was all about Jill—and Brad. As usual. He took a deep breath and shook his head.

"What makes you think Brad sent me?" he said, his voice coming out a bit harsher than he'd meant it to.

"You're his best friend." She frowned and looked pensive. "You were my best friend once, too."

There you go. Too many best friends. He was always the odd man out. That was exactly why he'd opted for

Singapore when he had the chance. And maybe why he would go back again.

He raised her hand and brought it to his lips, touching her gently with a kiss, then setting her aside and drawing away.

"Jill, you've had enough excitement for tonight. Let's talk in the morning."

"No, tell me. What does Brad want me to do?"

It was the question in her eyes that scared him—the hint of hope. She didn't really think that there was a chance that Brad might want her back....did she? It wasn't going to happen. He'd seen it with his own eyes.

Brad was a selfish bastard. It had taken him years to accept that. Maybe Jill didn't realize it yet. Brad was a great guy to hang out with. Playing poker with him was fun. Going waterskiing. Box seats at a Mariners game. But as far as planning your life with him, he wouldn't recommend it.

"Jill, I didn't come for Brad. I came to see you because I wanted to come."

Okay, so that was partly a lie. But he had to say it. He couldn't stand to see the glimmer of hope in her eyes, knowing it would only bring her more heartbreak. He had a message from Brad all right. But right now, he wasn't sure if he would ever tell her what it was. She thought he was on Brad's side, but she was wrong. If it came to a showdown, he was here for her—all the way.

He just wasn't sure how much she cared, one way or the other. She still wanted Brad. He could see it in her face, hear it in her voice. He shouldn't even be here.

No worries. He would leave first thing in the morning. He couldn't leave before six when the ferry started to run, but he would slip out while she was busy. No goodbyes. Just leave. Get it over with and out of the way and move on. That was the plan. He only had to follow it.

The couch was comfortable enough but he could only sleep in short snatches. When he did doze off, he had dreams that left him wandering through crowds of Latin American dancers in huge headdresses, all swaying wildly to exotic music and shouting "Mambo!" in his face.

He was looking for something he couldn't find. People kept getting in his way, trying to get him to dance with them. And then one headdress changed into a huge white parrot before his eyes, the most elegant bird he'd ever seen. He had to catch that parrot. Suddenly it was an obvious case of life or death and his heart was beating hard with the effort as he chased it through the crowd. He had to catch it!

He reached out, leaped high and touched the tips of the white feathers of its wings. His heart soared. He had it! But then the feathers slipped through his fingers and the bird was swooping away from him. He was left with nothing. A feeling of cold, dark devastation filled his heart. He began to walk away.

But the parrot was back, trailing those long white fathers across his face—only it wasn't white feathers. It was the sleeve of a lacy white nightgown and it was Jill leaning over him, trying to reach something from the bookcase behind the couch.

"Oh, sorry. I didn't want to wake you up," she whispered as though he might go back to sleep if she was quiet about it. "It's not time to get up. I just needed this manual. I'm starting to heat the ovens up."

He nodded and pretended to close his eyes, but he left slits so he could watch her make her way across the room, her lacy white gown cascading around her gorgeous ankles. The glow from the kitchen provided a backlight that showed off her curves to perfection, making his body tighten in a massive way he didn't expect.

And then he fell into the first real deep and dreamless sleep of the night. It must have lasted at least two hours. When he opened his eyes, he found himself staring into the bright blue gaze of one of the twins. He didn't know which one. He couldn't tell them apart yet.

He closed his eyes again, hoping the little visitor would be gone when he opened them. No such luck. Now there were two of them, both dressed in pajamas, both cute as could be.

"Hi," he said. "How are you doing?"

They didn't say a word. They just stared harder. But maybe they didn't do much talking at this age. They were fairly young.

Still, this soundless staring was beginning to get on his nerves.

"Boo," he said.

They both blinked but held their ground.

"So it's going to take more than a simple 'boo,' is it?" he asked.

They stared.

"Okay." He gathered his forces and sprang up, waving the covers like a huge cloak around him. "BOO!" he yelled, eyes wide.

They reacted nicely. They both ran screaming from the room, tumbling over each other in their hurry, and Connor smiled with satisfaction.

It only took seconds for Jill to arrive around the corner.

"What are you doing to my babies?" she cried.

"Nothing," he said, trying to look innocent. He wrapped the covers around himself and smiled. "Just getting to know them. Establishing pecking order. Stuff like that."

She frowned at him suspiciously. To his disappointment, she didn't have the lacy white thing on anymore. She'd changed into a crisp uniform with a large apron and wore a net over her mass of curly hair.

He gestured in her direction. "Regulation uniform, huh?"

She nodded. "I'm a Bundt cake professional, you know," she reminded him, doing a pose.

Then she smiled, looking him over. "You look cute when you're sleepy," she told him, reaching out to ruffle his badly mussed hair. "Why don't you go take a shower? I put fresh towels in the downstairs bathroom. I'll give you some breakfast before you leave."

Leave? Leave? Oh, yeah. He was going to leave as fast as he could. That was the plan.

He let the sheet drop, forgetting that his torso was completely naked, but the look on her face reminded him quickly. "Oh, sorry," he said, pulling the sheet back. And then he felt like a fool.

He glanced at her. A beautiful shade of crimson was flooding her face. That told him something he hadn't figured out before. But knowing she responded to him like that didn't help matters. In fact, it only made things worse. He swore softly to himself.

"You want me gone as soon as possible, don't you?" He shouldn't have said it that way, but the words were already out of his mouth.

She looked a little startled, but she nodded. "Actually you are sort of in the way," she noted a bit breathlessly. "I...I've got a ton of work to do today and I don't really have time to be much of a hostess."

He nodded. "Don't worry. I'm on my way."

He thought about getting into his car and driving off and he wondered why he wasn't really looking forward to it. He had to go. He knew it. She knew it. It had to be done. They needed to stay away from each other if they didn't want to start something they might not be able to stop. Just the thought made his pulse beat a ragged rhythm.

She met his gaze and looked almost sorry for a moment, then took a deep breath, shook her head and glanced at her watch.

"So far, so good. I'm pretty much on schedule," she said. "It can get wild around here. My assistant, Trini, should show up about seven. Then things will slowly get under control."

Despite her involuntary reaction to seeing him without a shirt—a reaction that sent a surge through his bloodstream every time he thought of it—there was still plenty of tension in her voice. Best to be gone before he really felt like a burden. He shook his head as he went off to take a shower.

It can get wild around here, she'd said. So it seemed. It couldn't get much wilder than it had the night before.

That reminded him of what those boys were capable of, and once he'd finished his shower, he took a large plastic bag and went outside to collect all the items the boys had thrown down from the bedroom. Then he brought the plastic bag into the house and set it down in the entryway.

"Oh, good," Jill said when she saw what he'd done. She looked relieved that he'd changed back into the shirt and slacks he'd been wearing the night before. "I forgot. I really did want all the stuff brought in before the neighbors saw it."

"This is quite a haul," he told her with a crooked smile. "Are you sure your guys aren't in training to be second-story men?"

"Very funny," she said, shaking her head at him, then smiling back. "There are actually times when I wonder how I'm going to do it on my own. Raise them right, I mean." She turned large, sad eyes his way. "It's not getting any easier."

It broke his heart to see her like this. If only there was something he could do to help her. But that was impossible, considering the situation. If it weren't for Brad... But that was just wishful thinking.

"You're going to manage it," he reassured her. "You've got what it takes. You'll do it just like your parents managed to raise you. It comes with the territory."

She was frowning at him. "But it doesn't always

work out. Your parents, for instance. Didn't you used to say...?"

He tried to remember what he'd ever told her about his childhood. He couldn't have said much. He never did. Unless he'd had too much to drink one night and opened up to her. But he didn't remember anything like that. Where had she come up with the fact that his parents had been worthless? It was the truth, but he usually didn't advertise it.

"Yeah, you're right," he said slowly. "My parents were pretty much AWOL. But you know what? Kids usually grow up okay anyway." He spread his arms out and smiled at her. "Look at me."

"Just about perfect," she teased. "Who could ask for anything more?"

"My point exactly," he said.

She turned away. She knew he was trying to give her encouragement, but what he was saying was just so much empty talk. It wouldn't get her far.

"Come on," she said. "I've got coffee, and as long as you want cake for breakfast, you can eat."

The cake was slices from rejects—Dutch Apple Crust, Lemon Delight and Double Devil's Food—but they were great and she knew it. She watched with satisfaction as he ate four slices in a row, making happy noises all the while.

The boys were playing in the next room. They were making plenty of noise but none of it sounded dangerous so far. Her batters were mixed. Her first cakes were baking. She still had to prepare some glazes. But all in all, things were moving along briskly and she was feeling more confident.

A moment of peace. She slipped into a chair and smiled across the table at him.

"You look like a woman expecting a busy day," he noted, smiling back at her and noticing how the morning light set off the faint sprinkling of freckles that still decorated her pretty face.

She nodded. "It's my biggest day ever. I've got to get cakes to the charity auction at the Lodge, I've got cakes due for six parties, I've got a huge order, an engagement party at the country club today at three. They want 125 mini Bundt cakes. I was planning to get started on them last night, but after the baby riot, I just didn't have the energy." She shook her head. "As soon as Trini gets here, we'll push the 'on' switch and we won't turn it off until we're done."

He grinned at her. "You look like you relish the whole thing. Or am I reading you wrong?"

"You've got it right." She gave him a warm look. "I really appreciate you being here to help me last night," she said, shaking her head as she remembered the madness. "That was so crazy."

"Yeah," he agreed, polishing off the last piece of Lemon Delight. "But nobody got hurt. It all turned out all right."

She nodded, looking at him, at his dark, curly hair, at his calm, honest face. She felt a surge of affection for him, and that made her frown. They'd been such good friends at one point, but she hardly knew anything about what he'd been doing lately. He'd walked out of her life at the same time Brad had. Both her best friends had deserted her in one way or another.

What doesn't kill you makes you stronger. Yeah, right.

"So the way I understand it," she said, leaning forward, "you've been in Singapore for the last year or so."

"That's right."

"Are you back for good?"

"Uh…" He grimaced. "Hard to say. I've got some options. Haven't decided what I want to do."

She thought about that for a moment. Did Connor ever have a solid plan? Or was it just that he kept his feelings close to the vest? She couldn't tell at this point. She resented the way he'd walked off over a year ago, but that didn't mean she didn't still love him to death.

Best friends. Right?

She narrowed her eyes, then asked brightly, "How about getting married?"

He looked at her as though she'd suddenly gone insane. "What? Married? Who to?"

She laughed. She could read his mind. He thought she was trying out a brand-new idea and he was ready to panic. "Not to me, silly. To someone you love. Someone who will enhance your life."

"Oh." He still looked uncomfortable.

"I'm serious. You should get married. You could use some stability in your life. A sense of purpose." She shrugged, feeling silly.

Who was she to give this sort of advice? Not only was she a failure at marriage, but she'd turned out to be a pretty lousy judge of character, too. "Someone to love," she added lamely.

His blue eyes were hooded as he gazed at her. "How do you know I don't have all those things right now?"

She studied his handsome face and shook her head. "I don't see it. To me, you look like the same old Connor, always chasing the next good time. Show me how I'm wrong."

She knew she was getting a little personal, but she was feeling a little confused about him right now. What was he doing here? Why was he sticking around?

In the bright light of day she thought she could see things more clearly, and that fresh sight told her he'd come with a goal in mind. If he'd just wanted to see her, make a visit, he'd have called ahead. No, Brad had sent him. Coming face-to-face in the hotel dining room had been a fluke. But what did Brad have in mind? Why didn't Connor just deliver the message and go?

She was beginning to feel annoyed with him. Actually she was becoming annoyed with everything. Something was off-kilter and her day was beginning to stretch out ominously before her.

"Okay, let's stop avoiding the real issue here." She stared at him coolly. "No more denials. What does Brad really want?"

CHAPTER FOUR

"BRAD?"

Jill saw the shift in Connor's eyes. He didn't want to talk about this right now. He was perfectly ready to avoid the issue again. Well, too bad. She didn't have all the time in the world. It was now or never.

"Yes, Brad. You remember him. My ex-husband. The father of my children. The man who was once my entire life."

"Oh, yeah. That guy."

She frowned. He was still being evasive. She locked her fingers together and pulled.

"So, what does he want?" she insisted.

Connor looked at her and began to smile. "What do you think Brad wants? He always wants more than his share. And he usually gets it."

She shook her head, surprised, then laughed softly. "You do know him well, don't you?"

Connor's smile faded. He glanced around the kitchen, looking uncomfortable. "Does he have visitation rights to the boys? Does he come up here to see them or does he...?"

"No," she said quickly. "He's never seen them."

For once, she'd shocked him. His face showed it clearly. "Never seen his own kids? Why? Do you have a court injunction or…?"

The pain of it all would bring her down if she let it. She couldn't do that. She held her head high and met his gaze directly.

"He doesn't want to see them. Don't you know that? Didn't he ever tell you why he wanted the divorce?"

Connor shook his head slowly. "Tell me," he said softly.

She took a deep breath. "When Brad asked me to marry him, he told me he wanted a partner. He was going to start his own business and he wanted someone as committed to it as he was, someone who would stand by him and help him succeed. I entered into that project joyfully."

Connor nodded. He remembered that as well. He'd been there. He'd worked right along with them. They'd spent hours together brainstorming ideas, trying out options, failing and trying again. They'd camped out in sleeping bags when they first opened their office. They'd been so young and so naive. They thought they could change the world—or at least their little corner of it. They'd invented new ways of doing things and found a way to make it pay. It had been a lot of hard work, but they'd had a lot of fun along the way. That time seemed a million miles away now.

"I knew Brad didn't want children, but I brushed that aside. I was so sure he would change his mind as time went by. We worked very, very hard and we did really well together. The business was a huge success. Then I got pregnant."

She saw the question in his eyes and she shook her head. "No, it was purely and simply an accident."

She bit her lip and looked toward the window for a moment, steadying her voice.

"But I never dreamed Brad would reject it so totally. He just wouldn't accept it." She looked back into his eyes, searching for understanding. "I thought we could work things out. After all, we loved each other. These things happen in life. You deal with them. You make adjustments. You move on."

"Not Brad," he guessed.

"No. Not Brad." She shrugged. "He said, get rid of them."

He drew in a sharp breath. It was almost a gasp. She could hear it in the silence of the kitchen, and she winced.

"And you said?"

She shrugged again. "I'd rather die."

Connor nodded. He knew her well enough to know that was the truth. What the hell was Brad thinking?

"Suddenly he was like a stranger to me. He just shut the door. He went down to Portland to open up a branch office for our business. I thought he would think it over and come back and…" She gave him a significant look. "But he never came back. He began to make the branch office his headquarters. Then you showed up and told me he wanted a divorce."

Connor nodded. His voice was low and gruff as he asked her, "Do you want him back?"

She had to think about that one. If she was honest, she would have to admit there was a part of her—a part she wasn't very proud of—that would do almost anything to get him back. Anything but the one thing he asked for.

She stared at him and wondered how much she should tell him. He was obviously surprised to know about how little Brad cared about his sons. A normal man would care. So Brad had turned out to be not very normal. That was her mistake. She should have realized that and never married him in the first place.

She also had to live with the fact that he was getting worse and worse about paying child support. There were so many promises—and then so many excuses. What there wasn't a lot of was money.

The business was floundering, he said. He was trying as hard as he could, but the profits weren't rolling in like they used to in the old days—when she was doing half the work. Of course, he didn't mention that. He didn't want her anywhere near the business anymore.

She knew he resented having to give her anything. After all, he'd given her the house—not that it was paid off. Still, it had been what she wanted, what she felt she had to have to keep a stable environment for the boys.

But now she was having a hard time making the mortgage payments. She had to make a go of her cake business, or else she would have to go back to work and leave the boys with a babysitter. She was running out of time.

Time to build her business up to where it could pay for itself. Time to stabilize the mortgage situation before the bank came down on her. Time to get the boys old enough so that when she did have to go for a real, paying job, it wouldn't break her heart to leave them with strangers.

So, yes. What Brad wanted now mattered. Had he gone through a transformation? Had he come up with second thoughts and decided to become a friend to the family? Or was it all more excuses about what he couldn't do instead of what he could? Women with husbands in a stable situation didn't realize how lucky they were.

Funny. Sometimes it almost seemed as though Brad had screwed up her marriage and now he wanted to screw up her single life as well.

She shook her head slowly. "I want my life back," she admitted. "I want the life I had when I had a loving husband. I want my babies to have their father. But I don't see how that can ever happen."

Her eyes stung and she blinked quickly to make sure no tears dared show up.

"Unless…" She looked up into Connor's eyes. "Unless you have a message from Brad that he wants it to happen, too."

Whistling in the wind. She knew how useless that was. She gave Connor a shaky smile, basically absolving him of all guilt in the matter. She saw the look in his eyes. He felt sorry for her. She cringed inside. She didn't want pity.

"Don't worry. I don't expect that. But I do want to know what he sent you for."

Connor shook his head. Obviously he had nothing

to give her. So Brad must have sent him on a scouting expedition, right? To see if she was surviving. To see if she was ready to hoist the white flag and admit he was right and she was wrong. She couldn't make it on her own after all. She should have listened to him. And now, she should knuckle under and take his advice and give it all up.

She bit her lip. She wasn't disappointed, exactly. She knew the score. But she was bummed out and it didn't help her outlook on the day.

A timer went off and she hopped up to check on her cakes. This was where she belonged, this was where she knew what she was doing. The realm of human emotions was too treacherous. She would take her chances with the baked goods.

Connor watched her getting busy again and he wished he could find some way to help her deal with the truth— that Brad didn't want her. He couldn't say it might never happen. Brad could change his mind. But right now, he didn't want Jill at all. What he wanted was to be totally free of her. At least, that was how he'd presented things a few days ago when they'd talked.

Brad wanted that, and he wanted her to give up her remaining interest in the company. That was the message he was supposed to make her listen to. That was the message he just couldn't bring himself to tell her. Maybe later.

He took his cup to the sink, rinsed it out and headed back into the living room. He was folding up the covers he'd used when the front door opened and a young woman hurried in.

Connor looked up and started to smile. It was Sara Darling, Jill's sister, and she stopped dead when she saw who had been sleeping on her sister's couch.

"You!" she said accusingly, and he found himself backing up, just from the fire in her eyes.

He knew that Sara and Jill were very close, but he also knew they tended to see things very differently. Both were beautiful. Where Jill had a head full of crazy curls that made you want to kiss her a lot, Sara wore her blond hair slicked back and sleek, making her look efficient and professional. Today she wore a slim tan linen suit with a pale peach blouse and nude heels and she looked as though she was about to gavel an important business meeting to order.

"What are you doing here?" she demanded of him. "Oh, brother. I should have known you'd show up. Let a woman be vulnerable and alone and it's like sharks smelling blood in the water."

"Hey," he protested, surprised. He'd always been friendly with this woman in the past. "That's a bit harsh."

"Harsh? You want to see harsh?"

He blanched. "Not really."

Okay, so Sara was being extra protective of her sister. He got it. But she'd never looked on him as a bad guy before. Why now? He tried a tentative smile.

"Hey, Sara. Nice to see you."

She was still frowning fiercely. "You have no right to complicate Jill's life."

He frowned, too, but in a more puzzled way. That was actually not what he wanted to do, either. But it seemed he was right. Sara was circling the wagons around her sister. How to convince her she didn't need to do that with him?

"Listen, staying for the night wasn't how I planned this."

"I'll bet." She had her arms crossed and looked very intimidating. "Just what *did* you have in mind, Casanova?"

What? Did she really think he was hovering around in order to catch Jill in an emotional state? If only! He wanted to laugh at her but he knew that would only infuriate her further.

"Listen, I saved your sister from a blind date gone horribly wrong. Seriously. Do you know the guy she went out with?"

Sara shook her head, looking doubtful.

"I think his name was Karl."

She shook her head again.

"Well, if you knew him, you'd see why Jill needed rescuing. He was flamboyantly wrong for her."

"Okay." Sara looked a little less intimidating. "Good. I'm glad you were there to help her out."

He breathed a sigh of relief. She was approachable after all.

"So I brought her back here, planning to drop her off and come back to see her in the morning, but there was a riot going on in the house. The twins had taken the babysitter hostage. I had to stay and help Jill regain the high ground. There was no choice."

It was as though she hadn't heard a word he'd said. She paced slowly back and forth in front of him, glaring like a tiger. It was evident she thought he was exaggerating and she'd already gone back to the root of the problem.

"So...what's the deal?" she said, challenging him with her look. "Brad sent you, didn't he?"

Uh-oh. He didn't want to go there if he could help it. He gave her a fed-up look. "Why does everyone assume I can't make a move on my own?"

She glared all the harder. "If he's trying to get her to come back to him, you can tell him..."

He held up a hand to stop her. It was time to nip this supposition in the bud. "Sara, no. Brad is not trying to get her back."

"Oh." Her look was pure sarcasm. "So the new honey is still hanging around?"

He ran his fingers through his thick, curly hair and grimaced. "Actually I think that was two or three honeys ago," he muttered, mostly to himself. "But take my word for it, Brad isn't looking for forgiveness. Not yet, anyway."

Her dark eyes flared with outrage, but she kept her anger at a slow simmer. "That's our Brad. Trust him to make life and everything in it all about him and no one else."

He nodded. That was one point they could agree on. "Brad does like to have things go his way."

Sara's gaze had fallen on the plastic bag of items picked up in the yard. She scowled, touching it with the toe of her shoe.

"What's all this?"

"Oh. Uh. I left it there. I'll get it...."

She looked up in horror. "What are you doing, moving in?"

Now he couldn't help it. He had to laugh. "Sara, you don't need to hate me. I'm not the enemy."

"Really? What are you, then?"

"A friend." He tried to look earnest. He'd always thought Sara liked him well enough. He certainly hadn't expected to be attacked with guns blazing this way. "I'm Jill's friend. And I really want what's best for her."

"Sorry, Connor. You can't be a true friend to Jill while you're still any sort of friend to Brad. It won't work."

His head went back and he winced. "That's a little rigid, don't you think?"

She moved closer, glancing toward the kitchen to make sure they weren't being overheard. "If you'd seen what she's gone through over this last year or so, you might change your tune."

"What?" He caught her by the upper arm. "What happened?"

She shook her head, looking away.

"Has Brad been here to see her?"

She looked up at him. "Not that I know of. But he manages to make life miserable for her by long distance."

He frowned, wishing she would be more specific.

She looked at him, shook her head and her shoulders drooped. All her animosity had drained away and tears rimmed her eyes. "Oh, Connor, she deserves so much better. If you could see how hard she works… And every time she turns around, there's some new obstacle thrown in her path. I just can't stand it anymore. It's not fair."

She pulled away and he let her go. And now he was the one whose emotions were roiling. Damn Brad, anyway. Why couldn't he just leave her alone?

He ran his hand through his hair again, tempted to rip chunks of it out in frustration. He had to get out of here. If he wasn't careful, he would get caught up in the need to protect Jill. From what? He wasn't even sure. Life, probably. Just life. As Sara had said, it wasn't fair. But it also wasn't his fight. No, he had to go.

He would drive back to his hotel, check out and head for Portland. He would tell Brad he couldn't help him and advise him to leave Jill alone. Maybe he would even tell his old friend what he really thought of him. It was way past time to do that.

Jill was in a hurry and things weren't working out. She had Tanner dressed in his little play suit, but she couldn't catch Timmy, and now he was streaking around the room, just out of her reach, laughing uproariously.

"Timmy!" she ordered. "You stop right there."

Fat chance of that. He rolled under the bed and giggled as she reached under, trying to grab him.

"You come out of there, you rascal."

She made a lucky grab and caught his foot and pulled him out, disarming grin and all. "Oh, you little munchkin," she cried, but she pulled him into her arms and held him tightly. Her boys were so precious to her. She'd given up a lot to make sure she would have them. Tears stung her eyelids and she fought them back. She couldn't let herself cry. Not now. She had a day to get through.

She had a huge, wonderful day full of work ahead. A day like this could turn things around, if it started a trend. She heard Sara's voice downstairs and she smiled. What a relief. Good. Sara was here. She would be able to help with the children.

She so appreciated Sara giving her some time like this. She knew she was applying for a promotion. She'd been a contributing editor to the design section of *Winter Bay Magazine* for almost two years and she'd done some fabulous work. If she got the new job, she would be working more hours during the week and wouldn't be able to help out as much. Still, she hoped she got it. She certainly deserved the recognition.

She was thankful for small blessings. Right now, if she had Sara here to help with the twins, and then Trini coming in a half hour to help with the baking and delivery, she would be okay. She would just barely be able to fulfill all the commitments she'd made for the day.

It was a challenge, but she could do it. In fact, she had to do it.

Sara appeared at the doorway just as she finished dressing her boys and sent them into the playroom.

"Hey there," she said, ready to greet her sister with a smile until she saw the look on her face. "What's the matter? What's wrong?"

Sara sighed and shook her head.

"Did you see Connor?" Jill asked brightly. "He looks

so much the same, you'd never know he'd been gone for a year and a half, would you?"

Sara gave her a look. "Jill, we've got to talk."

Jill groaned and grabbed her sister's hand. "Not now, sweetie. Not today. I've got so much I've got to get to and…"

Sara was shaking her head. "You've got to get rid of him, Jill."

She frowned. "Who?"

Sara pointed back down the stairs as though he were following her. "Connor. You've got to make him go right away."

Dropping her hand, Jill turned away, feeling rebellious. She'd been thinking the same thing but she didn't want to hear it from anyone else. Connor was hers. She resented anyone else—even her beloved sister—critiquing their relationship. She would make him go when she was good and ready to make him go.

Sara grabbed her by the shoulders. "You know he's just here spying for Brad," she said in a low, urgent voice. "You don't want that, do you?"

Sara had never warmed to Jill's ex-husband, even during the good times. And once he'd gone off and left her high and dry, she'd developed what could only be described as a dogged contempt for the man.

Jill took a deep breath and decided to ignore everything she'd said. Life would be simpler that way.

"What are you doing here so early?" she asked instead, trying to sound bright and cheery. "I appreciate it, but…"

"Oh." Sara's demeanor changed in an instant and she

dropped her hold on her sister's shoulders. "Oh, Jill, I came early to tell you...I'm so sorry, but I won't be able to help you today. They want me to fly down to L.A. There's just no way I can get out of it. I'll be meeting with the editorial staff from Chicago and..."

"Today?" Jill couldn't stop the anguish from bursting out as she realized what this meant.

Sara looked stricken. "It's a really bad day, right?"

"Well, I told you I've got a huge stack of orders and..." Jill stopped herself, set her shoulders and got hold of her fears. "No, no." She shook her head. "No, Sara. It's much more important for you to go do this, I'm sure."

Sara grabbed her hand again. "Oh, honey, I'm so sorry, but I really can't turn them down. They want to see how I handle myself with the visiting members." She bit her lip and looked as though she was about to cry. A range of conflicting emotions flashed through her wide dark eyes and then she shook her head decisively. "Oh, forget it. I'll tell them something has come up and I just can't do it. Don't worry. They'll understand. I think."

Jill dismissed all that out of hand. "Don't be ridiculous. Of course you have to go. This is your career. This is something you've worked so hard for."

"But I can't leave you if you really need me."

"But I don't." Jill dug deep and managed a bright smile. "Not really. Trini will be here soon and we'll be able to handle it."

Sara looked worried. "Are you sure?"

"Positive." She smiled again.

"Because I can stay if you really need me. I can tell them…"

"No." She hugged her sister. "You go. You have to go. I will lose all respect for you if you let silly sentiment keep you from achieving your highest goals. Say no more about it. You're gone. It's decided."

"But…"

"Come on. Do it for me. Do it for all of us. Make us proud."

Her smile was almost painful by now, but doggone it—she wasn't going to stop. Sara had to go. No two ways about it. And she would just have to cope on her own. Thank God for Trini.

"So she's really going?" Connor had watched Sara rushing off and then turned to see Jill come down from upstairs with a tense look on her face.

"Yes. Yes, she is."

He noted that her hands were gripped together as though she could hardly stand it. He frowned.

"Do you think you can do it without her?"

She took a deep breath. "It won't be easy. But once Trini gets here, we'll put our noses to the grindstone and work our little tushes off for the next twelve hours. Then you'll see."

He was bemused by her intensity. "What will I see?"

She looked up at him wide-eyed. "That this is serious. Not just a hobby job. It's real."

He frowned. He wanted to tell her that he respected her immensely and that he was impressed with what

she was attempting to do here, but before he could get
a word out, she went on, pacing tensely as she talked.

"You know, I thought I had everything pretty much
under control. My life was running on an even keel. I
was beginning to feel as though I might make it after
all." She stopped and looked at him with a sense of
foreboding wonder. "And then you hit town. And everything went to hell."

She was trying to make it sound like a joke, but
there was too much stress in her voice to carry it off.
He winced.

"So you blame me now?"

"Why not? There's nobody else within shouting distance. You're going to have to take the fall." She tried
to smile but her mouth was wobbly.

He looked at her, saw the anxious look in her eyes
and he melted beyond control. "Jill…" He took her
hands in his and drew her closer. "Listen, why don't
I stay? I could help you with the boys. I could run er-
rands, answer phones."

She was shaking her head but he didn't wait to hear
her thoughts.

He pulled her hands up against his chest. "I want to
help you. Really. I know you've had a lot of setbacks
lately and I want to help smooth over some rough spots
if I can. Come on, Jill. Let me stay."

Her lower lip was trembling as she looked into his
eyes. He groaned and pulled her into his arms, holding
her tightly against his body. She felt like heaven and he
wanted the moment to go on forever, but she didn't let

it happen. She was already pulling out of his embrace, and he could have kicked himself for doing it.

Too blatant, Connor old chap, he told himself ruefully. *You really tipped your hand there, didn't you?*

"No, Connor," she said as she pushed him away.

She looked at him, shaken. She'd wanted to melt into his arms. She still felt the temptation so strongly, she had to steel herself against it. She knew it had to be mostly because she was so afraid, so nervous about her ability to meet her challenges. If she let him hold her, she could pretend to forget all that.

And then there was the fact that it had been so long since a man—a real man, a man that she liked—had held her. Karl didn't count. And she hungered for that sort of connection.

But not with Connor. Not with Brad's best friend.

"No. It's sweet of you to offer, but I really can't let you stay. We are going to need to focus like laser beams on this task and having you here won't help." She smiled at him with affection to take the bite out of her words.

He stepped farther from her and avoided her eyes. The sting of her rejection was like a knife to his heart. "Okay then. I guess I'd better get going."

"Yes. I'm sorry."

He started to turn away, then remembered. "Hey, I didn't fix the door I kicked in last night."

She shook her head. "Don't worry. I've already called a handy man I use."

"Oh." He hesitated, but there didn't seem to be much to say. He was superfluous, obviously. Just in the way. Might as well get the hell out.

"Okay. It was good to see you again, Jill."

She smiled at him. "Yes. Come back soon. But next time, don't stop off to see Brad first."

He nodded. "You've got my word on that one," he said. He shoved his hands down into the back pockets of his jeans and looked at her, hard.

"What?" she asked, half laughing.

"I just want to get a good picture of you to hold me over," he told her. "Until next time."

The look in her eyes softened and she stepped forward and kissed his cheek. "Goodbye," she whispered.

He wanted to kiss her mouth so badly, he had to clench his teeth together to stop himself from doing it.

"Goodbye," he said softly, then he turned and left the house.

Outside, he felt like hell. He'd had hangovers that hadn't felt this bad. Everything in him wanted to stay and he couldn't do it. He looked down at the ferry dock. There was a ferry there now, loading up. He'd catch it and then it would be all over. How long before he saw her again? Who knew. He would probably go back to Singapore. At least he knew where he stood there.

Swearing softly with a string of obscenities that he rarely used, he slid into the driver's seat and felt for the keys.

"Goodbye to all that," he muttered, then turned on the engine. About to back out, he turned to glance over his shoulder—just in time to see a small economy car come sailing in behind him, jerk to a stop, and block him in.

"Hey," he said.

But the young woman who'd driven up didn't hear him and didn't notice that his engine was running. She flew out of the car and went racing up the walk, flinging herself through the doorway.

Okay. This had to be the famous Trini he'd heard so much about. She'd trapped him in his parking space and he wasn't going to make the ferry. Now what?

CHAPTER FIVE

JILL HADN'T RECOVERED from Connor leaving when Trini came bursting in. The boys ran to her joyfully and she knelt down and collected them into her arms, then looked up. Jill knew immediately that something was wrong.

"Trini, what is it?" she cried.

Trini was young and pretty with a long, swinging ponytail and a wide-eyed expression of constant amazement, as though life had just really surprised her once again. And in this case, it seemed to be true.

"You'll never guess!" she cried, and then she burst into tears. "Oh, Jill," she wailed, "this is so good and so bad at the same time."

"What is it, sweetheart?" Jill asked, pulling her up and searching her face. But she thought she knew. And she dreaded what she was about to hear.

"Oh, Jill, I just got the call and…" She sobbed for a moment, then tried again. "I got in. I was on the wait list and they just called. I got accepted into the program at Chanoise Culinary Institute in New York."

"But…hasn't the quarter already started?"

"Yes, but they had two people drop out already. So they called and said if I could get there by tomorrow, I'm in."

"Trini! That's wonderful! You deserve a space in the class. I always knew that."

But did it have to be today? She couldn't help but wish the timing had been different. Still, this was wonderful for Trini.

"What can I do to help you?"

Trini shook her head. "You've already done enough. You wrote the recommendation that got me in." She sighed happily, and then she frowned with worry. "The only bad part is I have to leave right away. My flight leaves at noon. The Jamison engagement party…"

"Don't you think twice, Trini. You just get out of here and go pack and prepare for the best experience of your life. Okay?"

Trini threw her arms around Jill's neck and Jill hugged her tightly. "I'm so excited," Trini cried. "Oh, Jill, I'll keep you posted on everything we do. And when I come back…"

"You'll teach me a thing or two, I'm sure." She smiled at her assistant, forcing back any hint of the panic she was feeling. "Now off with you. You need to get ready for the rest of your life."

"I will. Wish me luck!"

"I'll definitely wish you luck. You just supply the hard work!"

Trini laughed and dashed out the door. Jill reached out to put her hand on the back of a chair to keep herself from collapsing. She could hardly breathe. She saw

Connor standing in the entryway. She didn't know why he'd come back and right now, she couldn't really think about it or talk to him. She was in full-scale devastation meltdown mode.

What was she going to do? What on earth was she going to do? She couldn't think a coherent thought. Her mind was a jumble. She knew she was standing on the edge of the cliff and if she lost her balance, she was going over. She couldn't let that happen. She had to get herself together.

But what was the use? She'd fought back so often. So much kept going wrong and she kept trying to fix things. They just wouldn't stay fixed. She was so tired. Today, right now, she wanted to quit. There had to be a way to give up, to surrender to reality. She just couldn't do this anymore.

Looking at her reflection in the hall mirror, she muttered sadly, "Okay. I get it. I'm not meant to do this. I should quit banging my head against the wall. I should quit, period. Isn't that what a sane, rational person would do?"

She stared at herself, feeling cold and hollow. She knew Connor was still watching her, that he'd heard what she said, but she hardly cared. She was in such deep trouble, what did it matter if he saw her anguish? But a part of her was grateful for his presence—and that he was keeping back, not trying to comfort her right now. She didn't need that since there was no comfort, was no real hope.

She stared at herself for a long moment, teetering between the devil and the deep blue sea. That was how it felt. No matter what she did, disaster seemed inevitable.

Then, gradually, from somewhere deep inside, she began to put her strength back together and pull her nerve back into place. She took a giant breath and slowly let it out. She wouldn't surrender. She would go down fighting, no matter what it cost her. Let them try to stop her! She had glaze to prepare. She had cakes to bake. She would try her best to get this done and on time. She could only do what she could do—but she would do the best she could.

She looked at herself in the mirror again and gave herself a small, encouraging smile. She needed a joke right now, something to help her put things into perspective. She was a baking woman—hear her roar! They would have to pry her baking mitts off her cold, dead hands.

Revived and reinvigorated, she turned to face Connor. "There," she said. "I'm better now."

He still appeared a bit worried, but he'd watched her mini-breakdown and the instant rebuild in awe.

"Wow," he said. "Jill, you are something else."

She sighed. "You weren't supposed to see that."

"I'm glad I did. I've got more faith in you than ever."

She laughed. "I've got to get back to work." She frowned. "Why are you still here?"

"Because I'm not going to go while you still need me."

"What makes you think I need you?" Turning, she headed into the kitchen.

"So," he said tentatively, following her. "Now your

number one assistant has bailed on you. And your sister has bailed on you." He shrugged. "Who you gonna call? You need someone else. Who can come to your rescue?"

She met his gaze. "There's nobody. Really. I've tried to find backup before. There's really nobody. This island is too small. There aren't enough people to draw on."

He nodded. "That's what I thought." He picked up an apron someone had thrown on the chair and began to tie it on himself. "Okay. Tell me what to do."

Her eyes widened. "What are you talking about?"

His face was so earnest, she felt her breath catch in her throat. He really meant it.

"How can I help you, Jill? What can I do?"

This was so sweet of him, but it couldn't work. He didn't have the skills, the background. And anyway, he wasn't here for her. He was here for Brad. There was no denying it.

"Just stay out of the way." She shrugged helplessly. He shouldn't be here at all. Why was he? "Go back to your hotel. You don't belong here."

He shook his head. "No."

"Connor!"

He shook his head again. "You're like a fish flopping around on the pier, gasping for breath. You need help, lady. And I'm going to give it to you."

She shook her own head in disbelief. "You can't cook."

"The hell I can't."

Her gaze narrowed. "I don't believe it."

He stepped closer, towering over her and staring down with cool deliberation. "There are a whole lot of things about me you just don't have a clue about, Miss Know-it-all."

She shook her head, still wary. "Look, just because you can fry up a mean omelet after midnight for your Saturday night date doesn't mean you can cook. And it certainly doesn't mean you can bake."

"I'm not proposing to be your baker. You've got that slot nailed. I'm signing on as an assistant. I'm ready to assist you in any way I can."

He meant it. She could see the resolve in his eyes. But how could he possibly be a help rather than a hindrance? There was no way he could get up to speed in time. Still, she was in an awful bind here.

"So you can cook?" she asked him skeptically.

"Yes."

"There's a difference between cooking and baking."

"I know that." He shook his head impatiently. "Jill, you're the baker. But you need a support staff and I'm going to be it."

"But…what are you planning to do?"

"Prep pans, wash pans, drizzle on glaze, pack product for delivery, deliver product, go for supplies, answer the phones…"

She was beginning to smile. Maybe she was being foolish, but she didn't have much choice, did she? "And the most important thing?" she coached.

He thought for a moment, then realized what she was talking about.

"Keep an eye on the boys," he said and was rewarded with a quick smile. "You got it. In fact, I'll do anything and everything in order to leave you room to practice your creative artistry."

"My what?" She laughed and gave him a push. "Oh, Connor, you smooth talker you."

"That's what it is." He took her by the shoulders and held her as though she was very, very special. "I've eaten some of your cake wizardry, lady. *Magnifique!*"

The word hung in the air. She gazed up at him, suddenly filled with a wave of affection. Had she ever noticed before how his eyes crinkled in the corners? And how long his beautiful dark lashes were? Reaching out, she pressed her palm to his cheek for just a moment, then drew it back and turned away so that he wouldn't see the tears beginning to well in her eyes.

"Okay," she said a little gruffly. "We'll give it a try. As long as you turn out to be worth more than the trouble you cause." But she glanced back with a smile, showing him that she was only teasing.

"I won't get in your way, I swear. You just wait and see. We'll work together like a well-oiled machine."

She blinked back the tears and smiled at him. "You promise?"

"Cross my heart and hope to die."

"Ooh, don't say that. Bad vibes." She shook her head. "Okay then. Here's the game plan. I'm going to go back over all my recipes and check to make sure I've got the right supplies before I start mixing new batters. You go and see what the boys are up to. Then you come back and help me."

He saluted her like a soldier. *"Mais oui, mon chef."*

"Wow. Those sleepy-time French lessons really did do some good. And here I was a non-believer."

He looked a bit nonplussed himself. "Every now and then a few French words just seem to burst out of me, so yeah, I guess so."

He turned his attention to the twins not a moment too soon. There was a ruckus going on in the next room. The boys were crying. Someone had pushed someone down and grabbed away his toy. The other one was fighting to get it back. Happened all the time. They needed supervision.

But there was really no time today to deal with it properly. He went back to discuss the situation with Jill.

"If you can think of any strenuous activities, something that might make them take their naps a bit earlier…" she mused, checking the supply of flavorings and crossing them off a list, then handing the list to him to start working on an inventory of the flour she had in storage.

"Say no more," He gave her a wise look. "I've got a trick or two up my sleeve. As soon as I finish counting up the canisters, I'll deal with those little rascals."

Time was racing by. Her convection oven could accommodate four cakes at a time, but they had to be carefully watched.

"We've got to get these done by noon," she told him. "I can't start the mini Bundts any later than that. We've got to get the minis done by three, glazed and packed by four-thirty, and off for delivery by five."

He nodded. He knew she wasn't completely resigned

to him being there with her. This was her biggest day and her eyes betrayed how worried she was. Her shoulders looked tight. She wasn't confident that they could do it, even working hard together.

He only hoped he could—what? Help her? That went without saying. Protect her? Sure. That was his main goal. Always had been. If only he'd realized earlier that his vague distrust of Brad was based on more than jealousy. It seemed to be real in ways that were only now becoming more and more clear to him. It was a good thing she'd reconciled herself to accepting his help, because he knew he couldn't go. He couldn't leave her on her own. He had to be here for her.

Meanwhile, he had to find a way to wear out the boys. He tried to recall his own childhood, but eighteen months old was a little too far back to remember much. Still, he had a few ideas.

He took the boys out into the backyard. There was a big sloping hill covered with grass. Improvising, he set up a racetrack with different stations where the boys had to perform simple modified gymnastic elements in order to move on to the next station.

They loved it. They each had a natural competitive spirit that came out in spades as they began to understand the goals involved. Each wanted to win with a naive gusto that made him laugh out loud. They were a great pair of twins.

They were so into it. Running up the hill took a lot of their time. Shrieking with excitement was a factor. And Connor found he was having as much fun as they were.

At one point, he had them racing uphill, each pulling a red wagon filled with rocks to see who could get to the top first. He'd brought along lots of prizes, including pieces of hard candy that they loved. He knew they were sure to rot teeth, but he would only use them today and never again. Or not often, anyway. He also made sure to keep the winnings pretty equal between the two of them, so that each could shine in turn.

But, as he told Jill a bit later, the one drawback was— no matter how tired he made them, he was even more so. He was pitifully out of shape.

But it was fun. That was the surprising part. The boys were a couple of great kids, both so eager, so smart. He wondered what Brad would think if he could see them. How could he possibly resist these two?

He brought them back in and settled them down to watch an educational DVD while he went down to the kitchen to see what he could do to help Jill. She had recently pulled four cakes out of the oven and she was ready to put on a glaze.

"Show me how," he told her. "You're going to need help when you glaze all those small cakes for the engagement party, aren't you?"

She looked at him with some hesitation, and he saw it right away. Reaching out, he took her hands in his.

"Jill, I'm not here to take over," he said. "I don't expect to start making decisions or judging you. I'm here to do anything you tell me to do. You talk. I'll listen."

She nodded, feeling a little chagrined. She knew he meant well. He was just here to help her. Why couldn't she calm her fears and let him do just that?

As she glanced up, her gaze met his and she had an

impulse that horrified her. She wanted to throw herself into his arms, close her eyes and hold on tightly.

The same thing she'd felt before when he'd held her came back in a wave and she felt dizzy with it. She wanted his warmth and his comfort, wanted it with a fierce craving that ached inside her. She couldn't give in to that feeling. Turning away quickly, she hoped he couldn't see it in her eyes.

She was just feeling weak and scared. That was what it had to be. She couldn't let herself fall into that trap.

"Okay. I'm going to teach you everything I know about putting on a glaze," she said resolutely. "And believe me, it's simple. We'll start with a basic sugar glaze. You'll pick it up in no time at all."

He learned fast and she went ahead and taught him how to make a caramel glaze as well, including tricks on how not to let the sugar burn and how to roast the chopped pecans before you added them to make them crisper and more flavorful. She then showed him how to center the cakes on the lacy doilies she used in the fancy boxes she packed the cakes in before transporting them.

"Each cake should look like it's a work of art on its own," she told him. "Never ever let a cake look like you just shoved it into a box to get it where it needs to go. They should look like they're being carried in a golden coach, on their way to the ball."

He grinned. "Cinderella cakes?"

"Exactly. They have to look special. Otherwise, why not pick up a cake at the grocery store?"

That was when his phone rang. It made him jerk. He

knew before he even looked at the screen who it was. Brad. Brad wondering how things were going. Brad, wondering if he'd talked her into committing to his plan. Brad, trying to control everything, just like always.

He put the phone on vibrate and shoved it into his pocket.

Once they'd finished the glazing, he went back to babysitting, making peanut butter and jelly sandwiches for the boys. They looked so good, he made one for himself. Then he raided the refrigerator and made a cool, crisp salad for Jill.

"Lunchtime," he told her, once he'd set the boys down to eat at their little table in their playroom.

She gave one last look at her boxed creations, snuck a peek at the new cakes in the oven and turned to him with a smile.

"So far, so good," she said as she sat down across from him at the kitchen table. "Though one disaster can throw the whole schedule off."

"Relax," he said. "No disaster would dare ruin this day for you."

"Knock on wood," she said, doing just that. She took a bite of salad and made a noise of pleasure. "Ah! This is so refreshing." She cocked her head to the side. "The boys are being awfully good."

He nodded. "So it seems. I gave them their sandwiches."

She frowned. "You left them alone with food?"

"They seemed to be doing great when I looked in on them." He glanced toward the doorway. "Though they sure seem quiet."

Jill's eyes widened. "Too quiet," she cried, vaulting out of her chair and racing for the playroom. Visions of peanut butter masterpieces smeared on walls and teddy bears covered in sticky jam shot through her head.

Connor came right behind her. He didn't have as much experience with what might go wrong, but he could imagine a few things himself.

They skidded around the corner and into the room, only to find a scene of idyllic contentment. The peanut butter sandwiches were half eaten and lay on the table. The boys were completely out, both lying in haphazard fashion wherever they were when sleep snuck up on them. Jill turned and grinned at him.

"You did wear them out. Wow."

They lifted them carefully and put them down in the travel cribs that sat waiting against the far wall. Jill pulled light covers over each of them and they tiptoed out of the room and back to the kitchen.

"They look like they'll sleep for hours," she said hopefully.

"Maybe days," he added to the optimism, but she laughed.

"Doubtful. Besides, we'll miss them if they stay away that long."

"Will we?" he questioned, but he was smiling. He believed her.

She glanced at her watch. "We've got time for a nice long lunch," she said. "Maybe fifteen whole minutes. Those cakes have to be delivered by noon, but the church hall where they're going is only two blocks away. So let's sit down and enjoy a break."

She watched as he settled in across from her and began to eat his sandwich. She was so glad he'd talked her into letting him stay to help. Without him, she would surely be chasing her children up and down the stairs by now, with cakes burning in the background. She raised her glass of iced tea at him.

"To Connor McNair, life saver," she said. "Hip, hip, hooray."

He laughed. "Your Bundt cakes aren't all out of the fire yet," he told her with a crooked grin. "Don't count your chickens too soon."

"Of course not. I just wanted to acknowledge true friendship when it raises its furry head."

He shook his head and had to admit it was almost as covered with curls as hers. "Anytime," he told her, then tried to warble it as a tune. "Anytime you need me, I'll be there."

Her gaze caught his and she smiled and whispered, "Don't get cocky, kid."

His gaze deepened. "Why not?" he whispered back. "What's the fun of life if you don't take chances?"

She held her breath. For just a few seconds, something electric seemed to spark between them. And then it was gone, but she was breathing quickly.

"Chances. Is that what you call it?" she said, blinking a bit.

He nodded. "Chances between friends. That's all."

She frowned at him. "Some friend. Where were you to stop me from marrying Brad?"

The look in his face almost scared her. She'd meant it in a lighthearted way, but being casual about a subject that cut so deep into her soul didn't really work. Emotions were triggered. Her joke had fallen flat.

"I tried," he said gruffly, a storm brewing in his blue eyes.

He was kidding—wasn't he?

"What do you mean?" she asked, trying to ignore the trembling she heard in her own voice.

He leaned back in his chair but his gaze never left hers. "Remember? The night before your wedding."

She thought back. "Yes. Wait. You didn't even go to the bachelor party."

He snorted. "I went. Hell, I was hosting it." He seemed uncomfortable. "But I couldn't stay. I couldn't take all the celebration."

"Oh."

"So I went off and left all those happy guys to their revelry. I got a bottle of Scotch and took it to a sandy beach I knew of."

She nodded slowly, thinking back. "As I remember it, you were pretty tanked when you showed up at my apartment."

He took a deep breath and let it out. "Yes. Yes, I was. I was a tortured soul."

"Really? What were you so upset about that night?"

He stared at her. Couldn't she guess? Was she really so blind? He'd been out of his head with agony that night. He knew what a wonderful girl Jill was, knew it and loved her for it. And he knew Brad wasn't going to make her happy. But how could he tell her that? How could he betray a friend?

The problem was, he had to betray one of them. They

were both his best friends and he couldn't stand to see them getting married. And at the same time, he didn't think he should interfere. It was their decision. Their misfortune. Their crazy insane absolutely senseless leap into the brave unknown.

But he knew a thing or two, didn't he? He knew some things he was pretty sure she didn't know. But how could he hurt her with them? How could he explain to her about all the times Brad had cheated on her in the years they'd all been friends?

She would chalk it up to pure jealousy, and in a way, she would have been right. He was jealous. He wanted her. He knew Brad didn't value her enough. He knew Brad didn't deserve her. But how could he tell her that? How could he tell her the truth without ending up with her despising him more than she now did Brad? If she really did.

Besides, what could he offer her in place of her romance with Brad? He wasn't even sure he would ever be ready for any sort of full-time, long-term relationship. Every now and then he thought he'd conquered his background and the wariness he felt. But then he would see examples among his friends that just brought it back again. Could you trust another human in the long run? Was it worth the effort, just to be betrayed in the end?

And so—the Scotch. The alcohol was supposed to give him the courage to do what had to be done. But it didn't work that way. It made him sick instead, and he babbled incoherently once he had Jill's attention. She never understood what he was trying to say.

He couldn't even tell her now. She'd asked him a direct question. What was he so upset about that night? And still, he couldn't tell her the truth.

Because I knew you were marrying the wrong man. You should have been marrying me.

Reaching out, he caught her hand and looked deep into her eyes.

"Jill, tell me what you want. What you need in your life to be happy."

She stared back at him, and he waited, heart beating a fast tattoo on his soul.

"Connor," she began, "I... I don't know how to explain it exactly, but I..."

But then she shook her head and the timer went off and they both rose to check the cakes. Whatever she'd been about to say was lost in a cloud of the aroma of delicious confections.

The last full-size cakes came out and were set to cool and they began to fill the large mini Bundt cake pans. Twelve little cakes per pan. And each had to be filled to exactly the same level.

"They'll take about fifteen to twenty minutes," she told him nervously. "Then the ovens have to be back up to temperature before we put the next batch in. If we time it right, we might just make it. But it's going to be close."

One hundred and ten little cakes, she thought with a tiny surge of hysteria. Oh, my!

Connor left to deliver some of the full-size cakes. Jill checked on the babies. They were still sleeping in their travel cribs. She was thankful for that. Back to the kitchen, she began to prepare the rectangular boxes with the small dividers she was going to put the mini cakes in once they were ready to go. Then Connor was back and they pulled a batch out.

"These are perfect," she said with a sigh of relief. "You get the next batch ready. I'll make the Limoncello glaze."

They both had their eyes on the clock. Time seemed to go so quickly. Minutes seemed to evaporate into thin air. Jill was moving as fast as she could.

And then the phone started ringing. People who hadn't had their deliveries yet were wondering why.

"We're working as fast as we can," she told them. "Please, every minute I spend on the phone means your cake will get there that much later."

It was starting to feel hopeless. A batch overflowed its pan and they had to pull it out, clean up the mess and start again. She mixed up three batches of glaze and accidentally knocked them over onto the floor. That had to be done again.

And the clock was ticking.

She felt as though the beating of her heart was a clock, racing her, mocking her, letting her know she wasn't going to make it. Biting her lip, she forced back that feeling and dug in even harder.

"Last batch going in," Connor called.

She hurried over to see if it was okay. It was fine. Connor was turning out to be a godsend.

It was almost time. The phone rang. It was the Garden Club wondering where their cake was.

"Their party isn't until seven tonight," she said in full annoyance mode. "Can't they wait?"

"I'll run it over," Connor offered.

"You will not," she told him. "The engagement party is next. We have to deliver to them by five or we will have failed."

The twins woke up and were cranky. Connor tried to entertain them but there was very little hope. They wanted their mother.

Jill had to leave Connor alone with the cakes while she cuddled her boys and coaxed them into a better mood. She knew they needed her and she loved them to pieces, but all the while she felt time passing, ticking, making her crazy. She had to get back to the cakes.

Connor had his own problems. His phone was vibrating every fifteen minutes. Every call was from Brad. He knew that without even checking. He had no intention of answering the phone, but every time it began to move, he had that sinking feeling again.

Brad. Why couldn't he just disappear?

Instead he was texting. Connor didn't read the texts. There was no point to it. He knew what they said.

Brad wanted answers. He wanted to know what was going on. He wanted to get the latest scoop on Jill. All things Connor had no intention of giving him. But knowing Brad, that wasn't going to satisfy him. He was going to intrude, one way or another. And he wouldn't wait long to make his influence felt. Connor looked at his phone. If only there was some way to cut the link to Brad and his expectations.

CHAPTER SIX

IT WAS TIME. They had to move. But the twins wouldn't stop clinging to Jill.

Connor had an idea. He brought in a huge plastic tub he found in the garage, placing it in an empty corner of the kitchen, far from the oven and the electric appliances. Using a large pitcher, he put a few inches of barely warm water in the bottom.

"Hey kids," he called to them. "Want to go swimming?"

He didn't have to offer twice. They were excited, getting into their swimsuits and finding swim toys. Jill could get back to packing up her cakes and Connor could supervise the play area while he worked on glazing at the same time.

The long, rectangular boxes were filled with cakes for the Jamison engagement party. It was time to go. Connor packed them into Jill's van and took off. Jill sat down beside the tub of water to watch her boys pretend to swim and she felt tears well up in her eyes. They had made it. Now—as long as they didn't poison everyone at the engagement party, things would calm down. There were still a few cakes to deliver, but nothing was the hectic job the engagement party had been. She'd come through. And she couldn't have done it without Connor.

She wrapped her arms around her knees and hugged tightly. "Thank you, Connor," she whispered to the kitchen air. "You saved my life. I think I love you."

And she did. Didn't she? She always had. Not the way she loved Brad. But Brad was always such a problem and Connor never was.

She remembered when Brad had been the coolest guy around. The guy everyone looked up to, the hunk every girl wanted to be with. He drove the coolest convertible, had the best parties, knew all the right people. At least, that was the way it seemed back then. And he had chosen her. It was amazing how much you could grow up in just a few years and learn to see beyond the facade.

"Cool" didn't mean much when you had babies to feed in the middle of the night. And it only got in the way when it was time to separate your real friends from the posers. Back then, she'd been a pretty rotten judge of character. She'd improved. She had a better idea of what real worth was.

A half hour later, Connor was back. She rose to meet him, ready to ask him how it went, but he didn't give her time to do that. Instead he came right for her, picked her up and swung her around in a small celebratory dance.

"You did it," he said, smiling down into her face. "The cakes are delivered and the customer is in awe. You met the challenge. Congrats."

"We did it, you mean," she said, laughing as he

swung her around again. "Without you, all would be lost right now."

He put her down and shrugged. "What do we still have to get delivered?" he asked. "I want to get this job over with so we can relax." He looked down at the boys, still splashing about in the water. "Hey, guys. How are you doing?"

Timmy laughed and yelled something incomprehensible, and Tanner blew bubbles his way.

"Great," Connor said back, then looked at Jill. "Your orders, *mon chef?*" he asked.

"We do have two deliveries left," she said. "The last cakes are baking right now. We should be ready to call it a day in about an hour. Can you make it until then?"

"Only if I get a fair reward," he said, raising an eyebrow. "What are you offering?"

"I've got nothing," she said, making a face. "Unless you'll take kisses."

She was teasing, just having fun, but it hit him like a blow to the heart. "Kisses are my favorite," he told her gruffly, his eyes darkening.

She saw that, but it didn't stop her. Reaching up, she planted a kiss on his mouth, then drew back and laughed at him.

He laughed back, but his pulse was racing. "Hey, I'll work for those wages any day," he told her, and then he had to turn away. There was a longing welling up in him. He'd felt it before and he knew what it was.

He'd been yearning for Jill since the day he met her. His own background and emotional hiccups had worked against him letting her know over that first year, and by the time he actually knew what he wanted, Brad had taken over, and it was too late.

"What kind of glaze are we putting on these last cakes?" he asked her.

Jill didn't answer right away. She'd seen the look that had come over his face, noticed his reaction to her friendly kiss. For some reason, her heart was beating in a crazy way she wasn't used to.

"Those get a rum caramel with roasted chopped pecans sprinkled on top," she said at last.

They worked on it together, but there was a new feeling between them, a sort of sense of connection, that hadn't been there before. And she had to admit, she rather liked it.

He took out the last deliveries and stopped to pick up a pizza on his way home. She had the boys dried and put into their pajamas by then. They got their own special meals and then were put into the playroom to play quietly and get ready for bed. Jill set out the pizza on the kitchen table and she and Connor ate ravenously.

"Wow," he said with a groan. "What a day. I've worked in a lot of places, but I've never been put through the wringer like I was today."

"You did great," she responded. "I couldn't have met the deadlines without you."

He sighed. "What's the outlook for tomorrow?"

Tomorrow? She hadn't allowed herself to think that far ahead. Was he going to leave tonight? She didn't think so. He didn't seem to be making any of the pertinent preparations. And if he stayed tonight, what about tomorrow? Would he stay then, too? Should she let him?

"Just a couple of orders," she said. "And then, for the rest of the week, not a thing."

"Oh." He looked at her with a guilty grimace. "Uh, maybe you'd better take a look at some of the orders I took over the phone today. I wrote them down somewhere."

That started a mad scramble to locate the paper he'd written them down on.

"I have to set up a system," she muttered once they'd found it. "What if you'd gone and never told me about these?"

Gone? Where was he going?

Their gazes met and the question was there and neither of them wanted to answer it.

She looked at him, at his handsome face, his strong shoulders, and she felt a wave of affection. There was no one else she would have rather spent this day with. It had to be him.

She stopped in front of him and smiled, putting a hand flat on his chest. "Thank you," she said solemnly. "I can never stop thanking you enough. You really did make the difference today."

He didn't smile, but there was a dark, cloudy look in his eyes and he put his own hand over hers. "I wish I could do more," he said, and she could have sworn his voice cracked a little.

She shook her head, wishing she had the right to kiss him the way you would a lover. "You saved me from the nightmares," she murmured.

He frowned. "What nightmares."

She shrugged, wishing she hadn't brought it up.

"Sometimes I have this dream where I'm all alone on an island that's being attacked by huge black birds. They look sort of like vultures. They peck away at me. I run and run and they swoop down. Every time I turn to fight one off, others attack from behind me." She shuddered.

His hand tightened over hers. "Bummer."

She tried to smile but her lips were trembling. "No kidding."

"Hey." He leaned forward and dropped a soft kiss on her mouth. "I had a dream about birds last night, too. Only my dream was about a beautiful huge white bird with lacy wings. I was desperately trying to catch her. And you know what? That bird was you."

She smiled, enchanted, and he kissed her again. "Connor," she whispered warningly, trying to draw back, and a shout from one of the boys gave her statement emphasis. He straightened and watched as she left him.

They both went up to put the boys to bed.

"They're just going to climb out of these cribs again," Connor whispered to her.

"Shh. Don't remind them of the possibilities."

They covered the boys and turned out the lights and left, hoping for the best.

"How about a glass of wine?" he asked her.

She hesitated, knowing it would put her right to sleep. "I'd better not," she said. "But you go ahead."

The phone rang. She sighed. She was completely exhausted and ready to go to bed early and try to recoup. Hopefully this wasn't one of her friends asking about the date last night. She'd already ignored a couple of those calls on her cell. And if it was an order for a cake, she only hoped she would be able to get the facts straight.

"Hello?" she said, stifling a yawn. "Jill's Cakes."

"Oh, thank goodness," said the lady on the other end of the line. "You're there. Now please, please don't tell me you're closed for the night."

Jill frowned. What the heck did that mean? Was it someone at the engagement party who thought some of their order was missing? Or something different? "Well, uh, we're here and cleaning up but our workday is pretty much over. Was there something you needed?"

"Oh, Jill, this is Madeline Green," she responded in a voice that could summon cows. "You know me from the church choir."

"Of course." She pulled the phone a bit away from her ear and glanced up at Connor who had come close and was listening. She gave him a shrug. "Nice to hear from you, Madeline."

"Honey, listen. I'm here at the Elks lodge. We've had a disaster. Our caterer has failed us. We have one hundred and two people here for dinner and we have no dessert."

"Oh." No. Her brain was saying, *"No!"* Her body was saying, *"No!"* "I see. Uh....maybe you should go out and buy some ice cream."

"Impossible. We have to have a special dessert. It's traditional. People expect it. This is Old Timers' Night. Some only come to this annual award dinner because of the fancy desserts we usually serve. It's everyone's favorite part."

"But you had some ordered?"

"Oh, yes. They never showed up. The caterer disavows all knowledge of what the pastry chef was up to. He washes his hands of it entirely."

"I see." Her brain was still shrieking, "No!"

"Have you tried the Swedish bakery?"

"They're closed. In fact, everyone is closed. You're our only hope."

Jill blinked. "So you called everyone else first?"

"Well…"

"Never mind." She made a face, but the lady couldn't see it. She took a deep breath. "Madeline, I'm afraid we just can't…"

Suddenly she was aware that Connor had grabbed her upper arm and was shaking her gently.

"Say 'yes,'" he hissed at her intensely.

"What?" she mouthed back, covering the receiver with her hand. "Why?"

"Say 'yes.' Never ever say 'no.'"

He meant it. She groaned.

"You're trying to build up a reputation," he whispered close to her ear. "You need to be the go-to person, the one they can always depend on. If you want to build your business up, you have to go the extra mile."

He was right. She knew he was right. But she was so tired. She really didn't want to do this.

"Say 'yes'," he insisted.

She was too limp to fight it. Uncovering the mouthpiece, she sighed and handed the phone to him. "You do it," she said.

She turned around and looked at the mess they would have to wade through to get this done. Everything in her rebelled.

"You realize how many they need, don't you?" she asked when Connor hung up.

"Yes. We can do it."

"Can we? What makes you think you can say that?"

"I've seen you work. And I'm here to help you."

She winced. "How long do we have?"

"One hour."

Her mouth dropped open but no sound came out.

"Okay," Connor said quickly, hoping to forestall any forecasts of doom. "Think fast. What do you make that cooks in less than an hour?"

She shrugged. She felt like a wrung-out rag. "Cookies."

"Then we make cookies."

She frowned. "But that's not special."

"It is the way we make them." He looked at her expectantly. "What'll we do?"

She looked at him and she had to smile, shaking her head. She knew he was as beat as she was, but the call for desserts seemed to have given him new life. "You're the one who made the promises. You tell me."

"Come on. What's your signature cookie?"

She closed her eyes. "I'm too tired to think."

"Me, too," he agreed stoutly. "So we'll go on instinct instead of brainpower."

She began to laugh. This was all so ridiculous.

They'd just produced more baked product than she'd ever done before in one day, and now they were going to do more? Impossible.

"Cookies?" he coaxed.

"I guess."

They made cookies. Pecan lace cookies with a touch of cardamom, pressed together like sandwiches with mocha butter cream filling between them. Chocolate ganache on the base. A touch of white butter cream around the edges, like a lacy frill.

Connor used the mixer while Jill prepped the pans and got the chocolate ready to melt. Just as the first pan went into the oven, they heard the sound of giggling from the next room.

Jill looked at Connor. "Oh, no."

He nodded. "They climbed out again. We should have known they would." He looked at her. There was no time to spare and she was the chef. "I'll take care of them," he told her. "You just keep baking."

It took a couple of minutes to catch the boys and carry them back up, and all the while, he was racking his brain to think of some way to keep them in their beds. There was only one idea that just might work, but he knew instinctively that Jill wasn't going to like it. They didn't have much choice. He was going to have to do it and deal with the consequences later.

CHAPTER SEVEN

BY THE TIME Connor got back to the kitchen, Jill had at least sixty cookies cooling and was beginning assembly of the desserts.

"I don't hear the boys," she said. "What did you do?"

"Don't worry. I took care of it."

She stopped and looked at him through narrowed eyes. "You didn't tie them up or anything like that, did you?"

"No, nothing like that. I'd show you, but right now, we've got to hurry with this stuff."

She gave him a penetrating glance, but she was in the middle of the drizzle across the top of each confection and her attention got diverted.

"What do you think?" she asked him.

Connor looked the sample over with a critical eye.

"I don't know. It still needs something. Something to make it look special."

They both stared for a long sixty seconds.

"I know," he said. "We've got plenty of buttercream left. Get your decorating thingamajig."

"Why?"

"I've seen the flowers you can make with butter cream frosting. You're going to make one hundred and two rose buds."

"Oh." She looked at the clock. "Do you really think we can get them out in time?"

"I know we can." He grinned at her, then swooped in and kissed her hard on her pretty mouth. "We can do anything. We already have."

He took her breath away, but she stayed calm. At least outwardly. She stared at him for a few seconds, still feeling that kiss. Why was he doing things guaranteed to send her into a tailspin if she didn't hold herself together?

But she went back to work and she kept control and the job got finished. And at the end, they stared at each other.

"We did it."

"We did, didn't we?"

"But the delivery..."

"Quick. We're five minutes late."

He piled the desserts in boxes and headed for the door. Just before he disappeared, he called back, "Better check on the twins."

She was already on her way. There wasn't a sound as she climbed the stairs. When she opened the door, nothing moved. But somehow everything looked a little wrong. In the dark, she couldn't quite figure out what it was and she hated to turn on the light, but she had to. And what she saw left her speechless.

"What?"

One crib stood empty. The other had been turned

upside down. The mattress was on the ground, but the rest of the crib was above it like a cage. And on the mattress, her two little boys were sound asleep.

Her first impulse was to wake them up and rescue them, but then she realized they were probably better off where they were. After all, how was she going to get them to stay in their cribs without the bars?

She went back down, not sure what to do. She started cleaning up the kitchen, but then she heard Connor driving up and she went to meet him at the door.

He came in smiling. "They loved it," he announced. "People were asking for our card and I was handing them out like crazy."

She put her head to the side and raised her eyebrows as she listened to him. *"Our" card?* When had that happened? But she could deal with that later. Right now she had something else on her mind.

"Now do you want to explain what happened to the crib?"

"Oh." His face changed and suddenly he looked like a boy with a frog in his pocket. "Sure. I, uh, I had to turn it upside down."

"So I see."

He gave her a guilty smile. "Are they okay?"

She nodded. "Sound asleep."

"Good." He looked relieved. "That was the goal."

"But Connor…"

"They wouldn't stay in the cribs," he told her earnestly. "They kept climbing out. And that was just so dangerous. This was the only thing I could think of on the fly. And luckily, they loved it when I put them into their own special cage. I told them to be monkeys and they played happily until they went to sleep. Didn't they?"

"I guess so, but…"

"If I hadn't done it, they would still be climbing out and running for the hills. And we wouldn't have finished in time."

"Okay." She held up a hand and her gaze was steely. "Enough. I understand your logic. What I don't understand is how you could do such a crazy thing without consulting me first."

That stopped him in his tracks. He watched her and realized she was right. He thought he was doing what was best for her, but without her consent, it was really just what was best for him. He had no right to decide for her. They were her kids.

He'd goofed again and it pained him. Why was he always putting his foot in it where she was concerned? He had to apologize. He swallowed hard. That wasn't an easy thing to do. Taking a deep breath, he forced himself to do what had to be done.

"Jill, you're absolutely right," he said sincerely. "And I'm really sorry. I was wrong to take your agreement for granted. I won't do that again."

Now she had a lump in her throat. Few had ever said that sort of thing to her before, especially not a man. Could she even imagine Brad saying such a thing? Hardly. She felt a small sense of triumph in her chest. She'd asked for an apology and she got one. Wow.

"I guess the first order of business is to figure out

how to make a crib they can't climb out of," she noted, looking at him expectantly.

He feigned astonishment. "Who? Me? You want me to build a crib they can't climb out of?"

"Either that, or come up with a plan," she said, teasing him flirtatiously. "Aren't you here to help?"

His grin was endearingly crooked and he pulled her to him, looking down like a man who was about to kiss a very hot woman. She looked up at him, breath quickening, and she realized she really wanted that kiss. But a look of regret and warning flashed in his eyes. He quickly released her and turned away.

"You ready for that glass of wine now?" he asked, walking toward the wet bar at the end of the room.

She took a deep breath and closed her eyes before she answered. "Sure," she said. "Why not?"

He poured out two crystal glasses of pinot noir and they sat in the living room on a small couch. There was a gentle rain falling and they could see it through the huge glass windows that covered one side of the room.

"What a day," he said, gazing at her as he leaned back in his corner of the couch. The dim light left the wine in their glasses looking like liquid rubies. "It feels like it must have lasted at least a day and a half."

"Or maybe three and a half," she agreed. "And a few shocks to the system." She sighed. "But you came through like a trooper. I couldn't have done it without you."

"I'm glad I was here to help."

She met his gaze and then looked away too quickly. She felt her cheeks reddening and groaned inside. There was nothing to be embarrassed about. Why had she avoided his eyes like that? She coughed to cover up her feelings.

"So tell me the story of this cooking talent you seem to have discovered in the mysterious East," she said quickly.

He grinned. "So you can see the evidence of my expertise in my work even here," he said grandly.

The corners of her mouth quirked. "No, but you told me you were good, so I believe it."

"Ah." He nodded. "Well, it's all the fault of a young chef named Sharon Wong. We dated each other for most of the last year in Singapore. She taught me everything I know." He made a comical face. "Of course, that was only a small fraction of what *she* knows, but it was a start."

A woman was behind it all. She should have known. But it gave her a jolt. Connor had never seemed to have a special woman in his life. Lots of women, but no one special. Had that changed?

"A chef. Great. I'm partial to chefs. What kind of cuisine?"

"She specializes in Mandarin Chinese but she mostly taught me French basics. She claims every chef needs French cooking as a standard, a baseline to launch from. Sort of like learning Calculus for science classes."

She nodded. "That's why it's so important for Trini to go to the school she just left to attend. She'll get a great grounding in the basics."

He watched her for a moment, then asked, "Why didn't you ever go there?"

She shrugged and stretched back against the pillows, beginning to feel her body relax at last. "I took classes locally, but nothing on that level." Her smile was wistful. "Funny. I applied a few years ago. I got accepted on my first try. A scholarship and everything. But I didn't get to go."

"Why not?"

She gave him a bemused smile. "I married Brad instead."

"Wow, that was a bad decision." He looked pained at the thought. "You gave up going to the school of your dreams to marry Brad?"

"Yes." She threw him a reproving look. He was getting a little adamant about her life choices. "And I do regret it. So that's why I won't let her give it up for anything. She's got to go. She'll learn so much."

He was quiet and she wondered what he was thinking about. Something in the look on his face told her it still bothered him to think of her giving up her dream that way and she wasn't sure why he cared.

Everybody had to make choices. Everybody had to give something up now and then. It was part of life.

"I was just thinking about that time we went to San Francisco," she said a few minutes later. "Remember?"

He looked up and his smile completely changed his face. "Sure I remember. You had set up a weekend to celebrate Brad's birthday with a surprise trip to San Francisco and then you ended up taking me instead."

She nodded, still captivated by that smile.

"It was senior year, wasn't it?" he went on. "You got

a hotel just off Union Square and tickets to the ballet— or so you said."

She nodded again. "That was my big mistake. Once I told Brad that, he suddenly had somewhere else he had to be that weekend."

She could hardly believe it. What a fool she'd been in those days. "I was so mad, I told him I was going to take you instead. And he said, sure, go ahead."

Connor smiled, recalling that sunny day. He thought he'd died and gone to heaven. He was walking on air when she asked him to go with her.

A whole weekend with Jill and no Brad. He hadn't even cared if it was the ballet. But the beauty of it was, she was just setting up a surprise, because the tickets that she had were for the Giants in Candlestick Park. The ballet thing was just a ruse to tease Brad and the baseball game was supposed to be his big surprise. Instead it was Connor's.

She gazed at him speculatively. "Sometimes when I look back I wonder why I didn't notice."

His heart gave a lurch. What was she reading into his responses? "Notice what?"

She shrugged. "How little Brad actually cared for me."

Oh, that. It had always been obvious to most of those around her. Brad wanted her when he wanted her, but he didn't confine his activities too close to home. Still, looking at her now, he couldn't stand the haunted expression in her eyes. The last thing in the world she should do was beat herself up over the past.

"He cared plenty," he said gruffly. "He wanted you for himself right from the first. Don't you remember?"

She shook her head and gave him a sad smile. "I think you know what I mean. Anyway, we had a great time in San Francisco, didn't we?"

"Yes, we did." He let his head fall back as he thought of it. That trip had planted dreams in his head. You could say he might have been better off without them, but he didn't think so. His feelings for Jill were a part of that time, even if she never knew it.

"Remember that night? We talked until almost dawn, and then we slept until noon."

"Yeah." They had two rooms, but he never went to his own. There were two beds in hers, one for each of them, and he just stayed with her. He never touched her, but he sure wanted to.

And best of all, it was on that night that he knew he was ready to try to have a real relationship. He'd spent the first few years in college wary of making any sort of commitment to any girl. His background had argued strenuously against it.

But Jill was different. He made up his mind that night that he was going to tell her how he felt about her once they got back to the university. And he was resolved— he was going to take her away from Brad. Somehow, someway, he would do it. He spent hours going over what he wanted to say, how he wanted to make her understand his feelings.

And then they got back to school, and there was Brad on crutches. He'd gone waterskiing and broken his leg. Suddenly he needed Jill. Connor felt himself fading into the background, like some sort of invisible man, and wondering why his timing was always so bad.

It was shortly afterward that he signed up to go to Europe for a semester. When he got back, he learned that Jill and Brad had broken up just after he left. From what he could see, Brad was busy dating every pretty girl on campus while Jill was busy trying to pretend she didn't care.

He took her to his favorite little Italian restaurant and they ate pasta and talked for hours. He ended up with his arm around her while she cried on his shoulder about how awful Brad was being to her. He restrained himself. He was going to do it right. He was going to take it one step at a time.

But once again, the timing wasn't in his favor. By the next afternoon, Brad was back in her life and all was forgiven.

That was when he'd hardened his heart. It had happened to him one too many times. He wasn't going to let it happen again—ever. Even today he was wary. What seemed like the opportunity to strike so often ended up as the chance to fall on his face instead. It wasn't worth it.

"I think of that trip to San Francisco as an island of happiness in an ocean of stress," she said softly. She looked at him with gentle speculation and a touch of pure affection. "Everything is always so easy with you. And it was always so hard with Brad."

Really? Really?

He stared at her, wondering how she could say such a thing. If that was so, why had she married the hard guy? He was tempted to come right out and ask her that question. That just might clarify a lot of things between them. But before he could think of a way to put it, she spoke again.

"So, was it serious?" she asked him.

He was startled. "Was what serious?"

"You and Sharon Wong?"

"Oh." He laughed, then considered for a moment. "Who knows? It might get to be. If I go back to Singapore."

She turned away. Why did she have such a sick feeling in the pit of her stomach? Was she jealous? Ridiculous. He deserved to fall in love. He deserved some happiness. Hadn't she just been counseling him to find someone to marry? And now she was going to go all green-eyed over a woman he obviously had some affection for? What a fool she was acting.

Connor was probably the best man she knew. He'd always been there for her—except when he took off for places like Singapore. Still, he'd always been a playboy in so many ways. She couldn't imagine him in love.

"I never knew any of your girlfriends in college," she noted. "Why was that? You never showed up with a girl on your arm. I knew they existed, because I heard about them. How come you never brought them around?"

He gazed at her and didn't know what to say. He'd dated plenty of girls in college. But why would he take any of them to meet the one girl he cared about above all others? They would have seen through his casual act in no time.

Funny that she never did.

He stared at her for a long, pulsing moment. "You could have had me anytime you wanted me," he said in a low, rough voice.

There. He'd said it. Finally a little hunk of truth thrown out into this sea of making everyone feel good about themselves. What was she going to do about it?

"Connor!"

She didn't seem to want to take it as truth. More like teasing. Did she really think he was making a joke?

"Be serious," she said, waving that away. "You know that's not true. You didn't want anyone to be your steady girl. You wanted fun and excitement and games and flirting. You didn't want a real relationship. You admitted it at the time." She made a face at him. "You have to realize that back then, what you wanted didn't seem to have anything to do with what I wanted."

He shook his head sadly. "I don't know how you could have read me so wrong."

"I didn't." She made a face at him. "You just don't remember things the way they really were. I was looking for the tie that binds, just like a lot of women at that age. It's a natural instinct. Nesting. I felt a deep need for a strong male, someone to build the foundation of a family with."

He almost rolled his eyes at her. Was she really so self-delusional? "So you chose a guy who didn't want kids."

Her shoulders sagged. He got her on that one. What had she been thinking? He was right. She'd known from the first that he didn't want children. Somehow she had buried that fact under everything, pretending to herself that it didn't matter. Maybe she wouldn't want children, either. Or, more likely, he would change his mind. After all, once it was a clear possibility, surely he would think twice and begin to waver. After all, he loved her. Didn't he?

"I didn't say I chose wisely." She hated to face it, but he had hit the nail on the head. Her mistakes had been easy to avoid, if she'd only been paying more attention. Sighing, she rose. "I want to check on the kids. And I think I'll change out of this uniform. Will you still be up or should I not come back and let you get some sleep?"

He looked at her and realized he wanted her back above all else. He wanted her in his bed, in his arms, in his life. But for now he would have to do with the minimum.

"Sure, come on back," he said, holding up his wineglass. "I've still got a long way to go."

She was glad he'd said that. As she stopped in to look at her sleeping children, she sighed. The upturned crib was not a long-term solution. Something would have to give. She only hoped it wasn't her peace of mind.

She stopped by the guest room where she slept and changed into something more comfortable, then hurried back down, wondering if he would be asleep before she got back. But he was still staring at the light through his wine and he smiled to welcome her as she entered the room.

She flopped down on the little couch, sitting much closer this time. She was drawn to his warmth, drawn to his masculinity. Might as well face it. She loved looking at him, loved the thought of touching him. Would he kiss her good-night? That would be worth a little loss of sleep.

"Connor, how come I don't really know anything about your childhood? How come you never talk about it?"

He took a long sip of wine and looked at her through narrowed eyes. Then he put on his Sam Spade tough-guy voice. "It's not a pretty story, sweetheart. Full of ugliness and despair. You don't want to worry your pretty little head over it."

"Be serious for a moment," she asked. "Really. I want to know you better."

"Why? What more can there be? We've known each other for more than ten years and suddenly you don't know me?"

"Exactly. You've used our friendship as cover all this time. And now I want to know the truth. What were your parents really like? Not the cartoon version you dredge up for jokes. The real people."

He appeared uncomfortable for a moment, then thought for a second or two, and began.

"Let's just put it this way. As they say in the head-shrinking crowd, I've had lifelong relationship com-mitment problems, which can probably be traced back to my childhood environment."

"And that means?"

He stared at her. Did she really want him to go there? Okay.

"I learned early and firsthand just what kind of power women have," he said softly. "I watched my mother purposefully drive my father crazy. Payback, I think, for never making as much money as she felt she needed."

"Ouch." She frowned.

"Yes." He glanced at his ruby-red wine and thought back. "My father was a sweet guy in many ways. He tried hard to please her. But he just didn't have what it took to bring in a high salary, and she rubbed his nose in it every day."

"Oh, Connor," she said softly.

"I watched him go through all sorts of contortions to find some little way to bring a smile to her face, but that was virtually impossible. She nitpicked everything. Nothing was ever good enough for her." He threw her a lopsided grin. "Especially me."

"So she nitpicked you, too?"

"Oh, yeah. I think finding something to make me stammer out 'gee, I'm sorry, Mom,' was what made her day for her." He looked at her. "So I avoided going home. I hung around school in the afternoon, joined every sports team, every debating society, every club that would give me a place to hang out." His gaze darkened. "Meanwhile my father drank himself to death."

"Oh, Connor. I'm so sorry."

He nodded. "It was a waste, really. He was a smart guy. He should have had a better life."

"Yes."

He gazed at her levelly, wondering if he really wanted to get into the next level of this discussion. Did he want to cut a vein and just let it bleed all over the night? Not really. But he might as well explain a little more about why he'd been the way he was when they were younger.

"You know, for years I really was leery of having a relationship with a woman that lasted more than twenty minutes. It just didn't seem worth the risk from what I'd seen."

She wrinkled her nose at him, as if she thought he was being silly. Still, he plowed on.

"But I have a new perspective on it now. I spent the last eighteen months or so in Singapore working with a great guy name George who is married to a wonderful woman named Peggy. I lived in their house and saw their entire interaction, and it helped me understand that decent, loving relationships are possible. I had to look harder at myself and wonder if I had what it takes to have that. I mean, it may be possible, but is it possible for me?"

Jill stared at him. She'd had no idea he had such deep misgivings about lifetime relationships. It made her want to reach out to him, to hold his hand and reassure him. There were plenty of women in the world who didn't treat men the way his mother had. Didn't he know that?

"And what did you decide?" she asked tentatively.

He flashed her a quick grin. "The verdict isn't in yet."

She started to argue about that, but she stopped herself. How could she wrestle him out of opinions that had developed from real life experiences? She didn't have as many bad ones as he did. Maybe it got harder as they piled up.

"Where's your mother now?" she asked.

He shrugged. "I'm not sure. I think she moved to Florida to live with her sister, but we don't keep in touch."

She thought that was a mistake, but she held her tongue. Maybe later she would try to talk to him about how much could be lost when you lost your parents. Instead of going into it directly, she decided to tell him about her background.

"Here's what happened to me," she said. "And Sara. When my mother was alive, we were a happy family. At least, that's the way I remember it. But my father's second marriage was a horror show right from the beginning. That's why Sara and I never warmed to our stepmother, Lorraine." She shook her head.

"She was such a terrible choice for him. And it probably didn't help the marriage that we couldn't like her. He was a good guy, gentle, warm. And she was a shrew."

"Wow," he said, somewhat taken aback. He wasn't used to such strong disapproval from Jill. "That's a pretty negative judgment on the woman."

She shrugged. "Of course, I saw the whole thing through the perspective of a child who had lost her mother and found her father bringing home a new, updated version that didn't please her at all. We were very resentful and probably didn't give her much of a chance, especially after she had a baby. Little Kelly was cute, but it didn't make up for Lorraine. And she didn't like us any better than we liked her and she made it pretty obvious."

"Little Kelly is the one who died last week in a car crash?"

She nodded. "The one I wish we'd been kinder to." She shrugged, but her eyes were sad and haunted. "Too late now." She looked at him again. "And that's what I want you to think about. Don't wait until it's too late to contact your mother again."

He gave her a quizzical look. "Okay. Point taken."

She nodded, then yawned. He smiled.

"You look like a sleepy princess."

She'd traded in her uniform for a short fuzzy robe over the long lacy white nightgown and she looked adorable to him.

"What?" she said, laughing.

"In that gown thing. Even with the little robe over it. You look like you should be in a castle."

She was blushing. Connor had a way of letting her know how pretty he thought she was and she was so hungry for that, it almost brought tears to her eyes.

She smiled back. "I guess we'd better go to bed."

"You're right. We need sleep. I'm only glad we survived the day."

He rose and turned to pull her up beside him and he didn't let go of her hands once they were standing face-to-face, looking at each other.

"I'm glad you came back," she told him, her breath catching in her throat as her pulse began to race. Was he going to kiss her? Or was she going to have to do it herself?

"Me, too." His eyes went so dark, they could have been black instead of blue. He leaned closer, pulling her body up hard against his. "Jill…" he began, and at the same moment, the cell phone in his pocket began to vibrate.

She felt it right away. Sharply drawing in her breath, she stepped back and looked at him. He pulled the phone out, looking for a place to set it down. She reached out and took it from him. Flipping it up, she glanced at the screen and handed it back to him.

"Message for you," she said, and her voice showed no emotion. "How interesting. It's Brad." Her face didn't reveal a thing, but her eyes were strangely hooded as she turned away and started for the stairs. "Good night," she said over her shoulder.

He cringed, though he wouldn't show it. He stuck the phone back in his pocket and didn't answer it. He hadn't been answering Brad's calls all day. Why should he start now?

But he wished she hadn't seen that.

CHAPTER EIGHT

SLEEPING ON THE couch was getting old fast. Connor stretched and hit the armrest before he had his legs out straight.

"Ouch," he muttered grumpily, wondering why he was awake so early when he was still so tired. Then he noticed the problem. The twins were running around the furniture and yelling at the top of their lungs. He groaned. He really preferred a normal alarm clock.

He opened his eyes just enough to see them. They were pretty cute. But loud. He was going to have to give up any chance for more sleep. He stretched again.

"Great game, kids," he told them groggily, swinging his legs over the side of the couch and sitting up with a yawn.

The boys stopped and stared at him. He stared back. Tanner pretended to bark like a puppy. Timmy made a sound like a growling monster. He shook his head. They wanted him to respond. He could tell. And he couldn't resist.

Just like the day before, he burst up off the couch,

waving the covers to make himself look huge, and gave them a monster growl they wouldn't soon forget.

They screamed with scared happiness and charged out of the room, pushing and shoving to both fit through the door at once.

Jill came in and glared at him. "They won't be able to eat their breakfast if you rile them up too much," she warned.

He waved his sheet-covered arms at her and growled. She shook her head and rolled her eyes.

"How come you're not scared?" he complained.

"Because you look so ridiculous," she told him. She laughed softly, letting her gaze slide over his beautiful body. What on earth did he do in Singapore that kept him so fit? His muscles were hard and rounded and tan and a lot of that was on display. His chest was all male and his pajama bottoms hung low on his hips. He took her breath away.

"But you do look cute as a scary monster," she allowed, trying to avoid an overdose of his sexiness by looking away. "We might be able to use your skills at Halloween."

"Hey, no fair," he said as he looked her over sleepily. "You already changed out of your princess dress."

"I'm going incognito for the day," she told him. "They don't let princesses bake Bundt cakes."

"They should."

"I know." She smiled at him then asked with false cheerfulness, "What did Brad want last night?"

He shrugged. "I didn't answer it."

She stared at him for a moment, then looked away.

"I just checked my email. There are already two more orders from people who had cake last night. That makes four who want their cakes today, and two more for the weekend."

"I said you had star power. Didn't I?"

She reached out to take the sheet from him and he leaned forward and dropped a quick kiss on her mouth before she could draw back. She looked up into his eyes and the room began to swim around her.

"They should let princesses do whatever they want," he said softly, and then he reached out and pulled her closer and she slipped her arms around his neck and his mouth found hers.

Finally!

She'd been waiting for this kiss forever—or anyway, it seemed that way. She melted in his arms, taking in his taste and letting her body feel every hard part of him it could manage. His rounded muscles turned her on and his warm, musky smell sent her senses reeling.

And then the doorbell rang.

She collapsed against him, laughing and shaking her head. "Why does fate hate me?" she protested.

He held her close and buried his face in her hair, then let her go.

A timer went off.

"Oh, no, I've got to check that," she said.

"I'll go to the door," he offered.

"Really?" She looked at him skeptically, wondering who was going to get a stunning view of that magnificent chest and hoping it wasn't the church people. Then she rushed on into the kitchen to check her cake.

It definitely needed to come out. She set it on the cooling rack and looked around at the mess that still existed from yesterday. She usually made it a practice never to go to bed with a dirty pan left in the sink, but she'd broken that rule last night. Now she had a couple of counters full of pans that needed washing. She was working on that when Connor came into the kitchen.

"Who's at the door?" she asked distractedly.

Connor made a face. "The Health Department Inspector."

She turned to stare at him. "What? He just came last week."

He shrugged. "I guess he's back."

And so he was, coming into the kitchen and looking around with massive disapproval all over his face. Tall and thin, he wore glasses and had a large, fluffy mustache, along with a pinched look, that made him look like a bureaucratic force to be reckoned with.

Connor made a face at her and left to put on some clothes. The inspector sniffed at him as he left, then looked back at the kitchen.

"What the hell is going on here?" he demanded, looking at the pot and pan strewn counters.

Jill had a smart-alecky answer right on the tip of her tongue, but she held it back. This was the health inspector. He could ruin her if he wanted to. Shut her down. She had to be nice to him, much as it stuck in her craw.

"Look, this is such a bad time for you to show up. Unannounced, I might add. Aren't you supposed to make appointments?"

He glared at her. "Aren't you supposed to be ready at all times for inspection?"

She gave him a fake smile. "Sorry about the mess. I'm in the middle of cleaning it up. We had a huge, huge day yesterday. Things will be back in order in no time."

"That would be wise," he said. "I wouldn't want to have to write you up for kitchen contamination."

She gaped at him in outrage. "There's clutter, there's mess, but there's no contamination. Please!"

He shrugged, then turned as Connor reappeared, dressed in the same shirt and slacks he'd been wearing for three days now.

"What are you doing here?" he asked.

"Moral support," Connor responded simply. "I'm just a friend. I'm helping."

His eyes narrowed. "Helping how?"

Connor shrugged, instinctively knowing this might be a time to be careful and wary. "Odd jobs. Deliveries."

"Ah." He appeared skeptical. "Let's hope you aren't doing any of the baking. Because if you are, you're going to need to be screened for medical conditions. You'll need a blood test. And more. We don't want you touching the food if you're not healthy. Your papers must be in order."

Connor frowned at the man. "What papers?"

"The ones you need to qualify to do any cooking whatsoever."

Connor sighed and looked away. "Ah, those papers."

"Yes. Records of shots and tests, etc. Medical problems in the last ten years. You understand."

Connor made a face, but he said as pleasantly as possible, "Of course."

The man glared at him. "So? Where are your papers?"

"Really?" Connor said, beginning to get belligerent. "Hey, Mr. Health Inspector, let's see *your* papers."

The man produced a badge and a license and Connor stared at them, realizing he had no idea if they were authentic or not. But he was beginning to have his doubts about this guy.

Jill winced. Connor looked about ready to do something that would jeopardize her business and she had to stop him. Standing behind the inspector, she shook her head and put her finger to her lips, then jerked her thumb toward the other room. Connor hesitated, then followed her out into the hallway, leaving the inspector to poke around at will.

"Connor, don't antagonize him, for heaven's sake," she whispered. "He'll probably write me up for some little thing and then he'll have to come back to check if I've fixed it. But at least he'll go. So leave him alone."

Connor was frowning. "How often does this guy show up here?" he asked her.

"Too much if you ask me. I almost feel like it's harassment at this point. And the funny thing is, every time he comes, something seems to go wrong. I don't know if it's just that I get nervous and then I don't keep focused on what I'm doing or what."

Connor's gaze narrowed. "What sort of things go wrong?"

"Oh…one time the oven wouldn't work anymore and

I had to get a repairman out. Another time somehow the refrigerator got unplugged and it was hours before we knew it. A lot of supplies spoiled and I had to throw them out."

"No kidding." He frowned. "Is he the same official who comes every time?"

"No. But he does come the most. And he says the goofiest things. In fact, I called the health department to complain about him a few weeks ago. They claimed they hadn't sent anyone."

Connor's face was hard as stone. "That doesn't seem right."

"I know. But what can I do? I don't dare confront him. What if he pulls my license?"

Connor shook his head. "Jill, I don't buy it for a minute."

She stared at him. "What do you mean?"

"I think he's a phony. He's got to go."

"What?" She grabbed at his arm to stop him, but he pulled away and marched back into the kitchen, catching the stranger with a tiny camera in his hand.

"Get the hell out of here," he told the inspector in a low, furious voice.

"Connor!" Jill cried, coming in behind him. "You can't talk that way to the inspector!"

But the man seemed to take Connor quite seriously. He raised his hands as though to show he didn't mean any harm and said, "Okay, okay. Take it easy. I'm going."

And he turned around and left as quickly as he could.

Jill stared after him, then looked at Connor. "What the heck?" she cried.

He turned and gave her a look. "Jill, that man's not a real health inspector. Can't you see that?"

"No." She blinked in bewilderment. "What is he then?"

"A private investigator pretending to be a health inspector."

"But why would...?" Her face cleared. "Brad!"

Connor nodded. "That's my guess."

She sank into a chair. "Oh, my gosh. I can't believe that. Brad sent him to spy on me."

"And to sabotage your business, I would guess."

She closed her eyes and took a deep breath. "Why didn't I think of that? I knew there was something fishy about the way he kept showing up." She looked up at Connor. "I should have known."

But Connor was still thinking things over. "Okay, I'm ready to believe that was Brad at work. So the question is, what else has he been meddling in?"

She thought for a moment, then put a hand over her mouth. "Oh, my gosh." She grabbed his hand and held it tightly. "Connor, I don't know this for sure, but I was told that Brad tried to get them to disallow my license. Right at the beginning."

He lowered himself into the chair beside her, still holding her hand. "Why would he do that?"

"Well, he never wanted me to keep this house. He thought I ought to move to the mainland and get an apartment, put the kids in day care and get a regular job. He sort of acted like he thought I was trying to extort money from him by doing anything else."

His face was cold as granite. "Tell me more."

"It took a while to get started. At first, I didn't have any of the right equipment. I used every penny I got from Brad to help pay for the commercial oven, but I still needed to buy a three-unit sink and the special refrigeration I needed. When he found out what I was doing, he was furious."

"And stopped giving you money," he guessed.

She nodded. "Pretty much. Which only made it more important that I find a way to grow my business." She laced her fingers with his.

"You know, you hit a place where you can either move forward, or settle for something less, and get stuck in that great big nowhere land." She sighed. "In order to get to where I might make some actual profit, I had to take the chance. I needed funding. So..."

She met his gaze and looked guilty. "So, yes, I took out a loan so that I could finish buying the supplies I needed."

"What did you use to get a loan? The house?"

She nodded. "That's why it's so scary that this house is still underwater and they won't give me a mortgage modification."

"You've tried?"

"Countless times."

"You're in a tight spot."

She nodded. "I'm standing at the edge of the cliff, you mean. And the ground is starting to crumble under my feet."

His free hand took her chin and lifted her face toward his, then he leaned in and kissed her softly. "I'll catch you," he said, his voice husky. "I'm here, Jill. I won't let you hit the rocks."

She smiled, loving his generous spirit, but not really believing his words. How could he stop the chain of events that seemed to be overwhelming her? It wasn't likely. They'd had a good day yesterday and he'd made that possible. But goodwill—and cake sales—could only go so far. Every step forward seemed to bring on two steps back. She was beginning to lose hope.

He hesitated, then shook his head and drew back from her. "Okay, here's what I don't understand. This just really gets to me. Why do you let Brad still be such a huge part of your life?"

"I…I don't."

"Yes, you do. You're divorced. He's not even giving you the money you should be getting for the kids. He doesn't want anything to do with the children." He frowned, searching her eyes. "Why let him affect you in any way? Why maintain any ties at all?"

She blinked. It was hard to put this in words. How to explain how alone she felt in the world? In some ways, Brad was still her only lifeline. It was too scary to cut that off.

"The only real, legal ties we still have is the business," she said instead of trying to explain her emotional connection to her past. "I still own fifteen percent of it."

He nodded. He knew that. "Do you have a voting position on the board?"

She shrugged. "I'm not really sure if I do or not. I

think I'm supposed to but I've never tried to use it. I suppose I should ask a lawyer."

"At the very least."

"The only reason I keep it, to tell you the truth, is that emotionally, I just can't give up on it yet. It's still a part of my life, a part of my past, all those years we spent building it into the enterprise it is today."

He nodded. Did that answer the question? Her ties to Brad were still too strong. But were they that way from fear…or love? Hard to pull those two apart for analysis. And the answer to that meant everything.

Connor was so angry inside, both at Brad and at himself, he couldn't stay near her for now. Instead he went out and walked down to the ferry and then around the quaint little village and back again. He finally had something he wanted to say to Brad, but when he tried calling him, he found his old pal had turned the tables, and now he wasn't taking calls from Connor.

Voice mail was his only recourse. He waited for the beep.

"Hey, Brad. I just wanted to let you know that I know the health inspector is a phony. He's someone who works for you. If he comes here again, I'll have him arrested for impersonating a government employee.

"About those shares. If you really want them so badly, why don't you come and ask her for them like a man? Why don't you face her? And why don't you offer her something real? You never know what might happen.

"In the meantime, other than that, leave Jill alone. Go live your own life and forget about hers."

He clicked off and tried to tame the rage that roiled in him. Jill didn't deserve any of this. He only hoped she would let him stay here to help her get out from under all this. He knew she couldn't get Brad out of her system, but there wasn't much he could do about that. He didn't care about his own emotional involvement anymore. So, he was probably going to get his heart broken. So what? His love for Jill was too strong to try to deny any longer. And all he wanted was what was good for her. He had to stay.

When he walked into the house, he heard Jill singing in the kitchen. He had to stop for a moment and listen, marveling at her. What was she, some kind of angel? Whatever—she was everything he knew he wanted. And would probably never have.

"Hey," he told her as he came up behind her, putting his arms around her. She leaned back into him and smiled. "I'm getting pretty funky in these clothes," he said. "I think I'll run into town and get some fresh things from the hotel room. Can I bring anything back for you?"

She turned in his embrace and kissed him. "Just bring yourself back. That's all I need," she said.

He kissed her again and the kiss deepened. The way he felt about her grew every time he touched her. Right now, it seemed like fireworks going off in his chest. This was the way he wished it could always be.

Jill stood at the sliding glass door looking out at the grassy hill that was her backyard. Connor was outside playing with the twins, chasing them up and down the hill, laughing, picking up one and then the other to whirl about and land gently again. Her heart was full of bittersweet joy. Tears trembled in her eyes.

If only Brad could be this way. If he really met the boys, if he tried to get to know them, wouldn't he realize how wonderful they were? Wouldn't he have to love them? Wouldn't that make everything better?

As she watched, Connor fell, iron-cross style, into a huge bed of leaves, and the boys raced each other to jump on top of him. She could hear the laughter from where she was behind glass and it answered her own questions.

No. Brad would never love the boys, because he didn't want to. He wouldn't let himself. It was time she faced facts.

She heard the front door open and she turned that way.

"Jill!"

"In here, Sara." She frowned. Her sister's voice sounded high and strained. What had happened now?

Sara appeared, looking a little wild. "Did you get the letter?"

"What letter?"

"From Social Services." She waved an official-looking envelope. "Did you get one, too?"

"I don't know. Connor brought in the mail. I think he left it on the entryway table. Let me get it."

She stepped into the foyer and found the envelope Sara was talking about. Connor and the boys were coming back into the family room as she returned to it. The boys were jumping around him like puppies.

"I promised them ice cream," he said after nodding at Sara. "I'm hoping you actually have some."

"Don't worry." Jill put the envelope down and went into the kitchen. They all followed her and she pulled two Popsicles out of the freezer for them. "They'll accept this as a substitute," she said. "Now go on out and play in the sunroom. I don't care if you drip all over that floor."

They did as they were told, dancing happily on their toes. Connor laughed as he watched them go, then looked at Jill. They shared a secret smile.

Sara groaned. "Come on. Open the mail. You won't believe this."

"What does it say?"

"You need to read it for yourself. Go ahead. Read it. I'll wait."

Connor looked at Sara and said, "Hey, you look really upset."

Her eyes flashed his way. "Did Jill tell you about our stepsister? She died in a car accident last week."

"Yes, she did tell me. I'm sorry."

Sara nodded, then looked at Jill, waiting.

Moments later, Jill handed the letter to Connor and he noticed right away that her fingers were trembling. She turned and looked at her sister, wide-eyed. "I don't believe it."

Sara nodded, looking flushed. "Told you."

Connor glanced at the letter. It seemed to be about someone named Kelly Darling. Then he connected the name. It was the stepsister who had died the week before. Kelly Darling. It seemed that Kelly had a baby. A three-month-old baby. Jill and Sara were her only living relatives that could be found. Would either of them care to claim the child?

"A baby," he said. "And you didn't know?"

"No." Jill shook her head. "I guess she wasn't married. We hadn't heard from her for so long."

Sara nodded mournfully. "And now, a baby."

Jill felt tears threatening again. "Poor little thing."

Sara flashed her a look. "Kelly's baby." She shook her head. "I don't think we've seen Kelly more than three times in the last fifteen years."

"And that's our fault," Jill said mournfully. "We should have made more of an effort."

Sara shrugged. "Why? She never liked us. The last time I saw her, she was furious with me."

Jill looked surprised. "What happened?"

"She wanted to borrow five thousand dollars to help pay for a certification class she wanted to take."

"Some kind of computer class?"

"No. It was to qualify as a professional dog trainer. When I pointed out that I didn't see how she was going to be able to pay me back on the salaries beginning dog trainers make, she told me I was ruining her life and she never wanted to see me again."

Jill sighed. "Well, she was an awfully cute little baby."

Sara looked at Jill and bit her lip. "I'm sure they'll find some relative we don't even know about to take the child."

Jill frowned. "Maybe. But…"

"Jill!" Sara cried. "Don't you dare! There is no way you can take on another baby."

Jill looked pained. "What about you?" she asked.

"Me?" Sara's face registered shock. It was obvious that option hadn't even entered her mind. "Me?" She shook her head strenuously. "I don't do babies. I can barely manage to watch your little angels for more than an hour without going mad."

"Sara, she's our flesh and blood. She's our responsibility."

"How do you figure that? I don't see it. She was Kelly's responsibility, and now they'll find someone to adopt her. Tons of people want babies that age."

Jill was shaking her head. "I don't know...."

Sara groaned and looked tortured. Stepping closer, she took her sister's hands in her own. "Jill, I haven't come right out and told you this. I've tried to hint it, just to prepare you, but... I'm going to be moving down to Los Angeles. And my job is going to include almost constant travel, especially to New York. There's no room for a baby in that scenario." She had tears sliding down her cheeks. "And that also means I won't be here to help you. You can't even begin to think of taking this baby."

Jill looked at her and didn't say a thing.

Connor watched her. She was going to take the baby. He could tell. He tried to understand the dynamics here. This was another blow to Jill, another obstacle in her struggle to survive. And yet, that wasn't the way she was taking it. She didn't look at it as the end of her hopes and dreams, a financial and emotional disaster.

She was seeing it as another burdensome responsibility, but one that she would accept. He'd known her for years but he'd never realized how deep her strength went. Where had that come from? Where had she found the capacity to take on everyone else's problems? Was being the oldest sister the key? Or was it just the way her soul was put together?

"They'll find a good home for the baby somewhere, I'm sure," Sara was insisting. "Don't they have agencies to do things like that?"

Jill frowned. That just wasn't right and she knew it. "Sara…"

Sara closed her eyes and turned away.

"I've got to go. I'm expecting half a dozen calls and I've got to prepare myself." She looked back and hesitated, then said with fierce intensity, "Jill, you can't be considering taking that baby. I won't let you."

Jill winced. She knew what was going to happen. It was inevitable. She couldn't expect Sara to understand. Babies…life…family—that was what she'd been put on earth to deal with. So Brad hadn't worked out. Too bad. So her cake business was trembling on the brink and might just crumble. Okay. But turn down taking care of a baby? Her father's grandchild? Her own niece? No. Impossible. If Sara couldn't face it, that baby had only one chance.

She followed Sara to the door and touched her arm before she could escape. "Sara, I'm going to call them. I want that baby here with us."

A look of abject terror flared in her sister's eyes. Slowly, she shook her head, her lower lip trembling.

"You're crazy," she whispered. "Jill, I beg you. Don't do it." And then she turned on her heel and hurried to her car.

Jill came back into the house and went straight to Connor as though drawn by a magnet.

"Are you sure?" he asked her.

"About the baby?" She smiled. "Yes. There is no way I could let Kelly's baby go to strangers. I'm going to get in touch with these people right away. The sooner we get her here the better."

"Jill, your heart is definitely in the right place. But can you do it? You're already overextended. You're on the ragged edge with these two little boys. Can you take on another child like this?"

"I have no choice. I couldn't live with myself if I didn't do it."

His heart was overflowing with love for her, and he knew what she was doing courted disaster. His brain told him Sara was right, but his heart—it was all for Jill. "Come here. I have to hold you. You are so special..."

"Oh, Connor." She started to cry and he held her while she sobbed in his embrace. "It's scary, but it's wonderful, too. It's the right thing to do."

"I just hope it won't be too much for you," he said, kissing her tears away.

She kissed him back. "Sometimes I feel like I'm at my breaking point, but something always comes through to save the day. And right now, it's your arms around me. Connor, I'm so glad you're here."

And she started to sob again. He held her close, enjoying the feel of her and the sweet, fruity scent from her hair. He loved her and he would be there for her as long as she let him stay. But deep inside, he knew a time would come when she would want him to leave. He was prepared for that. He only hoped it didn't come for a long, long time.

CHAPTER NINE

AN HOUR LATER, Jill invited Connor to help her take the boys to the park to play on the swings and in the sandbox. They took little shovels and pails and made the trek on foot, through the residential streets and over the low-lying berm that marked the edge of the park area. The boys ran ahead, then came back for protection when dogs barked or a car came on the end of the street. Then they reached the park and the twins were in heaven.

When they tired of the swings, they got to work with the shovels, tossing sand and shrieking with happiness. After making a vain attempt to keep order, Jill and Connor sat back and let them play the way that seemed to come naturally to them. There weren't many other children around, so they gave them their freedom.

"I heard from Trini this morning," she told him. "I got an email. She's behind in a few classes, but she thinks she can catch up. She's thrilled to be there." She smiled happily. "She's going to keep me apprised with daily bulletins. That'll be great. It's just like vicariously going myself."

"I wish you could go yourself. We ought to be able to figure out a way...."

We? She looked at him sideways. But that seemed like a silly thing to have an argument about, so she moved on.

"So tell me more about what you were doing in Singapore all this time," she said, looking at the way his unruly hair flew around his head, much the way hers did, though his was dark as coal and hers was bright as sunshine. "You told me about the nice couple you lived with and worked for, and you told me about the chef you fell in love with—"

"Whoa! Hold on. I never told you that."

"Really?" Her eyes twinkled with mischief. "Gee, I don't know where I picked that up. I must have misheard it."

He knocked against her with his shoulder. "Come on, Jill. You know you're the only woman I've ever loved."

"Wow." She pressed closer to him. "It would be nice to think that was true."

He turned his head and said, close to her ear, "Count on it."

There was something in the way he said it that made her look up into his eyes. They were just kidding each other, weren't they?

"So tell me," she said after they sat down at the edge of the play area. She was sifting sand through her fingers. "Are you really going back or not?"

"That depends."

"On what?"

On whether I can make you fall in love with me. On

whether you can wipe Brad out of your calculations for your future. On whether you can believe in me.

But he sighed and actually said, "The company got bought out by a huge corporation. George made a fine haul on it. And under our contract, he gave me a nice chunk of change, too. So if I went back, it would be to link up with old George again and work on the next big idea."

She smiled with happy memories. "Just like the three of us did when we started MayDay."

"Exactly."

"Only Brad hasn't been bought out by anyone."

"No. Not yet."

She frowned, thinking that over. "And what are you going to do with your profits?"

He shrugged. "I don't know. Right now I'm pretty much looking around for a company to invest in. Some nice, clean little start-up. Preferably in the food business."

She looked at him suspiciously. "Are you teasing me?"

"Teasing you?" He looked shocked at the concept. "Why would I tease you?"

"Because you love to knock me off balance," she said with mock outrage. "You always have."

He leaned back against the rock behind him and laughed at her. She began to poke him in the ribs.

"You love it. Admit it. You love to have a good giggle over my naïveté. Fess up!"

He laughed harder and she began to tickle him. He grabbed her and pulled her down beside him and kissed her nose, making her laugh, too. And then he kissed her for real and she kissed him back and the warmth spread quickly between them.

"You're like a drug," he whispered, dropping kisses on her face. "I don't dare take too much of you."

"Good thing, too," she whispered back. "Because I only have that little tiny bit to give."

"Liar," he teased, kissing her mouth again.

She sighed, holding back the sizzle that threatened to spill out and make this inappropriately exciting. That would have to wait. But she had no doubt they would be able to explore it a bit more later.

"Hey," she said, pulling back up. "We're supposed to be watching the boys."

Luckily the two toddlers were still enchanted with the pails and shovels. Connor and Jill sat up and shook off the sand and grinned at each other.

"Okay," she said. "Now tell me what you're really going to do with the money."

"Just what I said. I've got my eye on a nice little Bundt cake bakery."

She didn't laugh this time. "No, Connor. I will not take charity from you."

He'd known she would react that way but it didn't hurt to start setting the background and give her a chance to think about it. "I'm talking about investing. I wouldn't put my money anywhere that I didn't expect to make a profit on it."

She was shaking her head adamantly. "I don't have shares to sell. That just won't work and you know it."

No, he didn't know it, but he had known she would be

a hard sell on the idea. Hopefully he would have more time to see what he could develop to do for her. "Jill…"

"Connor, I'm still bound to Brad by his company. I refuse to play that game again."

Ouch. That could make all the difference. He nodded slowly, frowning. "Jill, when you say you're still bound to Brad, what do you mean?" He looked her full in the face, searching her eyes for hints of the truth. "Do you still want him back?"

She thought for a moment, then looked at him, clear-eyed. "Connor, for a long time, I wanted Brad back. But not for me. I wanted him back for his children. What will it be like for them to go through life wondering why their father didn't want them? It breaks my heart." Her voice caught and she paused. "For so long, I was so sure, once he saw them, once he held them in his arms…"

He couldn't stand to see her still hoping. He wanted to smash something. Carefully he tried to tell her.

"He's just not made that way, Jill. Brad doesn't want to love a child. He doesn't want to complicate his life like that. He doesn't even want a wife at this point. He thinks he needs to keep the way clear so that he can think big thoughts and make cool-headed decisions. Human relationships only mess things up as far as he's concerned." He shrugged, grimacing. "I don't know why we didn't see that more clearly from the beginning."

"Maybe we did and we just didn't want to believe it."

She closed her eyes. She still had her dreams. She sometimes thought that maybe, if he saw her again, if they did come face-to-face, he would see what he'd once loved in her and realize what he'd lost—and want it back.

No. It wasn't going to happen. She'd given up on that fantasy a long time ago. So why did she still cling to the shards of that relationship?

"When did you start to figure out the truth about Brad?" Connor asked her softly.

Her smile was mirthless. "When I realized he was cheating on me."

He drew his breath in sharply. "You knew?"

She looked at him. "Connor, I'm not stupid. Gullible, maybe. Too weak to stand up for myself when I should, sometimes. But not dumb."

They were silent for a long moment, then Connor asked, "What do you think Brad will say about you taking on another baby?"

She laughed. "Luckily it doesn't matter what he says. Does it?"

The boys were tussling. One was hitting the other with a plastic pail and both were starting to cry. The inevitable end to a lovely time being had by all. Jill and Connor rose from their sitting place and started across the sand to mediate the battle, but on the way, they held hands.

Jill baked two more cakes once they got home and Connor put the boys down for their naps. They both fell asleep as soon as their heads hit their mattresses. He watched them for a while, amazed at how much he cared for them already. Then he went down to help Jill with the bakery business.

"So what's next?" he asked, sitting at the kitchen table and eating a nice large slice of Strawberry Treat. "What's the plan?"

She glanced back at him as she mixed up a fresh glaze. "Stay out of the way of the inspectors. Obey all regulations scrupulously. Grow my business. Hire some employees and get my own shop." She threw him a smile. "In other words, succeed."

He took another bite and nearly swooned with the deliciousness of it all. "You're the best Bundt cake baker on the island. Probably the best in all of Seattle. But all of Seattle isn't going to come here for their cakes. Your customers are basically the people on this island. Are there enough of them to let you be successful?"

She came to the table and dropped down into a seat across from him. "This is exactly my nightmare question. How can I get a large customer base?"

"And what's your answer?"

She shook her head. "I haven't really dealt with it because I'm scared of what it will take."

"And what is that?"

She frowned. "I have to branch out. I know it. I have to develop a full-blown bakery out of this. I have to make cookies and pies and éclairs and bear-claws and dinner rolls. I have to learn to do everything. It's my only hope."

"And your competition?"

She nodded. "There are two bakeries here, both run by older bakers who are about at the end of their bakery careers, I would think. So there should be room for me." She made a face. "If I can come up to the challenge."

He was impressed that she'd thought this out so fully. It gave him the reassurance that she really meant to make a go of it. Because she was going to have to work very hard to last.

"You've really developed a good business brain, haven't you?"

"I developed it right next to you. Remember when we used to brainstorm together during the early days at MayDay?"

"I do." He smiled at her. "But how are you going to do all this without someone here to help you? I can't even understand how you've done this much so far."

"It isn't easy."

He thought about that for a moment, then turned back and said, "You're going to have to have some help. Face it."

She nodded. "I know. I'm thinking of giving Mrs. Mulberry another chance."

"Great. I think she deserves it."

"She means well and she wants to do it. So there you go."

He nodded. "If you're with her most of the time, you can train her. And she'll begin to understand what the twins need. I'm sure it will go well."

She grinned at him. "I never realized what an optimist you are. Just a regular what-me-worry-kid."

"Sure. I learned long ago that being happy is better than being angry all the time."

He watched her work, nursing a cup of coffee and enjoying the smells of a working bakery. It all seemed too quiet and idyllic. Until you remembered that Brad was probably on his way. Most likely he would drive up from Portland. And then he would come here. Connor wanted to be here when he arrived. There was no way he was going to let Jill face him alone.

Jill was chatting about something or other. He wasn't paying much attention. He was too busy enjoying her, smiling at the flour on her face, watching the way her body moved, the way her breasts were swelling just inside the opening of her shirt, those long, silky legs. She'd always been his main crush, but now she was becoming something more. He wanted her and his body was letting him know the need was getting stronger.

From the beginning, it had seemed she was strangely dominated, almost mesmerized, by Brad. She'd been Brad's and he'd been crazy jealous, but he'd never thought he would have a chance with her. Now, he did. It all depended on how strong that bond between them still was.

He had his own bond with her—didn't he? Even if she didn't feel it, he did. She walked out toward where he was sitting at the table, talking about something he wasn't really listening to and stopping near him. Reaching out, he caught her wrist and tugged her closer. She looked down at him, saw the darkness in his eyes, and her own eyes widened, and then her mouth softened and she sank down beside him.

She hadn't hesitated. She'd come to him as soon as she saw he wanted her to. That filled him with a bright new sense of wonder. He wanted to hold her forever, make a declaration, make love to her and make her his own.

He wrapped her in his arms and she sighed as he

began to drop small, impatient kisses along the line of her neck. She turned, giving him more access to her body in a way he hadn't expected.

His heart was pounding now, filling him with a sort of excitement he hadn't felt for a long, long time. She was warm and soft and rounded in the best places for it. He kissed just under her ear and suddenly she was turning in his arms, moaning, searching for his mouth with hers, and then that was all there was.

The kiss. It took his breath away at the same time it put his brain into orbit. He couldn't think. He could only feel. And taste. And ache for her.

Jill felt his release, his acceptance of the desire swelling between them, and she was tempted to give way to it as well. She knew this had to stop but for the moment, she couldn't find the strength to make it happen. She hungered for his heat, longed for his touch, moved beneath his hands as though she couldn't get enough of him.

There was no way to stop this feeling. Was it love? Was it loneliness that needed healing? Or was it a basic womanly demand that smoldered deep inside all the time, hidden by the events of the day, and only revealed when the right man touched her?

That was it. She'd known passion before, but this was different. She not only wanted his body, but she also needed his heart and soul, and for once, she thought she just might have a chance to get that.

She was drowning in his kiss. His mouth tasted better than anything she'd ever known. She writhed with it, moaned and made tiny cries as though she could capture the heat and keep it forever in her body. And then reality began to swim back into focus and she tried to pull away.

It wasn't easy. His kisses were so delicious and his hands felt so good. But it had to be done. There were cakes in the oven. There were children waking up from their naps.

Reality. Darn it all.

"Jill," he murmured, his face buried in her curly hair, "we're going to have to find a way to do something about this."

"Are we?" But she smiled. Her body was still resonating with the trembling need for him, and she totally agreed. Somehow, they had to do something about it—soon.

The shadows were longer. Afternoon was flowing into evening. The boys were stirring and Connor went up to supervise their waking. He got them changed and brought them down to play in the playroom, listening as they called back and forth with what seemed like their own special language.

The doorbell rang and he stiffened. He didn't think Brad could have gotten here this fast unless he flew. But it was a possibility.

He went out into the entryway. It wasn't Brad. Jill was talking to the mailman and signing for a certified letter. She closed the door and ripped the letter open.

"What in the world is this going to be?" she muttered, her mind on her cakes. Then she looked at the letter. Frowning, she looked at it again.

"What does this mean?" she asked Connor.

He glanced over her shoulder and frowned. "It looks like the bank is calling your loan."

She gasped. "Are they allowed to do that?"

"Let me see the letter." He read it over more carefully. "Okay, it says here that their investigation has revealed that you have insufficient security and they don't trust your collateral." He looked at her. "You used this house, didn't you?"

She nodded, her eyes wide with alarm.

He went back to the letter. "They also claim that, if you study your contract, you will find it has a 'Due for Any Reason Clause' which allows them to call the loan without having to justify it." He stared at her in distaste. "Just because they want to." His face darkened as he thought that through. "Or because someone bribes them to do it," he suggested.

She stared at him and then she whispered, "Brad?"

He shrugged. "You probably won't ever be able to prove it."

She took the letter and read it again. That was what it said. Her loan was being called. There was no doubt in her mind that Brad had something to do with this.

She was shaking. Everything she tried to do seemed to fail. She wasn't getting anywhere. It was so hard—it was like running in quicksand. In her worst nightmares, she'd never thought of this. How could he do this to her?

"He won't ever cut me free, will he?" She raised her tragic gaze to Connor's blue one. "He doesn't want me, but he still wants to manipulate me. He still wants to control my life." Her voice got higher. "Am I doomed to be tied to this man forever? That's like being married without any of the perks. I just have to obey, forget the love and all that other stuff."

Connor took her shoulders and held her firmly.

"Jill, calm down. I know it's frustrating, but maybe if you find out exactly what he thinks he wants."

"Like what? For me to get rid of the boys?" She knew she looked wild. And why not? She felt wild. "You actually think I would consider something like that?"

"No, of course not." He hesitated. "But I don't think that's what he's after right now."

"Really? And why do you know so much about what he's after? Did he tell you?" Her face changed as she realized what she'd said. "That's it, isn't it?" She stared at him. "You know what he wants. You just haven't told me yet."

He had a bad feeling about where this train of thought was leading. He took a deep breath. "Jill…"

She backed away from him. "Okay, Connor," she said coldly, her face furious. "Are you finally ready to tell me what Brad wants from me? What he sent you to tell me?"

He tried to touch her but she pulled away.

"Tell me," she demanded.

He shook his head, knowing she was in no mood to hear this and think logically. But he didn't have any choice. He had to tell her. He should have done it sooner. But still he hesitated, not sure how to approach it.

"Brad asked me to talk to you," he admitted. "But I never told him I would. And once I saw you again, I knew I would never do his dirty work for him. If he wanted to ask you something he had to come and do it himself."

"I see," she said cynically. At this point, she was ready to believe the worst of anyone and everyone. "So you decided for some reason, I wasn't ready. I wasn't softened up enough. You decided to go slow. You needed to sweeten me up, flatter me a little, get me ready for the slaughter."

"Jill…" He shook his head, appalled that she would think that.

She drew in a trembling breath. "I can't believe you would gang up on me with Brad this way."

That was like a knife through his heart. "I'm not."

She wasn't listening. "So how about it, Connor? Am I ready now? Are you going to stop lying and tell me the truth?"

He shook his head. He might as well get this over with. "Okay, Jill. What Brad wants is those company shares he gave you when you divorced. He thinks he needs them back."

She looked surprised. "Why?"

He shrugged. "I think he's having a fight with some of the other shareholders. He wants to stop a power play by some who are getting together to outvote him on some company policies."

She pressed her lips together and thought about that for a moment. Then she glared at him again.

"Is that all? Really? Then why didn't you tell me the truth from the beginning?"

He turned away, grimacing. Then he turned back. "I asked you before, Jill, and I'm going to ask you again.

You've hinted now and then that you would take Brad back if you could. Do you still feel that way?"

She thought for a moment, pacing from him to the glass door and back again. "What I really want is to have my life back. Do you understand that? I chose Brad to be at my side forever and I gave birth to two angels, two gifts for him." She stared at him with haunted eyes. "So why did he reject them? Why did he reject me and the life we'd both created together? I want that life."

He winced. That wasn't really what he'd wanted to hear.

"I want things to be like they used to be. I want my life back."

"So you still want Brad back."

She didn't answer that.

Who was he to tell her it couldn't happen? Stranger things had.

"Nothing has changed?" he asked her, incredulous.

She shook her head. "Of course. Everything has changed." Anger flashed through her eyes like flames from a fire. "And now you've proven you stand with Brad."

He grimaced. He couldn't let her think he wasn't behind her one hundred percent. "Jill, listen to me. Seeing you again, I realized how much I care for you. How much I missed you and all you've always meant to me. I want you for myself. I don't want Brad to have anything to do with…with our relationship."

She stared at him as though she hadn't heard a word he'd said. "But you've kept in constant contact with him, haven't you? Isn't he always calling on your phone?"

"Yes, but..."

"Connor, you lied to me!"

"No, I didn't. That's ridiculous."

"Yes, you did. You led me to believe Brad didn't really want anything. And now I come to find out, he wanted it all."

Tears filled her eyes and she turned away, walking back into the kitchen. That was her default position. The kitchen was the center of her world. She went to the counter and turned to face him, hugging her arms in around herself.

"Jill," he said as he caught up with her. "I know this looks bad to you, but I didn't lie. When you asked, I just didn't answer."

"That's the same as a lie." She shook her head. "I can't trust you."

"Okay, Jill. I understand that you're really angry, and I'm sorry. But..."

She narrowed her eyes and hardened her heart. "I think it's time for you to leave, Connor. Way past time."

He shook his head. Pain filled him, pain and regret. "Don't do this, Jill. Wait until you've calmed down. Think it over. I...I don't want to leave you here on your own."

"You have to. I can't trust you. I want you to go."

His eyes were tortured but she didn't relent. She had to have some time and space to think, to go over all that had happened in the last few days and decide if she could ever, ever talk to him again.

He winced. "You know that at some time soon, Brad will be coming, don't you?"

She blinked at him. "Why?"

"Because he wants those shares. He's not going to rest until he gets them. If he has to come here to do that, he will."

She was seething. "If you knew that, why didn't you tell me before? Why didn't you warn me?"

He had no answer for that.

"Go," she said. "You've helped me with some things, but you've undermined me at the same time. I need you to go."

He started to say something, but she pointed toward the door. Shaking his head, he turned away. Then he looked back and said over his shoulder, "Call me if you need me," and he left.

She watched him walk away until tears flooded her eyes and she couldn't see anything anymore.

"Connor, Connor, how could you betray me like this?" she murmured.

The one person she thought she had in her corner, that she could count on when things got rough, the only one that she could really trust in this world besides Sara had turned out to be lying to her. And now it turned out all she had left was Sara.

She sank to the floor of the kitchen and hung her head and cried.

Connor was headed back to the mainland, but before he went, he had one last thing he had to do. He knew Sara lived only about a mile away, but her bungalow was right on the beach. Turning down the narrow road, he found her house easily. He'd been there before.

Walking up to the front door, he saw Sara in the side yard, trimming roses. He approached carefully but she still jumped when she saw him.

"Hey, Sara," he said. "We need to talk."

She backed away looking wary. "Connor, I don't want to talk to you. I already know how I feel about everything and I don't need you messing with my mind."

"Sara, come on. You know we both love Jill. Right?"

Sara made a face, but she nodded reluctantly.

"And you know that she's not going to let that baby go anywhere else, don't you? Not if she can help it."

Sara looked away.

"If you won't take her, your sister will. There's just no two ways about it."

Sara turned and looked at him pleadingly. "Can't you talk her out of it?"

"You know the answer to that. Nobody can talk her out of it." He looked down and kicked the dirt. "And we both know that taking on another baby is going to be hard. She doesn't need to have something that hard. She's already got far too much on her plate, far too much that she has to handle alone." He looked up at her. "So there's only one thing left to do. And you know what it is."

She shook her head with a jerky motion. Her face was a study in tragedy. "No," she said. "I can't."

He was quiet for a minute and she snipped off a few more dead blossoms. He listened to the water lapping against the shore not too far from where they stood. Seagulls called and a flock of low-flying pelicans swooped by.

Her hair was still slicked back into a bun at the back of her head. She'd changed into slacks and a fuzzy pullover, but she managed to look like a fully functioning professional anyway. There was something about her that spoke of competence and dignity. But when he looked at her face, all he saw was fear and sadness.

Finally he spoke to her quietly.

"Sara, come sit down with me."

She edged closer, but she still acted as though she was afraid he might have something catching.

"Come on." He sat down on a wicker chair and nodded toward the little wicker couch. She walked over slowly and sat down, but she wouldn't look at him.

"Thanks, Sara. I want to tell you about someone I got to know well in Singapore. Her name is Sharon Wong. She's a very fine chef. A few years ago, her neighbor died, leaving behind a three-year-old girl. Sharon had gotten to know them both during the neighbor's illness. She took her broths and things and watched the child for her at times.

"When the woman died, Social Services came to take away the child, and Sharon realized what a nightmare that baby faced. Who knew who would end up caring for her? Maybe someone good. Maybe not. Maybe she would be in an institution for the rest of her childhood. She watched how the Social Services people treated that little girl and she made up her mind that she couldn't let this happen.

"So she stepped in and took the baby herself. When I met her, the girl was six years old, bright as a penny and sweet as candy. A delight. And Sharon told me that this little girl had enriched her life like nothing she'd ever dreamed might happen to her."

"And then she told me about a saying she'd heard lately. No one on their deathbed ever says they should have spent more time at the office. When you get down to what really counts, it's family."

Sara turned tragic eyes his way. "But I don't really have that kind of family," she said softly.

"Not now. But that doesn't mean you won't."

She stared at him, shaking her head. "Connor, if I had a choice right now between having a terrific career, or meeting a terrific guy, I'd take the career. I've had enough disappointment with terrific guys."

He shrugged as he rose to leave. "Guys are one thing. Babies are another." Reaching over, he kissed her cheek. She didn't turn away. She caught his hand and held it for a moment, looking deep into his eyes.

"See you later, Sara. Do the right thing, okay?"

And he walked away.

Jill was wandering through her house like a ghost. It was after dark and she hadn't put on any of the downstairs lights yet. The boys were in bed and sound asleep. She was alone.

Her mind was a jumble of thoughts, none of them very coherent. She was so angry with Connor, and at the same time, she was so hurt that he would still be on Brad's side after all he'd seen her go through. Why had he come all the way back just to prove to her that she really wanted him—only to say, "Sorry, I'm with

Brad. He's such an old friend." That thought made her furious all over again.

She heard the front door opening and she stopped in her tracks, heart beating wildly. Who was this going to be?

"Anybody home?"

She let her held breath out in a whoosh. It was Sara.

Seconds later, Sara came into the family room where Jill was standing.

"What's going on? How come no lights?"

She wasn't going to tell her it was to hide her swollen eyes and tear-stained face. She would see that for herself soon enough.

Sara went ahead and turned on the overhead without asking permission. It must have seemed a natural thing to do.

"Hey, Jill. I've got to talk to you." Compared to the last time Jill had seen her, she seemed to be brimming with energy.

Slowly Jill shook her head, staying to the shadows as much as she could. "Sara, sweetie, not now."

She thought Sara would notice from her voice that this was not a good time, but no. Sara charged ahead as though she hadn't said a thing.

"Wait. I'm sure you're busy, but this will just take a minute and it may help take a load off your mind."

Jill threw up her hands in surrender. "Anything that will do that," she muttered and tried to smile. "What is it?"

Sara came and stood before her, looking as earnest as Jill had ever seen her look.

"I've thought about this long and hard. I've looked at all the angles. And I've decided. I want to take Kelly's baby."

That was a jolt from the blue. "What are you saying? You can't possibly do that and take the job in L.A. Can you?"

"No." She shook her head. "I'm turning the job down."

"What? Oh, Sara, no!"

"Yes. A job is just a job. A baby is a human being. And this human being is even a part of our family, whether we like it or not." She smiled. "And I've decided to like it."

It was true that she looked much better, much healthier, than she had earlier that day when she had been so frightened of the entire concept. That was good. If it was really going to last.

She took her sister's hands in hers. "But, Sara, why?"

"It's a funny thing. I wanted a traditional life so badly. I planned my wedding from the time I was five years old. You know that. But every romance I tried to have ended badly. I just couldn't seem to find a man who fit me. I finally got hurt one too many times and I gave up all that. It's just too painful. No more romance. No more man who was wrong for me."

Jill nodded. She'd been there and watched it all. "I know all this. But what does it have to do with taking the baby?"

"I decided maybe I was going at it from the wrong side. Maybe if I find a baby who fits me, I'll have my family without having to find a man first."

Oh, no. Sara had lost her mind.

"Sara, babies don't provide miracles. Please don't go into this thinking it's going to be a piece of cake. Don't depend on a baby to make you happy, to solve all your problems."

She waved that away. "Oh, please, Jill. Give me some credit. I know that. I've been with you enough with the twins to know that raising a child is no picnic."

"You got that right."

"But anyway, you're the one who always picks up the slack for everyone else. You do your big sister routine and go all noble on me, and I let you, because then I get out of doing things I don't want to do."

"Oh, Sara, please. We're not kids anymore."

"No, but we're still sisters." She gave Jill a hug. "So I decided. It's time I took my turn. I want Kelly's baby."

Jill took a deep breath and realized, suddenly what a weight she'd been carrying. "Oh, Sara, I hope you know what you're doing."

"I do."

She hugged her again and held her close, then leaned back and looked at her. "What changed your mind? What made you see it that way?"

"Connor."

"Connor?" She was thunderstruck.

She heaved a heavy sigh. "Yes, it was Connor. He gave me a good talking-to and then told me about a friend of his. Some woman in Singapore…"

"Sharon Wong?"

"That's the one. Do you know her?"

"No."

"Well, he sat me down and made me take a more realistic look at life."

"He did?" Jill felt dizzy.

"Yeah. Where is he?"

"He's a…"

"You know, that is one great guy. You'd better not let him slip away. He's a treasure." She looked around the room and toward the back porch. "So where is he, anyway?"

"I, uh, he left."

Her head swung around. "Left? Where did he go? What happened?"

"I told him to leave."

"Oh, Jill… You didn't!"

"I did. I told him to go. I was so angry."

"Why?"

She took a deep breath and tried to remember it all, including the incredible pain she'd felt. Quickly she explained to Sara about the loan being called, and how Connor thought Brad was behind it. Then she went on to fill in her problems with Connor.

"He didn't tell me the truth about what Brad wanted and when I found out that he wanted me to sell him the shares I swore I would never give up, I just…I felt like he was manipulating me. Like I couldn't trust him. Like he was on Brad's side again. Why didn't he prepare me to know what Brad was up to?"

"You think he's on Brad's side?"

Jill nodded.

Sara stared at her. "What are you, nuts? You do realize he's crazy in love with you, don't you?"

She shook her head. "Sara, I don't think—"

"You can see it in the way he looks at you."

She hesitated. "Do you really think so?"

"Come on, he's always had a crush on you. And now I think it's developed into full-blown mad love. He's insanely in love with you."

Jill was feeling dizzy again. "We've always been friends."

"No. It's more than that." Sara threw up her hands. "He wants you, babe. Don't let that one get away."

"I just got so frustrated. And…and so jealous."

"Jealous?"

She nodded. "I mean—is he my friend or Brad's? It makes a difference."

Sara nodded wisely. "I told him that the first day he was here. I told him if he was going to be your friend, he had to get rid of Brad. And you know what? He was ready to do it."

Jill wasn't so sure. Sara could go off like a runaway train at times. But she listened to her sister and they talked about how she was going to manage to take care of a baby, and after she left, she went back over what she'd said about Connor and she felt more confused than ever.

There was no doubt about it, she wanted Connor back. For the past couple of days, he'd been her shelter against the storm. Why on earth was she making him go?

But maybe it was for the best. After all, she didn't want him to be here if he was Brad's friend more than he was hers. What was the truth? She was overwhelmed by the emotions churning inside her.

But she knew one thing: it was time to face facts. She loved Connor. She'd probably loved him for years and hadn't been able to admit it to herself. But she could remember countless times that she'd been frustrated with Brad and wished he could be more like Connor. She'd known forever that Connor fit her better than Brad did. They looked at life through much the same lens. They liked the same things, laughed at the same jokes. Brad always seemed restless and disapproving. Why had she put up with it for so long?

And Connor was so darn sexy. She'd always felt a certain buzz around him. Brad was more demanding, more dominant. Connor was more easygoing. More her type. What a fool she'd been all these years.

She loved Connor. Wow.

Except for one little tiny problem. No matter what Sara said, she was pretty sure he didn't love her. He liked her fine, he always had. But he liked a lot of girls. And when push came to shove, he was better friends with Brad than he was with her. And that hurt.

In fact, it cut deep. Brad had been so awful to her. It had taken time, but she'd finally come to a place where she could look into the past and face the truth. She'd been blinded by a lot of things when she'd thought she loved Brad. A lot of those things were not too flattering to her. She'd been a fool. Now she could look Brad squarely in the eye and say, "Brad, you're a real jerk." At least, she thought she could.

She had to get that out of her system because, like it

or not, Brad was her boys' father. There was no hiding from that. Even Brad couldn't pretend it didn't matter. They would always be tied to him in ways he couldn't control.

So Connor had tried to help her in his way, and now she'd kicked him out. Maybe that wasn't the wisest thing to do, but she couldn't pretend with Connor. She was in love with him. What if he knew that? What if he saw it in her face, in her reactions? Would he use it against her? She didn't know, because she really couldn't trust him.

Why hadn't he told her the truth right from the beginning so that she could get prepared for any sort of attack from Brad? Now she was going to have to deal with Brad on her own.

That was going to be hard to do. Brad had a domineering way about him and she'd been trained over the years to yield to him. It almost came naturally to her. She was going to have to fight against that impulse. She couldn't let him walk all over her. And once he realized she wasn't going to obey him, what next? He would find some way to make her pay. Brad was capable of doing almost anything.

Life was becoming impossible. What was she going to do? She was probably going to lose her house and lose her business. She couldn't meet the loan call. She was going to go under like a small boat in heavy swells.

The only way out she could see was to sell her shares to Brad. She didn't want to do it. She especially hated to do anything that might make him happy. But she wasn't going to have any choice. Her options had just become even more limited.

Well, she might end up that way, but she intended to put up a fight as long as she could. She would see how well she could stand up to Brad when she really tried. Live and learn.

In the meantime, all she could do was sit here and wait for Brad to show up.

CHAPTER TEN

CONNOR CHECKED BACK into his hotel. As he started for the elevators, he heard "Mambo!" coming from the dining room dance floor and he couldn't resist looking in to see if Karl was back. Sure enough, and dancing with a bewildered looking redhead. Connor ducked back out quickly. He didn't want to scare Karl off.

He ordered something from room service and watched the news and then he turned off the TV and went out and walked the Seattle streets for a couple of hours. This was a city he knew well. He'd grown up not far away in a small town, and then gone to the University. The years after college had been spent right here. It was home in a sense. He could live here. He didn't need anything else.

Except Jill. He needed Jill more than he needed air to breathe.

His cell received a text and he flipped it out to see who it was. Brad had finally answered him.

"You're right," he said. "I need to come and get what I need myself. I'll be there in the morning."

So Brad was coming to work his magic on Jill. What

did he think—that he could walk in and hypnotize her into doing things his way? Or was he ready to give her what she'd always wanted—marriage and a promise to try to be a father to his kids?

That night he couldn't sleep. He spent the time staring at the ceiling and going over what had happened over the last few days. He knew he was following a familiar pattern. He'd begun to let his feelings for Jill come out and actually show themselves, but once Jill backed away, so did he. He'd walked off and left the field to Brad so many times, it seemed the natural thing to do.

But it wasn't. It was time he made up his mind, declared himself, and claimed Jill for himself. This was probably his last chance to do it. What the hell was he waiting for?

Damn it, she needed him. He was the only one who loved her the way she needed to be loved. He was the only one ready to protect her and make her happy, the only one who was ready to help her raise her kids. The only other person he needed to convince was Jill herself. And that was the only part he was still a little shaky on.

He was a realist and he knew there was a chance that Brad would offer to take Jill back, and he knew there was a chance she would take him up on it. She yearned to have the boys' father back fulfilling his role, giving them what they needed. Whether she yearned for the man himself in the same way, he wasn't sure. But he wasn't going to let things take their natural course and see what happened. No. Not this time. He was going to fight for the woman he loved.

He ate an early breakfast in the coffee shop and then he headed for the ferry landing. He got out of the car during the crossing and looked up at the house Jill and Brad had bought together when their marriage was young and the company was all they cared about. How quickly things could change.

He was pretty sure Brad would show up sometime today. And how Jill reacted to that would tell the tale. He meant to play a part, regardless. And if he had to tell a few home truths to his old friend, he was ready to do it. He drew in a lungful of sea air and began to prepare for what he was going to do.

Jill had the children up and dressed and ready to go first thing in the morning. She'd hardly slept at all but she had done a lot of thinking. She was definitely staring at a fork in her life's road. Would she bow to Brad, or would she fight for Connor? Could she find a way to make Connor want her more than he wanted to be friends with Brad? If she couldn't do that, it was all over. But if she didn't even try, how would she ever know?

She planned to leave the twins with Sara and then she was heading to the mainland. She was going to go and find Connor and tell him she loved him. Her blood pounded in her ears. She was so scared. But she had to take the chance. Like Sara said, she couldn't let him slip away.

She'd let the boys out to play in the backyard while she got things ready and she was just about to get them and put them into the car when she heard the front door close. She stopped, listening.

"Sara?" she called at last. "Is that you?"

There was no answer. She swallowed hard, glancing toward the side door and thinking of making a run for it, one child under each arm. But before she could try that out, Brad appeared in the doorway to the kitchen.

"No," he said, watching her coolly. "It's me."

It was still early and once Connor got across the channel, he decided to take a run around the island before he went up to the house. The trip was as pretty as it had ever been, with trees and a lush growth of flowers that was almost tropical in its glory. What a wonderful place to choose to raise a family.

As he came back around, he stopped at a light and looked down at the ferry landing. The next one had arrived, and the first car coming off was a silver Porsche. He knew right away that had to be Brad.

Staying where he was, he watched as the car climbed the hill and turned into Jill's driveway, then parked in front of the entryway. Brad got out and headed for the front door, and Connor gritted his teeth and counted to ten. He had to force back the rage that threatened to overwhelm him. If he came face-to-face with Brad right now, he would surely end up bloodying the man's nose. He had to give it a minute.

Once he was calmer, he turned his car up toward the house, parking on the street. He got out just as he saw Brad disappearing inside.

Striding quickly up the hill, he went around back,

quietly opening the door to the screened-in porch, which opened onto the kitchen. Ten to one she would be there. He stopped and listened.

Jill was shaking. She only hoped Brad couldn't tell. How many times had she imagined this scene? Here he was, in the flesh.

This was the first time he'd been back to their house since the divorce. The first time she'd seen him in over a year. She shoved her unruly hair back behind her ears and tried to smile.

"It's good to see you, Brad," she said breathlessly.

His eyes had been cold as steel when he'd first come in, but as she watched, they began to warm. "Jill," he said, and held out his hands to her.

She hesitated for a few seconds, but she took them. They were warm. He was so cool and confident. And here she was, rattled and skittish as a baby bird.

"I've missed you," he said.

She blinked at him. Why did his lies always sound so sincere?

"Where's Connor?" he asked.

"Oh, he…he left. Last night."

"Ah," he said, and she could tell he thought Connor had left because he was coming. "Probably a good thing," he said almost to himself. "Did he ever give you my message?" he asked.

She took a deep breath. "Why don't you just tell me what that message is?"

"I don't want to rush things. How about a cup of coffee while we talk over old times?"

He was so cool, so ready to treat her like dirt and pretend she deserved it. She dug deep inside. She couldn't let him maneuver her. This was her home and he was the invader.

"I…I don't have any coffee ready," she told him. "Why don't you just get on with it? I'd like to know where we stand."

He didn't like that. She could see the annoyance flash in his eyes. "Okay," he said shortly. "Here's the deal. I need those shares, Jill. You have fifteen percent of my company. I'm going to have to ask for them back."

"Really? And what if I want to keep them?"

He looked as though he could hardly believe she was being so obstinate. "No, don't you understand? I need them. I'm fighting off a mini rebellion and I need them to regain the advantage." He frowned. He could see she wasn't bending for him the way he thought she should. "Listen, I'll make it worth your while. I'm prepared to pay you quite handsomely for them."

He named a figure that didn't sound all that handsome to her. If he could pay that for shares, why couldn't he pay child support? But she knew the answer to that. Because he didn't want to.

"I'm being attacked by some of the other shareholders who are conspiring against me. I need those shares to defend myself. And of course, if you ever hope to get any more money out of me, you'd better help."

She found herself staring at him. The fear had melted away. He was just a big jerk. There was no reason to let him intimidate her.

"Brad, I'm not interested in selling. I feel that those

shares are a legacy of sorts for the boys. I want them to be there for them when they grow up, both as an investment and for traditional reasons."

His jaw tightened. "All right, I'll double the offer."

She shook her head. "But that's not the point. I want the boys to have something from their father. I'm just sorry you don't feel the same way."

"Are you crazy? What do those brats have to do with my company?"

She glared at him. Didn't he have any human feelings at all? "We built that company together, you, me and Connor. It was a work of joy and friendship between us all at the time."

"That's a crock. I had the idea, I worked out the plans, I did the development. You two were filler. The company is mine. You had very little to do with it." He grunted. "And those kids didn't have anything to do with it."

Her fingers were trembling but she was holding firm. "Whether or not you want to acknowledge them, those kids are yours. They have your DNA. They wouldn't exist without you. Though you may never be a real father to them, this will give them something to know about you, to feel they've been given a gift from you."

"That's ridiculous. It's sentimental garbage." He shook his head as though he just couldn't understand her attitude. "Jill, what's happened to you? You were once my biggest supporter. You would have done anything to help me. And now…"

For just a moment she remembered him as he used to be, so young and handsome, with the moonlight in his eyes and a kiss on his mind. She thought of how it was when they were first married and he had let her know how much he wanted her, every minute of the day. She'd thought it would always be like that. She'd been wrong.

But thinking about what used to be had the effect of cooling her anger. They did have a past. She couldn't ignore that. She took a deep breath and made her voice softer, kinder, more understanding.

"Brad, I did support you for so many years. But what you've done has undermined that. Lately you have done nothing but stand in my way. And you expect me to bend over backward for you?"

He controlled his own anger and tried to smile. "You know what, you're right. And that wasn't really fair of me." He tried to look sincere. "But everything I do is for the good of the company. You know that."

She shrugged. That wasn't good enough to justify what he'd done.

He stared at her for a long moment, then nodded and adjusted his stance. He was good at sizing up the other side and finding a way to adapt to new facts.

"Okay, Jill. I understand. You need something more." He nodded, thinking for a moment. "Here's the deal. I want full ownership of the company. I need it. I'm willing to take you back to get it."

She almost fell over at his words. "You'll take me back?"

"Yes, I will."

Unbelievable. "And the boys?"

He turned and looked at the twins playing on the hill behind the house. "Is that them?"

She nodded.

"Sure, why not?" He turned back, his eyes hard and cold as steel. "Have we got a deal?"

She stared at him. What could she say? Did she have a right to hand away her children's connection with their father? But what was that connection worth? Why hadn't she ever seen the depths of his vile selfishness before? His soul was corrupt.

"Brad, you've really surprised me with this. I never thought you would make such an offer."

"So what do you say?"

"She says 'no.'" Suddenly Connor was in the room with them.

"Hello, Brad," he said, his tone hard and icy. "She says 'no deal.' Sorry."

She looked from Brad to Connor and back again, confused. Where had he come from? She wasn't sure, but suddenly he was there and suddenly Brad didn't look so smooth and sure of himself.

"Connor," Brad said, looking annoyed. "I thought you were gone."

"I was. But I'm back."

Brad looked unsure. "This is just a matter between me and Jill."

"No, it's not. I'm afraid there's been a change." Connor stood balanced, his stance wide, like a fighter. In every way, he was exuding a toughness she didn't think she'd ever seen in him before. "I'm involved now."

Brad looked bewildered. "What the hell are you talking about?"

"You're not married to Jill anymore. In fact, since

you won't acknowledge your own children, and from what I understand, you hardly ever give them any money, the only real substantial tie they have with you is those shares."

He turned and looked at Jill. "Here's my advice. Give him the shares. Let him buy them from you. Once they're gone, and you and I are married, he won't have any reason left to contact you in any way or have any part in your life. You'll be free of him." He reached out and touched her shoulder. "But of course, it's up to you. What do you say?"

Jill stared at Connor. She heard his words but she was having some trouble understanding them. Did he mean…? Wait, what did he say about marrying her? A bubble began to rise in her chest—a bubble of happiness. She wanted to dance and laugh and sing, all at once.

"Connor?" she said, smiling at him in wonder. "Are you feeling okay?"

He gave her a half smile back. "I'm feeling fine. How about you?"

"I think I'm going to faint." She reached out and he caught hold, steadying her against him. She put an arm around his waist and pulled even closer, looking up at him with laughter bubbling out all over.

He gazed down at her and grinned. He had a good feeling about how this was turning out. There was only one last test. Was she ready to cut all ties to Brad? "What do you think about selling back the shares?" he asked her.

She nodded happily. Suddenly she knew that she just

didn't care about the shares. All her excuses had been hogwash meant to give her an excuse to not do what Brad wanted. But she didn't care about that anymore. She didn't have to care about Brad. She was going to care about her family, and he wasn't in it. He'd given up that chance long ago.

"I think you're right," she said. "I liked that second offer."

Brad looked uncertain.

Connor shrugged at him. "There you go. Hand over the money, Brad. Let's see the glint of your gold."

"Hey, she just said…"

"I don't care what you heard. She'll take the second offer. Or would you rather have her contact the people in the company who are fighting you and see how much they'll offer?"

Brad frowned at him, shooting daggers of hate, but he pulled out his checkbook. He wrote out a check and handed it to Jill. She looked at it, held it up to the light, then nodded and put it down, leaving the room to get her documentation. In a moment she was back.

"Here are the shares," she said. "There you go. It's all you now, Brad. You don't need me for anything anymore. Right?"

Brad didn't say a word.

"Let's make a pact," Jill said. "Let's not see each other ever again. Okay?"

He seemed completely bewildered. "Jill. Don't you remember what we once had together?"

She snorted. "Don't you remember what you did to me eighteen months ago?"

One last disgruntled look and Brad headed for the door. Connor pulled Jill into his arms and smiled down at her.

"I hope you don't feel like I coerced you into that."

"Not at all. I think it was the perfect solution. If he'd come and asked me in a humble, friendly way, I would have handed them back to him at any time. It was just when he acted like such a jerk, I couldn't stand the thought of giving in to him."

"At least you made him pay for them."

She shook her head and laughed. "It is so worth it to get him out of my life."

He searched her dark eyes. "You're sure there's nothing left? You don't love him?"

"How can you even ask that?" She touched his face with her fingertips. "I love you," she said, her voice breaking on the word. "It's taken a while to get that through my skull, but it's true."

He shook his head, laughing softly. "That's quite a relief. I wasn't sure."

She smiled and snuggled into his arms. "I'm not even going to ask if you still consider Brad your best friend. Actions speak louder than words. You showed me."

"You're my best friend," he told her lovingly.

She pursed her lips, looking up at him with her brows drawn together. "And the new baby?" she asked, just testing reality. "Are you really willing to take that one on with me?"

"Of course. It's going to be crazy around here with all these kids, but I think I can handle it." He went to the sliding glass door and called the boys and they came running.

"Well," Jill said, "the truth is, Kelly's baby is going to be living with Sara."

He turned and looked at her. "Ah. She came around, did she?"

"Thanks to you."

He shook his head. "She was going to get there eventually. It just took some time for the shock to wear off."

Jill looked at him with stars in her eyes. He was so good and so ready to be a part of this family and commit to them all, even to her sister. And the new baby. She hardly knew how to contain her happiness.

The twins roared in and headed for the sunroom and she went back into Connor's arms. This was where she really belonged. This is where she was going to stay. Forever was a long, long time, but she was ready to promise it.

"I love you," she whispered to him.

"I've always loved you," he told her, his gaze dark with adoration and longing. "So I win."

"Oh, no, my handsome husband-to-be. If anyone is a winner here, it's me." And she kissed him hard, just to make sure he knew it.

* * * * *

MARRIAGE FOR HER BABY

BY
RAYE MORGAN

To Patience Bloom, aptly named and endowed with talents for perception, encouragement and support that go above and beyond every day!

CHAPTER ONE

SARA DARLING WAS collecting donations for the Children's Sunshine Fund throughout her bayside neighborhood, and it wasn't easy over the last weeks of summer when everyone was gone on vacation. The beach was unusually warm today and the stairs to each cottage seemed higher and higher as she moved down the beachfront area. To make that climb and then come up with no answer to her knock was demoralizing. The only people who opened the doors were vacation renters, and they weren't interested in donating to a local fund.

"Collecting," she muttered sarcastically as fat beads of sweat began a race down her spine. "Begging would be a better name for it."

Somehow she let her sister Jill talk her into doing this every year, and every year, she swore it would be the last time. She walked past her own little house and smiled. She hadn't been living in it for the last few weeks. Renovations were underway. She could hardly wait to go in and see it all changed. Just a few more days and work should be over. She could pack up her baby and move back home.

The last house on her schedule was the one next to hers. The neighbors were in Europe on their annual trek, but they did rent out to short-term vacationers. She looked at the red door and sighed, wishing she could head back to her baby right now. One last climb.

She made it and gave a short knock on the door. No response. Oh, well. She started to turn away, but a sound from inside turned her back again. What was that? A siren? An alarm? Or was the tenant playing some sort of weird music?

What the heck, it was none of her business. She started to turn away again, but the door suddenly swung open as though someone had yanked it from behind. Sara found herself staring into a pair of icy-blue eyes beneath dark, intimidating brows.

"Yes?" the man asked shortly, as though she was already late answering him.

Unaccountably she was flustered and for a moment, she couldn't remember why she'd come. "I...uh..."

Maybe it was because he was so darn handsome. Or maybe it was because he was looking so fierce. Possibly also in the brew was the fact that his naked torso was muscular and manly and altogether breathtaking, and the way his jeans hung on his hips was enough to give a girl ideas. That might have been a contributing factor. But whatever the cause, her mind was completely blank.

"Hey, you're a woman," he announced gruffly, as though it was something of a revelation to him.

She tried to smile. "So I've been told," she said, attempting light humor that crumbled and died before the words even left her lips.

His frown grew fiercer. "I need a woman. Maybe you can help me. Come on." Reaching out, he grabbed her wrist and pulled her into the house, letting the door slam behind her.

"Wait a minute!"

"No time. All hell is breaking loose. Come on. Quickly."

Truth be told, she was pretty sure she would have resisted with a bit more spunk if it hadn't been for the oddly disturbing noises coming from the very room they were dashing toward. Curiosity was strong here, and it was rewarded. He threw open the double doors and ushered her into a little piece of madness.

The noise was overwhelming. Something was rotating and banging against the wall. Some form of food sizzled and spit on the stove, and thick waves of suds poured out of the dishwasher. A cat had climbed halfway up the inside of the screen door and was howling for escape. The refrigerator door stood open, creating an annoying electronic warning buzz. Meanwhile cans of soda were slowly rolling out and hitting the floor. Now and then, one burst open and shot carbonated beverage across the walls. A cloud of black smoke was emanating from the toaster and the smell of burning bread was in the air.

"You see what I mean?" the man shouted above the din. "Where do I start?"

Whatever was sizzling on the stove suddenly burst into tall orange flames, which shot toward the ceiling.

She gaped. The gates of hell might have looked something like this.

Sara took it all in and suppressed the scream of horror that wanted to push its way up her throat. This was no time to panic. She had to be cool, calm, collected.

But she wasn't perfect. "Oh, my goodness…what?" she cried, knowing there was going to be no answer until disaster had been headed off at the pass. "Are you crazy?"

He spread out his hands and shook his head. "Help," he said.

She looked at him. He was actually waiting for her to tell him what to do. She gulped. He wasn't the type. She knew that instinctively. But here he was, asking for assistance—from her. Help indeed!

She pushed back the panic and tried to think clearly. Wait. She knew all these items intimately. The situations, taken one at a time, were all things she'd dealt with before. Darn it all, she could handle this. Suddenly she realized it was true. She could take command. Why not? He was obviously clueless.

She grabbed his arm. "Okay," she shouted in order to be heard above the din. "Turn off the dishwasher. I'll take care of the fire."

He turned to look at it. The flames appeared fiery, leaping higher every minute. "You will?" he said doubtfully.

She didn't waste any more time. The lid to the frying pan was lying on the floor. She reached down to grab it, took a deep breath and plunged forward, firmly slamming it down on the pan, smothering the flames almost instantly. Quickly turning the knob for the gas, she doused its fuel. And then she took a deep breath of relief.

"Hey," he said, looking impressed.

"The dishwasher," she reminded him, jerking her head in that direction. They were going to be swimming in suds in no time if he didn't stop the flow. She could just picture the two of them waltzing across the slippery floor and landing on their backsides.

"Right," he said. He actually looked like he knew what he was doing so she headed for the washing machine at the far end of the kitchen. It was doing a spin cycle, but it was unbalanced and creating a terrible noise as it bounced around. Reaching out with a strange new confidence, she snapped off the juice. Like a crazed windup toy coming back to sanity, it began to wind down its banging cascade.

"How do I turn this thing off?" he was calling to her as he peered at the knobs and buttons on the dishwasher.

So she'd been wrong. He had no idea what he was doing. But wasn't that obvious by now? She strode over and slapped the off switch as she passed, never missing a beat, on her way to the refrigerator. There, she caught the last two cans before they hit the floor, unended them, placed them on a shelf and closed the door.

The awful noise from the washing machine had stopped. The sizzle was dying down in the frying pan. The refrigerator alarm had faded away and the suds were slowing down.

She looked at the toaster. A black cloud still hovered

over it, but nothing new was burning. At least he seemed to have unplugged it on his own, so that was taking care of itself by now.

However, the smoke alarm it had probably triggered was shouting a warning over and over. "Evacuate! Evacuate! There is smoke in the basement. Evacuate!"

She looked at him for an explanation and he shook his head. "There is no basement," he told her. "The thing's gone crazy."

"How do you turn it off?" she asked him, knowing there had to be a way and knowing at the same time that he wasn't going to know what that was.

"You got me."

She hesitated. It was up so high, she couldn't fan it with a towel like she usually did with hers. But something had to be done. It was getting louder and louder, as if it were angry they weren't paying enough attention. She looked around the room and saw a broom. Grabbing it, she placed it in his hand.

"Kill it," she said.

He almost laughed. "You're kidding."

She shook her head. She was feeling a little wild. "You're taller. Swing at it with the brush end of the broom. That might do it. If not, do you have a gun?"

He did laugh this time, but he swung at it, forcing air into its core and finally, like a gift, it stopped yelling.

"Oh, my gosh," she said, sagging against the counter. "What a relief."

"Almost done," he said, turning to look at the cat that

was still clinging to the screen door and howling at the top of its lungs.

"Is he your cat?" she asked, looking at the poor terrified thing with its claws stuck.

He shook his head. "Never saw him before in my life. He must have been hiding in here when it all began."

She nodded. She'd thought as much. She'd seen him around the neighborhood for ages.

"Okay. You're going to have to help me. This is going to be a two-part play."

He nodded, watching her. "Just tell me what to do."

She glanced into his eyes, expecting a touch of ridicule. He was the sort of man she would have thought would be ready to put her back in her place by now. But, no. His eyes were clear and ready. He really was waiting for her to tell him what to do.

For some reason, that made her heart beat faster. She scanned the room. "We'll need a towel," she said.

He turned and grabbed one from a pile of dirty clothes in front of the washer. It looked as though he'd just emptied a duffel bag right there. He handed her the towel and she regarded the cat. The only way she'd ever managed to take her cat—when she had one—to the veterinarian was by wrapping him firmly so that no claws were exposed. But that was a cat who knew and loved her. This one was a stranger. She only hoped she didn't end up a bloody mess when this was over and done.

"Okay. I'll grab him. You whip open the door."

"It opens to a back porch," he warned her. "You want

me to go all the way through that and open a door to the backyard?"

"Absolutely," she said, nodding. "Okay, here goes."

She drew in a deep, deep breath, muttered a little prayer and lunged for the cat. He saw her coming and yelled a threat, a deep, vibrant howl. If he'd been free to fly, he would have done it, but luckily his claws were stuck just enough so that he couldn't move.

The next part was tricky. She had to get him wrapped really well and do it fast, but at the same time, she didn't want to hurt him and his claws being stuck shifted from being an advantage to being a problem. She threw the towel around and hugged him, lifting slightly to loosen his claws. Somehow it worked out fine. Only a few claws continued to stick, and then only for a few seconds. As he came loose, she wrapped his paws quickly and clamped down tight. He howled and struggled but she gritted her teeth and held on, carrying him quickly out as the man opened the doors for her.

The cat was strong and he'd almost worked his way out of the towel by the time she hit the backyard and she didn't get to put him down as gently as she would have liked. But she hardly saw him at all. In a flash, he was gone. She looked around and tried to catch her breath. Then she turned and saw the man staring at her in wonder.

"Wow," he said. "You're incredible."

She stared back at him, surprised. He meant it. But she thought about it for a second. She sort of was, wasn't she? She'd handled all this pretty well, if she did say so herself. Now that things had calmed down, she couldn't believe that she'd been able to maintain that sort of control. She'd moved smoothly, with purpose and determination.

That really wasn't much like her. Hey. She was pretty proud of herself.

As for him…well, what on earth was that all about, anyway? She shook her head.

"How could you get so many things wrong at one time?" she asked, still amazed at what they'd just experienced.

He gave her a crooked grin that didn't seem to reach his eyes. "Pretty amazing, isn't it? I don't know. I just seem to have a talent for failure lately."

"I doubt that." She rejected his explanation out of hand. No, he had the look and feel of a man who did just about everything right. Only—today things had spun out of control for a bit. Interesting.

They were standing in the backyard and neither of them seemed to have any interest in going back into the kitchen. She shuddered when she thought of it.

"Seriously," he said. "I've spent most of my time living in hotel rooms or tents over the last few years. I've lost the knack of civilization."

She wanted to laugh but he wasn't even smiling. "Surely you didn't grow up in a cave," she said.

"No." He raised his bright blue eyes to meet hers. "It was more of a hut. And after my mother died, we didn't live much like modern people do. My father caught game and fished and we lived off that. People called us the

Wild Ones in my town. I resented it at the time, but looking back, I guess we deserved it."

She couldn't look away from his brilliant blue gaze. He had her mesmerized. She could see him living rough, like a twentieth century native. All he needed was a horse and a blanket and off he would go.

But the twentieth century was over and the modern world wasn't very open to living like a wild one. Very deliberately, she took a step backward, as if she could somehow make a move out of his sphere of suggestive influence by putting more space between them. It didn't work, and she found herself smoothing back her sleek blond hair like a woman primping for an encounter.

Ouch!

She wasn't going to do that. She was so far from being in the market for a flirtation, she hardly remembered what that would be like. She finally pulled her gaze away and shook her head.

"You've got a lot of cleaning up to do in there," she noted.

"Not me," he said decisively.

She frowned at him. "You can't just leave it. You're going to have to clean it sometime."

"Are you kidding?" His sudden grin was a revelation. "I'm not going back in there."

She gasped. "But…"

"I'll just go and rent a new place and start over, armed with all I've learned from you."

It took a moment to realize he was kidding. She shook her head, not sure what to make of him.

He was tall and hard and strong with a body that could have been chiseled from Carrara marble. That's what he reminded her of—the gang at the Parthenon. A Greek god for heaven's sake—with a face to match. His features were crisp and even—handsome in a hard, rough way. His eyes with their long, dark lashes had a sleepy, languorous expression. Very appealing.

But was there any warmth there? If there was, she couldn't find it. Was he as cold as marble, too? All in all, he was gorgeous, but he was also a little bit scary.

He watched her with one dark eyebrow raised.

"Tell you what, let's go down to the corner café. I'll buy you a cup of coffee."

That startled her. She'd sworn off men a long time ago. The aggravation wasn't worth the reward. She had other things in her life, things she valued. Besides, he might be a short-term renter in the house next to hers, but that didn't mean they were destined to be bosom buddies. Not at all. She took his offer as a cue to begin to back away.

"Oh, I don't know, I've got to…"

"Come on." He touched her. It was just a gesture, just a quick, passing touch. He probably didn't even notice when his fingertips softly slipped along her arm. But she did. It gave her a start and her breath was suddenly catching in her throat.

"Come on. I owe you one. You just did me a very big favor."

"Well…" She was weakening. A part of her stood aside and watched this with exasperation. What on earth was she doing? But she snuck a look at her watch and realized she actually had plenty of time. She knew her baby would still be napping at her sister's house for another half hour, at least. So…why not?

She glanced at him sideways. "Just for a few minutes," she conceded.

"Good," he said, sticking his hand out. "I'm Jake Martin. And I would guess that your name is Jill."

"Oh, no." She shook her head, wondering how he'd come up with her sister's name, then she realized she was wearing Jill's uniform shirt for doing the Sunshine Fund collecting. "Jill" was embroidered in big red letters right over the pocket. She laughed. "No, actually…"

"Come on, Jill," he said, taking her hand. "Let's go."

Her heart seemed to roll over inside her. She glanced at his muscular chest and knew she was turning bright red.

"You're going to need a shirt, aren't you?" she noted breathlessly.

"Oh." He stopped short and looked down at his lack of attire. "Hey, sorry. I hadn't realized I was being so informal. I'll grab something out of my car."

He turned to do just that and she gasped softly as she noticed the purple scarring on his back, a picture of past pain and agony she hadn't noticed before in all the commotion. She turned away and pretended not to watch as he pulled a dark blue T-shirt over that beautiful body.

"Listen, I left my papers and my purse in your house. I'm going to have to go in to get them."

He groaned. "Okay. But I don't want to see it. I'll meet you out front."

She made her way quickly through the mess, glad it wasn't going to be her job to clean it up, grabbed her things and came out the front door to meet him. He smiled and took hold of her hand again and they were marching toward the coffee shop.

"I really like it here," he told her, looking out at the gray-blue ocean that surrounded the Washington State island just across from Seattle where they lived—for the moment at least.

She liked it, too. In fact she planned to spend a long, long time here. That was why she was renovating her house to make room for raising Savannah, her nine-month-old baby.

A group of seagulls flew overhead, screaming in their usual argument. She looked down toward the other end of town. The ferry was coming in, bringing commuters home from their jobs in Seattle. Yes, this was where she wanted to be.

"Too bad I can't stay," Jake said, looking like he really did regret it.

"Where are you going instead?" she asked, just to make conversation.

He hesitated. "I'm not sure," he told her, staring right down into her eyes. "I haven't had time to think it through. But it will be somewhere different." His smile was crooked. "It always is."

She could see that he was telling her the truth. But

he was outside his comfort zone at the moment. She wondered why.

They went into the little café and took a booth, sitting across from each other. Coffee, he'd said, and she wasn't hungry, but she picked up the menu and began to peruse it, just to give herself something to do besides stare at him.

"You said you'd been living in a tent lately," she reminded him, peeking around the menu. "What was that all about?"

"I've been in the military," he said shortly, looking away as though it was something he didn't want to talk about.

"As if that wasn't obvious," she muttered, glancing back at the menu.

"Why?" he said.

She shrugged. "There's a military look about you," she said.

He frowned and she looked away again. So he didn't like the fact that she could see his military influence. Too bad. It was only obvious and she could have said more.

She could have mentioned that he had a noticeable restlessness in him, a sort of masculine urge to gaze at the horizon and wonder what might be out there. It was the sort of thing that made most women sigh with regret. He wasn't the sort to be tied down by anyone. It was written all over him. You fell for a man like this and you were playing with fire.

"Iced tea, please," she asked as the waitress stood poised, pad of paper in hand.

"Coffee for me," he said. "Black. And two pieces of cherry pie. Á la mode."

She looked at him and held back her smile. "You must be really hungry," she said.

"No. But I can see that you are," he shot back. Then he grinned and that took all the sting out of it. "You'll love the pie here," he said. "Trust me."

Trust him. That was just what she was having a bit of problem doing. And where did he get off telling her what the pie was like in her own little café? That did it. She'd known she should have rejected his offer from the first. The man was obviously insufferable.

But he was also right. The pie was great. She looked around the restaurant, surprised she didn't see anyone she knew. Only the girl behind the counter seemed familiar at all. But she usually stopped by for a large cup of coffee in the morning, and the crew in the afternoon were mostly different. It was odd to be in a place that was so familiar, and yet feel like a stranger.

Odd, but not unusual for her. She hadn't made many friends since she'd moved to the island, and the ones she did know didn't really know much about her. She kept things to herself.

And there was a secret about her that not even most of the people closest to her knew. She'd never been in love.

She'd been in pretty heavy-duty "like" a time or two. She'd known some very nice men and she'd had relationships. She'd even been engaged once. But somehow she'd always felt a little bit apart, as though she were an observer of her own talent at romance—and marking herself down critically every time.

Her engagement had been a high point. She'd really liked Freddy. He was fun and good-natured and liked to do many of the things she liked. His family was so nice. She could just see the trajectory of the life they would have together and it followed exactly what she would have expected for herself. It all fit. Why not? Why not go ahead and marry him and hope that it would all work out?

She became obsessed with pretending that she was in love. She tried so hard. But when he hugged her, she found herself craning to see what time it was. When he told her of his life plans, she found herself daydreaming instead of throwing herself into his ambitions the way she should have. And when he kissed her, there was no sparkle.

She told herself not to be so childish. Who the heck needed sparkle? And then she realized—she did. Just a little. Was that asking too much?

When they split up, she felt nothing but relief, and since then, she'd hardly given their relationship another thought. Looking back, she knew now that there had been very little love involved on either of their parts. There had been a longing for a regular, ordinary life, but it had very little to do with any strong emotional tie between them.

She just didn't seem to have what it took to create a loving relationship, and she'd resigned herself to concentrating on her career. Now there was something she was good at.

She had finished half her piece of pie and was trying to decide if she was going to eat the rest. It was awfully good, but the calories! She'd always been on the slender side, but that fit figure wasn't easy to keep that way. Pushing the plate away, she looked up at Jake instead.

"So you were telling me about living in a tent," she reminded him.

"Was I?"

"Yes. And then you got annoyed when I said I could tell you were military." She smiled. She was nothing if not helpful.

He gave her a disbelieving glance, but he willingly picked up the thread and went on. "I've been deployed mostly to Southeast Asia for the last couple of years," he filled in. "We did a lot of living off the land. Subsisting on roadkill and taro root."

She made a face. She didn't know whether to take him seriously or not, but the humorous glint in his eyes was a pretty big hint. "Don't they give you guys C rations anymore?" she asked tartly.

He leaned back and looked at her through heavy lidded eyes. "Now that would be giving away the military connection from the get-go, don't you think?" he drawled.

She narrowed her eyes, refusing to let him intimidate her. "So you were working undercover, were you?" she said, pleased with herself for making the connection.

But his eyes turned a stormy-gray. "Not lately," he

said shortly. "I was doing some time in a terrorist prison camp—as a detainee. And believe me, we were happy to get taro root. It was the fat, squishy insects that made you gag."

She gazed at him, not sure if he was still pulling the wool over her eyes or not. He seemed awfully serious. She decided to play along, regardless. "So that was why you said you had forgotten how to live like a civilized person?"

He nodded. "I felt I needed to get back in the groove. So I decided to try out all the modern conveniences I hadn't ever used before, all at once." His quick grin was self-deprecating and it left as suddenly as it had appeared. "Like I thought I could get the learning curve over with faster that way. As you can see, it didn't work very well."

"Okay," she told him sensibly. "So start over, only this time do one thing a day until you've mastered it."

He was shaking his head. "No time," he said. "I've got to learn fast. I'm going to need it all very soon."

She smiled. "Because you rented a nice little house with appliances?"

He didn't smile back. "No. Something more important than that."

She waited for a moment, but he didn't elaborate. She couldn't imagine what it might be, but she was curious. In fact, she was becoming more and more interested in this gorgeous, compelling man. There was no use trying to pretend. For the first time in years, she'd met a man who not only made her pulse dance, but made her think warm thoughts of all kinds.

Ordinarily that would make her back away and find an excuse to be somewhere else. But she couldn't do that with Jake Martin. She was starting to wish she could think of a reason to ask him over for dinner.

Wait. She had the perfect reason.

His house had practically exploded that afternoon. He couldn't go back there until something was done about the mess. So she wouldn't feel hesitant about asking him over—even if it was to her sister's house. She smiled again and waited for a chance to get an invitation in.

But meanwhile, there was the question of that important thing that made him want to learn how to run a house.

"Am I supposed to guess what it is?" she asked.

She was almost flirting now. Maybe she ought to hold that back for the time being. She'd forgotten how much fun it could be—that little surge of electricity as your eyes met his—that little bobble of excitement in your chest. Flirting. She was going to have to work on it a bit, but it could be an asset. She bit her lower lip and waited for an answer.

"No, of course not," he said, his blue eyes sparkling. "Sorry to be so secretive, but there are reasons."

"Go ahead," she said recklessly. "You can tell me anything."

He hesitated, looking at her as though trying to decide if he could trust her.

She smiled, trying to look trustworthy.

He shrugged. "Okay, I'll tell you why." He leaned forward so that he could speak more confidentially. "I'm about to become a father. And I've got to learn how to take care of my little girl as quickly as I can."

CHAPTER TWO

SARA GAZED AT Jake, amazed. A little girl—just like Savannah. Funny how similar their stories seemed to be. Maybe he was adopting his little girl, the same way she was adopting hers. Or maybe—she glanced at his hand, looking for a ring and he noted her interest with a crooked grin.

"No, I'm not married," he said. "But I do have a little girl and in a few days, she'll be with me. I've got to be ready to take care of her. I've got to learn all this stuff."

"Of course you do."

She smiled at him. Finally there was a flicker of warmth in his eyes and it had to be because he was talking about his baby. She knew the feeling. She'd considered herself a career woman for years until Savannah had come into her life. And now her entire reality was totally focused on that child.

She leaned forward, wanting to know all about it but not wanting to seem too nosy. She thought of her own nine-month-old baby, and her smile widened. He was in for such joy if his experience was even half as rewarding as hers had been.

Savannah had been the child of her younger half sister. After Kelly died in a car accident, Sara had volunteered to take her. She'd been reluctant at first. She and her sister Jill hadn't had any contact with Kelly for a long time and knew nothing about her baby. Besides, Sara was about to make a major step forward in her career, a job that would take all her time.

But in the end, the baby came first.

Now she couldn't even remember that struggle to decide very clearly. Her very existence revolved around this baby she'd only had for less than six months. She couldn't imagine life without her. In just a few minutes she would get a chance to tell Jake all about her. The anticipation made her smile.

"I've always been a quick study in my line of work," Jake said. "And since I didn't know anything, I decided the best thing to do would be to just start teaching myself how to cook and to clean and all the rest. Just go ahead and jump in with both feet. So today was the day." He threw his head back and groaned. "Disaster."

She had to admit that was pretty accurate. "Think of it as a learning experience," she told him. "I think you need more planning ahead of time. And maybe lessons would help."

"Lessons." He nodded, thinking that over. "Maybe you could teach me a few more tricks?" He looked at her, his face endearingly pathetic.

"Why not?"

That was her first, exuberant reaction, but it only took seconds to make her wonder what the heck she thought she was getting into. Her interior watchdog was yelling, "No, no, no, no!" That was exactly what she'd programmed it to do if she was ever in danger of falling for a man again. But she was very tempted to ignore it. Maybe her luck had changed. How would she ever know if she didn't try?

"So tell me about your little girl," she said, wondering if it would be a good time to ask him what his dinner plans were. Maybe not. Better wait another ten minutes or so. "How old is she? When did you see her last?"

He frowned. "I think she's about nine months old," he said. "I think that's what they told me."

Nine months. That was the same as Savannah. "You're adopting her?" Sara asked.

But he shook his head. "No. She's mine. I just didn't know about her until I got released from the camp and sent home to the States."

Somewhere deep inside, very near her heart, a new warning was beginning to send a small, nervous signal to her brain. She touched her breastbone with her fingers, gently pushing as though she could push the feeling back. But it just got stronger. Something wasn't quite right here.

But that was silly. She had no real reason to think that at all. He was telling her the facts as he knew them—why would that be threatening? She was being ridiculous. Probably because she wasn't used to talking to men like this.

"What's your baby's name?"

He shook his head. "Funny thing is, they never told

me that. I guess I'll be able to name her whatever I want."

"So you've never seen her?"

"No." His smile was brilliant. "But I've seen pictures, and she's a beauty—a little blonde with dark eyes and the biggest smile I've ever seen."

Sara was feeling sick. She wasn't sure why. But something was beginning to feel very wrong. Why did everything he said seem to have such a close resemblance to her Savannah?

Stop it, she told herself. *That's crazy. What he is describing is the picture of almost any little nine-month-old girl. Don't let your imagination carry you away. Just stop it!*

"What happened to her mother?" she asked, surprised to hear how raspy her voice sounded.

He shook his head. "She's out of the picture," was all he said.

What did that mean? That she didn't want the child? That she didn't want a relationship with Jake? That she was an unfit mother and he had to take over? It could mean a thousand things. It could also mean—no, she didn't want to go there.

"So they've told you that your baby is all yours?" she asked, feeling breathless. "Are you taking possession of her here? Or...?"

He grimaced. "Actually I'm not supposed to be here yet. I found out where she's staying and I came to get as close to her as I could. I want to be ready to go, as soon as the paperwork is all taken care of. We've just got to tie up a few loose ends, and I'll be taking custody of her."

As close to her as he could. Yeah, next door was pretty close. Pure, cold, electric panic was beginning to shiver through her system. It couldn't be. Could it?

"You said the mother is out of the picture," she repeated. Her voice sounded so strange and her mouth was so dry. "Permanently?"

He looked at her curiously, as though wondering why she cared. "Yes. She died in a car accident."

"Oh. I'm so sorry." Her words came automatically, but her hand rose and covered her mouth. Inside, she was screaming.

"Me, too." He shrugged. "But I really didn't know her very well. And now I've found she left me this wonderful gift." He shook his head. "Life is crazy, isn't it?"

"Yes."

She had to go. She had to get out of here. Maybe she was taking this completely wrong, but there were too many things that seemed to lead right to her situation—to her baby. *It couldn't be. Oh, please, don't let it be...*

She began to gather her clipboard and purse, preparing to make her escape.

"You know the neighborhood pretty well, don't you?" he was asking.

What? She blinked at him. It was almost as though he was speaking a foreign language. But she took a deep breath and forced herself to settle down and translate to her frightened mind.

"I...I've lived here for three years, but I traveled a lot

on business. So, no, I guess I can't claim to know the neighborhood really well. Why?"

"I was just wondering if you knew a woman named Sara Darling."

There it was—as though a huge gong of doom had been rung in her head. It was still ringing, echoing back and forth, deafening her. This was it. Everything she'd been dreading was coming down on her and she had to go. She began to tremble uncontrollably. She looked around, ready to run.

But at the same time, she couldn't give it all away. She couldn't let him know. She needed time to get away. So she tried to smile.

"Sara Darling?" Sara could hardly get the name out of her dry mouth. "I, uh, well, no, I…"

Ordinarily she would be laughing and explaining how he'd had her name wrong from the beginning, and that she was Sara Darling herself. But that didn't happen. She couldn't let him know who she really was. The shock of his question had pierced her heart and it was going to take some time to right herself again.

"She's supposed to be living next door to the house I rented," he went on, "but I've been there for two days and I haven't seen a sign of her."

"Oh." *Calm down, Sara,* she was telling herself. *You've got to make it through this. Calm down.*

She had to go. She had to get out of here. Her heart was pounding so hard, she was sure he had to hear it.

"Hey, I'm sorry," she said quickly as she slid out of

the booth. "I just remembered something I have to do. Thanks so much for the pie. I'll...I'll see you around."

She didn't stop to see how he took her sudden departure. She just went, walking quickly through the tiny café, then breaking into a run as she hit the street.

By the time Sara reached her sister's house at the top of the hill overlooking the ferry landing, she thought her lungs would burst.

"Sara, what is it?" Jill called, seeing her entrance from the kitchen where she was baking. "What on earth is the matter?"

She rushed out to greet her and Sara clung to her, trying to catch her breath.

"Where's Savannah?" she choked out as soon as she could speak.

"In her bed. She's still taking her nap." Jill frowned. "Honey, she's okay. What's wrong?"

"Nothing. I just...nothing."

Jill shrugged, searching her face. "Well, go ahead and check on her, but I just was up there getting the twins ready to go outside and play and she was snoozing away."

Sara nodded and started for the stairs.

"Oh, you had a couple of phone calls," Jill called after her. "One was from the Children's Home Agency. They wanted you to call back right away."

Sara turned to look at her. "Did you write down the number?"

"Of course. It's right by the phone." Jill frowned. "Sara, you don't look good. What's the matter?"

Sara held up her hand. "I'll tell you later. Right now, I've got to call the agency."

"Sure." Jill nodded, though she still looked concerned. "I'll be in the kitchen. I've got an order of Bundt cakes that need to go out by six."

Sara waved her off, turned to the phone and found the paper with the number on it. She dialed it quickly and got through to a real live agent almost immediately.

"We've been trying to get hold of you for the last few days," an agent named Linda told her. "You really must keep in better contact. If you're going to be away, you must let us know."

"Sorry. I'm sorry. I'll take care of it next time." Sara tried to stop her heart from racing so wildly. "Is there… is there something wrong?"

There was a pause and it nearly killed her. She put her hand over her heart and waited, trying to keep her breathing even.

"Well, I'm afraid something has happened," the woman said at last. "You've been doing so well with your quest to adopt little Savannah."

"My…my sister's child," Sara said, as though that was going to help her win.

"Yes, of course. But you see, there is a problem. Her, uh, her biological father seems to have turned up."

Sara closed her eyes and fought back the urge to vomit. The very thing she'd been afraid of from the beginning now filled her with a terrible dread.

"Are you sure?" she said, her voice raspy, her throat tight. "How can we know he's telling the truth?"

"DNA tests are being performed. We'll know the facts soon enough."

Soon enough. Soon enough. What was the woman talking about?

"But…I've done everything. I've met all the standards. I'm in the process of adopting her right now…."

"You do know that a DNA match will be determinative, don't you? If he can prove that he is her father, well, there's not much we can do."

Sara couldn't speak. She rocked back and forth, holding tightly. Tears were streaming down her face.

"Now don't you give up hope, my dear," the woman was saying. "The DNA might not match. And even if it does, he might decide he is unprepared to take on such a huge responsibility as raising a child on his own. But we do have to come to a conclusion, one way or another, before we can move forward."

"What's his name?" she asked, barely holding herself together.

"His name? Oh. Well, I guess I can tell you that. Jake Martin. He's been away in the military and didn't know that Savannah had been born. Or so he says."

She nodded. She wanted to say more, but she would begin to cry in earnest if she tried.

"I do have to warn you," the voice said, sounding tentative now. "Something happened the last time he was in here. You see, it seems he may have taken a file folder that included your address. It would be completely against regulations to give him your address, of course. But as the file has been missing since his visit... well...I thought you ought to be warned. He might try to contact you."

"Yes," she whispered. "He might." The woman was still talking, but Sara hung up the phone.

She had things to do. She was going to take her baby and run for shelter.

"Be calm," she repeated to herself over and over, breathing in through her nose and out through her mouth. "Remember how you were this afternoon in the crazy kitchen. You can do this. You can make it happen. But you have to stay calm."

They could do it. They would go to a new place and they would hide until the coast was clear, and then... She didn't know what would happen then. But there was no way she was giving up her baby to that...man.

She dashed upstairs and pulled out two travel bags. Working fast, she began to throw clothes into one, baby supplies into the other. They were going to run.

She looked into the crib where Savannah was sleeping. Her beautiful, beautiful baby. For just a moment she filled her heart with the look of her, her round baby cheeks, her perfect eyebrows, her adorable wisp of blond hair. Everything in her ached for this child. To hand her over? To never see her sweet face again? No! She could not, would not—give her up.

And then Jill was in the doorway.

"Sara! What are you doing?"

Sara shook her head and refused to meet her sister's

gaze. "Sorry, Jill. We've got to get out of here." She threw some little romper suits into the bag.

Jill grabbed her by the shoulders. "Why? Tell me what's going on."

Sara blinked back tears. "No time."

"Sara!"

"Okay, okay." She took a deep breath. "There's this man who is renting the Lancaster place next to me. His name is Jake Martin. He claims he's Savannah's father."

Jill gasped. "Oh, Sara! No."

"Yes. And he wants her." She set her jaw. "But I won't let him take her. I'm going to go."

"But, Sara, where?"

"Away. As far as we can go. Jill, you do see that I have to do this?"

But Jill was shaking her head. "No," she said softly. "Oh, Sara, no. You can't run. What good will it do? They'll find you. You won't get away. It's too dangerous. Stay here. We'll see what we can do. Maybe Connor will know someone…"

"Jill, he's here. He's looking for her right now. I have to go."

"No!"

"Jill, listen to me. You're the one who talked me into taking this baby. I didn't want to do it. But I saw the light and I did my duty to our sister Kelly. I took her baby. I put all my heart and soul into loving her, caring for her, making her feel cherished and safe. And now you want me to just give her up to some crazy man who doesn't have the slightest idea on how to take care of a child? No. I won't do it. I'm going."

"Wait until Connor gets home," Jill insisted. Pulling out her cell phone, she punched in her husband's number. "Wait. He'll have an idea. I know he will. We can all work on this together."

Sara didn't waste any more time talking. She pulled Savannah into her arms and headed for the changing table. Quickly she changed the diaper as her baby began to wake up and look around, cooing happily as she always did when she saw her mother's face. Sara pulled on a little playsuit and wrapped her in a blanket, then grabbed the suitcases and headed to the door.

She could hear her sister talking to Connor, giving him the facts and urging him to get home fast. But she couldn't wait for that. As she rushed out the door, her main fear was that Jake would already be coming up the hill to Jill's house. She looked quickly, but there was no sign of him, and relief surged in her heart. If she could get to the ferry before he found her, they just might make it. She strapped her baby into the car seat and off they went.

A good twenty minutes of high anxiety passed before sanity began to creep back into Sara's thinking. She was on the ferry by then, parked behind six cars and in front of two others and gliding across the water. The wait to board had seemed to go on forever. She'd sat behind the wheel, scanning the landscape, staring into her rearview mirror, jumping every time a new man appeared anywhere near.

But he didn't show up. They opened the gates and let her onto the ferry, and still she didn't see him anywhere. They started off across the bay and as time passed, she began to breathe again. Seattle lay off in the distance. Her thoughts had centered around losing themselves in the big city. As she calmed down, she began to realize how senseless that was.

Savannah was fussing a bit and she turned to reach out for her little hand. She hadn't thought to bring some snacks for her but she did have some fresh bottles. Once they got to the other side, she would pull over in a park she knew of and take care of that.

Looking at her adorable child, it came to her in a flash. This was crazy. It was a fantasy—a huge leap out into the great unknown without a safety net. In the modern world there were very few places where you could hide—especially if you were taking a baby with you. You had to have a way to make a living. You had to have someone to watch the baby while you did that. You had to have a place to live in. And all those things required identification. They would be found in no time.

It wouldn't work. She was endangering the welfare of her baby in order to keep control—and losing all control by doing it. This was nuts. Jill had been right. She was going to have to go back.

Her heart sank. She knew it was a sort of defeat. But at the same time, it was only recognizing reality. A thousand things could go wrong, and most of them might hurt Savannah. What had she been thinking? She couldn't risk it.

A sense of doom swept over her, catching in her throat, but she fought it back. There were other ways to fight this. It might take a bit of finesse, a talent for persuasion and a touch for manipulation. But she'd been there before.

Jake Martin wasn't domesticated. He was a wild man. He lived unconventionally. There was nothing in his background or experience that had prepared him to take care of a baby. Surely the powers in the agency would see that. Surely that would go into their decision-making. Or was biology all that mattered?

There was one counselor who had been very helpful to her before, a Mrs. Truesdale. She'd taken a special interest in getting Savannah settled with Sara and had said to call her if there were any problems. That was the one she should have talked to. Maybe she could help.

Her baby's fussing got more insistent.

"Okay, honey," she told her, clicking open her seat belt and opening the car door. "I'm afraid we're going to be turning around and going right back home again. But for now, let's go look at the water. You need some good old ocean wind in your face."

She bundled her baby in the blanket and carried her out onto the deck. A few other passengers were scattered along the railing, watching the icy blue-green water wash by. Lifting her face to the sun, she took a deep breath of fresh air. She was glad they were turning back. She needed to be with her sister. Together, they would think of something. She was sure of it.

She felt the large, hard hand take hold of her upper arm and she didn't have to look to see who it was. But she did anyway, whipping her head around and gasping. Jake seemed taller, his shoulders seemed even wider, his face harder. His hand had clamped down on her flesh like a vise and she knew there was no way she could get away from him.

CHAPTER THREE

"HI SARA," JAKE said, looking down at the bundle she carried.

She glared at him and clutched her baby up against her chest.

"So this is my little girl, is it?" he asked softly.

She quickly suppressed her original reaction. There was, after all, no place to run to while they were on the ferry.

"Hello, Jake," she said. She couldn't pretend to be pleased to see him, but she didn't think screaming would do her any good. "Fancy meeting you in a place like this."

He raised an eyebrow. "I'm sure you expected to see me again," he said, his voice low and not particularly friendly. "You didn't think you were going to get away that easily, did you?"

She gave him a look of round-eyed innocence. "Get away from what, pray tell?"

"You know exactly what I'm talking about. I'm sure you've talked to the agency by now." He shook his head, bemused. "I knew you were a runner from the start."

"A runner?" She held her temper with a lot of effort. "Why would I run from you, Jake? Is there something I should know?" Her gaze narrowed. "In what way are you trying to threaten me?"

His mouth twisted. "I'm sure you've figured it out by now. I'm that little girl's biological father."

She knew he thought that, but still, hearing him say the words made her cringe. For just a few seconds, she was breathless, but she pulled herself together quickly.

"No kidding? Where's your proof?"

He released her arm as though he'd decided she wasn't going to run just yet. "All in good time," he said softly.

She shook her head. If he thought he was going to bully her, he could think again. "Not good enough, Jake. You see, I've had this baby with me for six months now. I've mothered her. I've cared for her. I've loved her. I've done all the paperwork, paid all the fees. I've been inspected, injected and detected, as the old song might say. I've been found to be qualified." Her eyes flashed. "What have you been found to be?"

He blinked at her and she could tell she'd actually made him think for just a moment.

"It's coming," he said at last, sounding a bit more defensive. "It'll be proven soon."

That gave her a small surge of hope.

"In other words, you've got nothing. Meanwhile, I've got all the official seals of approval I could possibly get. This baby and I have bonded, big time." She had to stop to keep her voice from breaking. Taking a deep breath, she went on. "In order to even think about breaking that bond, you're going to have to come up with some heavy-duty evidence. I'm not giving up easy."

She glared at him. He glared right back. She could almost see sparks flying between them. This was no good and she knew it. But she couldn't stop. She had to let him know how much this meant to her. He couldn't be allowed to treat this as a lark of some kind. He had to know the consequences were serious.

He shrugged. "I may not have signed as many official forms as you have, but I've been tested. The DNA results will trump all your seals and certificates and..." He paused for a moment as though he regretted having to say it. "And all your emotional appeal, Sara. I'm sorry, but that's reality."

She knew he was right and it made her want to sob, but she couldn't let him see weakness. "We'll see about that," she said.

Funny, but she'd been so scared when she was running from him. Now that he'd caught her, the fear was gone. There was a dark, burning anger deep inside her, and a determination that was growing stronger every minute. She knew only one thing for sure—she would not give up her baby. She would find a way.

He gestured in her direction and she flinched. It was an obvious move. His gaze met hers.

"Why would I hurt you?" he asked her, seemingly irritated by her reaction.

"I didn't think you were going to hurt me," she said coolly. "I just don't want you to touch her."

A series of emotions crossed his face but she wasn't sure what it all meant. The only thought that came to her was, *So this is what it's like to have an enemy. Scary.*

He looked out toward Seattle and seemed to settle his anger down. When he turned back toward her, his eyes were cold but his face was smooth. No emotions showing at all.

"Could I hold her?" he asked quietly.

She pressed Savannah closer, holding her tightly. This was painful. She just couldn't do it. "She's sleeping," she said.

"No, she's not. I can see her eyes. They're wide-open. Just let me hold her for a minute."

"No," she said, feeling fierce. "Not here. Not yet."

He stared down at her, not saying a word, but warning her that he could do whatever he wanted to do if he felt like it. At least, that was the message she took from the look in his eyes.

"There's a security guard on this ferry," she said quickly. "I could yell for help."

His wide mouth twisted in half a grin. "You could. But you won't."

She looked away and rocked Savannah softly. "What makes you think you know so much about how I tick?"

"I'm a student of everyday psychology. I knew from the way you ran at the café that you would try to get away with your..." He stopped, realizing that was the wrong thing for him to admit. "With the baby. You knew from the first that I have an unshakable claim."

"I don't know anything of the sort." She shifted Savannah to her other shoulder. "We have a long way to go before we can tell for sure just who you are."

He turned away and looked out over the rushing water as though working hard on controlling his temper. It took him some time to get to the point where he could turn back and she wondered if he was counting to a lot more than ten. When he finally turned back, his face was calm but his eyes were flashing.

"When the DNA results arrive in my favor—which they will—you'll have to give way. How long did you say you've had her?"

"Six months."

"Six months." He shrugged. "Yeah, that's a good long time. But facts are facts. She's my baby and it's my responsibility to take care of her."

Sara pressed her lips together. She had plenty she could say but she wasn't going to muddy the waters right now. There would be time to make her case. Right now he had her in a corner. It looked like everything was going his way. But she was beginning to realize that she had many cards of her own that she could play. This thing wasn't a done deal yet.

"Look, Sara," he said impatiently. "I know you've checked this out with the agency. You know who I am. Let me hold her."

She shook her head.

He raked fingers through his thick, auburn hair. His frustration was clear, but she held her ground, realizing that she'd better put it into words so he could deal with it.

"Jake, you're a stranger right now. I don't know if

you're who you say you are. We're standing on a boat, right over the ocean. Anything could happen. I can't risk it."

He frowned and actually looked hurt. "I wouldn't do anything that could possibly harm her."

Sara held her ground. "I'm not letting you hold her."

For just a moment, anger flared in his eyes. She saw it and the sense of its intensity stopped her heart for a beat. He was scary in a way she'd never known with a man before.

"All right," he said at last, his voice raw. "I guess I can understand that." A muscle worked at his jawline, but he smiled. "I can even commend you for taking good care of my baby." He took a deep breath. "But we need to talk somewhere. Somewhere safe."

She didn't want to talk to him. What was the point? She knew what he wanted. He knew what she demanded. Neither one of them was going to budge an inch.

Mentally she shook herself. She was going to have to talk to him. That was the only way she could get him to see how crazy this was. There were so many angles to fight this from. Right now, she thought she had the strongest—he wasn't father material.

It was true. He didn't know the first thing about babies. She remembered how he'd been with a kitchen and she almost smiled. He wasn't domesticated in any way at all. He was hopeless. He had to learn that somehow. And who else was going to make him face it if she didn't?

"All right." She sighed, letting him hear her exasperation. "Come back to my sister's house with me. My brother-in-law should be home by now. I'd be more comfortable if he and my sister were there, too."

"Okay. You've got a deal." He seemed relieved, glancing at the rapidly approaching coastline and noting that they were almost at the end of this part of their ferry journey.

She hated that he went to the car with them for the ride back, but she knew it would be petty to insist he stay out on the deck. They got into the car and he looked around, his mouth twisted.

"What the hell did you think you were doing?" he asked her.

She lifted her chin and shrugged. "I'm taking my baby for a drive. I don't think there are any laws against that."

"That's not your baby," he growled. "That's my baby."

She blinked quickly and kept her composure. "We don't know that yet, do we?"

"I know it."

They didn't speak again for a long time. She drove the car off the ferry and then back on again. Savannah played with her fingers, made some noises that sounded like she was trying to sing, then dozed off. Jake sat twisted in his seat, watching her every minute.

Sara turned on the radio and soft music played, hiding the awkwardness of the silence. When they were about halfway back across the bay, she couldn't resist asking him a few questions.

"So how did you get on the ferry without me seeing you?"

He shrugged. "I was already on board. I've been waiting since you left the café."

"I see."

"Right after you left, I asked around the place to see
if anyone knew who you were. The girl working behind
the counter said she thought your name was Sara." He
shrugged. "So then I knew."

She nodded. "Of course," she said softly, staring in-
tently at the car in front of them.

"But I knew you weren't living in the house next to
me, as you were supposed to be. I didn't know where
to find you. So I hung around the ferry and waited for
you to make a run for it." He turned and narrowed his
eyes, looking at her. "Did you know who I was from
the start? Why didn't you tell me you had a little girl?"

She shook her head. "No, I didn't know. And until I
realized who you were, I was just waiting for a chance
to tell you about her. You were pretty much monopo-
lizing the conversation, you know. I could hardly get a
word in."

He looked surprised. "Funny. I usually think of myself as the strong, silent type."

She rolled her eyes. "Right."

He looked back at the baby, now asleep in the car
seat. "She's gorgeous," he said, his mouth turning up
at the corners. "You kind of fall in love with her at first
sight, don't you?"

Sara felt tears stinging her eyes but she would die before she let him know his words had affected her. She

stared at him for a long moment, wishing she could see into his heart.

"I have to be very careful around you," she said softly at last. "You're a seducer."

"What?" He was outraged. "I haven't touched you!"

She shook her head. "I don't mean that way. I mean that you're a seducer of the mind. If I'm not careful, I'll end up letting you convince me to do something I shouldn't."

"Oh." He relaxed, and then his mouth twisted in something resembling humor. "Well, I can't help that."

"Yes, you can. You're the exact reason it's going to happen."

He frowned at her, not sure what she was getting at. "Look, mind games are not my thing."

"Really?" This was good. He was unsure. Without that massive swagger and confidence, he seemed almost manageable. "What is your thing, Jake? What is important to you?"

"Right now? That baby." He jerked his head in her direction.

Sara's lips tightened. "Her name is Savannah."

"Really?" He frowned thoughtfully. "I was thinking about naming her Jolene. My mother's name was Jolene. Or so they tell me."

"Jolene," Sara said with scorn, glancing at him. "She isn't a Jolene at all. Just look at her."

"Oh, yeah? What's a Jolene look like?"

She threw up a hand. "Different from this."

He frowned, studying Savannah's face as though he

was going to find the right name for her if he stared hard enough. But instead, he went off in another direction.

"So why are you staying at your sister's house?" he asked.

"My house is being renovated."

He nodded. "I've seen the workmen come and go. It looks like you're adding on a whole wing."

"I am." She glanced at him sideways. "It's for Savannah. A bedroom, a bathroom and a playroom. All for her." She bit her lip and then continued, her voice shaking. "You see, we have a life planned out. How can you just swoop in and smash it to bits?"

He shook his head, looking almost regretful. "I didn't set this all up on purpose, Sara. There's nothing personal in it. It's just the way the cards fell. No one's fault."

No one's fault. Then whom did she go to in order to make her case?

They landed and the cars drove off, one after another. She turned hers toward Jill's street. Her house was high up on the hill, visible from everywhere on this side of the island. She got to the corner of the turn up to her sister's house and suddenly Jake held his hand out.

"Hold it," he said. "Pull over."

"What is it?" She did as he ordered, but looked around suspiciously. There was a large, tough-looking man standing on the corner. His nose appeared as if it had been broken a couple of times. His hair was clipped close to his head and he was dressed in worn black leather and torn jeans. He could have been a stand-in for a member of The Dirty Dozen. Just looking at him made her shiver.

She glanced at Jake. He and the man had made eye contact. Neither one of them gave any indication of greeting or of even knowing each other, but there was something about their body language that made it clear they were acquaintances. The stare was enough.

"Okay, I'm going to have to take a rain check on that meeting," Jake said.

She gaped at him. "What?"

How could he dismiss it like this? To her, getting some sort of resolution and doing it as soon as possible was as necessary as breathing. Her whole life hung in the balance, and he was ready to walk off and do it later? And all because of some guy standing on a corner?

"Who is that man?" she demanded.

"Someone I have to talk to," he said, unbuckling his seat belt. "I can't explain. Not now. I'll have to catch you later." He pulled out his cell phone. "Give me your phone number. I'll call you."

She recited it automatically, frowning and wondering what to make of this strange man. He punched in the numbers, leaned over the back of the seat and looked at Savannah, sighing.

"I need to get to know this little one," he muttered as he straightened and turned away. "That house there at the top? That's where you're staying?"

"Yes."

He hesitated, looking at her probingly. "You're not going to run again, are you?"

"I wasn't running before."

"Yes, you were."

She looked toward where the sea made a silver line on the horizon.

He grunted and looked there, too. "I'm going to have to trust you," he said. "But I think you know better than to go off again. I'll go to the end of the earth to find you, if you do. And the reunion won't be pretty."

She snapped her head back around to face him. "Oh, stop with the threats. Please! We're both grown-ups. We can talk things over without the TV show theatrics. This is real life, not some silly drama."

A reluctant smile broke out on his hard face. "You see, that's just the thing about you, Sara. I liked you from the beginning." His eyebrows rose. "I hope I'm not going to have to change my mind about that."

Her eyes flashed. "You know what? It doesn't matter if you do. We have an issue between us, something that has to be resolved. But whether we like each other is irrelevant. Who cares?"

"Right." He nodded firmly. "Who cares." He glanced at the man on the corner and looked back at her. "Okay. See you in the morning."

She watched him walk away. The man who had been waiting turned and walked with him. The two of them looked like something out of a 1930s gangster movie.

"What in the world?" she said aloud, shaking her head as she watched them go. This whole situation was getting stranger and stranger. Maybe it was going to be a silly drama after all. Who knew?

But the one thing she was sure of—she wasn't letting her baby go off with a man like this. Impossible to imagine. It would never happen. She would find a way.

CHAPTER FOUR

SARA FELT AS though every nerve in her system was quivering with energy. There was so much to think about, so many plans to make—so many traps to set. First of all she had to find out more about this man, this Jake Martin—and how he'd met her half sister Kelly, Savannah's mother.

Was he a good guy? Mixed evidence so far. Were things going to pop up that would be relevant and interesting to the agency as to his fitness to be a father?

Oh, come on. There had to be something.

In the morning, he would arrive and they would sit down in Jill's breakfast room, sipping coffee and eating one of her sister's wonderful Bundt cakes. And they would talk.

She turned the car up the driveway to Jill's, planning the assault on Jake's character as though it was the D-day invasion. This was a fight she had to win. The thought of giving her baby over to this stranger made her sick with revulsion. It couldn't happen. If she had only a few hours before she was going to see him again, she was going to spend that time preparing for battle.

* * *

Sara looked up from feeding her baby from a bottle and forced a smile as Jill came into the kitchen, clutching her long white robe around her.

"Morning," she said with brittle cheer.

Jill seemed incredulous. "What on earth are you doing up so early?" She paused to kiss the top of Savannah's head, then went on to the coffeemaker. "I've got twelve cakes to bake for the Alliance Ladies or I would still be happily sleeping away myself."

"Sleep?" Sara said groggily. "What is this thing you call sleep?"

Jill groaned. "You haven't slept a wink, have you?"

Sara shrugged. "I think I did get a few minutes worth around 3:00 a.m. My mind was whirring like a windup toy and I couldn't stop. I had to think, to go over all the possibilities. So I came down here where I could begin making lists." She nodded toward the three or four pages of wild note taking that were scattered across the table.

Jill poured herself a cup of coffee and came back to sink into the seat opposite her sister.

"Listen. We'll do it all. No stone left unturned. We'll research and brainstorm and write letters. We'll start calling people today and…"

Sara smiled lovingly at Jill and shook her head. "I've already been doing all those things. It's three hours earlier on the East Coast. I've called three different sources back there already."

Jill gaped at her sister, impressed. Sara had always been the careful one, her hair stylishly sleek, her makeup perfect, her goals clear and well-supported by her actions. Meanwhile, Jill seemed to be all over the place, just like her unruly mop of curly blond hair. And yet, Jill was the older sister and they both knew she would be there for Sara no matter what.

"Who did you talk to? What did you find out?"

"First I called the agency again to see if I couldn't get more information. I wanted to know about forms I could fill out and channels I could go through to file an appeal, just in case. They were adamant. There is supposedly nothing I can do."

"Nothing?"

"So I was told. If the DNA comes in his favor and he is deemed to be her father, that's it. Game over."

She stared at Jill with tears shimmering in her eyes. "I mean—that's it. He takes her. We wave goodbye and it's over. He walks off with her." Her face was tragic. "How can this be? It's just not right."

Jill nodded slowly. "I know, darling. It doesn't feel right at all. It feels unfair and dangerous. Maybe if we talk to the people at the agency..."

"That's exactly who I've been talking to. And I did leave a message for Mrs. Truesdale to call me back. She's the one who's always been the most helpful."

Jill closed her eyes, trying to think. "Who else can we call? Who else did you contact?"

"I called Mark Trainor. He's a lawyer at the magazine. I worked with him on a few features in the past. I've known him for years and I knew he'd give me the straight scoop."

Jill looked hopeful. "Well?"

Sara sighed. "He told me he'd be glad to recommend someone who deals with adoptions. He knows someone who would be especially good with the paperwork and going for appeals, or whatever." She shook her head sadly. "But he didn't advise going that way."

"Why not?"

"He didn't think there was much use fighting it. He thought I'd probably end up spending a lot of money and going through a lot of heartbreak with nothing to show for it in the end."

She looked down at the baby in her arms. Savannah had stopped drinking and let the bottle slip away. Her gaze was fixed completely on Sara's face. Suddenly she smiled and her pure, innocent love seemed to fill the room.

"Oh, sweetest heart, I just can't, can't…!" She stopped the words before they left her lips. She couldn't let her baby know in any way what loomed before them. Tears filled her eyes and began to make trails down her face.

Savannah's laugh sounded like a series of hiccups. She laughed as though Sara was the funniest thing she'd seen in ages. She laughed despite Sara's tears, and Sara began to smile because of her.

Jill watched, tears in her own eyes.

"Tell you what," she said. "Let's have a piece of cake. I've got something to tell you about."

Sara looked up at her and grinned through her tears. "Oh, you and your Bundt cake. You think it's like chicken soup, the cure for everything. Staying here with you, I'm getting fat."

Jill got down the cake anyway and began to cut slices with a long, beautifully carved cake knife.

"See, that's what I've always envied about you," she told her sister as she worked. "You never get fat. You're about as thin as those models your magazine plasters all over every page, wearing the latest outfits to come down the pike." She put a piece of Lemon Delight on a small plate and handed it to Sara. "Meanwhile, I'm pudging up. And it's going to be about nine months before I can really go on a diet again."

Sara stared at her. "Wait a minute. Do you mean…?"

Jill's face broke out in a joyful smile. "Yes. Connor and I are going to have a baby."

Sara gasped and looked stricken. "Already?" Jill and her husband had only been married for three months. Somehow Sara was starting to feel that everything was moving too fast, everything was spinning out of control.

All the joy drained from Jill's face and she frowned resentfully. She'd obviously expected a better response.

"I didn't know I had a schedule to keep," she snapped.

"No, I mean…" Sara shook her head, knowing she was handling this badly, but she was genuinely worried. She'd been here all along. She'd seen the chaos Jill's life had been only months before.

In fact, when the news about Kelly's death and Savannah's existence first came to light, there had been a discussion as to which sister could manage to take on this new little life, and Jill, though she'd been willing, had made it clear it would truly be a hardship for her. And now, only a short time later, she was ready to take on a new baby again. "Well, you can barely handle the twins as it is. Do you really think…?"

Jill glared at her. "No, Sara, you've got it wrong. That was the old me. That was the unmarried me." She read the concern on Sara's face and her attitude softened. Reaching out, she took her sister's hands. "Oh, Sara, look at me. Things are completely different. I've got a wonderful husband now. We can do this. Together." She smiled, coaxing out the Sara that she'd hoped to find there.

"Oh. Of course." Sara relaxed. She knew she was too careful sometimes. She really had to loosen up a little. "I guess that does make a difference."

"It makes all the difference in the world," Jill said.

"Okay then." Sara lifted her baby and rose, swinging her around the room in a happiness dance. "Savannah, you've got a new cousin coming." She looked at Jill. "Boy or girl?"

Jill shrugged. "We're going to wait until the six months mark and then we'll decide if we want to know ahead of time."

"Ah, you always were a sucker for tradition."

Jill rose and opened her arms and they had a group hug.

"I really am happy for you, sweetie," Sara said, giving her a squeeze. "It's just that I worry…"

"I know. So do I. But we're family and we'll make sure it all comes out okay. Won't we?"

"Of course."

They sat down again to finish their cake and talk over the preparations for the baby.

"How is Connor taking it?" Sara asked.

Jill laughed. "He's so funny. On the one hand, he's excited. On the other, he's scared."

Sara nodded. "Just the way I was when Savannah came into my life." She seemed stricken as she remembered the threat that was looming over her. "And now, the fear is so much greater," she said softly.

Jill reached out and covered her hand. "When do you think he'll show up?"

They both knew whom she was talking about.

Sara shrugged. "I know so little about him, it's hard to tell. He could show up for morning coffee, or he could wait until he gets some business cleared up in the morning. Don't forget, he's not supposed to be here at all. Not legally."

"Okay, so we'll just go on with our normal lives, drinking coffee and baking, etc, as though this hadn't happened."

"How can we possibly do that?"

"We can try. You want to keep Savannah happy and smiling, don't you?"

"Of course. Whatever else happens, that's the most important thing."

"Actually the most important thing is keeping Savannah safe."

Jill picked up their plates and started toward the sink with them. She stopped short just before she reached it, staring out the tall kitchen windows toward the play area of her backyard.

"Sara," she said sharply. "What does he look like?"

Sara made a face. "Tall and big and scary."

"Thick auburn hair?"

Sara looked up, alarmed. "Yes."

"I think that's him, then."

"What?" Sara slid out of the seat and moved quickly to stand beside her sister. "Oh, my gosh!"

There he was sitting in one of the larger swings hanging on the swing set, rocking a bit, back and forth.

She gripped Jill's shoulder. "Call the police."

"Sara! No. He's just waiting for you out there. He's not doing anything threatening."

"Just his existence is threatening." She folded her arms in tightly, trying to keep control of the fear she felt. "He has no right to stalk us."

Jill turned and searched her sister's eyes, taking her hands and looking worried. "Sara, darling, calm down. We have to be reasonable. He hasn't done anything wrong."

"Not yet, maybe. Just wait."

Jill sighed. "Listen, sweetie, he may be Savannah's father, and if he is, that means he was close to Kelly. Kelly's our half sister, and even though we were never very close to her, she was a part of our family. That makes his attachment to our family clear, doesn't it? You can't treat him like a total stranger. We owe it to him to at least be polite."

"Polite!"

"Yes."

Sara groaned. "I wish…I wish…"

"We all wish. But we have to take what we get and learn to deal with it." She hugged her sister. "Come on. Go on out there and invite him in."

Sara looked at her, horrified. "I will not. He'll want to hold Savannah."

"Of course. And we'll be here. He won't hurt her."

Sara was shaking her head. "I don't think I have to let him hold her. Not until he has proof."

Jill pulled back and shrugged. "It's up to you. But just remember, the harder you make it for him, the harder he'll probably make it for you if things change. Be prepared."

A shiver of nausea swept through Sara at her sister's words. She wouldn't even let her mind go there. She was not going to have to give up her baby. Somehow, someway…

Taking a deep breath, she turned toward the sliding glass door. "Will you watch her?" she threw back over her shoulder. Savannah was beginning to make "hey, don't forget about me!" sounds from her chair at the table.

"Sure," Jill said quickly. "Listen, I'll take her up to help me get the boys out of bed. If you decide to bring him in, we won't even be here in the kitchen until you signal you're ready."

Sara nodded and started out. This had to be done, but she was dreading it. Maybe she could get him to leave.

* * *

Jake had watched the sun come up over the mountains. He'd paced the waterfront and then turned up toward Jill's house. After waiting outside for what seemed like hours and finding no sign of life inside, he'd found his way into the backyard, hoping he'd get noticed and invited in. He didn't want to have to get tough about this. A nice friendly invitation would be better than an angry demand. But his patience was only human. The invite had better come pretty soon.

The yard was large and included a sloping lawn and a sand play area with a swing set. That seemed to mean there were other children here.

Children. What the hell did he know about children? Even less than he knew about kitchens. But he was going to have to learn. The question was—could he?

He hadn't put it that starkly to himself before. He'd been ignoring reality and living on dreams. He'd been riding along in the wash of the wave that had crashed over him the day he realized he had a child of his own. What had happened in his kitchen the day before had forced him to begin to face some home truths. He wasn't equipped to take care of a baby. He was going to have to get up to speed fast. Another life depended on it.

He had a baby. Wow. He looked up at the windows of Jill's house, wondering which ones led to the room where his baby slept. He'd been home from his time in South East Asia for almost two weeks before he read the letter that told him about Savannah. He knew he had a stack of mail from Kelly, but he'd avoided reading it.

They'd met when he was on R and R in Hawaii. They had a lovely time for almost two weeks. But they'd both said from the first that they wanted to keep things light and fun—nothing serious. Now here were all these letters from her. It looked like she'd changed her mind—but he hadn't.

Finally he steeled himself and opened up the first one. Just what he'd been afraid of—she was pregnant. He'd groaned. He was so careful to make sure things like that didn't happen. He knew what it was like to grow up without proper parenting and he would never want to inflict that on a child.

He opened the other letters and skimmed them quickly, noting her anger at first when he didn't respond, then her horror when she found out he was missing in action and presumed captured by the enemy. There was only one letter after Savannah was born, but it gave all the details. Kelly seemed to have accepted that he was probably dead and was just straightening out the loose ends of what had been their relationship.

He'd stayed up for hours, brooding about what to do. He tried to remember what she looked like. She'd been pretty with huge green eyes and lots of flaming red curls. As he remembered it, she'd been a vivacious sort, always ready to try anything from surfing to mountain climbing. She'd had a quick tendency to laugh—and a tendency to tease. He'd found her half adorable and half annoying. They'd had a lot of fun together. But he hadn't loved her, and she hadn't seemed to care at the time.

Later, she obviously did. But there hadn't been any

letters for over six months. He agonized over how to contact her. He even tried to talk himself out of doing it at all. Maybe she was married now. Maybe she wouldn't want him interfering in her life after all this time. But he always came back to the bottom line—he had a baby. A little girl. Someone that was truly tied to him in ways he'd never experienced before. He couldn't let go of that fact.

First thing in the morning, he tried to contact her. Her return address was in Virginia, not far from where he was in Washington, D.C. When he couldn't get a phone number, he went by the apartment and talked to the manager. And that was how he found out that Kelly had died in a car accident months before.

The tragedy of her passing hit him hard, but anxiety about the baby came even stronger. He started right away, haunting every Federal office he could think of that might have a bearing on this situation, and finally, he found the Children's Agency and found out that Savannah had been sent to live with her aunt in Washington State.

He began the process of proving his claim right away, but he couldn't stand the wait. Patience was not his main virtue, and he headed for the Pacific Coast as soon as he'd finished doing all he could at the agency. He quickly rented a house right next door to where Savannah was supposedly living, only to find it empty. And then, Sara had come knocking on his door.

He hadn't realized who she was at first, but now he knew. She had his baby. And he was going to have to force himself to wait. But not for long. Because Savannah was his.

He heard the slider and looked up to see Sara coming toward him. She wasn't carrying the baby, and that was all he cared about. But he had to admit the morning sun turned her hair into spun gold and she looked trim and determined walking toward him. She had something that belonged to him and he meant to end up with it, but all in all, she wasn't a bad sort. He'd actually liked her before he found out who she was.

She stopped a few feet away and stared at him. "Have you cleaned up your kitchen yet?" she asked.

"What?" He frowned at her, rapidly beginning to revamp his opinion of her. What a completely off-the-wall thing to ask. "No. Who has time to worry about kitchens?"

Now she was frowning, too. "You do. The Lancasters are nice people and you've ruined their kitchen. You're going to have to fix it."

He waved that away. "All in good time."

She didn't like the sound of that. If he was going to be a father, he'd better learn some responsibility. "I'll call someone to come over and give you an estimate," she said crisply.

He stared at her and half laughed. She was like a dog with a bone.

"Listen, I don't want to talk about kitchens. I want to talk about Savannah."

"Okay." She knew that, of course. She slid into the swing hanging next to his. "Talk."

He hesitated. What could he say that he hadn't already said?

She took advantage of the pause. "Here's the deal." She gazed at him levelly, her dark eyes snapping with intensity. "Savannah is officially mine. I've got the paperwork to prove it. There's nothing really to discuss about that." She waved an arm dramatically. "You appear out of nowhere and claim certain things. Who knows if you're telling the truth or not? I'm not going to move on your say-so. Once you have some paperwork to prove your case, we'll talk."

She settled back and began to move the swing as though that settled everything.

He shook his head. She was trying to fend him off, make him slink into the shadows and wait his turn. But she had a surprise coming if she thought he would go so easily. It wasn't his style.

"Not good enough," he told her stonily. "That could take another week or more."

She glanced at him sideways. "Look, be reasonable. We have no way of knowing anything about you. You can't expect us to welcome you with open arms. You're a complete stranger."

He shrugged. "So what do you want to know about me? Ask me anything."

She stopped the swing and turned to face him. "Okay. Why not? Let's start with this." She drew in a deep breath. "Who was that man last night? And why was talking to him more important than Savannah?"

For just a moment, there was an evasive look in his

eyes. "That had nothing to do with Savannah," he said quickly. "It...he's a buddy of mine. We were in the Rangers together. He came to ask for my help." He turned his face toward the distant ocean. "We've got the sort of relationship—well, when he needs me, I'm there for him." He turned back to meet her gaze, his own open and candid. "You can know that about me. Loyalty to the men I served with. That's number one. End of story."

She stared at him, then transferred her gaze to the ground. "So you're saying that your buddies from the service come first with you. Your priorities start right there with them."

"No, that's not what I'm saying." But he hesitated, wondering if that was true. "Your own child is in a whole different category. All that other stuff has nothing to do with her."

She nodded, listening. "I think it has a lot to do with Savannah," she said softly. "It has to do with you and what your motivations are. What drives you. What's really important in your life."

He shook his head, almost bemused. "Now you're reaching, Sara," he said. "Let it go."

Let it go? Hah!

"Tell me this," she said coolly. "Have you ever had a baby before?"

His head went back. "No, of course not."

She leaned toward him like a prosecutor. "Have you ever taken care of one?"

"No."

She leaned even closer, as though she was about to get in his face. "Have you ever lived with one?"

"Have you?" he shot back. "What did you know about babies? Before Savannah, I mean."

She pulled back but there was a triumphant smile just barely curling the corners of her mouth. "My sister Jill has twins. I helped her with them from the beginning." She sighed. "I had a pretty good idea of what I was getting into. And I don't think you have a clue."

He stared at her. Was she serious? "So that's the tact you're going to take, is it? I'm incompetent? I'm too clueless to know how to take care of a baby? I won't know what I'm doing, and therefore shouldn't be allowed to have her? Is that going to be the basis for your appeal?"

She stiffened. "Who says I'm filing an appeal?"

"Of course you will. You'll mount one as soon as I take charge of Savannah. I know damn well you've already called a lawyer."

She flushed.

He nodded. "Bingo," he said softly.

"Of course I've talked to a lawyer," she said. "And you should, too. We've got to make sure all the i's are dotted and the t's are crossed."

"Thanks for the warning." He looked up and stiffened. "Uh-oh. Looks like you're getting reinforcements."

CHAPTER FIVE

SARA LOOKED UP and saw Jill's handsome husband, Connor, walking toward them. His look was wary but not unfriendly.

"Jake Martin?" he said, holding out his hand. "I'm Sara's brother-in-law, Connor McNair."

Jake rose from the swing and extended his own hand. "It's a pleasure," he said.

"Jill would like to meet you," Connor said, looking at Sara but ignoring her ferocious glare. "Why don't you come on in and have some coffee? Jill's a baker and she's saved you a special slice of her latest Bundt cake." Connor smiled and turned his collar up against the stiff breeze. "It will be a more comfortable place to talk."

"Sounds good."

Sara pushed back the sense of outrage building in her chest. It sure seemed like she was outnumbered. Hopefully Connor had a plan. Otherwise, whose side was he on?

But she kept her confusion to herself. Jake was going to get his chance to hold Savannah. She knew it had to happen sometime. Might as well get it over with.

They walked up a brick path to the house and went in. Sara watched Jake as he met Jill, suddenly reminded of how good-looking he was. He was turning on the charm, but surely they could see through that.

"If you don't mind, I'd really like to see my…Savannah," he said, looking around the kitchen as though he thought she might be somewhere close.

"She's in the other room. I'll go get her."

"No," Sara said, so softly she wasn't sure if the others had heard her.

But Jill turned and took her hands. "Sara, I think it's only right. We're all here. Nothing will happen."

She knew her sister was right but it was killing her. She closed her eyes for a few seconds, then tried to smile. "Let me get her, then."

"All right."

Savannah was lying on her tummy in her play crib, playing with a touch toy. She looked up with a beatific smile when Sara came into view, her huge blue eyes set off by her golden curls. "Mama!" she cried, pounding her fist into the plastic toy. "Mama, Mama, Mama."

Sara's eyes filled with tears but she blinked them back. She wasn't going to let herself fall apart every time she looked at her baby.

"Come here, sweet thing," she said as she pulled her up and carried her to the changing table. She wanted to dress her in something pretty. There was no point in doing anything else. She was a pretty baby and no amount of downplaying that was going to work in dis-

suading Jake from taking her. He was going to love her
no matter what. How could he help it?

As she carried Savannah into the kitchen where Jill
was plying Jake with Bundt cake, she couldn't help but
feel a glow of pride.

"Here she is," she said, announcing her and holding
her up for inspection, right in front of the large, rough
person who claimed to be her father. "This is a man
named Jake Martin," she whispered in her ear. "Can
you smile at him please? Can you say 'hi'?"

Savannah stuck her fist in her mouth and stared at
him for a long moment. He stared back, looking thunderstruck, as though he'd never seen anything like her
before. At last, she smiled. He smiled back, and it was
like ice breaking in the Arctic. Something passed between the two of them, some flash of recognition or
acknowledgment, the establishment of a special bond—
Sara didn't know exactly what it was but she felt a pain
in her heart such as she'd never felt before.

Was it really so obvious…so simple? Did blood connect across the air between them? Would she just be
left behind?

He didn't ask to hold Savannah. Sara expected it, had
been tense, not sure how she would react. Waiting, she
couldn't breathe, but he didn't ask.

Then a thought flashed into her head like a bolt from
the blue. He hadn't asked to hold Savannah—because
now that he'd evaluated the situation, he was scared to.
He didn't know how to hold her. He didn't know what

to do and in front of her whole family, he wasn't going
to risk it.

Interesting. And somehow invigorating. Maybe all
wasn't lost, after all. Maybe she still had a chance in
this sweepstakes.

He'd come to take her baby away, but he just wasn't
ready. From what she'd seen, he'd done nothing in his
life that could prepare him for it. And even if he got beyond that, he would soon find out he didn't like what
child raising entailed. At least, she would bet that would
be the way he would go.

That was the angle she had to take. She had to learn
how to cajole him and convince him that this was not
what he wanted to do. Much better to use sympathy and
examples rather than confrontation and anger. There
might be a possibility of success that way. It would be
tough to hold back her temper, but she could do it if she
thought it could get her anywhere.

They sat in the kitchen and ate cake and watched
Savannah play with her toys in the middle of the floor.
Connor and Jill seemed to have a thousand things to
discuss with Jake. Sara didn't listen to most of it. She
was thinking, plotting, hoping.

At the same time, she did notice how friendly the
three of them seemed to be getting. That gave her a
weird feeling, almost like jealousy. Surely her own family wasn't going to end up being on Jake's side in this.
Were they?

No, impossible. They loved Savannah almost as much
as she did. There was no way they would help him take

her away from the place where she belonged. But Jill was concerned about keeping a happy face on things.

"Why don't you and Jake take Savannah to the park?" she suggested. She gave Sara a significant look, as if hinting they should get to know each other better.

"Oh." Sara wasn't sure how much she wanted to be alone with him.

The funny thing was, Jake appeared a little hesitant about it himself.

"Great idea," he said gamely. Then his blue eyes brightened. "Why not take the boys, too?"

Sara stared at him. Did he have any idea what he was suggesting? No, he didn't. And that was why she smiled and said, "Yes. Let's take the twins. They love the park."

She knew they would be a handful. There was more energy stored in the two of them than the average wind-mill could generate in a year. They could take apart a house in fifteen minutes and leave their keeper with days and days of rehab. Just a few months before, they'd locked their babysitter outside and ransacked the up-stairs, throwing things out of windows. She was pretty sure she could depend on them to create some sort of chaos.

The walk to the park was nice. She put Savannah in a stroller and they let the twins run free. The street they took only rarely saw a car and the boys stayed close enough so that it wasn't a worry. There were plenty of neighbors working in their yards. She waved to the ones she knew.

The boys were wearing their Danny Duck capes that

Jill had made them, held on by Velcro tabs. *Danny Duck* was their favorite TV show. They called him "Dandan Duck," but it worked for them. As they ran, their little capes spread out behind them, and they laughed and pretended to fly.

"Dandan Duck!" they called back and forth.

The end of summer was coming. She could feel it in the breeze. There was always a tinge of sadness at losing those lazy, hazy days, but it also meant the holidays weren't far away. She looked down at Savannah, laughing in her stroller as she spotted a cat across the street. Would she be able to spend her baby's first Christmas with her? Or would it all be over by then?

Jake had been silent so far, but now he spoke. "This is nice," he said, then made a face as though he regretted being so uninspiring. "I mean, it's great to get a chance to go to the park with kids. I've never done it before."

Good, Sara thought to herself. *This can be a learning experience for you.*

Out loud, she noted, "Children love going to the park. The problem is usually getting them to leave when time is up."

He shrugged, looking cocky. "Hey, they don't call me The Enforcer for nothing."

She frowned. She really didn't like the sound of that.

He saw her frown and winced, knowing he'd said something he shouldn't have again. But what else was new? He did it all the time. Usually it didn't matter. He expected people to take him as he was, or get lost. That was the way he'd always lived.

He gazed down at the little girl in the stroller and his heart swelled with some sort of emotion he couldn't even put a name to. His little girl. A lump rose in his throat as he thought of it. He'd have to make some changes. He had to throw out that old, rough way of living and learn to do things right. She deserved as much. He had to make himself worthy of her.

And how was he going to learn to do all these things? Who was going to teach him? There weren't a lot of women with child rearing experience in his life. Right now Sara was the prime candidate. He needed what she could do to help him. She was just about his only hope. The problem was, she didn't like him much.

He couldn't blame her. He was her worst nightmare. But he couldn't get bogged down in that. His goal was to make himself into the best dad Savannah could hope for. And he was beginning to realize, that was going to take a lot of work.

He glanced at Sara again. What did you do when you wanted to make a woman like you? He'd never dealt with this before. If a woman didn't like him, he shrugged and turned to a woman who did. There were always plenty of those. So what was his strategy to gain Sara's favor?

It made him grin to think of it. Good thing she couldn't read his mind. He moved closer so he could talk without others overhearing.

"Sara, I'm sorry about this. I didn't plan it this way. I didn't even know Savannah existed until last week." He shrugged and tried to look engagingly charming. "Things happen."

She nodded but she didn't plan to tumble to his charm offensive. "Yes, things happen. I understand that." She took a deep breath and plunged in. "And you want to be a father to this baby. I don't blame you. Who wouldn't want to be?" She gestured toward her, the proof if any was needed. "She's adorable and wonderful—everything you could ever want in a child."

She folded her arms and lifted her chin. "But the results of the DNA tests haven't come in yet." She eyed him warningly. He had to understand this was only the beginning. "What I think we need to do is take some time to get to know each other. Talk things over. See how it looks to you after some time here."

She gave him about half a smile. That was all she could muster. "We'll see how things work out."

He took what she had to say in good cheer, to her surprise. The confrontational man from the ferry seemed to have vanished from sight.

"I've got to hand it to you," he said. "I'm totally surprised that you're this open to a congenial arrangement. I thought you'd be ready to claw my eyes out."

The smile froze on her face and she couldn't seem to revive it. "You have to understand something." She sent him a flashing glance. "I'm open to congeniality because I'm hoping it redounds to my benefit. Nothing more. I want to be perfectly clear." She turned and held his gaze with her own steely version. "I want to keep this baby. I adore her. She's my life." Her voice choked but she pushed on, getting fiercer. "And she's mine. I will do anything I have to in order to keep her. Even claw your eyes out."

"Sara," he began, stepping toward her.

She held her hand up, stopping him.

"In the meantime, I want you to explore all the natural aspects of your paternal feelings. Go for it. Be a daddy for a day. Try your wings, so to speak."

He stared at her for a long moment, and then he started to laugh. "You're betting I'll punt, aren't you?"

She flushed. "I'm not betting on anything. I'm leaving it all up to you."

"Right." He shook his head, studying her more closely now. "Still waters run deep," he quoted. "I know you want me gone. I can understand that." He frowned thoughtfully. "Just don't try anything tricky, okay? Let's keep this struggle on the up-and-up."

She stared at him for a long moment, then nodded. "As you wish," she said crisply. "I'm not going to close any doors. I'm not going to be combative." She looked away, then swung around and stared at him again, hard. "But I am going to watch you like a hawk. Any chink in your armor will be duly noted."

He stared back, then gave her a lopsided grin. "Hey, you're on. May the best Mom win."

The park was filled with children. She glanced at Jake wondering how he was going to take all the high-pitched shrieking. It had taken her awhile to get used to it when she'd started out. The first few times she'd brought Savannah here, she'd thought her head would explode with

all the frenetic noise. But he seemed to be taking it
in stride, and when she tried saying something to him
about it, he laughed.

"You should try living in a jungle when the monkeys
start their daily chat," he said. "Now that will drive a
grown man crazy in less than a day."

They found an empty bench at the outskirts of the
younger children's playground. Sara held Savannah
while Jake supervised the boys playing on the equipment and climbing through the playtime tunnels.

"Nice kids," he commented when he came back to
sit beside her on the bench about half an hour later. The
boys had followed him and were playing some sort of
make-believe game in the sand in front of the bench.

"They're okay," she said modestly. After all, they
were her nephews. But she couldn't help but wonder why
they were so subdued today. And then she realized—it
was because Jake was here and watching them. They
knew a dominant male when they saw one.

Still, Tanner seemed to have a special charge of energy and pretty soon he was racing back and forth between the equipment and the bench, trying to organize
all the other children into platoons. Timmy sat down on
the sidewalk and began to make a sort of sand castle.

"We'd better keep an eye on them," she told Jake.
"Tanner will end up starting a war if we're not careful."

Jake nodded and grinned. "No weapons, though,"
he noted.

"Oh, you just wait," she warned.

She pulled some plastic cups and bowls and shovels

out of her carry-everything bag hanging from the stroller and gave them to Timmy to play with in the sand. She then put Savannah down beside him so that she could join in. The baby immediately began to pour sand from one container to another as though it was serious work that must be done.

Sara settled back and looked at Jake. He was staring out toward the ocean, which was just visible through the trees.

"Tell me about Kelly," she said out of the blue.

He stiffened. "What do you want to know?"

Everything. Nothing. She took a deep breath. "Did you love her?"

He thought for a moment, then decided to tell the truth. "No."

She recoiled as though he'd said something awful.

"She didn't love me, either," he said quickly. "It wasn't like that. We met, we had a great time together and we both knew it was just for laughs."

Sara thought about that one for a moment, pursing her lips. "How do you know for sure that she felt that way, too?"

He shook his head. "You can tell. I've known enough women in my time to know the signs. She said as much and I believed her. She knew the score, and so did I. We were a perfect match, but it was temporary."

Sara looked away and made a face. She'd been hoping for a more romantic story. "So what happened?"

"We met at a party in Waikiki. We hit it off right away. I was in Hawaii for a couple of weeks of R and R.

She was scoping out the job market, thinking of making the islands her home for a while. We got together and spent two weeks seeing the sights, swimming, eating fabulous food. We had a great time."

She searched his blue eyes. "So you liked her."

"Sure. I liked her quite a bit." He grimaced and tried to explain a bit more fully. "Listen, Sara, I've never been the marrying kind. I never expected to have a child. I thought I was being careful to make sure that didn't happen, and then, all of a sudden, there it was."

"There it was," she repeated softly, looking down at Savannah. Her sweet, sweet baby. What if she was really his? She bit her lip. She wasn't going to cry in front of him. Instead she rose, picked up Savannah and talked a bit of silly nonsense to her, then gazed at the playing children. She frowned.

"Wait a minute. Where's Tanner?"

Jake stood up beside her and shaded his eyes, surveying the scene. "I don't see him." He looked again and shook his head. "He's gone."

"What? He can't be."

Fear shook her, but she held it off. She searched again. He had to be there somewhere.

"Isn't there another area over the hill?" Jake asked.

"Yes, the play equipment for the older kids. But..." Could Tanner have gone there? He never had before. Still, if not there, where?

Her heart began to beat like a drum. "Oh, why wasn't I watching? Where did he go?"

"Would he have started for home on his own?"

She whirled and looked down the street. "I don't think so. And we should be able to see him. We can see all the way down to the corner."

Her breath was coming in gasps now.

She turned and thrust her baby into Jake's arms. "Here, hold Savannah. I've got to find him."

He seemed startled, not sure of what to do with the baby. "But, wait…"

She raced over to where Timmy was playing. "Timmy, where's Tanner? Do you know where he went?"

Timmy just stared up at her with huge eyes as though he didn't have a clue what she was asking him.

"Oh!" She didn't wait. "Watch the kids," she called back to Jake. And then she ran.

She'd learned from the first when she helped take care of the twins that losing sight of a child was one of the worse experiences you could have. The panic that started pushing its way up her throat was wrenching.

"Oh, please, please, please," she muttered in her own simple prayer that he might be okay—okay and found soon. "Oh, please!"

He wasn't near the preschool slides, nor the close-by junior merry-go-round. He wasn't at the bounce house.

"Have you seen a little two year old with a blue Danny Duck cape on?" she began to ask everyone she passed. "Reddish hair. Blue eyes."

All she got were shrugs and apologies.

"Sorry. Haven't seen him."

She knew it was fruitless. He was just like twenty other boys his age playing here. Her heart was beating hard and she ran past the rocky stream as she headed for the top of the hill.

And then she saw him. How on earth had he gone so far so fast? She'd reached the older kids playground with the heavy polished steel equipment as opposed to the soft, padded things the younger children dealt with. The pieces were huge and scary compared to what they were used to down the hill.

And there, at the top of the tallest, most dangerous-looking slide, sat Tanner, dangling his feet over the side and looking down as though he didn't have a care in the world.

"Tanner!" she cried, sinking to her knees in relief. "Oh, Tanner. There you are."

Rising again quickly, she began to race to the area beneath where he was.

"Tanner, wait! I'm coming."

He didn't look her way and the fear was coming back quickly. She reached the sandy area the slide was set in.

"Tanner," she called up. "Come on down, honey."

Tanner acted as though he'd never seen her before. He squinted his eyes. And then he rose, leaning under the bar and looking down on the wrong side of the slide.

"No!" She shaded her eyes against the sun. What was he doing? "No, Tanner. Come down the slide, sweetie. I'll catch you."

He bent over and looked down the slide, then he looked at her and shook his head.

"What's wrong? I'll help you. Come on, honey, we can do this."

He shook his head again, obviously scared to go down the big kid slide. And she could hardly blame him. It seemed so high! What little two-year-old would want to jump right into this crazy journey?

But paradoxically, he went to something even scarier. Instead of the slide, he turned back to the wrong side of the platform again and looked down at the sandy landing below. Sara's heart was in her throat again. It looked like—it couldn't be. But it was. The boy wanted to jump.

"No! Tanner, don't jump. It's too high."

He looked at her again, his eyes bright and shiny.

"Dandan Duck," he said happily, and he held out his arms so that his cape was ready to surge out behind him. He was going to try to fly down.

"No!" she yelled again, starting up the metal steps of the ladder to the top, going as fast as she could. She would never reach him in time. But she had to try. "Tanner, don't jump!"

"Dandan Duck!" he called back. He flapped his cape at her.

"No, Tanner," she called, climbing as fast as she could. She was almost there. "You can't fly. Stop!"

"I Dandan Duck."

And he stepped off the edge of the platform.

She screamed. She was terrified, barely clinging to the very top steps, leaning out as far as she could, as if she had a prayer of catching him. His small body fell past her, heading for the ground. She felt the earth begin to spin around her.

"No, no!" she cried desperately.

But then something happened. Everything went into slow motion, and there was Jake, down in the sand, holding Tanner.

He'd caught him! He'd caught him and he was already setting him down on the ground.

"Oh." She closed her eyes and everything went black. She lost her balance for just a moment, but that moment was long enough to make her lose her footing. The next thing she knew, she was falling, too. She grabbed at the railing, but it was too late.

She closed her eyes again, waiting for the jarring landing, praying she wasn't going to break anything. And she hit with a jarring thud, but not in the sand. Instead she found herself in Jake's arms, just like Tanner had.

She opened her eyes in surprise and stared up into his brilliant blue gaze. He was grinning.

"Wow, everybody's trying to fly today. What is it? A new trend?"

"Very cute," she managed to grate out. She struggled a bit, but he wasn't letting go. "Where's Tanner? Where's Savannah?"

"Everybody's right here," he said, turning so that she could see Savannah in the stroller and the twins sitting side by side on the cement walkway, their feet in the sand. Amazing. It seemed he'd taken care of everything.

She frowned, shaking her head as though to clear it. "How did you do that so fast?" she asked accusingly.

"Magic," he teased. "Magic and fast footwork. I'm a trained rescuer, you know. We have our ways."

She searched his eyes and tried to catch her breath. She'd been through an emotional meat grinder for the last ten minutes and she hadn't gotten over it yet. It actually felt good to be in Jake's big strong arms, safe and unharmed. She was tempted to close her eyes and rest her head against his shoulder while her system recovered.

Jake was laughing at first. It all seemed so comical, catching one person after another that way. But there was something in those dark eyes....

His smile faded as their gazes caught and they stared at each other in a strange, twisted sort of wonder. The feel of her began to sink in. Her body felt warm and her shape felt rounded and provocative in his arms. Her skin was so soft and her scent so clean and sweet. Her lips were touched with pink and slightly swollen. There was a glazed look in her eyes. Suddenly he wanted to kiss her more than anything in the world.

But that was nuts. If there was one thing he was not going to do it was get emotionally entangled with this woman. Kiss of death. He couldn't do it. And just like that—Savannah started to fuss, they pulled apart and he was snapped back to reality. He let her go, sliding to her feet, and they quickly backed away from each other.

It seemed like minutes had gone by, but it must have been only a few seconds. At least, she hoped so. She avoided looking at him again, embarrassed.

"Thanks for catching me," she muttered, busy with the clasp to Savannah's stroller. "And especially for catching Tanner. You lived up to your rescuer rep, I guess."

She glanced his way and found him frowning at her thoughtfully, as though what had just happened had given him food for thought.

He'd almost kissed her. She knew that. If the children hadn't been so close, he might have followed through. And to her horror, she also knew that for just a moment, she'd really wanted him to.

CHAPTER SIX

"LET'S GO," SARA said quickly, not wanting to talk about it any longer. She'd been hoping to catch Jake up in the difficulties of taking care of babies and she'd ended up being the one who hadn't coped all that well. He was the hero. And thank goodness he'd been there for them all.

"Time to go home."

They herded the children back and Jake was quite cheerful with them. She looked at him sharply, searching for evidence of getting tired or annoyed, but she didn't see any. That made her crosser than she normally was.

But they made it back to the house and then found themselves spending the next hour spinning their tales of adventure out for Jill and Connor and reenacting what they'd gone through—though they did skip most of the details concerning that spectacular last catch Jake had made.

The twins both told their parents all about it, one starting out the exposition and the other talking over him toward the end, beginning a new segment. They were so cute, but unfortunately, not a word of what they said was understandable. It was as though they spoke their own toddler language. But they were passionate and everyone gave them a good listen just the same, oohing and aahing over every incomprehensible detail.

"Is that right?" was repeated a lot. "Oh, my goodness." And that seemed to satisfy them. When it was over, they both looked very pleased with themselves.

Jill had fixed a nice lunch of grilled cheese sandwiches and tomato soup and the adults sat at the table while the children sat in pulled up high chairs. Sara gazed about the room as they ate, noting how Jake seemed to fit in much better than she'd expected. In fact, Jill and Connor obviously liked him a lot. They were talking and laughing with him as though they were old friends.

Why did that give her a hollow feeling in the pit of her stomach? Why did she keep thinking of herself as the odd man out?

And then, when she was hoping it was time for Jake to go to his own house and leave them alone for the rest of the day, she heard Jill inviting him to the birthday party for the twins they were having the next day.

"Their second birthday," Jill was saying. "I know they'd love it if you could make it to help celebrate. We're just having a few friends over."

"I'd be honored to come," he said. "These two little guys are about as fun to hang out with as short people get."

Jill loved it. Sara watched her, feeling a bit resentful. She'd been looking forward to the birthday party and now she was going to have to share it with him.

Even worse, tomorrow was the last day before the DNA report was due. She was planning to try to talk him into reconsidering his plans to take over raising Savannah, but she needed more time. She hadn't done enough groundwork to convince him yet.

She needed to make it up as she went along. The first thing she did, once lunch was finished, was call Jake over and tell him it was time for a lesson in baby management.

"You might as well learn how to do some of these things," she told him. "You might end up having to take over. Let's see if you're a quick study."

He seemed nervous. "What exactly are you talking about here?"

"Changing diapers. Giving a baby a bath. Putting her down for her nap. Dealing with her when she cries. Reading her favorite books to her. Keeping her busy and in a learning environment at the same time. Singing songs. Walking her when she needs to be carried." She shook her head. "I could go on and on. I just think you ought to get some taste of what you're signing up for."

"Of course. You're right."

He said the words, but he still looked more uncertain than she'd ever seen him look before. She smiled. Maybe this was going to be effective after all.

"Okay," she said. "You pick her up and bring her this way. We'll take her up to the room where she's staying."

"Pick her up?" he said, frowning.

"You managed at the park," she reminded him.

He nodded. "Sure. I can do that."

And he did. But he appeared scared to death for the first few moments. She smiled again. Then he began to hold Savannah like a real, live baby instead of a fragile and oddly shaped potato, and her smile dimmed a bit. He seemed to be catching on awfully fast.

"Okay, here's the deal," she told him quickly. "I'll walk you through everything today. Tomorrow you come in the morning and you'll do it all again, only this time, you'll be on your own. Got it?"

He nodded.

"How long did it take you to get up to speed?" he asked as they negotiated the stairs and headed into the upper bedroom.

"What are you talking about?" she shot back.

"Come on. You say you took care of your sister's boys so you know all about babies, but I don't believe it. I'll bet there was still a lot you had to learn."

She closed her eyes for a moment, thinking. She remembered her resolution—casual conversation, not confrontation. She was a lot more likely to get somewhere if he thought they were talking on a friendly basis. Honesty seemed the best option for her anyway.

"It was pretty hard at first," she admitted. "That was why we stayed here with Jill for the first week. She was there to help me over the rough spots."

She gestured for him to lay the baby down on the changing table and he complied fairly gracefully, then smiled down at the sweet little girl who grinned back at him and waved her arms, reaching for his fingers whenever they got close.

"So you would recommend having someone there with me at first?" he asked.

It was a simple question. She should have been able to handle it. But for some reason, resentment shot through her and she flushed. "What are you asking me? Advice on what to do when you steal my baby?"

He turned and stared at her. "Come on, Sara. It's not like that."

She couldn't help it. Suddenly it was all too real and menacing. "Yes, it is like that."

She turned away so that she wouldn't be actually glaring at him. Using every ounce of strength, she made herself calm down. "And yes, I would recommend very strongly that you have someone onboard who knows what she's doing. Probably someone full-time, because you're a man and men always seem to have things they have to do away from the house." She turned back and met his gaze rather defiantly. "And I certainly don't expect you to learn how to sit around rocking the cradle, so to speak."

He stared at her but he didn't say a thing and she flushed even redder, wishing she had held her tongue. She watched as he steeled himself for the job.

"Okay," he said quietly. "Tell me what to do. I'm ready."

He did great. Of course, he had her there to give him advice every step of the way. But she had to admit, he didn't waver. He watched as she changed Savannah's diaper. He was still hesitant to try that on his own. But he did walk her, humming a sweet song to help her go to sleep and then he lay her down gently in her little bed and she sighed and went right off to dreamland.

"How'd I do?" he whispered, looking pleased with himself as they made their way downstairs.

She nodded, feeling sad and lost. "You did just fine. Really. I'm impressed."

His grin could have lit up the sky. He took her hand and regarded her candidly.

"Hey, Sara," he said. "Thanks for today. I know it was hard for you to let me be a part of it. It must have cut into your heart to let me be this close to Savannah for so long. But you know what?" His grin was genuine and disarming. "This was one of the best days of my life."

And he walked off down the driveway, whistling as he went.

Sara stayed where she was, tears running down her face. There was no way she could spin this. He was basically a pretty good guy. She wanted to hate him, but even that had been taken away from her.

Sara went to her room and spent another hour in agony before she could get the tears to stop. She was very scared, but she couldn't let that stop her from moving forward with her plan to prove to Jake that he just wasn't father material. At least, not single father material.

Savannah was down for the night but it was still light outside. She decided to run over to take a look at the progress the workers had made on her house. She knew she'd been neglecting it lately. Other things had been on her mind.

She drove up, parked in front and went inside. It looked like her addition was almost completed. They were still working on the new bathroom, but it was gorgeous.

All the workmen had gone home for the night. She'd lived in this house for a number of years, but it had a strange, lonely feeling now that Savannah wasn't filling the place with love and laughter. If she lost her baby, would she be able to live here? She wasn't sure. It would be painful.

The new bedroom for Savannah was beautiful, powder-pink with white trim. She'd already begun furnishing it with a new crib and changing table. It was beautiful. The question was, would it ever be used by the little girl it was meant for?

She bit her lip and forced back the hopeless feelings. She was going to keep fighting so there was no use letting pessimism build up and handicap her spirits. She was going to win this.

She looked out the window toward the neighbor's house that Jake was renting. She'd heard music as she'd walked up to her own house. There seemed to be people visiting him. Noisy people. There was something going on.

Two huge Harley-Davidson motorcycles sat in the front, pulled onto the grass. What kind of people was he having over, anyway? It was none of her business. But she had to know.

No. She closed her eyes and took a deep breath and thought better of it. She had nothing to talk to him about that couldn't wait until morning. She would get into her car and drive away and leave it alone.

Sure she would.

She gave it a try. She walked to her car and opened the door and then someone shouted something borderline vulgar and she turned and made a beeline toward his front door.

A large jovial man answered the bell. He leaned out toward her appreciatively.

"Hey," he greeted. "You here for the party?"

"What party?" she snapped with disapproval.

"Oops. I guess not." He backed away, looking chagrined. "Sounds like a disgruntled neighbor to me. Help."

Jake came into the room and headed straight for the door. "Sara. What is it? Is there something wrong?"

"No." She frowned at him. "I was just checking out my house next door and I heard the music, so I thought I'd check out what was going on."

She glanced past him and saw two other large men filling up the couches. "So you're having a party?" she asked skeptically.

"Absolutely not," he told her. He looked back at the others. "Would you like to come in and meet my friends?" he asked, though he didn't look as though he really wanted her to. "They're guys who served with me in the Army."

"No." She shook her head. "Oh, no. I don't want to intrude. I just…" She shrugged helplessly.

He grinned and came out to join her on the porch, closing the door behind him.

A burst of laughter came from inside the house. Sara frowned. "Was that man on the couch the man from the other night?" she asked.

"My buddy Starman. That was him."

"What are they here for?" she asked.

"They just want me to join them on a little pleasure cruise," he said, his mouth twisting.

"What?" she asked, puzzled.

He sighed. "I was being sarcastic. They've got a project going, a quasi-military operation they think I should join them in. A sort of revenge plot off in the jungles of Southeast Asia."

Sara shook her head emphatically. "You can't do that."

He looked surprised. "I can't?"

"Of course not." Here it was, custom made for her purposes. He had to face the fact that taking possession of a baby would make all the difference. He had to come to terms with that before he tore all their lives apart.

He was shaking his head. "That's a knee-jerk reaction. You don't know what it's all about."

"No, I don't. But I do know that you can't go."

He frowned, looking almost angry. "Really?"

"Yes. If the DNA comes in as you expect it to, you can't go. You're Savannah's father now. You're not a lone wolf warrior type anymore. You've got a responsibility to your baby."

He blinked and raked fingers through his hair. "I

understand that. And believe me, it's not easy. I've got things tugging at me in more than one direction right now."

She reached out to touch him. It happened so naturally, she didn't realize what she was doing until it was too late.

"I can see that you're torn," she told him, her hand on his chest. She gazed earnestly into his blue eyes. "But you have to understand that Savannah has to be your first priority. She's the most important thing in the world. To both of us."

He raised his own hand and covered hers, but he was watching her in a strange way, as though he didn't quite get where she was coming from. And in truth, she didn't get it, either. Savannah was either his or hers. She couldn't have it both ways. Could she?

"Don't worry," he said, his voice husky with some raw emotion she couldn't quite place. "I understand how important she is. Believe me. I understand."

Something special passed between them, something human, a connection she'd never had with anyone before. It sent a thrill through her, but it sent a warning shiver as well. She and Jake had strings between them that could never completely be cut. It was very strange, but it was real.

"I'd better go," she said, pulling her hand away and looking toward the ocean. "I...I just wanted to stop by and...well, I was looking at the progress at my house."

"Oh," he said, following her to her car. "How does it look?"

"Great. You'll have to come over and see it soon."

"I'd like to."

She tried to smile at him. "I guess we'll see you tomorrow at the birthday party."

"Sure."

She nodded, got into her car and left. Looking in her rearview mirror, she could see him standing there, watching her go.

Jake was back first thing in the morning, out on a swing in the backyard again. Jill thought it was cute. Sara thought it was obnoxious. Connor didn't have an opinion.

"Do we have anymore of that Praline Rum Cake?" he asked instead of dwelling on it. "That would make a spectacular breakfast."

Jill smiled and mussed his hair. "I know. And that's why you're not getting any. Oatmeal for you, darling."

"What?"

"Somebody's got to keep an eye on your waistline."

"My waistline is doing fine," he grumbled, but he knew better than to push it.

Sara put on a jacket and went out. There was a cool breeze coming off the ocean. She marched out to where Jake sat, doing all she could not to respond to his wide smile.

"Where's my girl?" he said.

Sara gave him a look. "She's still asleep. You're early."

"Oh." His grin was sheepish. "Sorry about that. I'm so in love with that kid, I just can't stay away."

She stared at him. Here he was, casually planning to rip her heart from her body, and he didn't seem to know how offensive he was. If he kept this up, she would find it easy to hate him.

"Hey, I brought something you might want to see," he said, and he reached into his jacket and pulled out a set of four photos and handed them to her. "Pictures I took of Kelly during those two weeks in Waikiki."

She pored at them, startled to see her half sister smiling at the camera. She was so pretty and looked so alive. It was hard to believe…

"Oh!" she said. "I've got to show these to Jill."

He nodded, then rose and followed her back to the house.

Sara held the pictures out to her sister without saying a word, and within seconds, both women were crying. He looked away. He was tortured about it, too, but he didn't have any tears for Kelly.

That didn't mean he wasn't sorry she'd died. Of course he was. It was a horrible tragedy. And he had to admit there was a thread of remorse in his recollections of her. Kelly wasn't a bad memory—unfortunately, she wasn't much of a memory at all.

She was a fun date for a few days, and once he'd left Hawaii, he hadn't really thought about her again until he got back to the States from overseas and prison camp and found all the letters she'd sent. The pictures really didn't do much to bring her back to him in any meaningful way.

He tried to think if there was any way Sara looked

at all like Kelly. He couldn't see it. Or maybe he just didn't remember exactly what Kelly looked like—beyond the pictures.

Wait. Yes, there was one thing—her smile. Kelly had been blessed with a smile that drew people in. It made you want to share in her happiness. Sara's smile had been a lot like that at first. But he hadn't seen that radiance return once she'd known his identity. Would he ever see it again? Funny, but he wanted to.

It was a good thing the birthday party had been scheduled for afternoon, because Sara and Jill were emotionally wiped out for hours after seeing the pictures of Kelly.

"I'll never forgive myself for not having reached out to her more strongly," Jill said, tears in her eyes. "We should have brought her here. We should have made an effort to get to know her so much better than we did. I always thought we would, someday. And now it's too late."

"What do you think was behind it?" Sara mused, wiping away her own tears. "Why did we tend to have that lingering, simmering resentment of Kelly?"

Jill thought for a moment, then offered, "I think it was because of what she represented. She was our father's child with the woman who came to take our mother's place. We focused all our grief on her and we hated them both. It wasn't fair, but we did."

"I can't believe we did that. We were older. We should have known better. If we'd stopped and thought things through, if we'd stepped back and looked at the bigger picture…"

Jill hugged Sara and sighed. "But we never did. You just go on in life, so often, just taking day by day and not looking outward."

Sara frowned, thinking it over. What Jill had said still bothered her. "Hate is too strong a word, don't you think?" she ventured.

Jill hesitated, then nodded. "You're right. But we couldn't stand that woman. She tried to take our mother's place, and she was so bossy and unfriendly to us. And she didn't treat Daddy very well at all."

"Which is why their marriage didn't last."

"True." Jill managed a bittersweet smile. "Remember how we celebrated with hot fudge sundaes the day he told us they were separating?"

Sara nodded. "Yes. We must have been about fourteen and fifteen at the time. We were so happy the evil stepmother was gone." She sighed, shaking her head. "But that meant we never got to know Kelly very well, beyond her toddler years."

"Yes. It's such a pity."

"And that was part of why I decided to take Savannah when they asked us if we would. To try to make up—at least a little bit—for not being kinder to Kelly."

Jill groaned. "And now you may have to pay the price for us both."

"Oh, don't say that!" Sara said, hands to her mouth.

They stared into each other's eyes and both looked tragic and filled with remorse. Sara pulled Jill aside to where they could speak privately.

"You realize what this means, don't you?" she whispered to her sister. "These pictures prove he knew her and was with her right at the appropriate time. Look at the date stamp on the photos."

Jill nodded. "I noticed," she said. "Oh, Sara. What are we going to do?"

Sara's jaw tightened. "Convince him he doesn't really want to be a father," she said. "Unless you can think of something better."

Connor saw the way the wind was blowing and he asked Jake if he wanted to go along with him to the hardware store. He was looking for a new tool to use in making a tree house for the boys. Jake jumped at the chance to leave the agonizing behind. They talked about sports and cars and tools and had a great time, returning quite happy and refreshed, carrying a nice shiny new power screwdriver set.

Mrs. Truesdale, from the agency, called while they were gone. She deeply commiserated with Sara and promised to do all she could from her end of things.

"I know I have to be impartial," she told her. "But I put you together with your baby and I would hate to see that slip away. You are so perfect for it." Her voice was lower, almost secretive. "Now you keep track of anything that seems strange to you. Good documentation is important. I've often seen it win the day. And don't worry, I'll be in touch. We'll work on this together."

Sara was feeling a bit better after that conversation. She and Jill had pretty much gone through their catharsis by the time the men got back and were ready to move on with their day. It was time to start preparing for the party.

There was plenty to do, games to be set up, food to be prepared, play areas to be set out. Most of the children attending would be toddlers themselves, so the games would be completely basic and simple. Still, they needed to be thought through. Everyone was helping.

"Except for you," Sara told Jake. "I have something special saved for you."

He turned to look at her, his smile crooked and rather endearing. "Special for me, huh? Great. What do you want me to do?"

She stood watching him with her hands on her hips, wishing he didn't look like every woman's dream of the perfect guy. It would be easier to fight a man who gave you the willies instead of butterflies in the tummy area. "You're going to be a nanny for Savannah."

He frowned. "What exactly does that mean? I thought I did that yesterday."

"No, you just mostly observed yesterday. Today you'll be hands-on and on your own. Your job is to watch her. Help her when she gets stuck. Find her something to play with. Hold her. Change her when she needs it. Rock her when she cries. Feed her when she needs it. Put her down for a nap when she gets cranky."

Jake looked out toward where Connor was setting up the plywood clown panels for the sponge throwing game. "But I could be helping with the building crew," he noted wistfully. "I'm pretty good with a hammer."

"No time," she said blithely. "You're going to be in

charge of Savannah's health and happiness." She smiled at him. "I'll be watching."

"Great," he said halfheartedly, but he didn't argue. He knew that Sara had a double reason for wanting him to take on this challenge and he agreed with at least one of them. He had to learn this stuff. Having someone who'd been doing it for six months give him pointers was extremely useful and he couldn't waste that resource.

The second reason she was doing it was not quite as clear, but he thought he'd figured it out pretty quickly. She was hoping he would do a lousy job at it and get frustrated. Was she trying to make him feel like a loser? No, he really didn't think so. But she did want him to feel like this job was too big for him to handle. Well, maybe not too big, but too far out of his bailiwick. She wanted him to realize that it would be harder than he'd thought.

He had to admit he'd already had a few qualms along those lines. After all, the dream of having a child of his own was very different from the reality of actually dealing with one. He knew it was going to be hard. There was nothing easy about taking on responsibility for another human being, especially one that needed constant attention and care. He wasn't particularly talented in that direction and he'd had no experience. But he also knew that the connection he felt with Savannah was pure and clear and unique. He'd never known anything like it. And now that he'd felt it, he knew he couldn't walk away, no matter what.

Okay, he would do it. He would act as a nanny and

let Sara judge his talents. Why not? Anything for his little girl.

"I really do appreciate the effort you're putting into this, Sara," he said. "Believe me, the reality of this had hit me like a slap in the face. It's a whole different way of looking at the world when you've suddenly got someone else to think about. Someone who depends on you. I've never had that before."

Good, she thought, nodding in response. Another piece of ammunition. She had to file that away for future use. She would have to start making lists and keeping track of the things he said. This was war and she had to stay focused. Any sign of weakness was a point for her side.

She began preparing sandwiches for the kids, but she was keeping her eye on Jake's progress at the same time. She watched as he patiently fed her one of the sandwiches, making each bite zoom in like an airplane to make her laugh. When she was finished, he cleaned her up and found a toy and played with her for half an hour. By then, it was pretty obvious she needed changing.

Sara followed the two of them as they climbed the stairs to the room. Jake was looking very brave and determined. Savannah was happy in his arms. Sara followed and hung out in the doorway, just in case. He lay her down on the changing table and tugged off her jumper, then stared at the diaper for a long moment. He looked over at Sara and made a face.

"Maybe I ought to watch you do it one more time," he said.

She smiled. That was exactly the reaction she'd been hoping for. "Sure," she said, stepping up and taking over. "Why not?"

Once she'd put on a new diaper, she handed her baby over to Jake again. "Now pick out some clothes to put on her," she said. "On a nice late summer day like this, what would you choose?"

He stared at her, completely at sea. "Give me a hint," he said.

She grinned. "A sundress over tights. How about that?"

"Great." He looked at the open drawer and hesitated. "What exactly are tights again?" he asked.

She laughed and showed him, then guided him away from the purple leggings he was about to put on Savannah. "Try to find something that will go with her green dress," she suggested.

She watched as he finished dressing her. She liked the way he talked to her, half teasing, half loving. The way he looked, the tone of his voice, the expression in his eyes, touched her heart. He really did love that little girl. She could see that. This was going to be tough.

"All in all, you're doing quite well," she told him as he swung his baby up into his arms again. "I'm impressed."

Then she bit her lip. What was she doing praising him? She wanted him to feel inadequate, didn't she? Wasn't that the whole point? She had to be more careful. This was war and she couldn't give up ground too easily.

For the next hour as she watched him with Savannah, her mood darkened. He did things wrong and she pointed them out as they happened, but he learned quickly and the way he treated Savannah, his growing attachment to her couldn't be more clear.

Sara was losing all hope. He was her father and the only way she was going to be able to fight that would be to talk him out of wanting to take over her parenting. Was there any chance she could do that? She couldn't think about it too hard, not if she wanted to keep functioning for the rest of the day.

But her face told the story and Jake noticed. He'd just put Savannah down for her nap and was feeling pretty good about how things had gone when he caught sight of Sara. She'd slipped away and was standing in the den, looking out at the ocean in the distance. He came up behind her and touched her arm. She whirled and gazed up at him, tears standing in her eyes.

He took hold of her shoulders and frowned. "Hey, what happened? What's the matter?"

She shook her head, trying to avoid his gaze. "Nothing."

His hands tightened on her shoulders. "Come on. You can tell me."

She glanced up into his eyes, then away again. "I'm… I'm just upset."

"About what?"

She shook her head.

"Come on, Sara. If I've done something…"

"No." She took a deep breath. "It's not you. It's me." She took another breath and blurted out, "I really, really want to hate you. And I can't."

"Oh."

She was crying now. She hated that he was there to see it, but she couldn't stop. His arms came around her and he held her close, letting her sob against his chest, murmuring soft words of reassurance that she hardly heard. But she felt his comfort, and she relaxed within it, wishing…wishing…

No. She had to stop this. She forced herself to regain her balance and get back to her normal independent self. She couldn't show him this sort of silliness. She pulled away and gave him a watery smile.

"I…I'm just tired, that's all," she said, turning away. "I've got to get back to the kitchen. Jill needs help." And she escaped.

Jake stayed where he was for a few minutes, swearing softly and running his fingers through his thick hair. It wasn't often that he felt sympathy for another quite so strongly. But he could imagine what it would be like to be Sara and put in this position. It wasn't pretty.

He'd had his own moments of doubt, but that was over now. The better he got to know Savannah, the more sure he was. She was his and he had to take care of her. It was that simple.

CHAPTER SEVEN

FINALLY IT WAS party time, and for the most part, things went great. Friends of Jill and Connor began to stream in, most of them trailed by toddlers on their chubby, shaky legs. Sara watched them come and hid a smile. It was definitely a day for the short people of the island. Children under five seemed to rule the roost.

That meant noise, lots of noise, once the beginning shyness wore off and the children were playing in the backyard. Moms and dads hovered at the margins, rushing in to settle disputes or kiss an owwie.

Most were friends of Jill's that Sara didn't know very well. She helped organize games and supply party favors. The food Jill had spread out on the tables was super yummy and Sara took pity on Jake about an hour in, telling him she'd watch Savannah while he ate and did a little socializing.

She was just helping Savannah onto a rocking horse in the playroom when a friend of her sister's, a woman named Mary Ellen, stopped in to chat.

Mary Ellen had a bouffant blond hair helmet, scarlet

fingernails and a roving eye. The first thing she wanted to know was all about Jake.

"Okay, Sara," she said, giving her an air kiss and then standing back to look at her. "I understand that delicious man in the tight jeans is a friend of yours. What exactly does that mean?"

Sara bristled a bit. She'd never been all that fond of Mary Ellen. "What do you think it means?"

She shrugged. "I just want to know if you've got dibs on him, or is he fair game?"

Sara looked at her, chin high, eyes narrowed. This woman wanted Jake. How dare she?

And yet, she had to admit, Jake was a free man and she had no claim on him whatsoever. Still, Mary Ellen didn't have to know that.

"And if he is?" she asked. "Just exactly what are you planning?"

Mary Ellen looked out the picture window to where Jake was standing talking to some of the others and watching the children play.

"A lady never reveals her secrets, my dear." She laughed to show that was just a joke. "Oh, nothing. Everybody knows I'm hopelessly devoted to Hector. But a girl can dream, you know."

She winked as though the two of them had an understanding about these things.

If this woman doesn't stop, I'm going to throw up! Sara silently screamed. She had a sudden vision of Jake dating someone like Mary Ellen while raising Savannah and it sent a wave of sick agony through her. She would do almost anything to stop that from ever happening.

"Too bad," she said sharply. "Better luck next time."

"Oh." Mary Ellen looked disappointed. "So you *are* actually dating him, are you?"

"Yes, I am," she lied. But what could she do? The woman deserved what she got. "He and I have a very special understanding."

"Ah." Mary Ellen had no idea what that meant, but she accepted it with good grace and beat a hasty retreat toward the backyard. Straight to Jake, Sara noticed. He would have a good laugh when she told him about the "special relationship" the two of them supposedly had, but she couldn't help that now. Oh, well.

Still, it did point out a factor to be considered. Jake was attractive to women. If he took Savannah, there would be women, and maybe, eventually, a special woman. And no matter how many visitation plans Sara might have, it wouldn't last. If she thought anything along those lines might work, she was dreaming.

Savannah was getting fussy. She wanted to go back outside where the action was. Sara pulled her up into her arms and carried her out, and she found herself standing just behind where Jake was talking to another guest she didn't know.

"I hear you've been deployed in Southeast Asia for the last few years," the man, who she thought was a friend of Connor's, was saying to him.

Jake paused as though this was a topic he really didn't

relish getting into. "You might call it that," he said at last. "I was definitely in the area."

The man nodded wisely. "Something tells me that means you may have spent some quality time at the Mekrob Mansion. Am I right?"

She'd heard that name before. It seemed to her she'd seen it in news reports. She had a vague impression that is wasn't a very nice place.

"I've heard it called that." Jake seemed to shiver slightly. "What a benign name for the reality of that place."

"I had a buddy who spent some time there," the friend told him. "He came out a changed man, pretty much a shell of the person he used to be."

"I've had friends who had similar experiences," Jake said, starting to turn away. "Luckily I seem to be able to heal faster than most." And he began to make his way to the food table.

Sara watched him go, feeling sick. She knew he'd had a rough time over the last few years. He'd hinted at it often enough. But just how rough was it? She wasn't sure she really wanted to know the details.

She carried Savannah over to where the children were playing so that she could watch without getting too involved. Friends of Jill's stopped to talk to her and to admire her little girl. She loved showing her off. With her lively smile and her curly yellow hair, she looked great no matter what she wore.

Sara held Savannah close, trying not to think about how fast the time was going. In just a few hours, the agency would call and hand out the verdict. She was pretty sure she already knew what it would be. She looked down at her baby's beautiful face and sang her a soft song. She had to treasure every moment, just in case.

Savannah's legs began to kick and she pointed, laughing. Sara looked at the direction she was pointing in. Jake was helping to erect a piece of plywood with the figure of a clown painted on it, with a round cutout where the face should be. He looked through the hole and wiggled his eyebrows at Savannah.

It was time for the wet sponges!

This had to be the children's favorite game. Even two-year-olds could manage tossing a wet sponge. And when they had a target like Jake, making faces and pretending to be hit even when he wasn't, the laughter never stopped.

Savannah was still too young for this, but she laughed and laughed seeing Jake take the punishment from the other children. At one point, Sara put a wet sponge in her hand and took her right up to the clown form and let her press it to his nose.

He yelled as though it was his worse wound yet and Savannah turned red with laughter. Sara's gaze met Jake's and his eyes were filled with fun and happiness. She smiled. She couldn't help it.

Still, the feeling of dread was always there at the back of her mind. The time of reckoning was at hand.

By the time Jake had finished his turn in the target zone, he was drenched.

"Come on in," Jill said, guiding him into the kitchen, where Savannah was playing with balloons with two older children on the carpeted area of the floor. "Connor will let you use one of his shirts. Sara will show you where they are."

"Okay," he said, still laughing as he pulled a pack of breath mints out of his shirt pocket. The cardboard packaging was ruined and he spilled the mints out onto the coffee table so they wouldn't be ruined, too, and then he threw away the box.

Sara was already heading up the stairs and he followed her, pulling off the wet shirt as he went. She avoided looking at his beautiful chest as she took his wet shirt and traded it for one of Connor's, but as he turned, for the first time, she got a good look at his back in full light and gasped at what she saw.

There was a crisscross pattern of scarring all up and down the surface. The first thing that came to mind was the evidence left of a lashing. The long purple welts tipped in red looked awfully recent to her and she felt sick.

"What is that?" she cried before she thought.

He glanced in the mirror, saw what she was looking at and quickly pulled his shirt on all the way.

"Just a little memento of my prison camp days," he said lightly. "Don't give it a second thought."

She stared at him, hand to her throat. "I overheard you talking to that man in the yard," she said, her voice strained. "So you were at the Mekrob Mansion?"

"Sara, you don't want to hear about it. Believe me.

It's in my past and I don't even think about it much anymore. No problem."

No problem. Someone with scarring like that had to be affected in more ways than just the physical. She couldn't believe she hadn't noticed it before. But then, she'd spent a lot of time studiously trying to avoid looking at his naked torso, as if she thought it would have magic powers over her if she let herself gaze too long. And who knew? Maybe it did.

But somehow, now that she'd seen them and actually brought the scarring up to him, she couldn't seem to let them go.

"Jake, they don't look that old to me. Are you sure you're psychologically ready to take care of a child with that sort of damage done to you so recently?"

He looked at her for a second, then grinned, shaking his head. "Oh, yeah. I think I can handle it." Reaching out, he took her chin in his hand and smiled down at her. "Now you're clutching at straws, Sara. Cut it out."

She flushed but she didn't look away. Sure she was clutching at straws. She would try anything to win this fight. She wasn't the least bit embarrassed.

As they came back down the stairs, the first thing Sara saw was Savannah turning purple and making choking sounds, writhing on the floor, a sight that sent a shock of horror flashing through her. There was no adult in sight and the two children she'd been playing with were just going out the sliding glass door.

"Savannah!" she screamed, rushing to her. Somehow, Jake beat her to the child and had her in his arms, holding her from behind and pressing in the right place to get a burping sound out of her. Two breath mints came shooting out of her mouth, and just like that, she was breathing again.

Jill came in at the same time. "I just went out for a second," she cried, seeing what was going on. "Really! No more than a second. How did this happen so fast?"

But it wasn't Jill who Sara blamed.

"Who left those out where she could get them?" she demanded, sweeping the rest of them up in her hand.

"I did," Jake admitted. "I didn't think…"

"You didn't think!" She glared at him, anger hot and painful all through her body. Her baby, her little child, what if they hadn't found her in time? What if she'd died, or had brain damage, or some other horror? What if?

"How could you do that? You didn't think! She could have died if we hadn't come back in time!"

Jake's face went hard as stone. "I should have known better. Sorry. It won't happen again."

"Sorry!" Sara wanted to shake him. She was almost sputtering with her anger. "Sorry! What good is 'sorry' when…"

"Sara." Jill grabbed her hand and pulled her around as though to silence her. "Enough. She's okay. Jake will know better next time. Give it a rest."

Meanwhile, Savannah was back to normal. She'd reached up and put her arms around Jake's neck and she was babbling to him, nonsense words, but the meaning was clear. She might as well have been saying, "Thank you, Daddy. You saved my life."

Sara turned away in frustration. She was trembling with fear and anger. She glanced back at where Jake held Savannah, and she turned and headed up the stairs again, going to her own room and hoping to calm down once she was alone for a few minutes.

Jake watched her go. A black cloud loomed over him. How could he have done that, without thinking? It hadn't occurred to him—but that was the point, wasn't it? There was so much he had to learn—so much that didn't come naturally to him as yet. It wasn't going to be easy.

And Sara was right to yell at him. He deserved it. If his lack of care and knowledge did anything to hurt this adorable child in his arms, he would never forgive himself. This parenting thing was going to require a lot of work. Was he really ready to take it on?

The party was finally over. Large hunks of cake and dabs of frosting were littered all over the backyard, but the squirrels would get what Sara and Jill didn't get swept up. The men were putting away the tools and the plywood characters and the game structures that had been set up around the yard. Jill put away the leftover food and Sara tried to put the twins down. She soon gave up. They were much too excited from the party and all their new toys to think about something so boring as sleep.

Jake was holding Savannah. He'd been holding her almost continuously ever since the breath mint incident, as though constant apologies were needed for now. Sara watched and felt her anger drain away. How could she be mad at someone who loved her baby as much as she did—regardless of the consequences?

"I'm going to talk to him," Sara told her sister once the worst of the devastation had been cleaned up and they were outside, surveying the scene.

Jake was inside, holding Savannah. She could see him through the sliding glass door. Jill turned and looked at him, too.

"I'm going to confront him with what his life will be like and how he ought to leave the raising of Savannah to me."

Jill nodded, her eyes shadowed with sorrow. "Good luck," she said softly.

Sara went in to the room where he sat with the sleepy girl up against his shoulder and sank onto the ottoman in front of his chair.

"Jake, I need to talk to you." She was ready. Her heart was thumping. She had to do it now. There was no time left for avoiding this. The agency would be calling in the morning and by then, everything would be too crazy to get a serious conversation in.

"Is she asleep?" he asked softly.

Sara craned to see her face and looked at her eyes. They were closed. "I think so," she told him.

He smiled. "She feels asleep," he said, half whispering. "I can't tell you how much I love holding her like this."

That touched her heart. How could it not?

"Here, let me take her. I want to put her down in

her play bed. That'll keep her out of the line of fire for now." She settled the baby in the soft playpen, covered her with a blanket and turned back to Jake.

"I have to say something to you," she began, sitting back down on the ottoman. "I know you're not going to like it. But I have to say it."

He raised his gaze to hers and looked serious. "Go."

She drew air in deeply and began. "I want Savannah. I love her. I'm her mother. Please, please don't take her away from me."

He stared at her, then shook his head. "You're not going to like what I have to say, either," he warned. "Sara, I'm her father. And…you're not really her mother—you're her aunt. I have a more fundamental right to her than you do. It's that simple."

She drew in a shaky breath and held her head high. "No, it's not that simple. I'm a woman. I've learned how to nurture this child. You're a man. Your place in the scheme of things is very different. I know you love her. It's obvious. And she loves you. I'm not saying I want to tear that apart. I'm just saying, we each have our roles, and yours isn't to be her mother."

His blue eyes narrowed. "But yours is."

"Yes." She said it firmly. She wanted him to see how committed she was to this plan. "Yes, I really think so."

He shook his head. "Sara…"

"Hear me out. Jake, you're wonderful with Savannah. You're gentle and kind and good to her. But you're still a man. And she needs a woman to help her become one herself. There are a thousand different ways a girl needs a mother."

His frown became fierce. "That's nonsense."

"No. It's truth. You've spent the day taking care of her. Do you want to do the same thing again tomorrow?"

He grimaced dismissively. "What does that mean?"

"I'm trying to get you to think through what it means to raise a little girl. You have to watch her every moment. You have to be there for her for eighteen years, at least. You have to be her support in so many ways."

"I can do that."

"Yes, but alone? I don't think you realize how hard it will be."

"I can do it. I can." He glared at her. "No matter what, I can't walk away. That's not going to happen."

"Of course not." She touched him, putting her hand on his arm. She wanted him to see that she wasn't the enemy here. She wanted to be sure she kept open all lines of communication. "You're her biological father. You have to be a part of her life. But…"

"I know what you're saying, Sara. I understand traditional ways. Even though I wasn't raised that way, we all pretty much have that baked in the cake, don't we? But extraordinary things happen, and we have to make do. I'm adaptable. I'm ready to adapt to being a single father." He shook his head and stared into her eyes, emotion clear and determined. "I can't think of anything I want more."

She pulled her hand back. So far, she couldn't detect one gap in his armor, one area of vulnerability in his logic. She'd attacked and he hadn't retreated one bit. Was there really any hope lurking in there behind those brilliant blue eyes?

"How about money?" she challenged. It was the only unexplored thing she could think of. "Will you be able to afford her? Won't you have to get a job that pays enough to be able to pay for child care, too? What will her life be like with you?"

He stared at her for a long moment, then began to smile. "You know, the funny thing is, if this had happened a couple of years ago, I wouldn't even consider challenging you for her. And the money, just what you brought up, would have been the major factor."

"Really? What's changed?"

He shrugged. "My father died. My crazy father who made me grow up in a mountain cabin with no running water so I would be close to the earth." He shook his head, bemused. "Once he was gone, I found out he left me the royalties on a patent he'd taken out on an invention of his. It was a way to use a specially developed pulley for lifting extremely heavy loads." He shook his head again, almost laughing. "Go figure. Who knew he was a secret genius? It made a small fortune. And now that fortune is mine."

Her heart fell. He could counter every attack and push her back so easily. "Interesting," she said sadly. "So you're saying you can afford to fight for something you really want."

"Exactly."

She took a deep, trembling breath and fought back

tears. "You've got me beat there. I don't have any nice special pile of money."

"Sara..." He reached out and touched her cheek. "I'm sorry. What can I say?"

She shook her head, biting her lower lip and about to retreat. And then her sister, who had obviously been eavesdropping, came into the room like a chill wind.

"Okay, now I've had it," she said, standing before them both with her hands on her hips. "The two of you need to get beyond this stuff. The train is coming down the track. The whistle is blowing and the light is coming around the bend. There's no more time for nonsense. It's obvious what you need to do. Get real."

They both stared at her in surprise and she glared right back.

"You've both got great claims to this beautiful child—pending the DNA results, of course. But it looks pretty clear that you both deserve her. There's only one real solution." She shrugged dramatically.

"I'll tell you what I think. This is it. This will answer all your problems and make everyone happy. You've got to do it."

She paused for full effect, then threw out her arms. "You've got to get married."

It was as though an electric explosion had gone off in the room, almost flattening them both.

"What?" Jake cried out.

"Married!" Sara jumped up, shocked. "What are you talking about?" Her mind reeled.

"Oh, no," Jake was saying, shaking his head emphatically and brushing the whole concept off with his hand. "I don't do 'married.'"

"Maybe you didn't do 'married' in the past," Jill said, looking very stern. "But things have changed. You're not just thinking for yourself now. What Savannah needs is more important than what you may think you need. She needs a mom and a dad. Just like every child. Are you going to deny her that?"

Sara was shaking her head. "Jill, be serious. We're not getting married."

Jill held up a hand to her sister. It was Jake she was aiming at. "Do you have somebody else you want to marry?" she demanded of him.

"No!" He looked as though he was about to start tearing his hair out. "Don't you get it? I never wanted to get married. I never plan to. I'm not going to be tied down to a relationship with someone I might…" His voice faded and he flushed, not sure what he'd been about to say, but sure it really had nothing to do with Sara. Maybe he ought to just shut up for a while.

"Change your thinking, bud," Jill snapped at him. "Stop being so selfish. You've got to think for two."

Sara watched the scene, too stunned to say anything. Where on earth had this idea come from? Had Jill noticed how she was beginning to respond to Jake in a wholly inappropriate way? Was that behind all this talk?

It was a strange sort of love and hate blend that she felt for the man. That didn't do well in a marriage, she wouldn't think. But what did she know? She'd never been married before and Jill was on her second try.

She shook her head, trying to clear her mind. "Jill," she said, her voice choked with emotion. "Go. Please just go."

Her sister watched her uncertainly for a moment, then nodded. "Okay. But don't forget what I've said. Take it seriously."

"Go."

"Okay. Bye." And she left the room.

Jake rose and took Sara's hands in his. He looked at her with sadness and compassion in his eyes, but she could see that he was immovable.

"I am truly sorry, Sara," he said softly. "But it's a no go. She's my child. I need to be the one who takes care of her."

Sara nodded. For a moment, she couldn't speak. "Where will you go?" she asked when she could manage to control her voice.

"I don't know yet. I'll have to figure out where will be best for us."

She nodded, staring at the top button on his shirt. "Will you let me come see her?"

He squeezed her hands. "Of course."

She looked up into his eyes. Her own were swimming in tears. Was there anything left to say?

"I've got to go," he told her. "I've got some…meetings planned. I'm already late."

She looked at the clock. She was torn. A part of her wanted him gone so that she could go to her room and cry until she had it back under control. Another part just wanted him to stay. "It's almost dinnertime."

He gave her a crooked grin. "I ate enough at the party to last me for three days. I really need to go. I've got to prepare for tomorrow."

Her heart sank. She knew exactly what he meant.

"Okay. You'll be back tomorrow."

"Of course."

For just a moment, she thought he was going to bend down and kiss her. But he hesitated and then dropped her hands and turned away. "Goodbye," he said at the door, turning back to nod at her. "And, Sara, I really am sorry."

She watched him go and then she cried.

Hours later, she was still in agony but her tears were dry. She helped her sister prepare a light dinner, though she couldn't eat a thing. She played with Savannah, but her heart was pounding and her mind was reeling. She couldn't relax and she couldn't stop thinking about finding ways to keep her baby.

Jill could sense the turmoil she was in and was afraid she would have a stroke.

"Will you stop pacing and sit down? Take a bath. Watch a movie. Calm down. You're going to end up in the hospital."

Sara shook her head. "I can't stop thinking. I have to find a way to convince him...."

"You won't." Jill winced at her own words, knowing they were hurtful. "Oh, Sara, you won't. His mind is made up."

She stared at her sister as though she just didn't understand. "I have to."

Jill looked to Connor, appealing for help, but he shrugged and went out to the garage. She turned back to Sara.

"Well, think about it from his side…" she began.

"I don't want to think about it from his side!" Sara cried. "I just care about my side right now. Savannah's side. The important side." She shook her head in despair. "Jill, my side is to protect this baby. I have to keep her near me. I have to."

"Sara, six months ago we had to talk you into taking her. You didn't want to adopt. You didn't think you could handle a baby in your life."

Sara met her sister's gaze with a bit of defiance in her own. "Six months ago I was a different person."

"I know. You're right." Jill threw her arms around Sara and hugged her. "It was such a brave thing to do. And you are so good with her. You gave up everything to take her and it has worked out so beautifully."

Sara closed her eyes. "Until Jake showed up."

"Yes." Jill released her, watching her carefully. "But you know, it's possible…life can go on…."

"Really?" Sara turned on her sister fiercely. "You really think my life can go on without my baby?" She started off toward her room. "Then you don't know me as well as you think you do."

CHAPTER EIGHT

THE AGENCY CALLED to tell Sara that the DNA test results were in. The caller couldn't tell her what they were. Someone would be calling about nine the next morning to go over them with her. They just wanted to check that she would be there to receive the call when it came, and she promised she would.

She hung up trembling and looked at the clock. In fifteen hours her fate would be sealed. She had to talk to Jake. Had they called him, too? Or only her? And what would that mean?

She called his number. It rang and rang, and she'd almost given up, when a woman answered.

"Hello," she said smoothly. "Jake Martin's residence."

Sara nearly choked with outrage. He had a woman over while she was going through all this alone?

"Where's Jake?" she ground out hoarsely.

"Uh… He's taking a shower right now. May I take a message?"

So on top of everything else, he was going to have his women hanging around. Impossible! That was no way to try to raise a little girl.

"Tell him Sara is coming over," she said. To heck with their plans. "I'll be there in half an hour."

She freshened up, grabbed a jacket and started the walk down the hill, on her way over to the house next to her own. It took about five minutes. There was no strange car in the driveway, but that didn't necessarily mean anything. She went to the door and rang.

Jake opened the door and smiled at her. His hair was still wet from his shower and he wore a nice snug T-shirt and clean, but torn and faded jeans. He stood back and motioned for her to enter. She came in but she looked around suspiciously.

"Where is she?" she demanded.

Jake looked around, too, as though totally at sea. "Who?"

"That woman you had here."

He pretended to frown but his eyes were sparkling. "What woman?"

Her frown was real. "She answered the phone when I called."

His face cleared. "Oh. That woman."

"Yes."

"Her name is…let's see." He glanced down at a paper on the counter. "Patty Boudine." He tapped the paper and looked pleased with himself. "That's the one."

Sara frowned, knowing he was teasing her. "So where is she?"

"She's gone." He grinned again. "Sara, I was interviewing her for a job."

That stopped her short. "Really?"

"Yes, really." He mocked her tone. "I put out an ad for a nanny. She showed up. End of story."

She frowned again. "She said you were taking a shower."

"I was. I had to get rid of all that birthday party stickiness I ended up sporting," he said. "I left her out here filling out the application. Then I asked her a few questions, and she left." He shrugged. "Hey, I thought you would approve. You know I need help." Then he got an idea. "Maybe you should help me choose the nanny. You're the expert, after all. You know what I should be looking for."

He was acting as though it was all a done deal. Her heart was so broken. "You can't even wait a few weeks to see how this takes before you set up a whole support structure around this?"

He saw her despair and he reached for her, taking her by the shoulders and gently holding her in front of him. "Sara sweet Sara, how many ways do I have to tell you? I'm taking my baby with me. Even if it breaks your heart."

She nodded, holding back tears. "It does."

"I know."

She looked at him and everything in her wanted to melt into his arms and let him protect her—but at the same time, he was the one she had to be protected from. It made no sense. But emotions seldom did. She pulled away before she found herself letting temptation rule.

"Are your friends gone?" she asked, walking to the kitchen and peeking in, just to make sure he'd had the damage from the other day cleaned up. And he had. The room sparkled like new.

"They're gone for now. But they could show up again at any moment."

She turned to look at him. "Do they come over every night?" What a nightmare. First these huge, rough men would be hanging around. And then, the women. Despite the one she'd talked to on the phone turning out to be a job applicant, she was pretty sure other women would be showing up. It just fit the scenario. Savannah didn't belong here!

"Pretty much." Suddenly he seemed uncomfortable. "They're trying to talk me into something. I'm resisting for now." His smile was less casual. "They're working on me just like you're working on me. Everybody wants a piece of me. Maybe everybody ought to just leave me alone."

She looked at him speculatively. She wanted to talk to him, but she didn't want to be interrupted by his friends.

"Walk with me," she suggested. It would soon get dark, but the forecast called for a full moon rising and there ought to be enough light for quite some time. "Let's walk on the beach. Out to the point."

He shrugged. "Why not?"

And a few minutes later, they started off. The light was fading leaving the ocean a gorgeous midnight-blue. The regular beat of the waves on the sand seemed to echo their steps. A cool ocean breeze caught her hair and sent it out behind her like a banner. She lifted her face to it, breathing it in.

"Did they call you?" she asked him at last.

"Who?"

"The agency."

"Yes, they did." He turned to look at her. "I told them I'd be with you tomorrow for the call."

She nodded. That was what she'd thought he would want to do. "You don't plan to take her, though," she said, suddenly scared she might have misjudged him. "I mean even if they…"

"No," he said quickly. "Don't worry. All in good time." He shrugged. "I don't have all my ducks in a row yet. I need to make preparations."

Relief surged through her. She needed more time and so did he.

He stopped and gazed down at her, his face set and earnest. "I think you know what the verdict is going to be, though. I'm Savannah's father. There's no doubt."

She took a deep breath and summoned up all her courage.

"I am going to have to accept that, if the data comes in favoring you," she said, her voice a bit shaky. "And I can accept that legally, you have full rights to her, if that does happen." She looked hard into his eyes and said the hard part. "But regardless, I think you should let me keep her."

He made a face, as though he couldn't believe she'd said that.

"Sara…"

"I'm serious. Think about it. I'm a single woman. But you're a single man. You don't have a clue how to handle this. I'm ready. I've learned a lot. And we've bonded, she and I, big time."

He stared at her for a long moment, and then he began to walk again and she hurried to catch up with him.

"She's my baby, Jake," she said a bit breathlessly, having a hard time with the sand. "She's been mine for six months. If you take her away, it will be wrenching for her. You don't want to do that kind of damage to a child."

He kept walking. She noticed that his hands were clenched into fists at his side. He was angry, but she'd expected that. This was a gut-wrenching thing they were discussing. Of course he was emotional. So was she.

"I want her," he said at last, his voice a harsh growl of a sound. "More than anything in the world. I want my baby."

Her heart sank. He really meant it. There was no give in his tone, no hint of even the possibility of compromise. She was going to have to go further and think things through a bit more.

"I understand that," she said quickly. "You see, I think I can work out a plan where I can keep her but you won't have to totally give her up."

His grunt signaled disdain, but she didn't waver.

"Hear me out, Jake. You owe me that much."

He stopped and turned to glare down at her.

"Is it because of what happened this afternoon with the mint drops?" he asked. "Are you afraid I'm going to hurt her?"

She was surprised. Funny, but that was the furthest thing from her mind right now.

"I know you would never hurt her." She touched him, put a hand flat against his chest, just above the heart. There was only a thin sheet of cotton between her hand and a hard sense of pounding that spoke of life and determination. It almost scared her to feel it.

"I overreacted. I shouldn't have yelled at you like that." She tried to smile at him. "And you were the one who saved her."

He stared at her and placed his hand over hers, trapping it against his flesh. "So what's your plan?" he asked softly.

She took a deep breath, trying to focus. It was hard when he was so close, so warm.

"Listen, Jake," she said at last. "We could work something out. If...if you just leave her with me, you could go on with your life and not have to give up everything. I would have her here and you could come and go. She would always be here for you and..."

He was frowning. She knew without being told that he didn't like the idea. "It all sounds very nice but it just won't work. What if you get married?"

She brushed that away. "Oh, don't worry about that. I won't. I don't even want to—ever."

He grimaced and shook his head. "You say that now, but there will come a time..."

"No!"

He cupped her cheek with his free hand and gazed down into her eyes. "Sara, you're still so young. You need a man in your life. You know it. You're going to begin longing for it. You'll fall in love."

"No," she said, but this time it almost sounded like a whimper.

His mouth turned up at the corners, but his eyes didn't warm. "Yes. Deep down, you know it's true." His hand caressed the side of her face. "You feel a tug toward me right now. You want human contact. You want me to kiss you."

She was breathless now, and all she could do was shake her head. Her heart was beating like a bird in a cage.

"Don't try to deny it," he said so softly she could hardly hear his voice over the sound of the waves. "I'm going to prove it to you."

His mouth took hers with ease. She didn't put up much of a fight. Because he was right. She wanted his kiss. She'd been wanting it from the day she met him.

The contrast between the cool air and his hot mouth was the first thing that stunned her. And then there was his taste, like buttered honey in the sun, like a sip of red wine in the moonlight, like liquid gold, all wrapped into a racy sensation that sent her senses reeling.

She clung to him, her arms reaching up under his jacket to get as close to his heat as she could. His tongue rasped against hers in a gesture that made her moan low in her throat. His hands slid down to take control of her hips and pull them in hard against his and she welcomed it, pushing against him and hearing small whispered noises of pleasure coming from her own mouth.

She wanted him. Every part of her wanted him, every part of her was on fire. She was almost drowning in desire. She, who had always been so cool and collected, a reserved observer instead of a committed partner in affairs of the heart and soul, suddenly wanted this man with a sense of pure animal hunger that scared her witless.

Her mind finally fought its way back to the surface and she began to realize what she was doing. She cried out in anguish and pushed away from him, panting as she stared at him, hating him and adoring him at the same time.

"That wasn't fair," she managed to mutter at him, wiping her mouth with the back of her hand. "That was pure ambush. I wasn't ready to defend myself."

His grin was bittersweet and he tried to hide it. "Sara, my beautiful Sara," he said, shaking his head. "You've got something smoldering inside that's just waiting to break out into a forest fire. You can't hold it back forever. Someday, you won't be able to stop. You won't even want to. I think you just proved my point for me."

She glared at him. "You cheated," she said. "I'm not usually like that. And I won't be again. I can control myself. It won't happen again."

He shook his head. "We're talking years and years. You'll meet someone. The spark will light the flame. You'll want to marry him. And you'll have my child living with you." He shrugged. "How would we work that out?"

"No, I swear that will never happen."

He gazed down at her as though she were a recalcitrant child. "You can swear all you want. Life does things to us that we never expect. Happens all the time."

She knew he was right, but that didn't give her a tidy argument for her plans and ideas. She turned away and began walking toward the point as fast as she could go.

Once she'd reached the end of the spit of land, she found a rock and sat on it, looking out at the black ocean. It was dark now, and the mood was somber. Jake came up and sat on the rock next to hers. They stared out to sea, watching a boat in the distance, its lights shimmering over the dark waters.

"Tell me more about Kelly," she said, looking at him in the moonlight. "Tell me what she was like."

He frowned, concentrating on it, trying to wake up his memory. "You know, so many things happened to me right after I knew her, I have to admit, she doesn't stand out like she should. I mean, within a month I was back in the jungle, flirting with daily danger. And then I got caught and spent a lot of time being starved and tortured and trying to figure out how to escape. I wasn't mulling over my relationship with Kelly, if you know what I mean."

"Okay. You've made it clear that you two weren't exactly the love story of the century. And that's too bad, because we need a backstory on all that. We need to remember her better than we do now."

He frowned, shaking his head. "Why? What's the point?"

She turned to look at him. "There will come a day, not too far away, when Savannah will come to you—or come to me—and ask about her mother. And we need to be ready for that."

He stared at her, struck by the thought of it. "Oh, jeez. You're right."

She nodded. "So we ought to put together what memories we have right now, before they slip away, and be prepared to give her a bright, loving picture of the woman who is her true biological mother. Someday, she'll want to know."

He looked out at the ocean again and thought about it. "You know, I think I can remember a lot more than I was dredging up before. Kelly was fun and full of life. I'll work on it. I'll get some anecdotes together and we can go over them."

Sara stretched, feeling suddenly happier. "Great. I'll get Jill to help. I know we can come up with a great character sketch. We'll be ready for her when the time comes."

She smiled at him, but her smile faded quickly. After all, she was taking a lot for granted. What made her think that she would still be around Savannah when those questions began to pop up? Still, she could do her best to help. Savannah was the one who would benefit, no matter who gave her the picture she needed of her birth mother.

The trip back to Jill's house seemed to go by much faster than the trip out to the point had. They arrived in the front yard and Sara turned to face him again, wishing she could think of something to say, some way to cap off this day, that would change his mind and make him see how much better things would be if he left Savannah with her.

"Tomorrow will change everything," he said, almost as though he was warning her.

"Maybe." She searched his face, the lines around his mouth, and she remembered the kiss they'd shared. She could feel herself blushing, even though he probably couldn't see it in the dark.

But he was moving closer, moving with firm deliberation. He wrapped his hand in her hair, winding it slowly, then using it to pull her up close.

"Oh, no," she whispered, melting against him. "Not again. What are you doing?"

"Kissing you." His lips touched hers softly, then again. The feeling was completely different than it had been before. There was no fire behind his gestures, no sense of danger. Every move he made, every way he touched her, was filled with gentle affection. She felt as though she was floating on a cloud.

"No," she said, but there wasn't much force behind it. She was already under his spell.

"Yes." He tipped her chin up so that she had to look into his eyes. "I'm kissing you, Sara, because I need to. I need to hold you. I need to let you know how I feel in ways I can't put in words. Can you understand that?"

She was losing herself in his somber blue eyes. "Maybe," she admitted.

"I'm kissing you because I'm going to break your

heart and the way I feel about you now, I can hardly stand the thought of it."

"Then don't do it," she murmured.

"I have no choice. And it's going to kill me." He groaned, rocking her in his arms. "Sara, I like you. You're adorable. You've been so good for Savannah. And I'm going to hurt you so badly. I hate doing it. But there is no other way."

She sighed. She was already hurt beyond tears. "I should go in," she said.

"Yes." He released her and watched as she went to the door. "Good night," he whispered.

Turning, she wanted to kiss him again. Soaking in everything she was beginning to love about him, his thick, tousled hair, his handsome face, his strong, solid body, she took a step in his direction. Then she stopped, trying to read the look on his face, wondering…

No. Disappointment flooded her heart, and then chagrin. His eyes were hooded, his face could have been chiseled from stone. She couldn't do that. She couldn't let herself run back into his arms. Enough.

"Good night," she said, and she went inside and closed the door.

Jake awoke with a start. He glanced at the clock. It wasn't six yet. There was someone in his house.

He rolled out of bed silently, picked up a knife and made his way toward the living room. A shadowy figure was coming through from the kitchen. He pressed himself against the wall and waited.

He could see that it was a woman. He half wanted it to be Sara, but he didn't think it was. He waited. As she came closer, he tensed, and as she came even with where he was standing, he lunged forward and grabbed her, holding the knife to her throat.

She screamed.

"Who are you?" he rasped with his mouth against her ear.

"Jake! It's Jill. Cut it out."

He knew right away she was telling the truth, and he relaxed, letting her go and putting down the knife. Then he stared at her, shaking his head.

"What the hell are you doing?" he demanded. "I could have hurt you badly. You can't come in like that. Don't you know how to knock?"

She laughed, coming into full focus as he turned on a light. "Sorry. I'm really good friends with the people who own this house and I know where the extra key is hidden. I had to come in before this crazy day gets started and talk to you for a minute."

He shook his head. "You want me to make some coffee?" he growled.

"No. Thanks anyway."

He folded his arms across his chest and nodded. "Okay. Talk."

"I'm not going to make a long speech out of this," she began.

"Good," he muttered, making a face.

She hesitated, then added, "And I'm not very good at talking people into things."

"Good again," he said softly.

"But I need to say my piece. I need you to know how this looks to me. Jake, you know that you will probably be declared Savannah's father today. That means you have a completely new responsibility to that adorable child. It's going to be up to you to make sure she gets the launch into life she deserves. You need the best advice and the best help you can find. And I know how you can get it."

He looked at her coolly and waited for her to finish. He had a feeling he already knew where this was going. And sure enough, it went right where he thought it would. After all, Jill had tipped her hand before and she seemed to be like a bulldog with a very tasty bone.

"You and Sara need to get married," she declared, making it sound like a judgment from on high.

He groaned. "Sara and I barely know each other."

"So what? You'll grow together. Some of the best marriages in history started out that way. That means nothing in the long run. Lots of people who think they are madly in love then find out differently once they get married. I think you know that."

"I know it, and I don't care. I don't want to get married. I never wanted that. And I never will."

"Your baby needs a mother."

He groaned again. "Jill…"

"You know it's true. And if you won't provide one for her, you're going to regret it someday."

He shrugged. "So be it."

Her shoulders drooped. "Jake, don't be that way.

Think about it. You can both help each other and in the process, you'll be making life a lot better for your child. That is the best recipe for a good marriage. Mutual benefit. One of those marriage of convenience things."

He was shaking his head. "What makes you think that growing to love each other thing will work?"

"I know you both. You're good people, with good hearts. You both love someone better than you love yourselves." She was close to tears now. She was obviously completely invested in this emotionally. "It'll work. Believe me. You're fated to join together. It's written in the stars."

He stared at her for a long moment, then shook his head. "Okay, Jill. You said your piece. I understand your point of view. You can go now."

She nodded with a sigh. "I'm done. But I had to do it." She started for the door, then looked back. "Are you coming over for the call?"

"Yes."

"Good. See you then."

He closed his eyes and leaned against the wall, waiting to hear her car leave. Had her diatribe done any good in clearing up the way for him to do what he had to do? Not at all. He felt horrible about ripping Savannah away from Sara, but he didn't see any way around it. It had to be done.

Good. She was gone. He turned back toward his bedroom, but something stopped him. Had she come back? He looked out onto the driveway and saw one of his friends pulling up. He sighed.

"Doesn't anybody respect morning sleep anymore?" he muttered, and got ready for company. This one would want coffee. He was sure of it.

Sara heard the sound of knuckles knocking softly on the front door. She glanced at the clock. It wasn't even eight yet. He was early.

She went to let him in, opening the door and making a face as she saw him. It had been a long, sleepless night and she knew she looked terrible. She was pretty sure the startled expression on his face as he saw her gave evidence to that fact.

"Come on in," she said. "I do look like death warmed over and I know it."

He gave her a strange smile and said, "You look beautiful to me."

Something cloudy was swirling in his gaze and she couldn't get a read on what it was. Was he feeling awkward because of what happened the night before? No, she couldn't believe that.

She didn't feel awkward. She'd gone over it and over it in her mind, all night long, and she'd decided that she knew what had happened and why. She'd fallen in love with Jake.

The trouble was, he didn't love her. And that made all the difference.

"Would you like some Bundt cake?" she asked. "We've got plenty."

"I'd love some," he answered. "Give me a giant piece. I need sustenance for a day like this."

"For the phone call?"

"That," he agreed, "and so much more."

She squinted at him curiously, but his smile was enigmatic, and she turned to get him coffee and a slice of Chocolate Decadence instead of pushing the issue. She put his delicious breakfast in front of him, handed him a fork and stood back leaning on the opposite chair, watching him.

He was so beautiful; the most handsome man she'd ever known. Just looking at his square-jawed face and his gorgeously muscular body made her want to go ahead and swoon. Did he know how she felt about him? He had to know she was smitten, but he didn't have a clue about how deep the feelings went. She hadn't known until last night, but now she was sure of it.

Or was she just kidding herself? She'd only known him for a few days. Was that enough for falling in love? Of course not. It was just silly to think she knew enough about him to fall all the way.

Still, it had been a pretty intense few days they'd known each other. They'd done a lot of living, faced a lot of heartbreak, found a sort of comfort with each other that she'd never known before, all in that short time. And time was short. She probably wasn't going to be seeing him for much longer. She might as well live for love while she could.

Should she tell him how she felt? No. He would just pull back if she did. She couldn't risk that. But she did have one last play she was going to make, one last idea of how they could both keep Savannah in their lives. She wasn't hopeful, but she was determined.

"Have you got something new and interesting on your mind?" she asked, because it occurred to her that he appeared as though he did. There was definitely an idea brewing inside him. But he just smiled and said, "Let me eat first."

She slipped down into the chair and leaned forward, watching him. "So there is something new."

He swallowed a bite of cake and made a face indicating ecstasy. "Your sister is a fantastic baker lady," he mentioned in passing.

"That's not news," she said crisply.

"I realize that." He smiled at her. "Give me a few more minutes, okay? I do have something to talk to you about. I've had a couple of visitors this morning and I've done a lot of thinking. As a result, I've got a new perspective on some things. Tell you about it in a minute."

"Okay," she said, squirming impatiently in her chair. "And then I have something I want to tell you."

"What is it?"

"It's one last idea I've got for a solution to our problem. I've had some new thinking as well. I just want to run it past you and then let you think about it, too."

He shrugged. "Go for it."

She shook her head. "I want to hear your news first."

He smiled and reached out to take her hand in his. "Okay, I guess it's time to tell you."

"I'm ready," she said, smiling back and marveling

at this new affectionate look in his eyes when he spoke to her. She loved it.

Bringing her hand to his lips, he dropped a kiss in her palm, then released her so he could push away his empty plate. Sitting back in his chair, he grew serious.

"Okay, I'm going to tell you about my childhood and what I learned by growing up in some pretty tough circumstances." He looked at her. "I want you to know about it and how it makes me what I am today."

She nodded. "Okay."

He looked into the distance. "Sara, I was raised by a single father. My mother died when I was very young. I didn't have the advantage of a woman to nurture me. All I had was a mean, grouchy father who expected me to be a man at twelve. I know how much I lost because of that."

He drew back to look into her face again.

"I grew up in a house where a grunt meant 'good morning' and a glare meant, 'isn't it time you got the hell out of here and left me alone?' That was pretty much the extent of our communications when I was young. When it came to family, all I knew was what I saw at the movies."

"Oh, Jake!" She reached out to take his hand in hers and he leaned closer to her.

"I've always thought that my inability to fall in love, to really feel close to women I spent time with, was because my emotions were stunted by the way I was raised. I didn't know how to love. I didn't have that imprinting growing up. I was more like a wolf cub, just managing to survive in the woods. I thought I'd never get married, never have children."

Her fingers tightened on his hand. Her heart ached for that young boy, growing up wild.

"And then, a miracle happened. And there was Savannah." He shook his head, looking bemused, as though he still couldn't believe it. "My whole world changed. My first reaction was—this is ridiculous. I can't take care of a baby. I've never been around one before. I would have to give up my whole way of life."

He smiled at her.

"But then I looked at the pictures Kelly had sent me, and I began to fall in love. And I began to realize having that baby would connect me to humanity in a way I'd never connected before. She would be my lifeline. She would be my life."

His fingers curled around hers and held her tight.

"I'm not giving up Savannah. I think you understand that by now. She's mine and she's a part of me."

He blinked hard and she realized he was more emotional than she'd thought. His story of his childhood had touched her deeply. She knew he was right—she understood. He wasn't going to give his baby up, not for anything. She knew exactly how he felt.

She looked at him, hesitating and wondering how to approach this. As far as she could see, there was only one hope left. Reaching out, she took both his hands in hers and gazed at him with tears in her own eyes.

"I know, Jake," she said softly. "Believe me, I understand."

He cleared his throat and coughed, obviously not ready to go on, and she assumed he was finished.

"Jake, I know you can't give her up and I can't really ask you to. But I told you I had one last lone crazy idea to help solve our problem. Last night you were interviewing for a nanny to help you with her. You're obviously going to need somebody."

She shrugged and smiled at him.

"I want that job. Please." She held on to his hands tightly. "Please let me stay with her. I'll be quiet and discrete and won't…"

"No."

"No?" Her broken heart fell into pieces before him. "No?" It was a cry from her soul. "But, Jake…"

He tugged on her hands and pulled her up to face him as he rose. "No. Because, Sara, I've been thinking it over. And I think Jill is right. I think we ought to get married."

"You think…what?" Stunned, she could only stare at him, not sure she understood.

He stared down at her earnestly.

"I don't want my baby growing up without a mother like I did. I know from personal experience how important it is to have a mother behind you, to keep you strong and make you understand what is right and what is wrong. To give you love and teach you compassion for other living things. To teach you how to dream." He shook his head, about to get too emotional again. "She needs a father for a lot of things, but a mother is indispensible. Gotta have one."

He searched her eyes, gauging how she felt about it, but her mouth was wide-open and she was staring at him as though he'd suddenly turned green.

He touched her cheek. "I know you said you were dead set against getting married. But I know if you think it over and…"

"I said what?" she demanded, finally getting her voice. "Oh, no. That was then. This is now. I…I've been rethinking a lot of stupid opinions I once had."

A sudden grin broke on his face. "Sara…"

"See? I can change my mind, too."

"All the better."

"But, Jake, are you…? Do you really mean…?"

"I'm asking you to marry me, Sara. Please say yes."

CHAPTER NINE

IT WAS ALMOST nine o'clock and they didn't have much time for celebration, but they celebrated anyway. Jill came downstairs, carrying Savannah, who cried out with joy when she caught sight of Jake, spreading her arms to be taken up by him.

He took her and began to dance around the room, then grabbed Sara to join them. They were laughing and crying and explaining things to Jill, and then to Connor when he came into the room, when the phone rang.

The seriousness of the morning came surging back. Sara took one receiver and put it on speaker, while Jake took another, just in case. Mrs. Truesdale, the counselor on the line was the one they had each spoken to previously, and she launched right into it. Her explanation was filled with percentages and probabilities and all kinds of technical and scientific terms for the raw data in the results, most of it going right over Sara's head. She was too filled with happiness and wonder at Jake's proposal to have room in her heart or her mind to try to analyze things she only barely understood. But the gist of it all was pretty much what they had expected. Jake had been proven to be Savannah's biological father. It was all over on that score.

Mrs. Truesdale advised them to take a look at some forms she had sent them by email. She'd also posted the full document for them to look over and she advised them to take note of the final paragraph which described the grace period and what it meant.

"Here's what that is all about," she said. "There will be a grace period during which the father will take possession of the baby, but finalization won't be complete for three months. During this period, the previous guardian has the right to file an appeal. She might want to consult an attorney as to how she might do that and under what terms. It would be best if both of you were to familiarize yourselves with the rules and guidelines of our conditions so that you can judge whether the new guardian's activities and attitudes are in line with agency recommendations. I've emailed you that information."

"So I'm on probation?" Jake asked, a little startled by the news.

Sara frowned. She hadn't realized it but she had gone through the same trial period. Apparently she'd passed with flying colors. She made a mental note to check it out so that she could make sure Jake didn't do anything that might cause any problems.

For some reason, they didn't tell the counselor about their marriage plans. Maybe because they were so new—maybe for some other reason. Who knew?

They did hear about papers that had to be signed and

agreed to meet Mrs. Truesdale in Seattle within the week to do so. And then hung up and looked at each other with shining eyes and got back to celebrating.

Sara spent the next few days in a blur of happiness, interrupted periodically by moments of panic when she wondered if all this was really true. Could she be dreaming? Making it up in her own demented mind that might be trying to compensate for the horror she'd been contemplating if she lost her baby? It was all just too good to be true.

But then Jake would come by and the two of them would play with Savannah and take her on a picnic or a ride across the bay to a forest or a fun zone and she would know that this was what life was going to be like from now on. She couldn't imagine anything better.

There were other moments when she wondered if Jake was having second thoughts about it all. He was aloof at times, staring off into the distance, thinking hard about something he didn't seem to want to share with her. She wondered if he regretted what he'd done.

But there wasn't much time to worry about that. There was a wedding to plan!

Jill was in heaven. Sara had done most of the heavy duty planning on her wedding to Connor just months before, and now she was going to be able to pay her back with her own hard work.

Sara spent most of her time moving things back into her beach house. The workmen had finished and everything was gorgeous, but new furniture was a must—especially for the nursery.

At the same time, she could pop in and say "hi" to Jake next door any time she felt like it. And that was a lot. She got to know his friends better by being so close, and that was a good thing. They were all, without exception, remarkable men once she got to know the personalities behind the tough guys images. They all seemed to have nicknames, like Mr. Danger, or Two Speed. Jake was called Cool Hand and his best friend was a tall, handsome guy named Starman.

Sara asked him about how he got his nickname one day when he was helping her fold the sheets she'd just washed and dried.

"So why do they call you Starman?" she asked him.

He looked puzzled at her question. "Why not?"

She shrugged. "Does that mean you're interested in the stars? Or did you want to be an astronaut when you were younger?" She looked at him curiously.

"No." He frowned as though he was beginning to think she might have a screw loose. "They call me Starman because it's my last name. Kevin Starman."

"Oh." She laughed, chagrined. "I hadn't thought of that one."

He was a gentle giant, but she had a feeling she might not recognize the man he turned into in a firefight.

Jill was so busy preparing for the wedding, she hardly saw her long enough to say more than two words to until the day before the ceremony was scheduled.

"This has all been happening so fast," Jill said, look-

ing at her sister searchingly. "We haven't had any time
to talk." She frowned. "Are you sure about this?"

Sara's smile was glowing. "Are you kidding? It's saving my life."

"Yes, but…" She made a face of concern.

"Don't worry." She patted Jill's hand. "We get along
great, and we both love Savannah. Everything will be
fine."

Jill shook her head. "I don't know. I hate to think I
helped push you into something like this. I mean—you
should be marrying someone you love. Someone you
can build a life with…"

She waved that away. "Savannah *is* my life. This will
help her. That's all I care about."

"But, you'll be tied to Jake and…"

She hugged her sister. "Jill, don't worry. I haven't
even thought twice about that. Seriously. No second
thoughts at all. I'm ready. I want to do this."

She hesitated, wondering if she should tell her sister the truth. No, she would just worry even more if she
knew—that Sara was head over heels in love with Jake.
No doubt about it. No other man in the world would ever
cause her to waver. She loved him.

It was a strange place to be in, something she'd
thought would never happen to her. But it had, and right
in time, too. The trouble was, she had no idea how he
felt about her and it terrified her to make guesses. What
was he thinking?

"You don't really know him, you know," Jill said,
giving her a start. Was Jill reading her mind?

"Jill, aren't you the one who went cruising over to his house before dawn and set this whole marriage thing up?"

"Yes, but..." Jill frowned thoughtfully. "When you come right down to it, I don't really think I was the one who talked him into it."

Sara stared at her. "What are you talking about?"

"Oh, I tried all right. I tried very hard, because you were so miserable and I couldn't stand seeing you that way. But when I left him that morning, he was still totally unconvinced. At least, that was the way he seemed to me."

Sara shrugged. "Then what do you think sent him over the edge?" she asked.

Jill thought for a moment. "You know what? I think it was his friend, that Starman fellow. I saw him pulling up just as I was leaving the house that morning. I'd done all I could and I thought I'd failed." She shrugged again. "I left in deep depression, thinking all was lost. Two hours later, Jake was at our house asking you to marry him." Her eyes narrowed and she pressed her lips together as she thought about it. "Starman must have said something that convinced him."

Sara frowned as well. That seemed odd. She would ask Jake about it someday. Right now, she didn't want to risk upsetting any apple carts, so she wasn't going to ask questions about anything. Once they were married and it was a done deal, then she would get creative and curious. But until then, she was treading carefully.

But what did it matter? They *were* getting married.

Savannah was going to have a mother and a father. Whatever happened between her and Jake as a result— well, that was still to come, and they would deal with it as it happened. For now, she was a happy woman.

The wedding was on the beach in front of Sara's newly renovated house. And, incidentally, in front of the house Jake was renting. Very convenient. The ceremony was small and private. Jake had a small group of friends, mostly Army buddies that Sara had seen hanging out at his house—including Starman as his best man. Jill and Connor brought the twins and took care of Savannah. Luckily they had a family preacher they could contribute to the mix, and he turned out to be wonderful. Sara had invited a few of her friends from the magazine she'd worked for over the years. That was it. A small but elegant family wedding.

It was a beautiful morning. The sun was shining on the ocean and the blue of the water contrasted to the blue of a sky filled with white, puffy clouds. Sara felt like she was walking on air.

Jill had married Connor just months before and she'd loaned Sara her wedding dress. It was white and lacy and quite traditional. The bodice was form-fitting and encrusted with seed pearls, as was the edging on the veil. She carried purple irises and felt like a queen.

Jake had balked, but in the end, he'd agreed to wear a tuxedo. He was looking very handsome. But was he as thrilled as she was? Probably not. Still, she couldn't hold back her joy. She felt like one lucky girl.

Jill had baked the most gorgeous wedding cake she'd ever seen, and after the ceremony, their visitors did their best to eat it all as they stood around and chatted and congratulated the happy couple. She and Jake didn't seem to have any appetite. He kept looking at her and smiling as if they shared some secret joke on everybody else. She couldn't help but laugh. She was so happy.

Starman made a toast to their happiness and she could have sworn he had tears in his eyes. Jill had hired a string quartet who played lovely music during the ceremony and then more modern tunes during the reception, as they ate Jill's cake and laughed a lot. They kicked off their shoes and danced in the sand, with all their friends cheering them on.

A lovely day, simple and elegant. A day to remember, for the rest of their lives.

And then they were alone.

They'd decided to live in Sara's house. It was finished and beautifully decorated—just right to begin a new life in. Jill and Connor had taken Savannah with them for the rest of the day, so that Sara and Jake could settle in and get comfortable before they had to deal with a baby.

They explored the house and she showed off her favorite elements, like the reading nook in the stairway landing, and the glass-enclosed breakfast room that could have served as a greenhouse.

"This is really a nice place," he told her. "I'm beginning to feel downright civilized for the first time in my life."

She smiled at him. "I love this house," she admitted. "And now I'm going to love it even more with you in it."

He turned to look at her, startled, and she flushed, wondering if she'd said too much. There was a frisson of excitement between them. Every nerve she owned seemed to be sizzling. They were married now. What next?

She led the way back downstairs to the kitchen and she began a cheerful line of chatter while she cut them both pieces of their wedding cake and they sat down at her little counter to eat them.

What next?

The question was in the air and in her head. She was talking a mile a minute, but that wasn't helping. What next?

"So this is where we're going to live," he murmured, looking around approvingly. "I've gotta say, I like it. And it seems to be perfect for Savannah."

Sara nodded. "Renovated for her, custom-made." She glanced at him. "What do you foresee doing with your days?" she asked, suddenly wondering why they hadn't explored this topic before. It seemed pretty basic. "Just exactly what are you planning to do?"

He gazed at her levelly. "About what?"

She shrugged. "About earning a living." She'd never imagined that he might plan to just hang around the house. To her, that didn't seem like a proper man's position. Besides, they were going to need the money a job would bring.

"You want me to get a job?" He raised a dark eyebrow and looked at her cynically. "Is that it?"

She lifted her chin, not sure how he was going to react to her answer. "Yes. I think it would be a good thing."

He stared at her for a moment, and she began to get nervous. Then he laughed. "Oh, Sara, you're so conventional."

She smiled in relief. At least he found it funny, not offensive. "Exactly. The old ways are usually the best. Don't you think so?"

He pulled her off her bar stool and into his lap. He held her close and kissed the top of her head.

"Yes. I do think so. And a couple of my buddies and I are planning to start working on a small security firm. We want to emphasize research and development, working on new technology for keeping people safe. I learned to use a lot of technology in the Rangers and I think we can improve on some of the methods and equipment we had available. I'm really excited about our chances."

Well, there it was. Nothing to worry about. He had plans.

"Great. You're planning it for here in Seattle?"

He nodded. "Probably. We may start it out right here in the kitchen and then look for a headquarters in the city once we get going."

"Wow. That's really interesting. I'll help all I can."

He looked at her, considering. "You can work on ad copy when the time comes. You're experienced on that, aren't you?"

She nodded. "I've done PR work and marketing and

any kind of writing associated with magazine work. But I meant with start-up money. I've got some saved."

"No." He shook his head. "I would never ask you to risk your savings for my start-up. Besides, I've got my own stash. My father left me some, remember?"

"Oh, that's right. Good." She grinned at him. "Do a good job and we'll all be Seattle millionaires."

He kissed her neck. "You've got it." Gently he set her down and rose from his stool.

"So, shall we discuss the bed situation?" he said, gazing down at her.

Her breath caught in her throat. Now? Right here? She wasn't ready!

"I think I ought to take the guest bedroom for now," he went on. "What do you think?"

"Oh." Did her disappointment show on her face? She hoped not. "That's very considerate of you."

"This is a marriage of convenience, isn't it?" he asked her softly. "I mean, we didn't marry for love. We married to take care of someone we both love. That's different. Isn't it?"

She felt all the blood drain from her face. "Yes. I suppose so."

"So I think we ought to have separate bedrooms. At least for a while." He shrugged casually and didn't seem all that interested. "I mean, things may change."

"Of course. You're right."

She flushed and turned to hide it. It was for the best, of course. As he said, they hadn't married for love. There was no reason to hurry a physical connection.

If he didn't think the time was right, he was probably
on the right track. He was obviously much more experienced in these things than she was. She could wait—
wait in her cold, lonely bed. Would he ever want to
share it with her?

Maybe, someday. As he said, things may change.

But there was a cold, hollow feeling around her heart
that night.

Jake had been afraid he would be restless and uneasy
with another person living in his house. He didn't mean
Savannah, of course. But he did mean Sara. He was used
to having a buddy or two flopping in his place at vari-
ous times, but having a woman who actually lived with
him—no, that wasn't in his repertoire of experiences.

To his surprise, he adjusted very quickly. She enjoyed fixing him meals and that came as a sort of gift
he hadn't expected. She kept things picked up, which
he'd never quite gotten the knack of. And she wasn't one
of the chatty types who talked your ear off. She was as
quiet as he was most of the time. All in all, he enjoyed
having her around.

He watched her feeding Savannah. The joy in her
face, Savannah's happy laugh, the sunshine coming in
through the breakfast room windows, all contributed
to his feeling of happiness and well-being. He didn't
deserve to be this happy. He still had promises to keep.

He'd done the right thing—hadn't he? He thought
he had. He couldn't have left his child behind, and he

needed someone to help take care of her better than he could ever do. So he'd enlisted Sara in the endeavor. Was that fair to her? Maybe not. But so far, it was working out fine.

Still, he wasn't totally sure he'd done the right thing. Was it right to marry Sara, to tie her up in this relationship? Would he have felt as close to any other woman he'd involved in it this way? She seemed so perfect for this role and she shared his joy in Savannah day by day in ways probably no one else could. For now, it seemed all was right with the world.

But there was going to be a big test of that sense of calm coming up soon and he didn't feel he ought to do anything to bring the two of them closer until then. He couldn't completely commit to this relationship until he saw how that came out.

When Sara realized he was going back to the jungle to take care of unfinished business, the truth would be plain for all to see. Could she handle it? Only time would tell.

He had to go. He was going with his mates. There was a job they had to take care of. They'd left too many people behind. The bastards who had treated them so badly had to pay, and they had to make sure that could never happen again in that place. He owed it to his buddies, he owed it to himself. He owed it to the world. That hellhole in the jungle had to be purged.

And once that was done, if he came back alive, they would see where things stood.

* * *

Days fell into a pattern of mundane happiness. Sara cared for Savannah, which was her greatest joy, and she took care of Jake, which was getting to be a sweeter task every time she performed some little service for him. She was beginning to understand how doing things for other people could be a precious gift—as long as it was appreciated.

She took Savannah to put her toes in the ocean at least once a day. She took her to the playground. She took her along when she went grocery shopping in the little island market that she loved. She signed up for a "Mommy and Me" swimming class at the local Y and spent time finding just the right outfits to make Savannah the cutest baby on the island. She spent a lot of time cooking up special baby food versions of meals for her child.

But best of all, she shared every minute she could with Jake. No one else in the world could understand how special their baby was. Only Jake. And he joined right in. It was wonderful.

Sharing with Jill and Connor had been fun, but that had nothing on the deep, abiding joy sharing with Jake had for them both. This was what a family ought to feel like. This was as close to heaven as real life could get.

The only problem that nagged at her was the question—how long was Jake going to deny that the two of them should be a total and complete unit as well?

She was afraid there was an answer to that—and not one she was going to like. The truth was out there if she only let herself face it. He didn't love her. And he didn't want to raise her expectation that someday he might.

She had to admit he was generous with kisses, as long as they were simple and affectionate. His hugs were warm and welcoming. But they hadn't had a repeat of the burning encounter they'd had out at the Point that night before he asked her to marry him. Hopes were dimming that real married life was in the cards for them and she wasn't really sure what she could do about it.

So her nights were still empty, though she couldn't really complain. Her days were warm enough to make up for it. And her husband was always there for her in every other way. Maybe that would be enough.

She was getting to know his friends better all the time and she liked them more and more. Starman had a way of showing up just when she needed help to carry in groceries or start the barbecue. She knew Jake felt very close to him.

"I'd say he's my best friend," Jake agreed. "We've been through a lot together. We've saved each other's neck a few times, and we'll probably do it a few times more."

That gave her a chill, but she didn't question it.

One day, about a month after the wedding, she was trying to dig into soil that was hard as a rock in order to prepare for planting a rosebush. Starman showed up and did it for her, giving her a large, perfectly round hole that would leave lots of room for planting mix.

"Thank you so much," she told him. "I was going

to ask Jake to dig it for me when he got back from his morning run, but now I won't have to bother him."

Starman put down the shovel and looked at her earnestly. "Sara, I just want to thank you for what you're doing."

"Really?" She smiled at him. "What am I doing?"

"You're really helping us out here. You marrying Jake is going to make all the difference. I know it had to do with the kid and everything, but now he'll be able to relax about that. He's just whacko about that kid."

"Oh, I know. We both are."

"Sure. She's a great kid. But the point is, now that you're someone he can trust to take care of her, he's starting to think straight again. So I just wanted to thank you for that."

He turned to go but she stopped him.

"Wait, Starman. I'm not sure I understand. What was Jake worried about?"

"Who would take care of the kid." He stepped back closer and spoke confidentially. "He was saying he couldn't leave little Savannah alone while we went on missions. But now he's got you to take care of that. He was turning us down, telling us he had new responsibilities and such. We told him we couldn't imagine going without him. And we got him back in gear." He winked at her. "He told me the other day that he'll be coming along." He grinned. "So all is right with the world. Because of you."

He gave her a crisp salute and headed out. She stood

staring after him, trying to make sense of what he'd said and very much afraid she understood it only too well.

That night was the first night she heard Jake cry out in the dark. It wasn't a scream exactly. More of an angry yell. It sounded like swearing, only she couldn't make out the words. When she went in and woke him, he seemed angry about it, and in the morning, he didn't want to talk about what had happened. The whole thing left her more worried than she'd been since the day they'd decided to get married. How could she help him if he wouldn't let her in?

CHAPTER TEN

WAS JAKE PREPARING to go on a mission to Southeast Asia? Was he planning to attack the prison camp where he and his friends were once held? It made Sara sick to think of, but she was afraid he was actually doing exactly that.

What were the chances that he would come back alive? How could he even contemplate doing something so dangerous? Leaving behind Savannah—leaving behind the life they'd begun to build together? It was unthinkable.

She didn't care what the other men did. If they felt they had to go back to the prison camp, maybe to get revenge for the way those guards had hurt them, fine. Let them go. But they didn't have wives and children to think of. Jake did. How could she convince him that this was just wrong?

He'd grown up, as he always said, uncivilized. And this wild sort of living had been his existence for much too long. So maybe he didn't understand that there was a point where a man had to give up the excitement of revenge and fighting.

It was one thing to be a military man, trained and protected by a system. It was another to go off into the jungle with a bunch of guys you palled around with and hope to get the chance to succeed at destroying a prison camp on your own. It was crazy. That much she understood. But did he?

He'd never told her all about what had happened in that Pacific jungle when he was an Army Ranger. She'd seen his naked back up close and personal, studied the scars, even traced one with her finger the day before when they were at the beach and he was lying on his stomach in the sand. Savannah was playing with sand toys and Sara was watching her but paying just as much attention to the man beside her.

"What happened?" she asked him at the time. "Who did this?"

He turned to her. "You don't really want to know," he said dismissively. "It's not a pretty story." Looking beyond her, he said, "Hey, look at Savannah. She pulled herself up beside the beach chair. That girl is going to take off walking any day now."

Sara swelled with pride for her baby like she always did. "Oh, she's too young for that," she said.

"Are you kidding? Look at her. She wants to run!"

"You should have seen the twins. They were both running at ten months." She laughed. "I was told I was fifteen months before I would trust my legs to carry me. I took my time." She smiled at him. "How about you?"

He shrugged with a sort of studied disinterest. "I

didn't have much of a mother. Nobody ever told me stuff like that about my baby days."

Her smile faded and she looked away. "No baby book, huh?" she noted.

He shook his head and she realized he'd turned the conversation away from those scars on his back once again. But now she had to know. It was time he filled her in on the background.

That night she was determined to get to the bottom of it all.

"All right," she said after the sun had gone down and Savannah had fallen asleep for the night. "Savannah is down, we've had dinner and cleaned up, there's nothing either of us want to watch on TV—it's time for you to open up and tell me a few things I need to know." She pinned him with her steady gaze. "You are going to talk."

"Oh, yeah?" He couldn't help but smile at her, she looked so cute and serious. "What do you want me to talk about?"

"Tell me about what you were doing in the Pacific area for the last couple of years. I know you were an Army Ranger and that you spent some time in a prison camp in the jungle, and I know you've been discharged recently. But what was it you did back then? And why do you have those scars on your back?"

He looked away for a moment, then made a face. "Okay. I guess it is time." He sank down onto the couch and she sat at the other end. "You're right about me being an Army Ranger. We had a special mission in our unit. We rescued people."

"From what?" she asked in all innocence.

He took a deep breath, searching her face before he told her. "From being kidnapped and tortured by the bad guys."

"Oh." She recoiled. Maybe she really didn't want to know all the details.

"I've been working rescue operations for years. I got pretty damn good at it, too. I rarely got hurt or caught or in any sort of trouble. Until this last time."

"You mean, after you knew Kelly?"

He nodded. "We managed to negotiate a couple of good situations in the Philippines. Then we were sent to a trouble spot in Southeast Asia. A pair of missionaries had been captured by rebels. No one knew where they'd been taken. We spent weeks tracking down their location. We were undercover, pretending to be hippies looking to commune with nature and do drugs."

"What?" She had a hard time seeing him that way.

He threw a half smile her way. "We were pretending, Sara. Trying to blend into the countryside. We made friends with the more primitive people of the area and finally we got a fix on the location we were looking for. It was in the jungle and we executed a beautiful text-book-ready operation. But when we finally got to the site where the missionaries were being held…"

He hesitated, then shrugged and went ahead and told her the truth. "We found nothing but bodies. They were already dead. And left as bait for us." He sighed. "At that point, we were so upset when we saw what had been done to those good people—a man and a woman whose only goal was to help others—we got careless and screwed up and ended up getting captured by the militia of the local strong man who didn't like foreigners coming in. He immediately threw us into his prison camp and tried to get ransom for us."

"Wow." She could hardly breathe. He was sitting here so calmly, telling her things that should only be in movies. No real human beings should have to go through these things. Her heart broke for them all.

"They held us for a few months. They didn't feed us much, but most of the time, they weren't exactly cruel. Just not very nice. But the first time a few of us tried to escape—me and Starman, among them—they caught us and then the really ugly stuff began."

"Is that when you got those scars on your back?" she asked him, wincing as she thought of it.

"Yeah. Starman has the same. They thrashed us the old-fashioned way. They wanted to make sure we didn't do that again."

She shook her head. She didn't want to think about it. It made her sick. "But you did do it again, didn't you?"

He grinned. "Of course we did. That's how stubborn we are. We bided our time and saw another chance and escaped. This time we made it to a city and got help." He moved as though his back was bothering him. "But the punishment lives on," he murmured softly.

"They do look…horrible. Those scars, I mean. I'm

surprised you lived through that." She felt nauseous thinking about it.

"I'm kind of surprised, too. And actually, Punky, a friend of ours, didn't. His back got infected and he died."

He said it so simply, as though it was a common thing. Could have happened to anyone. She had to catch her breath to speak. "I'm so sorry."

"Yeah. Well, that's the breaks. Other guys were there, guys who didn't get away. People we had to leave behind." He grimaced. "They need to be rescued," he said softly.

She bit her lip. She didn't want to hear that.

"See, that's what I have to get you to understand," he said, looking at her with his luminous eyes. "That's what we do. We rescue people."

She stared at him. "But you're not in the service any longer."

He nodded. "I took a discharge. I thought I wanted to move on." He shook his head. "But the faces haunt me, Sara. All those people. They need to be helped. Somebody's got to save them."

Emotion welled in her chest. "Not you."

He turned away and didn't say a word. She moved closer to him on the couch.

"Your friends are planning a trip back there, aren't they?" she said.

He nodded, still looking away.

"Are you going with them?" she asked in a strangled voice.

He winced and ran fingers through his thick hair.

"Wow. Listen, I've been meaning to talk to you about that." He looked at her. "I won't be gone long."

Her heart seemed to stop. What was he talking about? He couldn't predict the future. If he went, he might be gone forever. That was impossible. It couldn't happen. She felt a sense of hysteria rising in her throat.

"You know very well you might get killed. Just when Savannah has her father back, you want to take him away again? Are you crazy?"

His face was tortured. "Look, I love Savannah. She's my life. But there are other things in my life, other responsibilities. There's old business that has to be cleared up."

She felt a sense of despair. What could she do to prove to him how wrong this was? "Then take us with you," she demanded.

"What?" He stared at her. "Now you're the one who's sounding crazy."

"We're a family unit. We go where you go. If you need to go so badly, take us with you." She glared at him, daring him to answer.

He shook his head slowly. "You don't have a clue what you're asking. The place where we're going is hell on earth. I wouldn't let you or Savannah within a hundred miles of the place. It can't happen."

"If it's really so bad, you shouldn't go, either!" she cried.

He stared at her, hard. "I have to go. It's my responsibility. I owe too many people to turn back now."

His tone was final and she knew going on with this

train of thought was only going to make them both too angry to be rational. She took a deep breath and forced back all the things she wanted to say.

"When are you going?" she said as calmly as she could.

"Monday." He glanced at her and then away. "We'll fly out of Seattle to the Philippines and go down from there."

Her heart was breaking. "How long will you be gone?"

"Not too long. Two weeks at the most."

"Or forever."

He turned to look at her. "Sara…" Reaching out, he grabbed her hand and held it tightly, as though he might be able to convince her by touch.

"What makes you think you can succeed?" she asked him fiercely. She pulled his hand up to press it to her cheek, looking at him with all her agony plain to see in her eyes. "Why can't you just notify the authorities in that place? Why can't someone in an official capacity take care of it?"

He appeared pained. "See, Sara, you don't understand how things work in places like that. There is no official authority taking care of civil rules and regulations. Everyone's being paid off by someone. The only rule is the rule of gold. Rich people get their way, the others scrabble to stay alive. Regular Joes don't have a chance."

"But then why…?"

"Unless they get together and form a unit, like the guys and I are planning to do."

She shook her head. Tears flooded her eyes. "Jake, you said it felt like you'd stepped into civilized behavior by moving in here. Can't you understand that part of civilized behavior is having an authority force that can keep the order and make sure bad things don't happen? When people take the law into their own hands, society falls apart."

He nodded solemnly. "I hear your words and I understand what you're saying. I even agree with what you're saying." His gaze rose to meet hers. "But then I come back to what my heart tells me to do, and my heart says, go." He shrugged as though he knew there was no way he could make her understand.

"These are my friends, my fellow soldiers, and I owe them my allegiance. Some of my buddies are still in that prison camp. We can't leave them there. We have to rescue them."

She took a shuddering breath and dropped his hand, pulling away. "If you go, if you do this thing, I'll never forgive you."

He watched her. He saw the fire in her eyes and he knew the threat behind it. A dark, burning anger simmered in him that she would be thinking that way, but he knew that she was—and he thought he had some idea why. After all, marrying him hadn't been her first choice.

He knew what he was risking. He'd wondered about it ever since he'd heard about the three-month grace period during which Sara could file a complaint against him. She'd wanted Savannah all for herself from the beginning. If she could get Savannah without him attached, she would probably like it better that way, even now.

"What are you going to do, Sara? File a grievance with the agency? File a lawsuit to get me disqualified?"

She stared at him, stung that he would think such a thing, but she didn't answer.

Suddenly his eyes filled with fury. "So that's it. You've been hoping for something like this, haven't you?" He rose and started to leave the room. "Well, here you go. Have at it. See you in court." And he was gone.

Sara sat in shock. How had it come to this? How could he think that she was just waiting for an excuse to catch him out? Didn't he understand how she felt about him?

Obviously not.

He barely looked at her the next day and didn't speak to her at all. She was in misery, but she didn't know how to approach him. She couldn't weaken on the trip. She couldn't give him her permission to go. And yet, what did she have if he left this way? She had to find a way to talk him out of it.

She found out where Starman was staying. Leaving Savannah with Jill, she took the ferry to the mainland and found the rented room, knocking on the door. A very surprised and startled Starman opened it to her, and she surprised him even more by insisting she wanted to come in.

"I have to talk to you," she told him. "I know about the mission you guys are planning to the prison camp."

Starman scowled. "Jake shouldn't have told you about that."

"You're the one who gave me the alert," she noted. "And I've talked to Jake. And now I want to ask a favor of you. Please, please convince him that he can't go."

He looked shocked at the thought. "But, Sara, he's our best man. Without him, the entire mission will fail."

"No, it won't." She wished she knew how to be more persuasive. "You can keep it on an even keel. You've been his right hand man all along. You can do it."

Starman thought for a minute, then nodded. "You're right," he said. "I can do it. But do I want to do it without Jake?"

"I don't know. Do you?"

"No." He scowled at her. "No, I don't." He glared at her for a moment, then added grudgingly, "But I will."

She nodded, smiling in relief. "Good. Because, Starman, you know he's done it before. He's done his part. He's never shirked, has he? It's just that his circumstances have changed. He can't go do this sort of thing anymore."

Starman didn't look happy about it. "I guess you're right."

"Yes. Now here's the hard part. You have to talk him out of going."

He frowned, shaking his head. "But I just talked him *into* going."

She shrugged, tugging nervously on the buttons of her sweater, one after another. "Tell him you've changed your mind."

He looked confused. "But I haven't."

"No. But I have. I don't want him to go."

"Oh. Right."

"He's got a baby now. He's got me. He can't act like a footloose adventurer. He needs to be here, building a life, building a business, finding ways to make this all work. The prison camp should be in his past, not his future. Can't you explain that to him?"

"Sure." He straightened his shoulders and looked tough. "I can do that." He wavered for a moment. "Doesn't mean he'll listen."

"I know. But you can try."

He nodded, looking emotional. "You know I'd do just about anything for you and that little girl. Okay. I'll try."

And he did.

But it didn't do any good. Jake came to her right away to tell her that Starman had failed.

"Listen, Sara," he said, holding her hand. He didn't want to get into a fight if he could help it. "I know you mean well, but you can't get to me through my friends. It won't work."

She shrugged, searching his beautiful face, wishing she knew the right words. "I had to try," she said softly. "Oh, Jake, I'm so scared."

He looked at her in surprise. Her eyes were huge and filling with tears. He wanted to pull her close, but he hesitated.

"I wish I could make you understand," he said. "It's a matter of honor. It's a matter of loyalty and camaraderie. They need me. I'm there for them if I possibly can be. I owe them that. We've got to go. We've all got to go. We've got to make those bastards pay for what they did to us and rescue those we left behind."

She shook her head, tears coming fast. "I think I do understand. Being a rescuer is part of who you are, and you don't want to lose that part of your identity. But, Jake—you have a new role now. You're a father. And for the next few years, that has to come first."

She was right, and yet... He couldn't do it. He couldn't turn his back on his friends. He reached down to kiss her and her arms came around his neck, pulling tightly.

A shiver went through him. He realized that he was risking more than losing Savannah. He was risking losing Sara, too, and that was becoming more and more important to him. For just a moment, he wavered.

But Jake left on Monday, just as he'd planned. She was still totally against it and she didn't let up, but she kissed him goodbye and wished him luck, and then stood with Savannah in her arms as he drove off toward the ferry. He looked back and saw her and everything in him wanted to turn around and go back. But he couldn't do that.

Sara went on, living the next few days just the way she had been doing for the last two months. But she felt like a robot. No emotion. No joy. Everything she did was under a cloud of doom. She was sure something terrible was going to happen.

Mrs. Truesdale called to check on how things were

going and Sara tried to put on a calm front. Unfortunately the woman saw right through it.

"All right, Sara. Tell me what's happened. I can tell there's a problem. Let me help."

There was no way Sara was going to tell her where Jake was or what he was doing, but she couldn't hide the unhappiness, no matter how cheerful she tried to appear.

Mrs. Truesdale could smell out dissension in the ranks. "My dear, whatever it is you're going through, believe me, I'm on your side. We've been through a lot together in getting this situation squared away, and I was so sorry things seemed to be ruined when Jake appeared out of nowhere. I made sure you two had the grace period in your contract, just in case. And if you find that you need to exercise that clause, you call me right away. I'll do all I can for you."

"Oh, but there's really nothing wrong…."

"Just remember, you have a duty to that little girl. You are the gatekeeper for her future welfare. If you feel something is going awry, you must take action."

Sara hung up the phone feeling worse than before she'd talked to the woman. Jake had accused her of wanting to use the grace period clause when he'd been angry with her, but she'd never even imagined doing such a thing. No. Jake was Savannah's father. She couldn't take that away from her—or him. Jake was who he was, and no matter how angry she got with him, she would never betray him. Didn't he know that?

She packed Savannah up and headed for Jill's house, hoping to get some reassurance and moral support, but

Jill was in a frenzy over a last minute order for her Bundt cakes and Sara kept her misery to herself. Jill had enough to contend with.

She took her baby home and watched her play as she fixed her dinner. She watched the international news, in case there was anything on about the Pacific area, but nothing out of the ordinary seemed to be happening. She turned off the TV and started to gather the plates. For just a second, she happened to look up, and there was Savannah, taking her first step.

She clamped her hands over her mouth to stop the scream that wanted to alert the world, and then she laughed and ran to her girl, helping her back up when she fell, and coaxing her to do it again.

"Wow," she said. "Barely more than ten months and a half and you're walking! If only…" Her voice choked and tears filled her eyes. Jake should have been there to see this. How could he miss a milestone like this? It wasn't right.

Suddenly she was angry. Her tears melted away. What good were they, anyway? This was all Jake's doing and he was paying the price.

But so was Savannah! It wasn't fair. Her daddy ought to be there for her special achievements. It made her so angry that he'd voluntarily walked out on that.

She put Savannah down for the night and then went out to sit in the living room. She left the lamp off so she could see the lights across the bay. Should she consider doing what Mrs. Truesdale obviously thought she should—file a complaint against Jake? Did Savannah deserve it? Did Jake?

She wasn't sure. She didn't want to. But if he was off doing what he felt was his duty, maybe she ought to be doing the same. She looked at her phone and tried to decide. She knew she could call Mrs. Truesdale's number and get her answering machine. All it would take was a couple of words, and the gears would begin to grind.

Was she really that angry with Jake?

She closed her eyes. She couldn't do it. With a sigh, she got up and went to bed.

It must have been about three in the morning when she woke up and realized there was a man in her room. She wanted to scream but he was already sliding onto the bed to sit beside her. Leaning down, he whispered in her ear.

"It's me, Sara. It's Jake."

She gasped, trying to shake the cobwebs from her sleepy brain. "What?" she said, then lowered her voice, thinking of Savannah. "Jake! How did you get here?"

"I flew into Seattle a few hours ago. I didn't want to call and wake you up."

"Jake…" She reached for him. "Oh, Jake. You're safe. You're back." Clinging to him, she burst into sobs.

He held her, but his voice was full of surprise. "Sara, what's the matter? Are you okay?"

She sobbed harder, rocking the bed with it.

"Why are you crying? There isn't anything wrong with Savannah, is there?"

She shook her head. Finally she managed to get a word out.

"Oh, Jake, you didn't die."

He thought about that for a few seconds, then asked, incredulous, "Do you really care that much?"

She only pressed against him harder, her face buried in his chest, her fingers clutching at his muscular arms. He was back. Those words kept echoing in her head. He was back. He wasn't out in a jungle waiting to be killed. The relief she felt proved how utterly shell-shocked she'd been by his going.

He stroked her hair and murmured sweet words and finally she pulled back, hiccupped and sniffed deeply. "You jerk!" she cried at him. "You claim to know all about the nuances of women's emotions. Hah!"

He looked bewildered. "When did I ever claim that?"

"Numerous times." She sniffed again, feeling around for a handkerchief. He provided one. "If you're so good at it, how come you can't even tell if your own wife loves you? Huh?"

He drew back, astonished. "Seriously?"

"You!" She threw a pillow at him. "Yes, seriously. I completely love you and you…you…"

"Wow." He stared at her in wonder. "Who knew?"

"Anyone with half a brain," she muttered, using the handkerchief and handing it back. Then she stared at him in the darkness. "Is it over? Did you do what you went to do?"

He pulled her back into his arms. "No. I only made

it as far as Hawaii. We met there and I decided to come home."

Home. It had a good sound. So he considered this place home, did he? She felt a glow beginning in her heart.

"And the others?"

"They went on. They're prepared and well-equipped. And I decided I had more important things to do at home."

That word again! It was like gold to her.

"I talked to Starman. He set me straight. Sort of slapped me around and told me to wake up." He grinned. "Figuratively speaking, of course."

"Of course."

"I've been on these missions before. I'm usually one of the ones saying we've got to do it. But there was something missing. I began to realize it wasn't fair to you, or to Savannah. And that was when I decided I could use money instead of flesh and blood. The more money they have, the less chance something will go horribly wrong."

"Oh." She tried to understand, but her mind was fuzzy. She only knew that he was here with her and not over there and that was all that mattered right now.

"Well, nowadays, I've got money," he reminded her. "I can do my part that way, funding the guys and making sure they have all the supplies they need. Giving them a little bribe money to grease a few palms and make sure they don't get held up for ransom. Things like that."

"A financial backer," she said sleepily. "A philanthropist."

"Maybe. I was torn, Sara. But now I'm not. I know what is most important to me. It's you, you and Savannah. It's home. That's where I have to be."

She sighed with happiness, stretching next to him. He kissed her mouth and she sighed again.

"I love you, Sara," he said, his voice husky with emotion. "I realized that while I was in Hawaii, missing you and your warm smile. I love you like I never thought I could love a woman. You taught me how."

"I feel the same way," she said with a sigh. "I was never going to love a man, and then there was you."

His kiss was deep and hot and had all the sparkle she would ever need.

"How's Savannah?" he asked her, pulling back to look at her in the golden lamplight. "I stopped in and looked at her on my way here. She was sleeping like a rock."

She smiled, then giggled as she remembered their baby taking her first steps. "She's fine. She's going to have a surprise for you in the morning."

"Is she?" There was a smile in his voice, too. "I can hardly wait."

"Me, too." She turned to face him. His hand slipped beneath the straps on her nightgown. "How about you, Sara?" he asked softly. "Do you have a surprise for me?"

Her pulse began a wild race through her entire system. She caught her breath at his touch. "Yes, Jake. Yes, I do."

She reached up to kiss him again, but only for a moment. He began to unbutton his shirt and pull it off, then went to his belt.

"Are you inviting me into your bed?" he asked her softly.

"I'm inviting you into *our* bed."

"That is an offer I would be a fool to refuse," he said as he came to her.

She laughed and turned in his arms, letting him pull her nightgown off and then pressing herself against his naked body. She'd never felt anything more exciting. Her breasts against his hard, rounded muscles, her skin against his smoothness, his mouth on hers—this was what she'd been waiting for ever since their wedding. She lost herself in his heat and closed her eyes, living for the moment.

He was home.

* * * * *

SINGLE MUM SEEKS...

BY
TERESA HILL

Teresa Hill lives within sight of the mountains in upstate South Carolina with one husband, very understanding and supportive; one daughter, who's taken up drumming (Earplugs really don't work that well. Neither do sound-muffling drum pads. Don't believe anyone who says they do.); and one son, who's studying the completely incomprehensible subject of chemical engineering. (Flow rates, Mum. It's all about flow rates.)

In search of company while she writes away her days in her office, she has so far accumulated two beautiful, spoiled dogs and three cats (the black panther/champion hunter, the giant powder puff and the tiny tiger stripe), all of whom take turns being stretched out, belly-up on the floor beside her, begging for attention as she sits at her computer.

To all mothers who've survived raising teenagers.
You have my complete admiration.

Chapter One

"I just don't see what all the fuss is about," Lily Tanner told her older sister, Marcy, as she scrambled to hold the phone to her ear with her shoulder while making sandwiches for her two girls' school lunches.

"Fuss?" Her sister seemed disbelieving. "That's what you call it? Fuss?"

"No, I don't call it fuss," Lily said, smearing peanut butter on the bread too fast and tearing a gash in the last slice she had, save for the heels. Her girls acted like she was trying to feed them some kind of brick when she had nothing but the heels of a loaf of bread to offer.

"Who's fussing?" her youngest, Brittany, who was six, asked.

"No one's fussing," Lily assured her, as her daughter moved like a sloth through the kitchen, slowly sipping a cup of milk, like she had all the time in the world before Tuesday's designated carpool driver arrived.

"And no one's getting any fuss," Marcy told her. "Which is

fine for a while and completely understandable, given what that rat Richard put you through. But after a while, a woman's just got to have a little fussing."

"Oh, for God's sake, I am not going to call it fussing," Lily said, trying to salvage the torn slice of bread. Anything but the heel. She wasn't taking lip from her daughters today about a heel of bread in a peanut butter sandwich.

"You said nobody was fussing," Brittany reminded her.

"Fussing? Who's fussing?" her oldest, Ginny, asked, looking worried, as she too often did these days. "Is it Daddy? Are you and Daddy fussing?"

"No. I told you. No one's fussing," Lily promised, rolling her eyes in exasperation. "Your aunt Marcy and I were just talking, and we weren't actually talking about fussing at all. We were talking about—"

"Yes, please. I can't wait to hear," Marcy said, laughing. "Tell me what we were talking about."

"Fudge," Lily said, thinking it was the farthest thing from fussing she could come up with on short notice.

Marcy roared at that.

Lily shoved sandwiches into lunch boxes as Ginny looked like she didn't quite believe her own mother.

Then Brittany piped up and saved the day, announcing with absolute sincerity, an unwavering sense of optimism and six-year-old innocence, "I like fudge."

"There," Lily said, managing a smile for her girls. "Everybody likes fudge."

"Everybody certainly does," Marcy said. "So for you to tell me that you're perfectly fine without—"

"Marcy!" she yelled into the phone while she shooed the girls toward the front door.

"Wait," Brittany said, stopping short and tugging on the right leg of Lily's shorts. "Do we have fudge?"

"No, baby. Not right now. But maybe tonight," Lily said.

"Here. I've got the front door. You two have to get outside. Mrs. Hamilton will be here any minute."

She hustled the girls out the door, waved to Betsy Hamilton, who was already at the curb, then closed the door and turned her attention back to the phone.

"Honestly, Marcy! Fudge?"

"Hey, it was your word, not mine. But now that you've coined the term, we're stuck with it. It's perfect. It'll be our code word forever."

"We don't need a code word. We don't need to talk about it at all. I am perfectly fine," Lily insisted.

After all, it was just…fudge. Nothing to get all that excited about. Not when she had fifteen things to do every minute of the day and the girls ran her ragged and Richard was still as annoying as could be.

Who had time for fudge?

"May I remind you," Lily said, "that I have a year to get out of this house? Not even that, anymore. Just a little over ten and a half months to do everything I can to upgrade it before I have to sell it and hope I get enough out of my half to get me and the girls into another house. Which is going to take every bit of time and energy I have for the next ten and a half months."

"I know. I know."

"And where am I supposed to find a man anyway? You know what it's like in my neighborhood. Everybody's married, with kids the girls' ages, and if they do happen to get divorced, the wife ends up here in the subdivision with the kids while the cheating husband moves out to some little love nest of an apartment with his new, pretty, young thing. Until the wife has to sell out for lack of money and then some new married couple moves in. These are the suburbs, in all their glory. I could easily go a month without seeing a single, eligible man, and then even if one did show up, I don't have time to date anybody. I hardly have time to drink my coffee."

She gave a big huff at the end of her little speech, tired and spent.

Did her sister know nothing of Lily's current life? Of her world?

It was maddening and annoying and more than a little sad to feel so alone and to be living in such aggravating circumstances, just because Richard met a girl barely out of her teens on a business trip to Baltimore.

"Oh, honey. I'm sorry," Marcy said, and Lily could hear Marcy's own kids in the background now. "I wasn't trying to make things harder for you. I was just trying to warn you that it's fine to go without…fudge for a while, and then…well, then it's not. I mean, you're still human, and you're only thirty-four years old. We all have needs. We all get lonely."

"I am not lonely," Lily insisted, clearing the table of half-eaten bowls of cereal and bread crumbs from the peanut butter sandwiches and half-empty glasses that seemed to multiply like rabbits all over the house when Lily's back was turned. "At least not for…fudge. Now, a bubble bath, I could handle. Someone to cook dinner every now and then or a good book, plus enough time to read it without interruptions—that I could handle. But fudge is—"

Lily broke off as she straightened up, having put four cups in the dishwasher and found herself looking out the window above the sink, which faced the house next door, which had been empty for weeks.

It looked like it wasn't going to be empty anymore, because in the driveway was a moving truck backed up to the garage, the big back door of the truck open, a pair of sun-bronzed, muscular arms handing a table out of the back of the truck to someone Lily couldn't quite see because of an overgrown rhododendron bush.

"What?" Marcy asked. "Where did you go?"

"Right here," Lily said, watching as the arms kept coming out, soon to be followed by a really nice, perfectly muscled shoulder.

First one.

Then the other.

Lily was afraid her mouth dropped open, and she just couldn't seem to shut it.

Legs. Long, masculine legs, encased in well-worn jeans that hung just a tad low on a taut waist, above which was what looked to be the most beautifully formed washboard abs she'd ever seen, and above that, nice, broad, extremely capable looking shoulders.

"Oh," Lily said, all the breath going out of her in a rush.

"What?" Marcy asked. "Are you okay?"

Lily felt like she'd been burned.

A wave of heat came over her, blossoming in the pit of her stomach and spreading like a flood to every cell in her body.

There was an absolutely gorgeous male creature at the house next door, muscles flexing beautifully, a little sweat on his brow, chest gloriously naked, and all of a sudden she got it. Everything her sister had been trying to explain to her about loneliness and needs and how some things were fine for a while and then, they just weren't anymore.

Suddenly, they were urgent, burning, overwhelming.

"Oh, fudge!" Lily said and dropped the phone.

She was afraid he'd seen her watching him through the kitchen window or that somehow he'd heard her phone clattering on the hard tile floor. Which seemed impossible at this distance and with the walls of her house between them.

But his head shot around and he stared right at her before she gulped and dropped to her knees, feeling guilty and confused and hot all over.

Like she'd suddenly developed a fever in mere seconds.

Maybe she was coming down with something.

Lily touched her hand to her forehead to see if it felt hot.

A mother could tell those things just by the touch of her hand, after dealing with as many feverish kids as she had.

But she couldn't tell this time. Not for sure.

Rattled, she stood back up and looked cautiously out the window once again, to see nothing but the open back of the moving truck and a few boxes.

No sign of *him.*

Had to be one of the movers, she told herself as she searched the cabinet above the stove, where she stored medicines to keep out of her girls' reach.

Men in her neighborhood did not look that good without their shirts on. They didn't have those kinds of muscles or those kinds of tans.

They were strictly suit-and-tie kind of guys.

Desk jockeys.

Pencil pushers.

A man didn't get muscles like that in corporate America.

Lily found the thermometer and put it in her mouth, just as her phone rang stridently.

She must have dropped the phone just right to disconnect the call as it landed.

Which meant this had to be her sister calling back.

And Lily didn't want to talk to Marcy.

Not that Marcy would really give her the option of refusing. She'd just keep calling until Lily answered. Either that or get in her car and drive the twenty minutes between their houses to make sure Lily was okay.

Marcy tended to be a tad overprotective since Richard had moved out.

"Oh, fine," she muttered, picking up the phone, thermometer still in her mouth. "Hewwo."

"What happened?" Marcy demanded to know.

"Sowwy. I dwopped d'phone," Lily said as best she could. "Huh?"

"Wait…." The thermometer beeped and she took it out. No

fever. How odd. "I was just taking my temperature. I felt a little warm, and I dropped the phone."

Not necessarily in that order, but Marcy didn't have to know every little thing.

"You think you have a fever? From just talking about... fudge?"

Lily rolled her eyes. Marcy's kids must still be there. They left for school about fifteen minutes later than Lily's.

"No, not from just talking about it. I just felt...warm, that's all."

"You're not telling me something," Marcy insisted.

"There's a lot I don't tell you or anyone else," Lily admitted, leaning every so slightly to the left, so she could see out the kitchen window again.

And there he was, unloading a kitchen chair.

Lily sighed heavily, unable to help herself.

"I knew it!" Marcy pounced on the sound. "What's going on? Do you have a man there?"

"No, I do not have a man here, and I don't want a man here. I just got rid of one, and he was enough trouble to last me a lifetime," she insisted.

"Honey, we just talked about this. You are not off men for a lifetime. You think you are, but I promise you, you're not. You're just in deep freeze right now."

"Deep freeze?"

"Yes. Where men are concerned. But you won't always be there. One day, some man will come along and bam! No more deep freeze on your...fudge life."

"Aunt Lily has a fudge life?" she heard Marcy's youngest ask through the phone.

Lily started laughing.

"What's a fudge life?" Stacy asked. "Do you just eat it and eat it and eat it all day?"

"No," Marcy insisted.

"'Cause I like fudge. Could I have a fudge life?"

"No. No one spends her life eating fudge," Marcy said, then hissed at her sister, "Fudge life? I will never hear the end of this. She'll probably tell the other kids at school, and I'll be getting calls from the other moms. All their kids will want a fudge life, and the moms will want to know what I'm doing, telling kids they can just eat fudge all the time. How am I ever going to explain this?"

"Sorry. Gotta go," Lily said, hearing her sister growl at her before she hung up the phone.

A fudge life?

Lily laughed again.

At least she could do that now. Laugh at times.

She hadn't for a while. It had been too hard, too scary, too overwhelming, to think of being mostly alone in the world except for two little girls depending on her for just about everything.

But it was getting less overwhelming as time went on.

She was down, but she wasn't beaten.

Lily peeked out the window again, and he was still there, a big box perched on one shoulder, the muscles in his arm looking long and sleek and glistening with sweat.

Had to be a mover, she reassured herself.

Something looking that good would never move in next door to her.

And it was getting hot out.

They probably didn't have anything cold to drink in that house, which had been empty for three months, since the Sanders got transferred to San Diego.

It would be neighborly to drop by and offer them a little something, and maybe the owners would show up while she was there. Or she could pump the moving men for information on the new family.

Her girls were always eager to have more friends to play with. The first thing they'd ask when they walked in the door after school would be whether the new neighbors had girls their age, and a good mother should be ready to provide the answers for her children, shouldn't she?

Lily opened the refrigerator door, thinking…a pitcher of iced tea?

Yes, she had one, very nearly full.

And some cookies?

She checked the cabinets. No cookie mix. Lily dug a little deeper, then sucked in a breath, feeling uneasy once again.

No, she didn't have any cookie mix.

But she had what she needed to make a batch of fudge.

Neighborly, she muttered to herself, as she marched across the yard with the pitcher of tea, four plastic glasses tucked under her arm, and a batch of still-warm fudge.

Just be *neighborly.*

Nothing more. Nothing less.

She made it to the back of the truck and could hear someone swearing softly from inside the enclosed space, and when she paused right behind the truck and looked in, she found him, eyes narrowed in concentration, right shoulder pressed up against a huge box that had snagged on the corner of another one and then didn't want to budge.

Up close, in his face she saw a toughness and a certain strength, eyes so dark they were almost black and flashing with irritation at the moment. He had an ultra-firm jaw, a head full of thick, dark brown hair that he wore a little too long, and what seemed like miles and miles of bare, brown skin.

It was all that skin and muscles that did it to her.

She started to feel hot all over again and thought about cooling her forehead with the tea pitcher, which was already sweating with condensation from the heat.

She'd be taking her temperature again when she got home, just to make sure. Because something wasn't right here.

"Hi. Can I help you, ma'am?" a deep voice said from behind her.

"Oh!" She startled, nearly spilling the tea before the nearly grown teenager, all arms and legs and hair, grabbed it and saved it.

"Jake!" the man who had made her feverish called out from behind her.

"Sorry," the kid, Jake, said. "Didn't mean to sneak up on you."

"Oh. No. It's all right. I just…didn't hear you." *I was too busy becoming feverish, possibly over your father.*

How embarrassing.

Did the kid know women reacted this way to his father?

Did his gorgeous dad know?

Lily wanted to sink into the rhododendron behind her.

"It's okay." The kid pointed to the plate of hot fudge in her hand. "Is that for us?"

"Jake!" The man, standing at the edge of the truck bed and looking down at them both, made the name sound like an order, not to be ignored.

A mind-your-manners-or-else order.

Lily glanced up at him nervously, then quickly looked away. Tall, hot, all muscles and no smile, she saw in a flash.

"Sorry." The kid looked properly apologetic. "I just… It's hot, and we've been at this for hours, and I'm hungry."

"You're always hungry," the man said, command still evident in the voice.

"Yes," Lily said, jumping in to save the boy. "I have nephews who are about your age. I know teenage boys are always hungry, and I thought I'd come over and…introduce myself."

"Sweet," Jake said, sounding truly appreciative as she held out the plate to him. "Jake Elliott. This is my uncle, Nick Malone."

Uncle.

Not *dad.*

Did they have a moving company together? Or maybe Jake and his family were moving in, and Uncle Nick was just helping out?

"I'm Lily Tanner, from next door." She nodded toward her house, then held up the pitcher. "Would you like some sweet tea?"

"Oh, yeah," Jake said, his mouth already full of fudge. "Hey, it's still all warm and gooey. Did you just make this?"

"Yes," Lily said.

"Sweet!"

Which she knew was his generation's current equivalent of *cool*.

"I bet she was thinking the fudge might make a good snack for later on," his uncle pointed out. "And before you stick any more of it in your mouth, you could say thank-you."

"Thanks," Jake muttered with a mouth full of fudge. "Really, ma'am. It's great."

"You're welcome." She offered him a plastic cup and then filled it with tea.

Lily braced herself to face Uncle Nick, who'd just jumped down out of the truck bed and onto the ground, landing just a tad too close for her own comfort.

He immediately grabbed a worn, white T-shirt from the truck bed and pulled it on in what Lily could only describe as a truly impressive rippling, flexing mix of muscles in his arms and chest.

She appreciated that, she told herself, he would cover up that way. And she'd have thought maybe her mysterious fever would have gone away, once he was more covered up. But no, it hadn't.

If anything, it was even hotter now that he was closer and staring at her with those intense, dark eyes of his and a jaw like granite.

"Sorry," he said. "I feel like I've told him a million times already to say please and thank-you, and it just never seems to sink in."

"I know. It's the same thing with my girls."

"You have girls?" Jake piped up at that.

Lily smiled at him. "Much too young for you, I'm afraid."

"I'm only fifteen," he said.

Which had to be impossible, it seemed. He was positively overgrown, this big, awkward, hulking thing who towered over her. The only thing boyish about him was his face.

"I know. I just look older," Jake said.

"You do. But my girls are only six and nine."

"Oh." He shrugged, like it was no big deal.

Lily was sure he had more girls than he could handle flirting with him, just like they must flirt with his uncle.

"I'm gonna go inside. Get out of the sun for a minute," Jake said, turning to leave. "Thanks again, Mrs. Tanner. This is great."

"You're welcome," Lily said, then found herself completely tongue-tied.

Flustered.

Flushed, she feared.

Feeling foolish.

She held out a cup to Mr. Tough-and-Sweaty, thinking sweat had surely never looked so good as it did on him.

"Thank you," he said, taking the cup and holding it out for her to fill, then shook his head. "That little rat escaped with all the fudge, didn't he?"

Lily smiled, not too big a smile, she hoped. Not like she was trying to flirt or anything. "I think he did. You should probably hurry inside. If he's anything like my nephews, he could down the whole plate easily inside of five minutes."

"Sounds like Jake," he agreed, tipping his head back as he took a long swallow of tea. "Wow, that's good."

"You're welcome to keep the pitcher," she offered. "I thought your refrigerator must be empty, and it's supposed to be in the nineties today, so... I just thought this was a good idea."

"It was. Jake and I appreciate it."

"So…are you moving in? Or is Jake and his family?" She hoped she sounded neighborly and nothing more, and that the flush on her face didn't give her away.

"Just Jake and me," he said, his expression if possible becoming even more stern. "My sister and her husband died in a car accident six weeks ago. They have twin boys in college at Virginia Commonwealth. Jake's their youngest. Other than the twins, I'm what passes for his family now."

"Oh. I'm so sorry," she said.

And here she had been admiring every bit of him, right down to the sweat on his brow. Admiring the sweat of a grieving man with a grieving teenage boy.

"Thanks. It's still a little raw, but—"

"Of course. I'm sorry I even asked—"

"No. I'm glad you did. Glad you asked me and not him. He's…uh…well, it still throws him, getting the question and not knowing what to say."

"Of course. My girls were the same way when my husband and I divorced. I mean, I know it's not the same thing, but…they hated having everyone ask, and then having to explain about their father not living with us anymore."

He nodded, quiet and understanding.

The kind of man who'd take on raising his fifteen-year-old nephew alone.

Which, if possible, only made him even more attractive. Maybe that stern expression was simply a result of what he'd been through in the last six weeks.

"Well, I should let you two get back to work," she said, handing him the pitcher. "Let me know if you need anything else. I'm almost always at home."

"Thanks again. This was really nice of you," he said quietly.

Nice.

Fine.

He thought she was nice.

She hoped he didn't know she was gawking like a smitten teenager over him, all while he was grieving for the loss of his sister and brother-in-law and taking care of his poor parentless nephew.

What is wrong with you? Lily muttered to herself, trying to hide her dismay behind a forced smile.

He nodded toward the house. "I'm going to get inside and have some of that fudge."

Yeah. She nodded goodbye.

Fudge.

Chapter Two

Jake was shoving fudge into his mouth like there was no tomorrow when Nick finally got into the kitchen of their new house. He stopped only long enough to hold out his now empty glass, wanting Nick to refill it for him before putting the pitcher down on the counter.

"Hey, she was kind of cute for somebody's mom," Jake said. "And she can really make fudge."

"I wouldn't know. I haven't had any yet," Nick said, hoping his voice wasn't too gruff.

He didn't mean for it to be. Too many years of snapping out orders to soldiers in his command. It was habit now, though he tried his best to tone it down for Jake and his brothers. They really didn't need anybody who sounded like they were yelling at them or mad at them, and Nick knew he could sound like that without even trying.

Jake handed over what was left of the fudge and Nick bit into it, a flavor akin to ecstasy exploding in his mouth.

"Oh…sh…man!" he said.

He was trying to quit cussing, too, trying to set a good example for the kid. Not that he was doing all that well with the no-swearing bit, either.

"I know," Jake said appreciatively. "What do you think we'd have to do to get her to make us dinner?"

"Doubtful. She's a single mother with two little girls," Nick said, still savoring a mouthful of fudge. "She probably doesn't have a lot of extra time."

"Still," Jake said hopefully. "I bet she'd do it for you. Did you see the way she looked at you? Like she didn't really mind that you're—"

"Old?" Nick guessed.

"I was going to say practically ancient." Jake grinned, reaching for the last piece of fudge.

"Touch it and die," Nick growled. "You already had a plateful."

"I know, but I'm still hungry," he complained.

And it wasn't even ten o'clock.

Lily Tanner knew what she was talking about. Teenage boys were bottomless pits. Nick hadn't noticed so much in the first week or so after his sister and brother-in-law's death, because neighbors kept bringing over food. It seemed like a mountain of food, but it hadn't lasted long with the twins and Jake in the house. It seemed nothing, even grief, dimmed the appetite of a teenage boy for long.

"Let's finish getting everything out of the truck before it gets any hotter, and then we'll go find something to eat," Nick said. "Who knows? Maybe by that time, another one of the neighbors will show up with lunch. Just try to look pitiful and weak and underfed."

"I can do that," Jake said, guzzling another glass of tea and then heading outside.

Nick put down his own glass, grabbed the last piece of fudge and popped it in his mouth, then looked around the house, empty of everything but boxes and furniture that hadn't yet been put into place, and he hoped for what had to be the thousandth time that he was doing the right thing in coming here to Virginia and trying to raise this kid.

And wondered what in the hell his sister had been thinking of to name him the boys' guardian in her will.

They got everything out of the truck by noon, and then went inside and moved just enough boxes to allow them room to collapse on the sofa that had landed temporarily right under a ceiling fan.

Nick had to hand it to the kid. He could do some work, and he was really strong, although Nick had to think he could take the kid in a fight, if he really had to. And from the mountain of unsolicited advice he'd received in the last few weeks on raising teenagers, Nick had been led to believe it might just come down to who was stronger physically at least once. Although, he couldn't see Jake refusing to listen to him to the point where the two of them got into a fight.

Still, what did Nick know? Next to nothing about raising kids.

Thank God they were boys.

If they had been girls, he wouldn't have had a prayer.

Of course, if his sister had daughters, she probably wouldn't have left them to Nick to raise.

"I'm starving," Jake said, sprawled out on the couch, eyes closed, head resting heavily against the back, long legs stretched out in front of him.

"Tell me something I don't already know," Nick said, thinking of what kind of fast-food restaurants he'd seen on the drive over here in the truck.

And then, the doorbell rang.

Jake sat up and looked insanely hopeful. "Do you think it might be more fudge?"

"I think we could use something more substantial than fudge. Don't you?"

"Guess so," Jake said, dragging himself up to answer the door.

Which was a good thing, because every muscle in Nick's body was protesting the very idea of moving, which the kid would no doubt give him hell about.

Nick didn't want to be fifteen again for any amount of money in the world, but the body of a fifteen-year-old... That, he could handle, especially on days like today.

Jake opened the door and grinned like crazy.

Must be food.

Nick forced himself up and to his feet, trying to make it without a grimace as his back protested fiercely. At least the kid didn't see. He was focused completely on the baking dish placed in his outstretched hands.

They made nice to the neighbor lady with the chicken cheddar noodle dish for a few minutes, then headed for the kitchen and scarfed it down right out of the pan, leaning over the kitchen countertop with a fork for each of them and nothing else.

Jake's mother would be appalled, Nick was sure, but hey, the kid was hungry and he was being fed.

They washed it down with some more of Lily Tanner's tea, Jake all but licking the chicken pan clean, like a puppy who hadn't been fed in days.

"I think I like this neighborhood," he said. "Do you think someone will show up with dinner?"

"We can hope," Nick said.

Lily had meant to get some work done that day. Truly, she had. She'd come home from next door and taken her temperature again, finding it still oddly normal, but still felt all flushed and shaky and...weak.

Was she coming down with something?

Had to be, she decided.

What other explanation could there be?

And then she went to work in her dining room, where the

walls were nothing but Sheetrock, ready for taping and spackling, then wallpaper, paint and wood trim.

She'd been an interior decorator before the girls were born, then a stay-at-home mom and then kind of fallen into the whole rehabbing thing. She'd convinced Richard they should sell their smaller house and buy a larger one in need of remodeling three years ago and hadn't looked back since.

A year there and a lot of work, mostly on Lily's part, which she found she truly enjoyed, and they'd sold the house at a nice profit and bought another one.

This was their fourth, bought just weeks before Richard announced he was leaving her, and as part of the divorce settlement, she owed him half the equity they had in the house when they'd first purchased it. But she had a full year in which to finish renovating it and she got to keep everything she got over the original purchase price.

She'd worked hard to get that agreement and was counting on the profits from the house to allow her to outright buy a much smaller house for her and the girls to live in.

So she did not lack work to do that day, but the phone never stopped ringing. It seemed half the neighbors in the cul-de-sac had seen her talking to that gorgeous specimen of man next door and wanted to know a) If he was really moving in, b) If the teenager was his son, and c) If the gorgeous man could possibly be single.

Having all the answers to all three questions, Lily was a very popular woman that morning. Not to be outdone by a gift of fudge and iced tea, her neighbors promptly went to work.

By noon, there was a veritable parade of women marching to the house next door, casserole dishes in hand, bright smiles on what looked to Lily like perfectly made-up faces and clothes more suited for a fancy lunch out than a casual drop-in on a new neighbor.

"Shameless," Lily muttered to herself, again at that kitchen window, watching Jean Sumner from three doors down show up in a low-cut sweater that hugged her more than ample curves. "Absolutely shameless."

Her new neighbors would enjoy the view much more than what Lily would bet was Jean's curried turkey, which Lily knew from experience tended to be quite dry.

Sissy Williams just happened to drop by in her little white tennis outfit, practically bouncing in enthusiasm as she presented them with what looked like a cake.

Jake would like that.

But the most shameless one of all, as far as Lily was concerned, was Audrey Graham, showing up at their front door in jogging shorts and a jog bra!

"You could at least put a shirt on!" Lily muttered, knowing good and well the woman couldn't hear her.

At least Lily had shown up with all her clothes on, and she hadn't dressed up. She felt vastly superior to the parade of neighbors she'd seen so far just because she hadn't fussed over her appearance or shown an excessive amount of skin.

She wondered if her neighbors, too, had felt a little feverish after their visits, because Nick's shirt had come back off while he was unloading the truck. Lily couldn't help but notice, being right next door and all.

But she hadn't gawked at him or anything like that. It was just that in passing by her kitchen window, which she did on a regular basis on any given day, she happened to glance out and there he was, him and Jake and a parade of food-bearing, scantily clad women.

Lily had never known her neighbors to behave in this way. This was a very respectable street, in a well-respected neighborhood, after all.

Lily's sister called again, but Lily got away with being remarkably vague about her day, and there was no more talk about fudge of any kind. The girls came home from school, happy and full of energy until after she fed them and mentioned homework. At which point, they pled an overwhelming case of fatigue and collapsed on the floor of the family room, watching a Disney Channel movie until she shooed them off to bed at eight-thirty.

Lily was loading the dishwasher a few minutes later when she caught sight of Jake cutting through the side yard and heading for her kitchen door.

She didn't fuss. Not really.

Patted down her hair, checked her shirt to make sure she wasn't dusty or really dirty, because she had gotten a little work in on prepping the dining-room walls that day, and then she pulled open the door.

Jake stood there about to knock, looking like a giant puppy, all hair and ears and feet.

"Hi. Get everything moved in?"

"Yes, ma'am," he said, coming inside.

"You must be tired," she said.

"A little," he admitted, like it would take more than a day like this to make a boy his age actually tired.

"What can I do for you?" she offered.

"Well…I kind of messed up, and I'm not sure what to do about it," he confessed. "See, we had all these people come over and bring food. All kinds of good food—"

"Yes. I noticed," Lily admitted.

"Nothing as good as your fudge. But good stuff, and my uncle told me to keep a list of who brought what and what it was in, so we could get the plates and pans back to everybody and thank them, and I…well, I kind of have a list, but…not really."

"Ah." Lily nodded. "You got hungry and got distracted and…"

"Yeah. I did. And now, I'm not sure what to do. I have cards and things with names on them, but they're not all attached to dishes anymore, and I think I remember what some of the women looked like who brought certain things…."

Like Audrey in the jog bra.

Lily bet Jake remembered her.

"I can probably match up most of the dishes to the cards," Lily assured him. "We tend to bring over the same recipes when we do meals for people. I know everyone's specialties."

He looked so grateful she wanted to hug him.

Poor baby.

He must have had a long day and a really bad six weeks or so.

"Look, my girls are upstairs asleep—"

"I could stay here, in case they wake up," he offered.

"Okay," Lily said. "It won't take me a minute. Everything's in the refrigerator?"

He nodded. "And the cards and stuff are on the counter by the refrigerator. I left the side door open, and my uncle went to drive the truck back to the rental place, so the house is empty."

"Okay. Be right back."

She knew the house from when the last couple lived there, and her kitchen faced theirs, so all she had to do was get around the low row of bushes and she was there. And everything was right where Jake said it would be.

Sissy had indeed brought a cake. Something fancy with fruit and glaze on it.

"No way you made that yourself," Lily muttered. Sissy wasn't much in the kitchen. And she should have known it was much fancier than a teenager boy cared for it to be.

Jean's turkey looked tastier than usual. It was easy to match that dish with Jean's card. A half-dozen others, and Lily was left with only Audrey's card and one with absolutely awful handwriting that looked like it might even be the work of teenage girls.

Even the teenagers were flaunting their baked goods along with their bodies these days?

The two dishes left were a container of homemade macaroni salad and a baked chicken thing.

With that body, Audrey probably didn't touch carbs, Lily reasoned. The baked chicken was likely hers.

She decided to ask Jake just in case. After all, he wouldn't have forgotten Audrey in that little outfit. Whether it had blinded him to everything else, including what she brought, Lily didn't know, but she'd find out.

She took the container of baked chicken to show Jake, opened the kitchen door and there was Nick.

She had to work fast to keep the chicken from landing on the ground. He was more worried about her landing on the ground, because while she caught the pan of chicken, he caught her with lightning reflexes and the kind of strength she couldn't help but admire.

She'd have pitched backward, if not for him.

As it was, he had her, his big hands on her upper arms holding her easily, a wry, maybe slightly amused expression on his face.

"Lily," he said, much too close. "You okay?"

"Yes," she whispered.

"Sorry I startled you."

His hands lingered for a long moment, her arms feeling odd and tingly. Only once he was sure she was firmly planted on her feet, did he let her go and he step back.

"No. It was me. I wasn't looking where I was going," she admitted, a funny little catch in her voice, finding herself oddly breathless and seeing nothing but wide shoulders and well-muscles arms.

Feeling pure heat coming off his body.

Not such a shock, she decided.

After all, she hadn't been this close to a man other than her ex-husband in years. So she supposed it wasn't all that surprising.

She blinked up at him, a little confused and a lot embarrassed and…she wasn't even sure what else.

What had she been thinking? Doing? Saying? Her mind was a blank.

"I doubt you're the kind of woman to come over here and steal baked chicken, so…"

"Oh," she rushed in. "No. I wasn't. I swear."

"I didn't think you were, Lily."

No. He just probably thought she was nuts. "Jake got a little confused about which dish came from who, and I told him I'd help him sort it out."

"Yeah. He ripped off the cards and lids and was eating out of the pans before he even thought about keeping track of who brought what."

Lily nodded. "He seems like a really sweet kid. He's at my house, to make sure my girls don't wake up and find themselves alone. I'm sure I know who brought everything except this and one other thing."

She held up the baked chicken.

"I remember that one," he said.

"A woman wearing…"

"Next to nothing," he said plainly and if anything, a bit confused by it all.

"Shorts and a…"

"Bra-like thing," he said.

"Audrey Graham," Lily said, turning around and heading back into the kitchen. "I'll just put her card with this dish, and—"

"Does she often show up at strangers' doors dressed like that?" he asked.

Lily laughed, couldn't help it, then reminded herself that she might not have dressed as provocatively as Audrey and the rest of the neighborhood ladies, but she'd been first in line at his door this morning.

What did that say about her?

What did it make him think about her? That she was just like all the others?

"Well…Audrey is…I guess you could say…she's turned into a physical fitness buff since her divorce was final." It was the kindest thing Lily could come up with to say. "She runs most every day now, and it's been so hot, so…"

She turned around, having finished labeling dishes, and found Nick Malone leaning against the kitchen counter, looking like a man with a lot of questions he wasn't sure he wanted answered.

"Friendly neighborhood," he said.

"Yes. Very."

"I've never lived in a place like this. Didn't expect such a welcome," he said carefully, like they were treading all around all sorts of subjects now. "Is it always like this when someone moves in?"

"Well…" She supposed she should warn him. Or give him the good news, depending on how he felt about things. "There aren't a lot of single men in the neighborhood."

"Okay," he said, looking even more confused.

"Mostly married couples and divorced mothers," she explained.

Lonely, divorced mothers.

Mothers with certain unmet needs.

Of which, she wouldn't have said she was one. Would have said she was fine. In need of nothing. Wanting nothing except a long, hot bubble bath and a good book.

And now here she was, with a gorgeous neighbor and that funny, slight fever again that she'd proven to herself wasn't a fever. At least not the first two times she'd taken her temperature today.

Lily looked up at him as innocently as she could manage.

"And all those women who showed up today are single?" he asked, like the idea frightened him a bit.

"No. Not all of them," Lily said, and then thought that meant she'd spent all day watching his house from her kitchen window.

Wait…no. That she'd looked at all the cards that came with the food.

She hoped that's what he thought she meant.

Not that she was spying.

"They're just...always happy to welcome a new neighbor," she said.

New man, she'd meant, but hadn't said it. Though he had to know that's what she meant. He could have a different woman for every day of the week, if he wanted, if she was any judge of what just happened today.

Did he want that? A rotation of different women from Sunday to Saturday?

Was he that kind of guy?

And what about Jake? Surely he wouldn't have women parading through the house with Jake here?

"Well, Jake is certainly happy," he said finally. "Unfortunately, I'm not much of a cook and neither is he."

"So, this is a good thing. All this...friendliness and neighborliness."

Was that even a word? *Neighborliness?*

Like this was about nothing but food.

Lily was embarrassing herself and a little confused.

Did the man not know how good he looked? Especially with his shirt off? Surely this wasn't the only place where women flirted with him?

Was there a world out there somewhere, outside of Lily's existence in the suburbs, where this man wouldn't be admired for his physique?

She couldn't imagine that there was.

Granted, she'd lived a fairly sheltered existence of kids' birthday parties and neighborhood cookouts and volunteering at her kids' schools, but she wasn't that out of it. Was she?

Not that she was going to ask *him* about any of this.

He probably thought *she* was one of *them.*

Not as blatant as Audrey Graham and her little jog-bra, but still one of them.

And maybe Lily was.

"Well, I'd better get back," Lily said, slipping past him and out the door, trying not to look like she was fleeing.

"Thanks for everything," Nick said.

"You're welcome. I hope the two of you like it here." Not a woman-a-day kind of like it here, but…like it. She blushed just thinking about him and what he might do with all those women. "I'll send Jake right home."

Chapter Three

Four days later, Nick waited just inside the front door of his new house. It was just before sunrise, and he was dressed to go running, but instead he was peeking out the front window like a man expecting to be accosted in the early-morning light, right here in one of the quietest subdivisions in town.

Not by a mugger, but a grown woman in a jog-bra.

She'd followed him for the whole five miles he'd run two days ago, followed him through the quiet streets, talking the whole time, when he'd been counting on clearing out his head of everything, on having a time when he had to do nothing but keep breathing and putting one foot in front of the other. And if that wasn't enough, the woman had followed him home, followed him inside.

Before he'd known what she was up to, she'd been all over him, right there in the kitchen. Okay, he'd been pretty sure what she was up to. He just didn't expect to be attacked in his own kitchen that morning, and before he could do anything about it, Jake had walked in. Though starving and still half-asleep, the kid had nearly gotten an eyeful.

Something Nick did not care to repeat.

He also didn't want anybody chattering to him the whole time he ran.

Which was why he was staring out the window, wondering if Audrey Graham was out there, waiting for him, despite the fact that he'd told her—politely but plainly—that he wasn't interested.

Obviously, whatever he'd said, it hadn't been enough.

"What are you doing?" Jake asked from behind him.

Nick nearly jumped out of his skin.

Too many years in the army before he joined the FBI.

Jake yawned. "Sorry. I forgot."

"One day, you're going to sneak up on me, and I'm going to crush your throat before I figure out who you are," Nick told him.

"You can really do that?" Jake asked admiringly.

"In a heartbeat," Nick boasted, hoping the kid would believe him and remember the warning next time. He'd really come close to hurting him once already when Jake startled him.

"Sorry. I thought you heard me." Jake shrugged, like the possibility of a crushed throat was no big deal. "So, what are you doing? Did you go run?"

"Not yet."

All of a sudden, Jake looked very interested. "Wait a minute? You're not…you know. Sneaking somebody out of the house, are you?"

"Sneaking someone out?" Nick repeated.

"You know. Like…a woman?"

"No, I am not sneaking a woman out of the house," Nick said.

"'Cause, if you want somebody to sleep over, I'm fine with that. Is it that Audrey woman? The one with the giant—" Jake lifted his hands up and held them about a foot away from his chest. "And the really cute daughter? 'Cause, I'd really like to know the daughter."

"No, it's not her. It's not anybody."

"Not anybody I know, huh? Okay—" Jake looked way too interested.

"Not anyone at all. No one was here. I wouldn't do that."

Nick started to say not with Jake in the house, but that sounded a bit hypocritical. Was he supposed to pretend to be a monk? Just because he was single and raising a kid? One who happened to be a teenage boy, no doubt with raging hormones of his own?

Nick didn't think so, but what did he know about the etiquette of single parents and their sex lives?

Not much.

He'd never been seriously involved with a woman with kids. Hardly been seriously involved with any woman.

"So, you're just going to do without until I'm eighteen?" Jake asked, like he couldn't quite believe it. "'Cause I thought you'd be really cool about things like that. I thought…you know. You'd bring your ladies over here, and I'd bring mine, and we'd both be cool with that."

Nick did a double take. "You have ladies? Plural?"

"Well, not exactly," Jake said. "Not at the moment."

"Okay, one? You have one? Who you intend to entertain in your bedroom? At fifteen?"

"Well…maybe."

"No way that's gonna happen," Nick insisted.

"Really?" He looked crushed.

"Really," Nick said, barking out the word.

"Jeez," Jake grumbled, looking all put out. "I thought—"

"Well, you thought wrong."

Jake grumbled as he made his way into the kitchen, no doubt hungry already. After all, it had been a whole six hours or so since he'd eaten. Nick had found him in the kitchen at midnight, gulping down a giant bowl of cereal. Now the kid was already up and hungry again.

Nick couldn't sneak a woman into and out of this house, even if he'd wanted to. Jake got hungry too often to make that work.

And had ideas of entertaining, all of his own.

"Jesus!" Nick said, more of a prayer for help and understanding than anything else. "What am I supposed to do about that?"

And he couldn't even go for a decent run, because when he opened up the door to do that, he saw Audrey lurking behind a tree at the house next door, looking for him, no doubt.

Nick slammed the door and wondered if he could wait her out.

Didn't the woman have to go to work? Or take care of her kids? Did she have nothing better to do than stalk him?

He'd either have to find a way to avoid her, by finding out her schedule and running at a different time, or convince her he wasn't interested, and he'd bet she hadn't heard that from many red-blooded American males. It might be hard to convince her it was true.

"Damn," he muttered.

He was mowing the grass later that morning when Lily pulled into her driveway and got out of her little SUV, neither of her kids in sight.

He waved and kept on mowing, wanting the job done before it got too hot. But then he saw her open the back of her SUV and start wresting with a pile of wooden trim, and he cut off the mower and went to help.

"Here," he said, coming up behind her and catching an errant piece that was dragging on the ground. "Let me help."

"Oh." She whirled around, but the trim wasn't all the way out of the vehicle and didn't quite move with her.

Nick had to move fast to keep it from going all over the place and from hitting the ground and getting scuffed up.

"Sorry. Didn't mean to startle you," he said, wondering if she was naturally jumpy or a bit of a klutz.

"No. You didn't. I just…forgot I was holding all that and then…well, you know the rest."

"I've got it. Let me carry it in for you," he said, wiping the sweat off his face with his forearm and hoping the trim didn't slide out of his hands.

"Okay. Thanks."

She fished out her keys and headed for the back door, leading him through the kitchen and into the dining room, the top half of the walls freshly painted a muted gold tone and ready for the wide, white trim.

"Anywhere here is fine," she told him.

He piled the wood in the far corner. "You doing all this work yourself?"

"Yes. I like it. I used to be an interior decorator, but I found out I liked making all the decorating decisions myself, much better than following someone else's orders, and I like doing the physical work on a house myself. So after the girls were born, I started rehabbing houses and selling them."

He looked around at the room in progress and the kitchen that she'd obviously already done. "You do good work, Lily," he said.

"Thanks. How are you? How's Jake?"

"Jake's…as good as can be expected, I think," he said. "But what do I know? How do you think he is?"

"Sweet. Smart. Eager to please," she said. "He offered to mow my lawn in exchange for another batch of fudge."

"Hey, sorry—"

"No, it's great. I get tired of mowing the lawn, especially by this time of year. Believe me, it's worth a lot more to me than a plate of fudge to have someone else do it."

"You're sure?"

"Absolutely." She walked into the kitchen and grabbed a couple of glasses from the cabinet. "Would you like something to drink? You look like you've been out there in the heat for a while."

"Water. Thank you."

She handed him a glass, which he downed in one, long swallow. She watched as he did it, looking like she wasn't quite sure what to make of him or if he made her uneasy or something.

But then she just smiled and refilled his glass again.

"So, if it's all right with you, I'll make a deal with Jake? Food in exchange for lawn-mowing duty?"

"Fine with me. Just don't let him take advantage of you or your time."

She shrugged, smiled a bit nervously. "I like to cook, and it's just as easy to make something for five people as it is for me and the girls. What's his favorite meal?"

"I don't even know," Nick said. One more thing he didn't know about kids in general and this one in particular. "I mean, I haven't found anything the kid won't eat. I do remember being at my sister's a year or so ago, and she'd made a pot roast. Jake ate plates full. I came into the kitchen not an hour and a half later to get something to drink and found the pan of leftovers still on the stove, cooling I guess, and Jake was eating out of the pan. Kid's got no manners when it comes to food, and that he could be hungry again after eating so much at dinner…"

Nick just shook his head in wonder.

"Okay," Lily said. "A pot roast, it is. Everything else going okay?"

Nick hesitated, needing to talk to someone, but…Lily?

He didn't know her that well, and as open about their sexuality as some women were these days, he suspected Lily wasn't one of them. She seemed sweet and a little shy, and Jake had volunteered that she hadn't been divorced from her husband for that long.

Nick just couldn't see asking her how she handled her sex life with two little girls in the house.

"I'd like to help, if I could," she said, all sweetness and earnestness.

Nick frowned, thinking he could at least find out a little more about Audrey Graham to help him avoid her.

"Well…" He hesitated. "I don't think there's any easy way to say this, and I really don't want to make you uncomfortable, but…"

Ahhh!

Lily thought she was going to die of embarrassment right there on the spot.

He knew!

He knew she'd been practically slobbering all over him, and he wanted to talk about it?

"Ahhh," she whimpered.

She didn't mean to. Not out loud at least, but she must have, because suddenly, he looked concerned. He took her by the arm and said, "Lily? You okay?"

"Yes," she lied and not at all convincingly.

"You sure?" he asked.

"Yes. Really. Just go ahead. Tell me. It's about—"

"Audrey Graham," he said, looking like it pained him to even say the name to her.

"Oh! Audrey?" Lily smiled, so relieved she could have fallen to her knees and said a prayer of gratitude right then.

She'd been certain he knew she'd been all but drooling over him while he moved in and then while he'd been doing yard work the other day. She was so grateful it hadn't gotten that hot yet, and he still had his shirt on this morning.

Him shirtless in her kitchen was probably more than she could have handled.

"Yes, Audrey. Did you say something about her running every morning?"

"Yes," she said.

Did he want to watch?

Because the woman was certainly putting on a show.

Her outfits got skimpier by the day. She must have gone shopping after Nick moved in.

Someone had even said Nick and Audrey had run together the day before, and that when it was over, Audrey had followed Nick into his house. But people said a lot of things, and Lily made a policy to discount at least half of what she heard, just on principle alone, and it must have been one of the few occasions when Lily hadn't been watching his house, because she hadn't seen a thing.

"Do you know where she runs? Like how far and the route she takes?" Nick asked, looking really uncomfortable with the question.

"Not really. I'm not a runner. I mean, I see her go by our houses sometimes," Lily said.

More often, now that Nick moved in.

Did that mean he hadn't run with her the other day?

"And…uh…I guess there's no easy way to say this, but…if I wanted to run without…running into her?"

"Oh," Lily said, relieved, but puzzled.

He wanted to avoid a woman with a body like Audrey's?

She didn't think anybody who looked like him would want to avoid someone who looked like Audrey.

"I like to run alone," he said. "That's all. Really. It's just time to clear my head, and she followed me the other day and…well, she talked the whole time."

"Oh. Of course." Lily nodded, gleeful at the thought of Audrey, half-dressed and nearly bouncing out of her bra and annoying Nick every step of the way.

It shouldn't make Lily so happy, because Audrey's husband had walked out on her just like Lily's had, and Lily knew how awful that was. Lily felt bad for everything Audrey had gone through, but still… She didn't want Audrey to have Nick.

"If you cut through my backyard on the side farthest from yours, then take the first left, then a right, it will take you out of the neighborhood the back way. From there, you might be able to run without seeing her, because I think she stays in the subdivision."

He grinned. "That would be great. Thanks."

"Sure," she said. "Anytime."

He looked like there might be more he wanted to say, but then thought better of it and just put his empty glass down on the counter and said, "Well, I guess I'd better be going, finish the lawn before it gets any hotter."

"Okay."

Lily went to open the door for him, and he reached for it at the same time, which meant they ended up almost bumping into each other, and when they pulled away, she went left and he went right.

Which meant, they ended up even closer.

He gave a little chuckle. "Hang on." And caught her by the arms, to keep her from moving again the same way he did, she thought.

Which was fine.

It was…almost a polite gesture.

Nothing more.

She didn't move at first, didn't want to if she was honest with herself, just stood there breathing in the scent of him, a big, strong man who'd been outside doing manly things, and the sheer heat of him, which seemed to be radiating from his body.

And then he froze. "Damn," he muttered, turning his head back to her.

"What's wrong?"

Had she done something? Completely given herself away?

Would she be forever embarrassed in his company and have to live with him being right next door forever and knowing she wanted him as much as Audrey? Would he be getting tips from someone else on how to avoid Lily?

Still, he held her gently by the arms, mere fractions of an inch from being pressed up against him, and he wasn't moving away.

"Audrey's out there. I saw her through the kitchen door," he said.

"Oh."

"And she sees us," he said.

Okay?

So?

"I don't understand—"

"Lily, she followed me into the kitchen two mornings ago and practically jumped me as Jake was coming downstairs."

"Oh!"

"I thought I made it clear, as politely as possible, that I wasn't interested, but maybe I didn't. Because she's been stalking me ever since, and Jake is daydreaming about going out with her daughter. So I'd rather not piss her off completely, if I don't have to."

"Okay." Lily said, still frozen there, half an inch from him and liking it. Liking it a lot. "But what does that have to do with...this?"

He took a breath, chest and shoulders rising, coming that much closer to actually touching her, and she wanted him to touch her. She was tingling all over, like her body was singing, it was so happy. Like she'd already anticipated this slight touch a dozen times in the few seconds they'd been standing here, her waiting and waiting for things she couldn't bring herself to ask for.

He was just so big and strong. So much...a man.

And it had been so long since she'd been this close to a man.

If she was really honest with herself, she'd admit she'd never been this close to a man as appealing as him. In a completely physical way, of course. She didn't really know him. She just knew that her body really wanted to know his better.

"Well," he said, dipping his head ever so slowly until his lips were resting somewhere near the base of her throat.

Not touching her.

Not really.

Doing something oh so sexy that was almost like touching.

Breathing on her, breathing in her, like a man taking a moment to savor a great meal he knew he was going to love before he ever took the first bite.

Bite!

She couldn't think about him taking a *bite* of her.

Men didn't take bites of her!

She wasn't that kind of girl.

Maybe she should have been.

Maybe she regretted that right this minute, but still...

"If I could just do this for a moment," he whispered, his arms sliding carefully around her.

"Mmm-hmm," she said, her voice coming out a little squeaky and weird.

"And you were to put your arms around me, just for a minute...."

"Okay." She was all too happy to comply.

She'd been thinking about touching him for days. Touching him in all sorts of ways, in all sorts of places that made her blush.

And actually touching him was even better, she found.

His body was solid as could be, all hard and sexy, muscles curving and sloping one into another, her hands sliding up his biceps, to cup his broad shoulders, one hand even sneaking onto the base of his neck and into the ends of his hair.

"There you go," he said, like he really liked that. "Just like that."

Oh, yes.

Just like that.

Lily took a giant gulp of air, her breasts rising to the point where they just barely brushed his chest.

He sucked in a breath, then gave a shaky little laugh.

"She's watching everything we do," he said. "And if it's okay with you, I think if I just do this for a few moments...."

And then he stroked the tip of his nose along the side of her neck, lips so close they left a trail of heat and longing in their wake.

Lily whimpered. Couldn't help it.

If this didn't stop soon, she'd be begging him to stop putting on a show for Audrey and just kiss her already and be done with it.

As it was, she could imagine his mouth opening and then landing right there in that spot where the base of her neck met her shoulder, a spot that was already tingling with longing. She thought about his warm, moist mouth teasing, caressing, his beautiful, hard body plastered up against hers.

Lily stretched her neck out to the side, like she was giving him that spot, giving him anything he wanted, and let her body settle in against his. His arms tightened around her ever so slowly and carefully, like he was determined not to take advantage of the situation.

Or she hoped that's what it was.

That he was a nice man.

A very nice, wickedly sexy man.

His nose nuzzled her ear, teased her hair, his hand cupping one side of her face and his lips settling as gently as a whisper against her temple before he slowly drew back, a wry grin on his face.

Lily tried not to whimper or to beg for more. Tried to stand on her own two feet without any help from him and tried not to look too thrilled by what he'd done or too devastated that it was over.

"So…she got an eyeful?" Lily asked, reminding herself what this had all been about.

"Yes, she did." He grinned easily, the way a man might look at a woman he considers a good friend. "I hope that was okay? I mean, I hope I didn't offend you…."

"No. Of course not," she said. "Anything to help out a neighbor."

"Well, she's gone so…" He waited, like he wanted to say more.

She waited, too, hoping, wanting, needing, thrilled and a little bit scared.

But then he shook his head and all he said was, "I should be getting back to work. Thanks again, Lily."

"You're welcome," she said.

She waited until he was out the door and she heard his lawn mower start before she sank down to the floor in her kitchen, leaning back against the cabinets, closed her eyes and relived every glorious second of what had just happened.

Sadly, it was the sexiest thing that had happened to her in years.

Chapter Four

Jake hadn't been trying to spy on them.

Honestly.

He'd been spying on Audrey Graham, the woman who wore all the skimpy tops and had practically attacked his uncle in their kitchen, because Mrs. Graham had an absolutely gorgeous sixteen-year-old daughter, clearly miles out of Jake's league and who'd never so much as looked down her nose at him at school.

But still…a guy had to have hope, didn't he?

If nothing else, Jake could look and hope.

At the moment, he'd been looking at Mrs. Graham, hoping her daughter might be with her, but she wasn't. He'd seen Mrs. Graham staring into Lily's house and looking none too happy at what she saw, and then Jake wondered what was going on, and that's when he saw them.

His uncle and Lily?

It looked like Nick was licking Lily's neck or something, and it sure looked like Lily liked it.

Women liked to have their necks licked?

Jake frowned.

He didn't exactly know a ton about women, but he'd sure never heard that one.

Kissing necks, yes.

Licking?

Not that he had a problem trying it.

He was open to pretty much anything, especially with Andie Graham.

He would be her willing slave, fulfilling her every wish, if he ever got to the point where she knew he was alive and was willing to have him close enough to do things to that pretty neck of hers.

Jake took one more look at his uncle and Lily, not quite sure what he thought about that. One, he didn't want his uncle to make Andie's mother mad, just on the off chance that Andie might one day have anything to do with Jake. And he liked Lily. She was sweet, and she'd been kind and understanding and made the most incredible fudge Jake had ever eaten. He didn't want anyone to hurt her, and if she knew his uncle was all over Mrs. Graham in the kitchen the other day, and now all over Lily, Lily wouldn't like that. Would she?

Women didn't like to share.

It was one thing Jake was pretty sure about.

And he didn't like thinking his uncle was the kind of man who'd hurt someone like Lily. Was he that kind of man? Jake frowned and—

"Excuse me? I'm looking for the Malone house? Is this it?"

Jake thought for a second he must be dreaming, because he was pretty sure he knew that voice. He *dreamed* about that voice. About more than the voice.

He turned around really slowly and hoped he didn't look too stupid as he stared for a minute and wondered if he was actually dreaming or if Andie Graham was actually standing in front of him. If she'd actually spoken to him.

"Uh…" was all he managed to get out before he had to take a breath and try to calm down.

She was wearing some really short shorts and a little white top with spaghetti straps and a scooped out neckline, and truly, it was hard to breathe this close to her. Especially with her looking the way she did. Looking as good as she did.

Had to be a fantasy come true.

She was looking for *his* house?

"No way," he muttered, out loud he feared.

She gave him an odd look, one he no doubt deserved, like he might have the IQ of a piece of fruit.

"The Malone house?" he repeated, his voice doing that weird, cracking thing that it hadn't done since he was fourteen. He hated that stupid cracking thing.

She nodded, like she feared words might be too much for him.

"That's my house," he said, still thinking this had to be a mistake.

No way she'd come looking for him.

She frowned, like maybe she didn't believe him or was really confused. "Your dad is Nick Malone?"

"Uncle," he said, his voice still sounding funny.

"Oh. And this is your house?" She pointed to Lily's.

"No, this one," he said, nodding in the other direction.

"Oh. Okay. I was actually…" She looked thoroughly exasperated, not so much like the blond princess of his fantasies. More like a real person who might actually have normal problems like everyone else. "I was looking for my mom."

And she didn't like admitting that. Or maybe it was…thinking her mom was here with his uncle? That something was going on between them?

"She's right over…" It was Jake's turn to frown. She wasn't there anymore. "She was there just a minute ago."

Andie sighed, like she dreaded the next part, then asked, "Do you think she went inside?"

"No. My uncle's not there," Jake told her, not adding that his uncle was at Lily's, licking Lily's neck or something like that, and that Andie's mom had seen them and hadn't been happy about it.

"Oh," Andie said, sighing once again. "Your uncle? Is he married?"

"No," Jake said. Why would she care if his uncle was married?

"Well...thanks, I guess. I'll just... I'll be..." She paused for one more moment, then looked him over one more time. "Do I know you?"

Jake shook his head, then woke up to the fact that this was his chance. She knew he was alive, even if it was just to help her find his house. "I'm Jake. Jake Elliott. We go to the same school. I mean...I'm pretty sure we do. Jefferson?"

"Yeah, I go to Jefferson. What are you? What year?"

"Sophomore," he admitted, knowing she was a junior.

Just one more way in which she was way out of his league.

"Oh," she said. "Well, I've got to go find my mom. See you."

Jake mumbled goodbye, and then was treated to the sight of her walking away from him in those short shorts, with those long, tanned legs, her long, blond hair swinging as she walked, wishing he could start this whole conversation over again and not sound like an idiot, not act like one, not be one.

She'd talked to him.

She knew his name and where he lived.

Jake suspected he'd be dreaming of her tonight, dreaming in more vivid detail than ever before.

Okay, maybe that wasn't the best idea I've ever had, Nick told himself, safely back in his own house, out of sight of any prying eyes and not mere centimeters away from being plastered up against Lily.

Luscious Lily.

He made a face, trying to get that particular description out of his head.

He did not need to be thinking of his neighbor as *luscious*.

Particularly with a teenage boy in the house who had visions of entertaining his own ladies in his bedroom.

So, no…nuzzling Lily's neck was definitely not a good idea.

It had just felt like one.

A great one.

Nick tried to breathe and turn his thoughts to something else, anything else but how long it had been since he'd been involved with a woman or had one in his bed and the utter unlikelihood that he'd ever talk Lily Tanner into joining him there.

Audrey, of the skimpier and skimpier jogging outfits, he could have, if he wanted her. Which, unfortunately, he didn't.

Lily, he suspected, was firmly off-limits.

He'd bet the woman had never had casual sex in her life. She was too sweet, too nice, too kindhearted. Softhearted, he was sure.

Not at all his type.

And yet…pretty was the word that came to mind, and it both seemed to fit and not do her justice at the same time. She had pretty blond hair and gorgeous skin, an easy smile and an openness and genuineness. She seemed real. That's what it was. Not fussy. Not fake. Not pushy. Not playing any kind of games. Real and nice and surprisingly appealing.

He opened up the refrigerator and poured a cold glass of water from the pitcher he kept there, wishing it was that easy to cool himself down.

Damn, Lily.

She'd felt so soft and fragile beneath his hands, smelled so good, trembled ever so slightly, blushed a bit, and all he'd been able to think about was devouring her right there in her kitchen.

He took a long swallow of that cold water, but it didn't seem to do anything to cool him down.

One by one, he thought of all the women who'd shown up at his door with offerings of food, drink and, though unspoken, companionship. Surely he could think of one he'd like to kill some time with, one who wouldn't object at all to killing time with him.

And yet he found himself discarding one after another and staring out the window toward Lily's house.

He'd just have to stay away from her. That was all there was to it.

He had Jake to take care of, parenting stuff to figure out, legal issues to sort through having to do with his sister and brother-in-law's estate, determining the boys' finances and whether there was enough money to see them all through college and if there was time, his own life to see to.

More than enough to do to keep a grown man busy and his mind off one, quietly pretty, sweet-smelling woman.

Yeah. He'd just have to stay away from her.

Three days later, Lily was trying to explain to Jake the finer points of scraping old wallpaper off the kitchen wall, when he started asking her about Audrey Graham.

What did she know about Mrs. Graham?

Lily frowned.

Was the woman still chasing after Nick? Even after the… *incident?*

Lily was trying very hard not to call it what it was.

Neck-nuzzling.

Oh! She practically shivered, just thinking about it. How good it had been. How delicious it had felt.

Better than sweet, warm, gooey fudge, as far as Lily was concerned.

"You do know her, don't you?" Jake said again, giving her a funny look.

Like she'd gone off into la-la land.

"Yes," Lily all but groaned. "I know her. Is she…bothering your uncle?"

Lily hated asking the question, but there it was. It had just popped out, oh so innocently. Okay, not so innocent. Probably not innocently at all. She felt really bad about it, but there! She'd asked.

Jake looked puzzled. "I don't know. Maybe."

Lily went back to steaming the wallpaper in hopes it would just peel off the wall, wishing quite firmly that she hadn't asked. She hadn't seen Audrey Graham lurking around the Malone house, but that didn't mean it hadn't happened. Audrey was sneaky and quite determined. There was no telling what Lily had missed.

And then she wondered if maybe Jake was trying to look out for her, to warn her that Audrey had been hanging around, and maybe she wasn't bothering Nick. Maybe Nick was enjoying himself.

Maybe he'd changed his mind after the neck-nuzzling incident. Maybe Audrey had done something to change his mind.

Lily made a face, then tried to wipe the look off her face before Jake saw.

She really hated the idea of Nick with Audrey Graham. Having to see them next door. Hear them. Think about them.

Nick neck-nuzzling with Audrey Graham.

Lily wasn't sure if she wanted to scream or cry.

"Are you okay?" Jake asked.

"Of course," Lily lied, not too badly she hoped.

"So…Mrs. Graham has a daughter, right?" Jake asked, as he scraped the wall clean of the residue left on it, despite Lily's careful steaming and peeling off of the old wallpaper.

Daughter?

"Yes," Lily said. Had she completely misread the whole conversation so far? Was she so obsessed with Nick Malone that she'd completely jumped to the wrong conclusions? "I think she probably goes to high school with you."

Jake turned an interesting shade of pink, and Lily didn't think it was coming from the heat of the steamer.

Okay, now she got it.

The Graham women captivated men of all ages.

Lily rolled her eyes. "Andie," she said. "You know Andie?"

"Well...yeah. I mean, I doubt she remembers I'm alive. But...I've seen her around."

Oh, I just bet you have, Lily thought.

She tried to think of the last time she'd seen Andie Graham and if the daughter took after the mother in her wardrobe choices.

Lily hoped not, for Jake's sake.

"Isn't she a little old for you, Jake?" Lily tried, because he was so adorably awkward and sweet, and if Andie was anything like her mother, she'd chew him up and spit him out without thinking twice about it. Lily hated to see him hurt.

"Only a year older," Jake said.

Lily nodded.

"Do you know...like...what she likes to do? I mean, where she might hang out? Or anything like that?" Jake asked.

"I think I've seen her at the mall a few times," Lily told him.

Andie really looked like a mall kind of girl.

She had a feeling Jake would be spending every spare moment there, hoping to run into Andie.

Trying to let him down easily, Lily told him, "I think, last I heard, she had a boyfriend who's in college now. Someone who went to her high school last year."

"Oh." Jake looked completely dejected.

A college boy.

Lily kept steaming. Jake attacked the wall, scraping so hard Lily was afraid he was going to gouge the Sheetrock underneath.

"Hey, why don't we take a break while I start dinner, okay?" she suggested.

"Dinner?" He perked right up at that.

"What would you like?" Lily asked, shutting off her steamer and heading for the refrigerator. "Come on. You can pick."

If he couldn't have Andie Graham, he could at least have a good dinner.

They dug through Lily's refrigerator, Jake settling on a chicken and rice dish Lily had made last week that he'd particularly enjoyed. She'd bought twice as much as she had the week before, astonished at how much he could eat and wanting to have enough to send home to Nick, too, and maybe for leftovers.

She'd learned Nick and Jake lived on takeout and her leftovers, and decided she was going to teach Jake to cook. Otherwise, they might not survive.

He was cutting up chicken, and Lily was assembling ingredients when the girls burst into the kitchen, arguing as they went.

"Cannot!" Ginny said, heading for the refrigerator.

"Can, too!" Brittany said, her bottom lip sticking out in a pout so adorable, it was all Lily could do not to laugh.

It was a good thing she looked cute when she pouted, because she pouted a lot and whined. The whining got really old, but the cute pout often saved Lily from getting too irritated.

"Cannot!" Ginny said, standing in the open refrigerator and blocking her sister's view of all the goodies inside.

"Can, too!" Brittany folded her arms and glared at her sister.

"What is it that Brittany cannot do?" Lily asked, giving her oldest daughter a look that used to have the power to silence her instantly, but was quickly losing that magical effect.

"She cannot have a horse for her birthday! She doesn't get a present like that!" Ginny said.

A horse?

Lily gaped at her baby girl, tears filling her eyes now as she tried to turn on the charm and get her way.

"Oh, honey," Lily said. "A horse?"

Brittany nodded hopefully. "Mattie Wright got a horse, and a special outfit to wear to ride it and riding lessons for her birthday!"

"Mattie Wright's father owns half the county," Lily said. "Including a farm on the edge of town where Mattie's horse can live. We don't have a place where a horse could live. We just have the backyard."

"He could live there," Brittany said.

"Honey, it's just not big enough for a horse."

"We could get a little horse," Brittany reasoned. "A baby horse. He wouldn't need much room."

Ginny started laughing at that. "A baby horse? You are so silly. A baby horse grows up into a big horse, Britt. Everybody knows that."

Brittany glared at her and started to cry.

Jake jumped in then, trying to help. "You know, Brittany, horses are really big. They can be kind of scary. One of my brothers was on a horse once, and he fell off and the horse stepped on him and broke his nose."

Brittany looked highly skeptical. "Did he really?"

Jake nodded. "Maybe it would be better to wait until you're bigger to have a horse."

Jake looked to Lily to see if that was a mistake or not. To imply she might get a horse later.

Lily nodded. Anything that got her daughter off the horse thing for now was okay with her.

"Isn't there anything else you'd like for your birthday?" Jake tried.

"Well." Brittany sighed, like it was quite a lot to ask, that she give up on the horse and go to her second choice. But she liked Jake and gave him an answer. "I thought about…a tree house."

Her eyes lit up once again, a new dream replacing the horse just that quickly.

Lily frowned once again. "A tree house?"

"Yeah," Brittany said, like it sounded like the greatest thing in the world.

"Oh. Great."

* * *

"Do you know anything about building tree houses?" Jake asked three nights later as they wolfed down take-out Chinese food for dinner.

Nick made a face. "You want a tree house?"

"No!" Jake looked disgusted. "Lily's daughter, the littlest one, Brittany, does. It's her birthday next week. I heard her talking to Lily about it when I was over there helping her with the wallpaper."

"Oh."

Lily.

Stay away from Lily.

Nick might need a flashing neon sign.

"So, do you know anything about 'em?" Jake asked.

"Not really. I mean, we had one when your mother and I were growing up, but it wasn't much more than a platform in a tree and a ladder to reach it."

"You think I could build one?" Jake said between shoveling a huge mouthful of curry chicken into his mouth.

"Have you ever built anything?"

"Not really."

"Then I don't think you should start with something in a tree. That's something you want to get right, especially if little girls are going to climb up there and play in it."

"That's what Lily said," Jake mumbled, mouth still half-full. "That she wasn't sure if she trusted herself to do it and have it be safe for Brittany. I mean, Lily knows how to do lots of stuff. She's fixing up her house all by herself and everything, but I guess the tree thing is different."

"Yeah," Nick said, thinking, *Stay away, stay away, stay away.*

If he could quit thinking about her neck, that would be even better.

"So, could you do it?"

"I don't know if that's a good idea, Jake," Nick said, trying to think of what he could use as an excuse, other than the fact that he'd decided Lily was hot and that he was getting really lonely fast.

"Why not?" The kid dumped the last of what Nick had thought was an impressive pile of chicken and rice onto his plate and resumed eating at a rapid pace.

Nick frowned.

"Did you want some of this?" Jake asked, holding out his plate.

"No. I'm good. Go ahead."

Gotta order more food next time, Nick told himself.

More food.

And stay away from Lily.

He could do those things.

"So…I don't get it. Why is it a bad idea?" Jake asked.

"I just…have a lot to do," Nick said. "We're barely settled in here, and I have things to take care of."

Best Nick could come up with.

He wondered if the kid could see straight through him and knew Nick was just trying to avoid Lily and why, but Jake just gave him an odd look.

"It's just that the poor kid's had a tough year, you know?" Jake said. "Her father moving out on them. And it's her birthday. She wanted a horse, but Lily said that was impossible, and the next thing she wanted was a tree house, and… I don't know. I just don't want her to be sad on her birthday. She's a little bitty kid, and she lost her dad, and… I just wanted to try to help."

Jake was practically in tears by the end of it, and Nick had a feeling they were talking about more than Lily's daughter feeling bad because her father moved out.

He had a feeling they were talking at least in part about Jake losing both a mother and a father and feeling pretty lousy about it and wishing there was something that would make him feel better.

If Nick knew what it was, he'd give it to the kid in a heartbeat.

A horse, a tree house...not on Jake's list, Nick was sure.

But it was sweet that the kid was thinking of Lily's little girl and what she'd lost and wanting to try to make it better.

He was a good kid.

A really good kid with a good heart.

Nick looked at him for a long time. Should he pat the kid on the back? Or do one of those manly, nonhug kind of things that men did, like hit him on the shoulder or something. Or did this call for an all-out hug?

Nick wasn't sure.

He wasn't sure about anything, so he just said the first thing he thought of.

"That's nice of you, Jake. To want to help her like that. Your mother would be proud of you."

Jake's head came up at that. "You think?"

"I know she would."

"So you'll help me help Lily with the tree house?" Jake asked, cornering him but good.

"We'll work something out," Nick said.

Maybe he could help without actually being there.

Help from a distance of some kind.

Or maybe Lily could leave, and he and Jake could build the thing, with Lily and her neck nowhere near them as they did it.

That was it.

Or something like that.

He just had to be strong.

Don't start anything.

And stay away from Luscious Lily.

Chapter Five

"So, big weekend alone, huh?" Marcy said suggestively over the phone to Lily, who was repacking for her girls' stay with their father. "What are you going to do?"

"Nothing, really," Lily said, wondering how her youngest expected to make it through the weekend with no socks, no underwear, no pajamas and three hair bows and a half a dozen toys. *Honestly.*

Lily dug into the sock and underwear drawer, grabbing a handful of both for Brittany.

"Lily, you can't just sit there and wait for life to come to you. You have to get out and meet it sometimes," Marcy claimed.

"I may meet my hairstylist and get my hair done," she said. Best she could do.

Marcy sighed heavily, as if Lily's life was such a chore that Marcy had to manage.

"I like getting my hair done!" Lily said.

Truly, she did.

It was nice and quiet in the salon, and she loved having someone else fuss over her hair. Just getting it washed felt good, and that little bit of scalp massage, and then having someone run their fingers through her hair....

It was Lily's turn to sigh in anticipation.

"There. What was that?" Marcy asked.

"That was me, thinking about getting my hair done. I really do like it."

"Is your hairdresser by any chance straight and male?"

Lily laughed, getting down on her hands and knees to look under the bed for Brittany's other shoe. "I wish!"

Having a cute, straight, single man fussing with her hair sounded really, really good.

She closed her eyes, seeing herself in the chair at the salon, practically purring with happiness, saw *him* smiling appreciatively at her in the salon mirror, felt big, strong, capable hands running through her hair....

Lily sighed once again, maybe groaned a bit.

Her imaginary hair-guy leaned down, lifting a handful of her hair to his face to smell it, then let his warm mouth settle against her neck. She watched in the mirror and then realized...

It was Nick.

"Ahhh!" Lily cried, coming out of her little stupor in the blink of an eye.

"Oh, wow. You must have a cute, straight hairdresser!" Marcy cried.

"I do not!" Lily insisted.

She had a cute—and she felt certain—straight neighbor who'd nearly nibbled on her neck to keep another woman away from him, and she'd been having wicked, wildly distracting thoughts about him ever since.

That was all.

"If you don't tell me everything right this minute—"

"Gotta go," Lily interrupted. "I hear Richard's car in the driveway."

"Spit on him for me," Marcy said. "Bye."

Lily got off the phone, grabbed the girls' bags and hurried downstairs, hating this whole exchange-of-the-children ritual. She tried to be civil, tried not to be nervous or mad or sad or anything, tried to be as neutral in her emotions and her speech as could be, and yet it was just so awkward and so hard.

To think that she and Richard would ever be shuffling their girls back and forth this way, disrupting their lives, changing everything, was still unbelievable.

The girls were in the family room playing on the computer. Lily yelled to them that their father had arrived as she carried their bags downstairs to the front door. She wanted to hand them over quickly, smiling somehow as she did it, and then hide in her house for a while, trying not to think of how quiet it was, how odd, how sad.

She made it outside, bags in hand, to find Richard standing on the driveway surveying the place like he was trying to figure out what it was worth at the moment, then looking uneasy as he saw her.

He pulled out his phone, checked it or at least pretended to, probably just trying to avoid talking to her, and then got a funny look on his face. Lily tried to remember what the admittedly handsome face had looked like when he'd so coldly told her he was walking out on her and the girls and had the nerve to think she shouldn't have been surprised or particularly upset. To remember that pretty packages didn't necessarily hold good things or good men inside of them, and that she didn't ever want to be fooled in that way again. That attraction could fizzle out and disappear so quickly, and a woman might be surprised at how little was left.

And then before she got too mad, she tried to just get the exchange over with.

"The girls are on their way," Lily said, talking too fast. "I double-checked their bags. They should have everything they need, including some cold medicine, in case Ginny's nose is stuffed up tonight. Don't worry. It's the grape-flavored kind. She likes it and won't give you a hard time about taking it. Dosage information is on the bottle. She weighs forty-six pounds—"

"Lily, wait—"

"Brittany's pillow, the one she won't sleep without, is in the bag. Please make sure it comes back with her on Sunday—"

"Lily, I'm trying to tell you—"

"And try not to load them up on sugar when you do the birthday thing with Brittany. A piece of cake at a restaurant is plenty—"

"Lily, I can't take them this weekend," he said.

She stopped talking at that, mouth hanging open, annoyance building inside of her like mercury rising in a thermometer on a scorching hot day. "What do you mean, you can't take them?"

"I mean, I can't. Something came up."

"Richard, it's Brittany's birthday!"

"Not until next Thursday. I'll come by then. Or the day before."

"You said you were going to take her to the zoo this weekend for her birthday. She's been looking forward to it for two weeks."

He didn't even have the grace to look embarrassed. "I'm sorry. I have a job to do."

"And you have a daughter who's turning seven!" she said, glaring at him.

Jake was home, standing in the kitchen with the door wide-open, staring outside, when Nick came downstairs to see if there were any leftovers from the previous night's dinner that had survived this long.

"Hey," Nick asked, grabbing a glass and hoping there was something to drink, too. "What's going on?"

Everything simply disappeared around Jake the human disposal unit.

"Lily's ex is giving her a hard time," Jake said, still standing there.

Nick turned around and went to stand behind the boy, staring at Lily on her driveway with a guy in a really expensive suit who was up in her face about something.

They weren't yelling, so Nick couldn't hear what was going on, but he didn't like how close the guy was or the look on his face.

"You sure it's the ex?" Nick asked.

"Yeah. He was supposed to take the girls this weekend, but he's backing out," Jake said, then looked like Nick might have thought he was doing something wrong. "I was walking home when he showed up, and I just wanted to make sure Lily was okay."

"Good for you," Nick told him, putting a hand on the kid's shoulder. "A man should always look out for a woman. Some of them won't ever thank you for it, because they think they're invincible, but they're not. And some men are just asses. This guy looks like one of 'em. What else did you hear?"

"He doesn't even want to go in and tell the girls himself that he's backing out on their weekend. He wants Lily to do it for him," Jake said.

Which meant Nick had a choice.

Stay away from Luscious Lily.

Stop wondering why that fool of a man would ever have left her, and stop being mad that he'd apparently decided to walk out on their kids this way, too.

Or go do something about it.

Nick definitely tended to be the kind of man who'd do something about it when anyone was doing something he didn't like to a woman.

And surely teaching her ex some manners was one thing he

could do without getting distracted by how much he wanted to nuzzle Lily's delectable neck.

Surely there was no danger here.

Still, he knew it was better to keep his distance, and Lily struck him as an immensely capable woman. She might not thank him for interfering. She might not even want him to know she was fighting with her ex about something like this.

"Let's give it a minute. See how this plays out," Nick said.

"Why? The guy's a real jerk," Jake said, still staring.

Now he had a scrawny, little finger that he was shaking in Lily's face, and then it looked like he was poking her in the shoulder with it, trying to get her to back away from him.

Nick saw red.

"You're right. We're not going to stand here and let him get away with that," Nick said. "Come on. Go to Lily's house. Get her girls and ask them to come outside."

Jake hesitated. "You're sure."

"Oh, yeah. This jerk can explain things to them himself, if he has the nerve," Nick said.

"But—"

"Go on. I'm right behind you. I'll handle him."

With pleasure, Nick decided.

With great pleasure.

Lily didn't see Nick or Jake until Jake walked past her and went in her kitchen door. She was starting to ask him where he was going when Nick walked up to her side and slid an arm ever so casually across her shoulder, like he belonged there, like he greeted her this way every day.

"Hey, Lily. Everything okay?" Nick asked, dropping a light kiss on her temple.

And then it was like he just took up too much space or sucked up all the air or something, because Richard backed up three steps. His stupid finger disappeared altogether, too

quickly for Lily to reach out and snap it off, which she'd wanted
to do ever since he stuck it in her shoulder to make a point. And
then as she watched, it was like Richard just shrank or something, looking smaller and more pathetic every second.

Lily was so happy with the way Richard backed off, she
forgot all about needing to take care of this herself and wanting
to both scream or maybe throw something at Richard's four
thousand dollars' worth of dental work or his perfect suit.

She remembered that everything had been up to her for so
long and that no one had helped her with anything in months,
and that she was tired and frustrated and exhausted and decided
she could have reached up and kissed Nick Malone right then
and there on the driveway and enjoyed it very much.

Enjoyed Richard's reaction to it, too, she thought.

But Lily resisted, settling for letting herself lean into Nick's
side, like she did it every day, and smile as she said, "Just a little
difference of opinion between me and Richard. He says he
won't be able to take the girls for the weekend, and here they
are all packed and ready to go."

"Oh," Nick said, like he belonged in this discussion, too.
"Must be something really important to keep a man from being
able to see his daughters. Especially this weekend."

Richard finally came out of his stupor and stopped staring
at Nick and how cozy he seemed to be with Lily, and said,
"Who are you exactly?"

"Nick Malone, Lily's new neighbor." He called himself a
neighbor, but the hold he had on her said something else entirely.

Richard frowned and looked confused. "You didn't tell me
you were seeing someone, Lily."

"Well, I didn't know you still cared, Richard," Lily said as
sweetly as she could, finding a smile easy to come by in that
instant, leaning against a truly gorgeous man who made her ex
look as insignificant as a fussy, pouty, scrawny boy.

Richard looked even more confused then, like he couldn't

quite believe another man was attracted to Lily? Or that this particular man was?

Lily really wished she had something to throw on that suit then.

The door opened behind them, the girls walking out, and Nick let her go and moved a step away. Brittany gave her father a big hug and a pretty smile, but Ginny hung back, still cautious around him since he'd moved out.

Brittany started talking about a trip to the zoo, something Richard had promised them, and Lily wanted to strangle her ex, who looked like he wanted to strangle either Jake or Nick. She realized Nick had made sure Richard at least had to face them before disappearing on them. Either way, it was going to hurt, that he wasn't going to keep his promise to them, and Lily wasn't sure how she felt about Nick deciding to make Richard do the telling.

She started to jump in and try to explain, but Nick's hand settled against the small of her back. He leaned over and whispered, "He should at least have to face what he's doing to them, Lily."

And then Richard finally started a fumbling explanation.

Lily fumed quietly.

So he really could turn them down to their faces.

That rat!

She hadn't been sure he would be able to, but he did.

Ginny looked like she wasn't surprised and glared at her father, but Brittany started to protest.

"You promised!" she said, tears filling her pretty eyes.

Richard tried again to explain, then looked at Lily pleadingly.

Now he wanted her help?

The weasel!

But it was Nick who jumped in and saved the day.

"Lily," he said, but looked at poor Brittany. "Maybe it's better that the girls are here this weekend. I mean, I know you wanted it to be a surprise, but it is going to be Brittany's present, and this way, she can design it herself and even help us build it, if she wants. It'll be fun."

"What?" Brittany asked, eyes still watery, but perking up at the word *present*.

"You're building my daughter a present?" Richard asked.

Now she was *his* daughter.

That was great, Lily thought. Just great.

Richard didn't even remember what his own daughter wanted, Lily suspected, though she had told him, but Nick apparently knew.

"Yeah. We'll make a weekend of it," Nick said, like he couldn't wait to get started. "We'll need to come up with a design tonight and head to the home builder's store for supplies, and we'll start building first thing in the morning. What do you say, Brittany?"

"You and Jake are gonna build me a tree house?" she asked, sniffling and drying her tears.

"That's the plan. It was going to be a surprise, but maybe its better this way. Since you're going to be here," Nick said, shooting a look at Richard that had him squirming, "you can tell us exactly what you want and pick out paint colors and everything."

Lily watched as her daughter's face went from sad and stormy to happy and excited. Ginny looked relieved, Jake extremely pleased. He must have told Nick about Brittany wanting a tree house and Lily being unsure if she trusted herself to do the project.

"I want to help," Brittany told Nick.

"Okay. Let's go to the backyard and see what kind of tree we have to work with."

She put her little hand into Nick's and followed him into the backyard, Ginny and Jake going after them.

Lily just smiled up at Richard. "Well, I guess we'll see you...whenever."

He looked all put out, then practically yelled, "This is my weekend with them, after all."

"I know, but if you can't make it, you can't make it, Richard."

He threw his hands up in the air. "And exactly who is that man?"

"He told you. He's our new neighbor. Isn't he just great?"

And then Lily turned around—leaving her ex standing there fuming—and followed the weekend tree house construction crew into her backyard.

By the time Lily made it into the backyard, Nick had the kiddie construction crew organized and heading off to follow his orders.

Brittany was headed upstairs to find a book with a picture of exactly what she wanted for her tree house. Ginny was getting a tape measure from the kitchen, and Jake was headed to his house for a ladder.

Nick stood leaning against the biggest tree in her backyard, waiting, looking a little unsure of his reception.

"You mad at me?" he asked, when Lily made it to his side.

She thought about it, then admitted, "No. Not really."

"You sure?"

"Gee, Nick, why would I be mad?"

"Because I jumped into a situation that was none of my business," he said. "Gave your ex the idea there was something going on between us, when there really isn't. Made sure he had to face the girls before walking out on them this weekend, which was really not my decision to make, and then promised your daughter a tree house that you might not want her to have."

Lily nodded. "Yeah. You did. That's quite a list."

"So, I'd say you have a right to be mad." He looked a bit sheepish, as if to say he just couldn't help himself. "I just want you to know, I would have stayed out of it if he hadn't started shoving you backward with that little finger of his. Besides, it's not like I hit him or pushed him up against the side of the house or anything, and believe me, from where I stood, he deserved it and I sure wanted to give it to him."

"Okay." Lily would have freely admitted Richard poking her in the shoulder had really annoyed her. "But I could have handled him."

"I didn't say you couldn't have, Lily. I just thought...you shouldn't have to."

"Well, he's my ex. I was crazy enough at one point to trust him and marry him, to have children with him. That means I have to deal with him," she reasoned, not wanting to think about how it felt to have another man act like he had the right to protect her from the big, bad world. That was too much to think of at this moment with so many other things going on that she had to deal with.

"All right. I'm sorry," Nick said. "I have trouble standing by when a guy is manhandling a woman."

Lily wasn't sure what Richard had done would qualify as manhandling, but she let that one go.

"Tell me to stay out of it in the future, and I will," he said, sounding like he meant it. "Unless I see him put his hands on you in a way I don't like, and then you're just going to have to be mad at me. Because if I see him do that to you, I'm not walking away from it."

"Well, if that's as reasonable as you get..."

He rolled his eyes in surrender, blew out a long, slow breath and finally backed down. "Maybe we could work out a signal or something. One for me to stay the hell out of it and one that says I can do what I want with him?"

"That I'd accept," she said, laughing. "What did you say you do for a living, Nick?"

"I don't think I did."

"Mommy?" Ginny came running toward them, holding out a tape measure. "Is this what you and Nick needed?"

Lily took it from her. "Yes, sweetie. That's it."

She looked back at Nick. "I forgot the paper and the pencil. I'll go back."

And then she turned and ran back to the house before Lily could stop her. All because one take-charge-kind-of-man had taken over and started issuing orders.

Lily looked back at him and said, "Let me guess. Cop?"

"Army for a long time," he admitted. "Most recently, FBI."

"Oh." Even more dangerous than she thought. But she could see it in him. A man who didn't stand by while someone pushed a woman around, and one who was used to sticking his nose into unpleasant situations.

"I'm on leave right now, to get Jake settled," he said. "But I've worked Missing Persons in D.C. for the last three years. There are a lot of nasty people in this world, Lily."

"Richard's an insurance agent. I think by definition, they're not very dangerous."

"You never know. People you'd never think would do something violent can get pushed too far, especially when strong emotions are involved—like in a divorce. And then they can do things you wouldn't believe possible."

"Then we're perfectly safe, because the only real emotion Richard seems to have left toward me or the girls is annoyance," she shot back, then immediately wished she hadn't.

Because it hurt to say it, to admit it and to have anyone else know it.

"Oh, damn," Lily said, feeling it like a fist in her midsection.

It happened like that sometimes. She could be going along, living her life, taking care of her girls, thinking they were all just fine, and then some nasty little memory popped into her mind of great times or awful ones. And then it felt like someone had shoved a fist into her belly, catching her completely unaware, and it just hurt so bad she could hardly stand it.

She shot Nick an exasperated look and then put her back to him, wishing she could just disappear.

Chapter Six

He gave her a minute to get herself together, for which she was grateful, and she took the time to lean against the tree, fighting for a steadying breath of her own.

She was supposed to be a strong, capable woman after all.

She'd just argued that very thing to Nick, and here she was ruining it all by nearly dissolving into tears at the idea that her ex didn't give a damn about her and the girls.

"You okay?" Nick came to her side, put an arm around her shoulders.

Lily fought against that, too. Honestly, she did.

No one held her anymore. No one had in a very long time.

And it felt so good to have someone close, a grown-up, someone big and strong who wasn't depending on her to take care of him. Who actually seemed interested in taking care of her.

He would have no idea how seductive that idea was to a woman in Lily's shoes. Someone to take care of her for a change.

"You can just cry it out, if you want," he offered. "I can

handle a few tears. I mean, I don't like them, but I'm tough enough to take it. Go ahead."

Lily laughed through a shimmer of tears in her eyes and she thought she might be able to hold back now.

"You're not one of those men who just dissolves into nothing at the idea of a woman crying?"

"Now what kind of man would I be if I did that?" he said easily, still holding her pressed against his side.

Okay, Lily thought. *Just for a minute.*

She leaned into him, feeling how solid he was, how capable he seemed, how calm in the face of her little emotional storm and Richard being such a jerk.

It was like something inside of her was inching ever closer to Nick, the sweetness of him, the steadiness, the strength, the temptation of him, and she wasn't sure she had the strength to pull away.

What would be so wrong with it? she asked herself.

"Ah, Lily, I'm sorry," he said, giving her a little squeeze, his chin, his nose, then his lips nuzzling against her forehead.

Lily got herself together and backed away, shakily, but she did it.

Because of how very much she wanted to stay right there in his arms.

She shrugged, tried not to look like she'd just lost it and then had to tear herself away from him. "It just…sneaks up on me sometimes…how bad it can still feel to think of everything that's happened."

"I'm sorry, Lily. Really, I am. Especially if I made things worse by getting in the middle of it," he said, still too close for her own comfort.

She was grateful in a way for the high-handed way he'd gotten in the middle of everything with Richard, to have Richard see her as someone who'd have a new, gorgeous man by her side. And she appreciated the way Nick had stepped back immediately when he heard the girls coming. She didn't think they'd seen any of it.

But it was sheer pretense, and it needed to stay that way. Because it was dangerous to depend on anyone else but herself. Richard had taught her that very well. She no longer believed a woman could count on promises of any kind from a man.

Which made Nick Malone an obviously very nice, but very dangerous man.

Lily took one more step back to try and save herself.

"This is not your fight, Nick," she said quietly.

"I know," he agreed. "I won't do it again unless you ask me to intervene. I mean it."

"Okay." Lily nodded. "And it's really not up to you to decide whether I tell my girls their father's a jerk or he shows them that he's a jerk."

"Yeah. I know. I thought he probably wouldn't be able to look them in the eye and walk away from them today, and then I thought, if he's really going to do that, he should at least have to face them."

"He deserves that, yes, but I'm not sure if that's the best thing for my girls right now, and that's my decision to make," she insisted.

"You're right. It is. I'm sorry, Lily. The guy just really pissed me off."

"Well, join the club," she said.

She was trying to figure out where they went from here when Jake yelled from the back of the driveway, "Hey, did you mean this one?"

He was carrying a small ladder.

"No, the big one," Nick yelled back, and Jake disappeared, ladder in tow. "So," Nick said to her, "the way I see it, I have a lot to make up for. And Jake and I owe your daughter a tree house."

"No, you don't."

"Yeah, we do. I'm the one who promised her one. Oh, hell, I don't even know if you want her to have one," he admitted.

"I don't mind her having one, I'm just not sure if I trust myself to build her one that's safe."

He shrugged, grinned ever so slightly, like he knew he was pushing. "Well, then…there is something I can do to make this up to you. What do you say? We could make a project of it. You, me, the girls and Jake?"

"I'm sure you have better things to do than build a tree house this weekend," Lily said.

He shook his head. "Well, I could start going through massive amounts of paperwork having to do with my sister and her husband's estate to try to get it settled. I could try to figure out how much money's going to be left for the boys. Hopefully, they can get through college on it, but I'm not sure yet. I could start getting used to the idea that all that's left of my sister and her husband's lives is a house full of stuff, a bank account here and there, bills left to be paid, forms to fill out, a sum of some money, and three boys…. Believe me, I'd much rather build a little girl a tree house."

"Okay, but you have to let me pay you and Jake."

"No way. I'm not going to take money from you for building a tree house, especially when I'm the one who told your daughter I'd make sure she got one."

"I will pay you for your time," Lily insisted.

"How about we take it out in trade? Jake and I have had takeout three nights in a row. It's getting old really fast."

Lily knew that would make Jake happy, and she'd just double what she was making for herself and the girls. "Okay. Deal."

Lily hadn't quite known what she was getting into.

Her daughter wanted something akin to a kiddie mansion in a tree. A lavender and pink kiddie mansion.

But they soon figured out that as long as it was lavender and pink, with some scalloped trim along the roofline and a balcony, Brittany would be happy.

"Balcony?" Nick whispered in disbelief to Lily as they stood perusing shades of lavender at the paint store later that night.

"So she can play princess," Lily explained. "Little girls go through a phase where they still want to play princess on a balcony with the prince down below, begging for their hand."

Jake stood back from the overwhelming rows of paint shades, close enough to Lily and Nick to hear, and said, "You're kidding, right?"

"I wish I was," Lily admitted.

"But…like…most houses don't even have balconies, right? I mean, how's a guy supposed to do that, if the girl doesn't even have a balcony?" Jake looked really confused, then turned to Nick. "You never did the balcony thing, did you?"

"No way," Nick said.

Jake looked mightily relieved. "Whew."

Brittany came back with a paint strip with a horribly bright purple on it and held it up to Nick. "I like this one."

"Well…that's…an interesting color." Nick took it from her, then went two colors down on the paint strip, to something decidedly less bright "But the thing is, you've already picked a really bright color for the trim. The pink. And I think your mother, as a decorator, will tell you that colors with a lot of contrast look best together."

"Contest?" Brittany asked. "The colors are gonna have a contest?"

"No, contrast. More like…different. Really different," Nick tried. "And one way to make the colors really different is to use a bright color for one and a lighter color for the other. So if we did the bright pink, like this one, for the trim, we should probably go with a lighter purple. Like this."

He put Brittany's bright pink next to a lavender that was almost white, it was so light.

"See how well they go together?" he asked.

"I guess so." Brittany frowned a bit, then went back to the brighter color. "But I still like that one."

"Well, we might need a second trim color. So I guess we could get some of that, too. We'll use all three."

"Okay," she said, happy again.

Jake muttered something about girls being so weird and about being hungry. Brittany skipped the rest of the way through the home building store. Ginny kept throwing suspicious looks at Lily and Nick, like she was wondering if something was up between the two of them. Nick clearly didn't understand princess balconies or princess colors, but was obviously committed to doing what he'd promised, to build Brittany a fabulous tree house.

And Lily?

Lily was thinking stupidly that Nick was really good with her girls, much more patient than her ex, and that he was good with Jake, too, and that she was having fun in the store, buying supplies for their project, and looking forward to the weekend spent with all of them working together to build Brittany's tree house.

Like Lily was anywhere near the point of wanting another man in her life or her children's.

And then Nick Malone had to come along and build play places in pink and purple with princess balconies, even though he clearly thought it was a silly idea, just because it was what her daughter wanted.

Don't do this to me, Nick, Lily thought. *Don't.*

But he just kept right on. Charming her daughters. Guiding Jake with a blend of gentleness and firmness she couldn't help but admire, and acting like he was perfectly at home with Lily this way. Like this could be their little family, and the story had a happily-ever-after ending, and Richard and her life with him was nothing but a bad memory, fading away to almost nothing.

It was like she sat back and watched it all unfolding in front of her.

And she had a wicked craving for fudge.

Much as she tried, there was no way for Lily to hide the tree house's construction from her sister, because it was all that Brittany talked about, nonstop, all weekend, and Brittany loved to answer the phone.

So by Saturday morning, Lily found Brittany on the phone telling her aunt Marcy all about her wondrous tree house and the most wondrous tree house builders, Nick and Jake.

Marcy must have broken all landspeed records in getting to Lily's house to see the wondrous tree house builders for herself. She found them all in the backyard, Marcy's youngest, Stacy, who was a year older than Brittany, exploding onto the scene, giggling and chattering and dancing around the base of the tree as Brittany told her all about her princess tree house.

At that point, Nick was shirtless, having worked up a manly sweat from his construction efforts, and hauling a stack of two-by-fours from the driveway into the backyard, his back thankfully to Marcy, as Marcy stood on the edge of the driveway, her mouth gaping open in a look of complete and utter awe.

"Who is that?" she finally managed to say.

"My new neighbor," Lily admitted, planting herself between Nick and Marcy, trying to have a few words with her some-times-pushy, always-talkative older sister, before Marcy charged the scene and started talking to Nick herself.

Marcy's mouth gaped open even further. "Thaaaatttt moved in next to you?"

Lily nodded.

"And you didn't tell me?" Marcy nearly yelled that.

Nick's head swung around, along with the boards, muscles rippling in his arms and shoulders from the effort in a way that had Lily going weak in the knees. Marcy might have been drooling. Lily couldn't be sure. She waved at Nick to tell him everything was fine and to go on moving what he was moving, because that would take him farther away from Marcy, at least temporarily.

"Please," Lily begged her sister. "Please, please, please do not embarrass me."

Marcy had the nerve to look offended at that.

Lily sighed and begged some more. "Please!"

"He's the Fudge Guy!" Marcy figured it out right away. "He's the reason you sounded so funny on the phone that day we were talking about fudge!"

"Yes."

"When you thought you had a fever that day, you were looking at him!"

"Yes, I was! All right! Now you know. Could we just…not do this right now in front of him?" Lily said in a furious whisper.

Marcy huffed and puffed some more, like she had reason to be offended. "And you let me think it was your hairdresser, and that you were going to do nothing but get your hair done this weekend, when this…absolutely gorgeous man is in your backyard, sweating and flexing his muscles, stripped down to nothing but his jeans and all that gorgeous man-skin. Oh, my God! Men just stop looking like that at some point, you know? I mean, I'm sure you and I can't stop traffic like we used to when we were…I don't know. A few years younger—"

"You might have stopped traffic, but I never did," Lily insisted.

"I'm not going to argue with you about that, because you've never seen yourself as you really are. But for now, my point is, men just stop looking that good when they reach a certain age, and it's just a shame, you know? Because it's really nice to look around and see really good-looking men. It's just a little perk to a woman's day to have that kind of scenery around her."

"I'm sure you look enough to know," Lily said.

"I like to look, so what? It's not a crime. I don't touch. It's nice to have something good to look at, and that man…he is worth looking at. Which you've obviously been doing and keeping it from me."

"Yes, all right? I did. I didn't tell you because—"

"Mommy, look!" Stacy called out, a look of pure glee on her face. "A princess tree house!"

"I know, sweetie," Marcy said, grinning for all she was worth as she looked from her daughter to Nick, who was bent over a board doing something, his nearly perfect backside encased in a worn pair of jeans.

Marcy just gaped for a moment.

"Mommy!" Stacy yelled impatiently.

It was all Marcy could do to tear her gaze away. "What? What, sweetie?"

"I said, I want one, too. Can I have one?"

"We'll see, Stace. We'll talk to Daddy and look at the trees in our backyard, okay?" Marcy turned back to Lily and was practically fanning herself. "Is this his line of work? Construction? Is he taking orders? Not that I'm sure I could handle having him in my backyard, looking like this. I might forget my look-but-don't-touch policy, which would be a shame, because I really do love my husband."

"I know you do. And don't worry. Nick is just doing us a favor. He doesn't work in construction. He's an FBI agent," Lily told her.

Marcy gave one of those aching sighs again, like it hurt almost, just to think of Nick, gorgeous and some kind of cool, dangerous government agent. "This man just gets better and better."

Which was the last thing Lily needed to hear or think about, because she was afraid she felt the same way. The more she saw and knew, the more she liked.

"So, why did you not tell me all this?" Marcy demanded.

"Because… I just didn't. I wasn't sure what I thought about the whole thing yet myself, and—"

"You don't know what you think about having this beautiful specimen of man living right next door to you? Lily, are you absolutely nuts?"

"No. I'm sure I have all the appropriate thoughts a woman might have when someone like him shows up next door."

"And they're all decidedly inappropriate, I hope."

"Yes, Marcy. Yes." Lily's face flamed, and she got even more flustered. "I am having decidedly inappropriate thoughts."

Marcy's lips spread into a wide, satisfied grin. "I take it he's single?"

"Yes."

Marcy's gasp was practically orgasmic.

Lily buried her face in her hands and wished she could disappear right then and there.

"Oh, honey," Marcy said. "I think this man is your reward for all you suffered through with that pig, Richard."

"My reward?"

"Yes. You don't think the universe sends us little presents from time to time? Because you've been through such a hard time, and you've worked so hard to keep the girls happy and out of the nastiness between you and Richard. You've been a great mother, but you're still a woman, and this beautiful creature is your reward."

Lily had never known the universe to offer such a reward, never imagined it delivering a man to her, to meet her womanly needs.

Oh, she thought she was a lucky woman, despite all the mess with Richard. She had her wonderful girls and a job she enjoyed and they were all healthy and happy most of the time. She had a big, loving—if nosy—family, and she thought she was blessed in many ways.

But to deliver her a man like Nick?

"Marcy, you can't possibly think the world works that way."

"Sure I can. He's here, isn't he? And looks to be the perfect…Fudge Man."

"Somebody say something about fudge?" a decidedly male voice asked.

Marcy's and Lily's heads both swung around to see Jake, a thinner, younger version of his uncle, heading from his garage to Lily's backyard, a power saw in hand.

"Lily, you're going to make more fudge?" Jake asked hopefully.

"Uh…sure, if I have everything I need, I will," she said.

Jake grinned widely. "Lily makes killer fudge."

Marcy shot Lily a knowing look. "You already made him fudge?"

"For Nick and his nephew, Jake, as a housewarming gift," Lily said, once again daring Marcy to say anything else before turning to Jake to introduce him to Marcy.

Marcy pumped Jake for as much information as she could before getting onto the subject of how Jake came to live with his uncle, and then Lily stopped her as fast as she could.

"Jake, I think your uncle needs that saw."

"Oh, sure," he said, nodding his head to Marcy. "Nice to meet you, ma'am."

"Ma'am?" Marcy said woefully. "Oh, my God, I'm getting 'ma'am-ed' by pretty boys. My life has come to this."

"You poor thing," Lily said. "Maybe you could just not talk to Jake anymore."

"Well, I had to try to find out some things. I know I can't trust you to tell me anything," Marcy reasoned.

"I will tell you that his parents were killed in a car accident two months ago, and that's why he's now living with his uncle, so try not to ask him about it, okay?"

"Oh. How awful for him. And how wonderful that the gorgeous man in your backyard is the kind of man who'd step in and raise his nephew like that," Marcy said, showing new interest in Nick.

Lily groaned.

"What? He's obviously a nice guy, not just a gorgeous one. Responsible, kind, likes kids—"

"Marcy, stop."

"Do you know how rare this is in a man?"

"I know my ex-husband hasn't been gone a year, and he didn't have all those qualities, and I'm not sure if I believe any man really does," Lily told her.

"Oh, honey." Marcy sighed and put her arm around Lily's waist. "We're just going to have to work on that, because a man like this does not come along every day."

"So, he's gone from being my gift from the universe to fulfill all my womanly needs to being family-man material in…what? Two minutes? Honestly, Marcy. Slow down. I barely know him."

"Well, you're just going to have to fix that. Women are going to be showing up in droves to snatch him right out from under your nose."

"They already are," Lily admitted. "I swear, the temperature rose ten degrees in a six-block radius the moment he moved in. You wouldn't believe how many women showed up on his doorstep bearing gifts and looking like they were dressed up for New Year's Eve or something."

"See, you have no time to lose! You have to grab this man before anyone else does."

"I don't grab," Lily insisted, as she saw Nick striding toward them, having finished whatever he'd been doing with his two-by-fours. "I'm not a man-grabber."

"Well, it's time you started," Marcy said, as Nick came to stand by Lily's side.

Lily shot her sister one more warning look, then tried to appear as composed as she could manage and said, "Nick, this is my sister, Marcy, and the little girl is her youngest, Stacy. Marcy, this is Nick."

Nick held out his hand and shook Marcy's.

Marcy managed not to melt at his feet, but just barely. "Hi," she said, a silly, breathy sound she used to make when she was sixteen and in complete awe of a boy. "I'm so glad Lily has a man next door."

She made the word *man* sound like *Greek God.*

All because he had a few muscles and a nice tan.

Lily tried to tell herself that and the fact that she was not a man-grabber. She just didn't have it in her. Never had, never would. And the competition for this man was sure to be fierce.

And yet, the man was obviously much more than a few muscles and miles of gorgeous skin.

He was a nice man.

A really nice man.

And gorgeous.

Lily couldn't deny that part.

He was building her daughter a tree house, saving Brittany's birthday weekend, and had stood up for Lily and Brittany to Lily's ex, which had been really, really nice. And he smelled really good, especially when he'd nuzzled her neck the other day.

Lily had given a great deal of thought to that neck-nuzzling, despite how hard she'd tried to forget it.

Gorgeous, nice to small children and his nephew, handy around the house, great-smelling, single and a neck-nuzzler.

Marcy was right.

Where would she ever find another man like that?

Chapter Seven

A little more than twenty-four hours later, Nick was stretched out in a surprisingly comfortable wooden chair in Lily's backyard, the masterpiece of a tree house completed.

Nick was now pleasantly sore from using muscles he hadn't used in a while, enjoying a perfect fall evening in Lily's backyard, complete with pleasantly cool temperatures, a bright, starry sky and a full moon.

The girls were playing happily in the tree house. Jake had gone to his room to play video games. Lily had grilled steaks to absolute perfection and served them for dinner.

When she showed up in the backyard a few minutes later with a small cooler with two ice-cold beers in it for Nick, he decided his life was complete at the moment.

"Lily," he said, sighing happily. "I have to say, you really know how to treat a man. And your ex has to be an idiot."

She laughed, as he'd hoped she would, and settled into the

chair beside him, holding a glass of wine for herself. "I fed you and gave you a couple of beers."

"Fed me extremely well," he corrected.

"It was a steak on the grill," she reminded him.

"Yeah. What do you think a man really wants? A hunk of red meat, a big baked potato, a few icy beers, and we're happy. Very happy. Plus, it was a great steak. What did you do to it?"

"Marinated it in some teriyaki sauce for an hour and threw it on the grill. Surely you can grill a steak."

"Not and have it turn out like that."

"So you're completely hopeless in the kitchen?"

"Yes," he admitted.

"How did you survive all these years?"

"Takeout, the deli counter at the grocery store—"

"Women to take pity on you and feed you?"

"There weren't that many women," he told her, taking a nice, cold drink of his beer.

"I have trouble believing that," she said. "Especially given your reception in this neighborhood."

"You forget, normally I would never be in a neighborhood like this."

"Okay, but still…"

Did she really want to know about him and the women he'd known? Nick supposed he should tell her, just so she knew what she was getting into.

If she was even thinking of getting into anything with him.

He was sure thinking of getting into some things with her. Maybe it was inevitable. She was right next door, right here all the time, and so appealing.

"I spent all but the last three years in the army, all over the world, really. It's not exactly the kind of life that makes for stable relationships," he told her. "I've seen more marriages break up from the stress of it all than most people have seen get started."

"It sounds like you liked the all-over-the-world part."

"Who wouldn't?" he asked, but then could see the idea didn't particularly appeal to her. "You never wanted to just get away from everything and keep on moving?"

"Every now and then, for a little while. I'd love to go to Florence and Rome for a couple of weeks. Not for my whole life."

He shrugged, then admitted, "Okay, yeah. I liked it. I liked it a lot for a long time."

"So what happened? Why'd you stop? Seen everything there was to see?"

"Maybe."

"Didn't ever find what you were looking for out there?" she tried.

"That's what my sister said," he said. "I never told her she was right. I'm not even sure myself if she was right. I just… I was ready for a change, and it was nice, the last three years to be in D.C. with the Bureau and be able to get down here to see more of her and the boys. Now that she's gone, I'm really glad we had that time. I never really understood how she did it— made a marriage work with the same man for twenty-three years—but she was a happy woman. She loved her husband, and her boys are great. She would have said she loved her life."

"And she thought your life needed to be more like hers?"

"You have a sister like that?" he asked. "Who thinks she knows everything, especially what you need?"

"You've met mine. What do you think?"

He nodded. "Yours is…interesting."

"Bossy, interfering, nosy," Lily added. "I mean, I love her, but sometimes I imagine just being able to block all her calls for a while without her just showing up on my doorstep and demanding to know what's going on with my life."

"Annie was more subtle than your sister, but she did have a way of making you understand what she thought you weren't doing what you should be doing with your life. She just kept waiting for me to…I don't know. Figure it out? She was sure I'd get tired of roaming the world one day, and I guess I did, finally. But she was still waiting for me to do…I don't know. Something different. Something more," he admitted. "And she was always trying to fix me up with women."

Lily laughed. "She didn't approve of your choices?"

"No." Nick thought about it, going back and forth with himself, thinking back through the years over the ones he'd introduced to his sister. "I mean, don't get me wrong. I like women. But they can be a lot of trouble, a lot of work."

Lily really laughed then.

"Maybe I just never found one I thought was worth all that effort."

"Ooh." Lily made a face.

"Okay, I sounded like a jerk. I didn't mean it like that, really. I've just… I've never met a woman I couldn't live without. Never met one who made me feel like it was absolutely necessary to have her in my life. That I'd be miserable without her. I'm not sure I ever will." He shrugged. "Some people just don't make those kind of connections, you know? Did you feel that way about your husband? Like he was the only one for you?"

"I thought he was in the beginning, but…maybe I just really wanted to feel that way about someone and there he was, right time, right place, right… I don't even know now."

"You must have been really young," he said.

Lily nodded. "Richard and I met in college, got married right after we graduated. We'd been together for ten years when he left."

Which had Nick wondering if maybe Richard was the only man who'd ever truly been in her life.

In her bed.

Which was a dangerously appealing thought.

It had him wondering if the man was as selfish and stupid there as he seemed to be in the rest of his life. Wondering if the man had taken as lousy care of Lily in bed as he obviously had out of it.

Which had Nick thinking about having Luscious Lily to himself, in his bed, showing her what it was like to have a man truly take care of her in bed, at least.

Would she be sweet and a little shy?

He'd bet she would.

She'd practically melted in his arms the day he'd done nothing but breathe in the scent of her and nuzzle her neck.

Ah, Lily. You're killin' me.

And then he thought, why did he have to fight so hard against this?

She was right here. He was here. They were obviously attracted to one another.

He just had to figure out how to ask for what he wanted.

Nick was up to something.

Lily knew it, and he was making her nervous.

He'd been half-naked and sweaty and grinning happily all weekend, as he worked to give her little girl a birthday weekend that was truly special.

For which Lily was grateful.

But now, it was just the two of them, Jake gone and the girls close but out of sight, playing inside the tree house.

Just her and Nick, and a dark, starlit, fall night, the man a little too close for comfort.

"So, it's been just you and the girls since your ex left?" he asked.

Lily went still. Was he asking if she'd been with anyone else since her husband walked out on her?

Surely he wasn't asking her that.

Maybe he just wanted to know that there wasn't anybody else right now. Could that be it?

Oh, he was going to ask her out!

Lily grinned like crazy, hoping the dark was enough to hide it from him.

She felt like getting up and dancing around the yard, she was so happy. Forget being so cautious and scared. Richard had been gone for more than a year, actually for a long time before that, truth be told, and her sister was probably right. She couldn't be alone forever. She had to get out there in the dating world sooner or later.

So, they'd have dinner or see a movie.

What was the big deal?

It was just a date.

"I haven't dated or anything," she said, trying for all the world to sound calm. "It took a while for everything to sink in, that Richard was really gone, and he wasn't coming back. And then there was just so much to do, to make sure the girls were okay and deal with the separation and divorce, and make sure we'd be okay financially. I haven't felt like I really had time to…do anything for myself."

He nodded, going slowly, picking his words carefully. "And, I guess it would be hard to find time to get out and meet someone with the girls to take care of."

"Yes," she agreed.

Which made it so convenient that he'd just shown up next door.

Maybe Marcy was right. He was like a little present from the universe.

Which made her think of unwrapping him very, very slowly. *Bad Lily. Very bad Lily.*

"And I imagine you might not want the girls to know you were seeing anybody? I mean, that you might not know how they'd take that?"

Lily nodded. "Or worry that they might get attached to someone and then see him leave, too. Honestly, I hadn't given that much thought to the whole idea of dating. But it would be complicated with the girls."

"And for me, with Jake," he said.

"You think Jake would have a problem with you dating someone?" Lily was surprised. Jake seemed pretty reasonable.

"Oh, he wouldn't have a problem with it. He just thinks we'll have…open house, I guess you would say. I'm free to have my women sleep over, and he's free to have his do the same thing."

Lily burst out laughing, it was so ridiculous.

Nick looked pained, then shook his head and took another drink of his beer. "I think he was serious. He said it just like that. Like he didn't expect me to have any kind of problem with it. What am I supposed to do about that?"

"You're asking me? My girls are seven and nine. No one's asking me for coed sleepover privileges. And I'm very glad about that right now."

"I didn't know what to say to him. I mean, I told him he was crazy if he thought he was bringing teenage girls home for the night—"

"Good. That's exactly what you should have said."

"But what if I want to start seeing someone? Do I sneak around behind his back? That seems kind of silly, too. I mean, he's not a child, but he is only fifteen. I'm thirty-eight. Am I supposed to live like a monk or do I get some kind of pass on this?"

"I don't know if I'm the person to ask about this," Lily said. "I really don't have any experience with this kind of parenting problem. I mean, I guess you could hope to find a woman with no kids and a place of her own and make an early night of it. So Jake isn't home alone for long."

Nick grinned and put his beer down in the grass beside him, then turned to look at her. "Not gonna work. The woman I've got my eye on has two little girls."

"Oh." Lily nearly dropped her glass of wine.

Nick saved her by taking it out of her hand and putting it down in the grass, too. Then he took her chin in his hand, and very slowly, giving her time to pull away if she wanted to, leaned in close, his nose nuzzling hers, lips practically on hers.

"It's you, Lily. The woman I want is you."

Lily might have grabbed him and kissed him then.

Or he might have grabbed her and kissed her.

Actually, now that she thought about it, he wasn't a grabber.

He was exquisitely gentle and smooth and very, very sure of himself.

So it must have been her who reached out and wrapped her arms around him and hung on to him for dear life.

Anything to mean that he kept kissing her the way he was.

Warm, soft, sexy lips on hers, the heat of him seeping into her bones, his arms so strong and sure around her. Making her feel like it had been about a million years since a man had held her this way, kissed her this way, excited her this way.

She felt the same way she had when she'd looked out her kitchen window and seen him in the bright sunshine, all gleaming skin and muscles, dark golden hair and dark eyes, sexy as can be and a little bit scary.

Because it didn't feel safe to feel this way about him or any man.

But at the same time, it felt so very good.

Lily sank into him, opening herself up to him, greedy for the taste and feel of him, like a woman who'd been alone for decades.

Honestly, that's how it felt. Decades.

She clung to him, drinking in those sweet, drugging kisses of his, imagining hands all over her body, clothes stripped off, her welcoming him into her bed.

If they'd been alone, she feared that was where they'd be in five minutes flat.

The man's appeal was that potent. Either that, or she had become the proverbial sex-starved divorced woman, sleeping alone in the suburbs for way too long.

He started pulling away long before she was satisfied, his arms slowly disentangling himself from her, taking her face in his hands, his lips grinning against hers as she tried to get in one more kiss and then another and another before this was over. Like she absolutely could not get enough of him.

"Lily, honey." He laughed. "We can't do this right now. Believe me, I want to. But we can't. Jake's at my house, and your girls on the other side of the yard, and you don't want them to know anything about this. Remember?"

Lily laughed, too, because she was so happy. Because she felt alive again, after being half-dead for so long. Because a gorgeous man had moved in next door to her, and he was kind and sweet to her girls and good to his nephew, and right now, he did seem like a present from the universe, delivered right to Lily.

"Sorry. I… Oh, geez." She was embarrassed now. Happy, but embarrassed.

"I know. Believe me, I know," he said, drawing in a long breath and letting it out slowly. "At least, they have to go to sleep at some point. I don't guess you'd feel comfortable with me slipping in the back door after you get the girls to bed tonight?"

Lily still had what felt like shooting stars inside of her, felt every little zing as they zipped around inside of her, bringing her back to life.

It was like she could still feel his lips on hers, was still drowning in all the sweet sensations, so she didn't quite get what he said the first time.

"What?" she asked.

"Me, slipping in the back door after the girls go to bed tonight. You wouldn't be comfortable with that, would you?"

She looked up at him dumbly through the darkness.

All those little tingling sensations were still there, all the excitement, all the joy, but it was starting to fade and fade fast.

He expected to be in her bed tonight?

Just like that?

Lily was starting not to feel so good.

She was starting to feel foolish.

"I thought..." *Oh, no.* "You meant...when you said...and you..."

"Yeah, but I understand. I mean, I didn't think you'd be comfortable with that. What about tomorrow? While the kids are in school? It'll be just the two of us. No one ever has to know."

Lily felt like all those really good, tingly feelings drained right out of her, along with all the air in her lungs.

He wasn't asking her to go out on a date with him.

He just wanted to sleep with her.

She sat back in her chair, wishing she could disappear into the darkness.

Was this what people did these days? Just jump into bed together? Did nobody date? Maybe not. What did she know? She hadn't been single for a dozen years, after all.

Maybe she should feel flattered instead of shocked and embarrassed.

"I'm sorry," she said, just wanting to flee. "Really. I am. But, I can't—"

"Lily?"

"I just... I didn't know...uh. I have to go." She jumped up, ready to flee.

He reached for her, got a hold of her hand, but Lily pulled herself free and ran.

He called out to her as she ran, but didn't try to follow her, for which she was thankful. Lily got inside the kitchen and locked the door behind her. Which seemed ridiculous, but she did it, then put her back to the door and sank down to the floor, just wanting to hide.

It wasn't like he was going to chase her inside and demand to speak to her, or like the man was overcome with lust for her.

He'd simply…made her a proposition, she supposed. One many women might consider quite reasonable, even inviting.

One that made Lily feel like a fool.

She thought he wanted to date her, maybe romance her a bit, flirt with her, tempt her, and then after an appropriate courtship of some sort—whatever that was considered these days—she might let herself fall into bed with him.

But, no!

He just wanted her to run upstairs and take her clothes off for him.

Was that how it was done these days?

She sat there on her kitchen floor, back to the door, feeling absolutely miserable, then realized she'd left the girls in the backyard alone after dark. She stood up, unlocked the door and threw it open, to see if she could hear them playing in the tree house, and there he was, standing in the dark getting ready to knock on her door.

"Damn!" Lily cried. "I didn't want to leave the girls alone."

"They're fine," he said.

"And I just can't talk to you right now. I'm sorry. Really. I am. Please don't make me talk about it."

"I'm not going to make you do anything you don't want to do, Lily. I'm not that kind of man," he said, sounding ever so reasonable and calm.

"I know you're not. I didn't mean to imply that. I feel foolish enough as it is, and right now, I just don't want to talk about this anymore."

"Okay. How about I sit out here and keep track of your girls, so you can have some time to yourself. And when you're ready, you can call them to come inside?"

She sniffled, fighting back tears that would have made her feel even more ridiculous, and said, "That would be nice."

"Okay. I'll do that."

Try as she might, she couldn't read any kind of inflection

into his words. Not amusement, not mockery, not anything close to annoyance.

He seemed to be the most reasonable man in the world right now, which prompted her to add, "I know I'm being ridiculous. I'm sorry."

"Okay," he said.

"I just…" She took a shaky breath, and then turned her face away.

"Lily, I'm sorry I upset you. I thought we wanted the same thing, but obviously, I was wrong. I'm going to sit in the backyard until the girls come in, and if you change your mind and want to talk to me, that's where I'll be. And if you don't ever want to talk about this again, that's fine, too. I'm sorry I offended you."

Chapter Eight

Lily stood there and watched him walk back to the yard, and then she closed her door and locked it again, just because she wanted to. Then sank back down to her floor, as hot, stupid tears rolled down her cheeks.

She was so mad at the world she could hardly stand it.

Then she grabbed the phone off the countertop beside her and called her sister.

"I am so stupid!" she announced when Marcy answered the phone.

It sounded like complete chaos in the background, which it often did at Marcy's house. Kids yelling, the dog barking, the TV going.

"John!" Marcy yelled to her husband. "Do not say another word," she told Lily. "Not until John gets here to take care of the kids and get them fed, because I want to hear every word. Every single one."

"Okay," Lily agreed, thinking to use the time to pull herself together.

"John, I have to talk to Lily. Please just take care of things for a few minutes."

Lily could hear Marcy moving through the house, probably going to hide in the garage, which she often did to get away from all the noise in her house.

"There," Marcy said, nothing but quiet in the background. "Now, tell me. What did he do? I know he did something! I knew he would! Tell me everything right this instant!"

Lily sighed, all the words getting stuck in her throat. "You don't understand. It's not good—"

"What do you mean, it's not good? I saw the way the man looked, and the way he looked at you. Of course it's good."

"I thought he was asking me out on a date," Lily admitted pitifully.

"Yes. Dates are good," Marcy said, ever cheerful. "They're a very good way to start. So? Tell me."

"He wasn't asking me out. He just wants to sneak into my house after the girls go to bed, to sneak into my bed. Tonight, hopefully. Or maybe tomorrow while the girls are in school!"

"Oh," Marcy said.

"Oh? What do you mean, oh? You don't even sound surprised. Am I not supposed to even be surprised by this? I mean, is this what dating is like these days? Someone asking if you'd like to hop into bed with them? Of course, I guess you wouldn't call that dating, would you? I'm so out of touch, I don't even know what to call it, Marcy. What do I call it? Just so I know, because apparently, this is what my life is going to be like. I should at least know what to call it!"

"Lily, honey, breathe," Marcy said. "Take a big, slow breath."

Lily, instead, tried to hold back more tears and ended up hiccupping and sniffling in Marcy's ear.

"Now, tell me again, very slowly. I mean, the man just didn't walk up to you and ask if he could let himself in the back door later, did he?"

"No," Lily admitted. "We were talking…about how hard it is to date with kids. Or I thought we were talking about how hard it is to date with kids. I guess he was talking about how hard it is to have a sex life when you have kids, and I was agreeing that…you know…it would be awkward, and that I wasn't sure if I was ready to have the girls know I was…seeing anyone. They're not even done getting used to the fact that we're divorced. And then…I don't know. I thought we were going out to dinner. He thought we were going to bed."

"Oh, honey. I'm so sorry."

"So, is this it? Am I supposed to just…go along with this or be alone forever?"

"You are not going to be alone forever," Marcy insisted.

"I don't know how to do this," Lily cried. "I just don't fit in this world anymore. I've been married forever, and I thought it was going to last forever, and it didn't, and now… I don't know what to do."

"Lily, I know it's been just rotten for you, and I'm so sorry—"

"And I didn't even want this," she complained. "I didn't go looking for it. I was fine, just fine, right here with the girls and my house and my family. I was fine! And he just showed up next door, all big and gorgeous and sweaty, making me remember all these things I didn't want to remember. Making me want things I'm scared to want! It's all so unfair, and it just makes me so mad. And I feel so ridiculous right now!"

She was crying again by the time she was done.

"I hate this," Lily said. "I just hate it!"

"I know. I'm sorry. But it's going to get better, I promise."

"How can it possibly get better? I just made an absolute fool of myself, and it's not like I can avoid the man. He lives right next door!"

"I'm sure it's not as bad as you think," Marcy reasoned.

Lily groaned. "I ran away from him. I ran inside my house and locked the door behind him and hid behind the door, so he couldn't see me. I'm sitting on my kitchen floor, behind a locked door, hiding from a grown man. It's bad. It's so ridiculously bad."

"Well, we all make mistakes…." Marcy tried.

"And he was even nice about it. I was stupid and crying and practically incoherent, and he was nice even then. He's a nice man, and even he doesn't want anything except to have a woman hop into bed with him," Lily cried.

"Honey, you're just out of practice with men, that's all—"

"Well, if this is what it's like, I don't want to practice." Practice implied doing something over and over again until she got it right, and there was no way Lily was going to do something like this again and again until she understood it and could play this game.

She had no desire to play this game.

But then…

The word *desire* stopped her right in her tracks.

Because he'd kissed her. Really and truly kissed her, and it had been…absolutely…delicious.

There was no other word that applied.

Extravagantly, wonderfully delicious.

"Wait?" said Marcy. "What was that? You must not have told me everything."

Lily sighed. "Okay…he kissed me."

"There we go." Marcy was happy now.

"And…" *Damn.* "I felt like I was sixteen years old again and had never been kissed before," Lily admitted.

"Ohh, geez," Marcy groaned. "That good?"

"Absolutely that good."

"So, then…I'm sorry, but I have to say this. What would be so wrong about thoroughly enjoying yourself with this man?"

* * *

Jake was putting Lily's lawn mower away the next weekend when he spotted Andie spying on his house once again.

At least, it looked like she was spying.

Why would she be spying on his house?

Jake pressed his back against the side of Lily's garage, nothing but half his face sticking out, so he could watch without her seeing.

Andie walked by the front of the house once, going really slowly, like she was trying to see inside the front windows or maybe around the side to the deck.

No way she was looking for him. He could hope, but he'd be wrong.

Did she really think there was something going on between his uncle and her mother? And if she did, why all the sneaking around like this? Why didn't she just ask her mother about it?

"Jake?"

He jumped at the sound of the voice off to his right, when he'd been looking left, and turned around to see Lily standing there, giving him an odd look.

"Yes?" Then he remembered Andie spying on his house, and jumped back to press his back against the inside of the garage.

"Are you okay?" Lily asked.

"Yes," he claimed. "Just... I was... I think... Andie's out there."

"Oh," Lily said, like it made sense that he'd hide in Lily's garage, rather than take a chance Andie Graham might notice him and say something to him.

Jake made a disgusted sound. "I guess that's pretty stupid, huh? Her being out there, me hiding in here. I was just...surprised."

"Believe me, I know what that's like," Lily said.

Yeah, he thought she might.

Because something was wrong with Lily, something that

started the day after they finished the tree house. Lily had made them all dinner, steaks on the grill that were fabulous, and then Jake had gone inside, leaving her and his uncle and the girls outside.

His uncle had been a bear ever since, and Lily had been... quiet and kind of sad, Jake thought.

He wanted to ask if they'd had some kind of fight, if Lily was mad, and if Jake could do anything to help, then thought of Andie spying on his house.

Was this about Andie's mom and his uncle Nick?

Was Andie looking for her mom at Jake's house? And Lily mad because she thought there was something going on between Nick and Andie's mom?

"He's not seeing Andie's mom," Jake just blurted out.

Lily looked completely taken aback, aghast and then trying to cover, failing miserably.

"Sorry," Jake said. "I thought you and my uncle had some kind of fight, and then I thought it might be about Andie's mom. But it's not. I mean, I don't know what it's about, but if it is about Andie's mom...he's not seeing her. I mean, I haven't seen her at the house or anywhere with him. Not since that first time in the kitchen.... You did know about that time in the kitchen, right?"

Lily nodded. "Thanks, Jake. But it wasn't about Andie's mom."

"Okay. Just trying to help."

"I know." Lily smiled gently at him.

"If you like, I could talk to him for you," Jake offered. "I mean, if there's anything I could do...I'd try. He's really grumpy and unhappy, if that helps."

Lily shook her head. "I don't want him to be grumpy and unhappy."

"Then you should talk to him, because he's been that way ever since Sunday night."

"Making your life miserable, is he?" Lily asked.

Jake shrugged. "He's certainly not any fun to be around like this."

"Sorry. Really, I am."

Jake glanced back outside. "There's Andie again. I don't get it. What's she doing? I mean, it looks like she's looking for her mom. That's what she was doing last time I saw her over here, but I was just at the house. Her mom's not there, and I haven't seen her mother there in weeks."

"Why don't you just go ask her?" Lily suggested.

Jake took a breath and told himself to act like a man—not like his grumpy, unhappy uncle—and just go talk to the woman.

"What do I say?" he asked, completely at a loss.

"Ask her if there's anything you can do to help her."

"Oh." That seemed simple enough. "Okay. I'll do it."

Lily laughed, looking not quite miserable for the first time in days, and wished him luck.

He walked right up to Andie, remembering at the very last second that he'd just finished mowing Lily's lawn, that he was drenched in sweat and a little grease from the mower and had yard clippings clinging to him in all sorts of places.

"Aw, hell," he muttered.

Andie whirled around, apparently close enough to hear, and looked really unhappy to see him.

Way to go, Jake.

"Hi," Jake said, because it was too late to back out now.

"Hi," she said cautiously, looking so sad.

"I was just next door, mowing the grass, and saw you walking by," he said, which he supposed made it sound like he was spying on her, which he was. But he sure didn't have to tell her that. "Are you... Do you need something? Can I help? Because, I would, if there's anything I could do."

She shrugged and shook her head. "I'm just looking for my mom."

Jake nodded.

She couldn't keep track of her mom?

What was that about?

He'd never really spent any time keeping track of his mother. It had always been the other way around—her trying to keep track of him.

"Well, I haven't seen her around here in a few weeks. And I'm pretty sure there's nothing going on between her and my uncle, if that's what you're worried about."

"I'm not worried," she insisted, though everything about her expression said she was. "I just... Sometimes she takes off and...forgets to tell me where she is, and... I just need to find her."

"Oh. Not answering her cell phone?"

Andie shook her head.

"Well, when's the last time you saw her?" Jake tried, thinking this was getting weirder and weirder.

Her mom just disappeared and left her daughter all alone and worrying about her?

"Last night," Andie whispered.

Jake was sure he'd misunderstood. "She didn't come home last night?"

Andie nodded. "Okay, you have to swear you won't tell anybody about this—"

"Sure. Okay. I swear."

"I'm not sure if she came home or not. She went out, and then I went to bed, and...uh...when I got up this morning, she wasn't there. I mean, she might have come home and gone to sleep and just gotten up early and gone out again. I'm probably being silly. I mean...she's a mother. What's she going to do? It's not like she has a curfew or friends she's not allowed to see. I just...sometimes I worry about her. That's all."

"Well, sure you do," Jake said.

He'd never really worried about his mother or father, and look what had happened to them. They'd gone out to the store and never come back. Andie's mother disappearing overnight sure sounded like reason to worry to him.

"You want to come inside, and we can talk about this and maybe figure out what to do?" he offered.

Andie hesitated. "I just really want to find my mom."

"Well, we can go inside and make sure she's not there," Jake tried.

"Okay," Andie agreed.

Lily watched from the garage as Jake talked to Andie and was happy for him when the girl followed Jake inside.

At least things were going well for someone.

She'd been steadfastly trying to avoid any contact with Nick, which was hard, and she knew she was being silly, but she still hadn't managed to make herself talk to him and try to clear the air.

She just felt so foolish and wished she could just disappear into thin air.

Honestly, to be a grown woman and feeling this way was beyond ridiculous.

She went inside, grabbed a glass of water, after working in the yard most of the afternoon, and was thinking of finding something to eat when the phone rang, and she answered it without even looking to see who was calling.

"Lily?" The voice was nothing but a whisper, but she knew who it was.

Nick.

"I'm sorry. I know you don't want to talk to me, but… I didn't know who else to call," he said, still whispering.

"What's wrong?"

"Jake has a girl here."

"I know." Lily laughed, because he sounded so flustered. Over a teenage girl? "It's Andie Graham. I saw them talking outside."

"Graham? Jake actually has Audrey Graham's daughter here?"

"Afraid so."

Nick groaned. "Is she anything like her mother?"

"I don't know. Why?"

"Because Jake brought her inside and then made up some story about wanting to show her the house."

"So? What's wrong with that?"

"Why would he care what she thinks of this house, and why would she care what the house is like?" Nick reasoned. "Come on. He's a fifteen-year-old boy. I know how they think. He walked her around the downstairs, and then they headed upstairs to the bedrooms and didn't come back down."

"Oh," Lily said. Now she got it.

"Help me," Nick growled. "What do I do?"

"You make sure the bedroom door stays open and you find excuses to walk upstairs every now and then and walk past the open doorway," Lily suggested.

"That's it? He can just waltz up to his bedroom with a girl?"

"I don't know. Can he?"

"Oh, hell, I don't know. Lily, I have no idea what to do," Nick pleaded.

Lily looked out the kitchen window, to see if she could see anything, and there was Nick, standing in his own kitchen window, staring back at her. She missed him, she realized. Missed him something fierce.

Missed even talking to him.

"Come on, Lily. It's for Jake."

"I know. I'm just not at this stage of parenting yet. Let me think," she said, trying to keep her mind on the problem at hand and not how much she missed him. "Did you ever tell Jake he can't entertain girls in his bedroom?"

"I didn't know I needed to. I mean, I told him he wasn't having girls sleep over, but we didn't exactly touch on the whole entertaining-in-the-bedroom thing. Do I have to tell him that?"

"Apparently, you do, since he's doing that right now," Lily

said. "But don't go tell him now. You'll embarrass him. Wait until she leaves, and then tell him."

"Okay, I'll wait."

"And I don't think you need to worry that much. He barely knows Andie. He was scared to even talk to her earlier, so I don't think he's going to put the moves on her the minute they get into his room."

"He's scared of her?" Nick didn't like the sound of that.

"What? You're scared of her mother," Lily said, not able to help herself from teasing him a bit.

"I am not scared of her mother. I'd just rather not have to have anything to do with her."

And then, it wasn't any fun anymore, teasing him.

It was hard, because she still felt like a fool, but she missed him, too, and she couldn't imagine it would be hard for him to find a woman to give him what Lily wouldn't.

"Audrey would let you slip in her back door after her daughter's asleep," Lily said.

Nick swore softly. "Audrey practically attacked me in my own kitchen while Jake was here. Not that it matters, because Audrey isn't the one I want."

To which, Lily had no idea what to say.

Did he expect her to believe she was the only one he wanted?

Because Lily would really love to believe that, much as it scared her at the same time.

She'd taken his offer to be nothing but the most casual of suggestions. He'd taken a look around the neighborhood and decided he'd rather have her.

But thought quite honestly that if she wasn't willing, he'd simply find someone else. All very casual and adult and not what Lily was feeling at all.

She wouldn't have been surprised to see him with Audrey Graham after that. In fact, she'd been bracing herself for that very thing to happen.

And now, he seemed to be telling her it wouldn't happen, no matter what.

"Lily, we have to talk about this. We live right next door. Jake's in and out of your house all the time, and we can't go on ignoring each other when we're living this close to each other."

"I know," she said.

"I'm sorry I hurt your feelings. It was never my intention," he said. "How about you let me deal with this girl in Jake's bedroom, and later, we'll talk."

"The girls are here," she said. "Richard backed out on them again—"

"Tonight. Will you meet me in the backyard after they go to sleep."

Backyard.

Dark.

Alone, but not quite alone.

Surely Lily wasn't afraid to meet him in the backyard.

"Okay. I'll call you when they go to sleep."

"Thank you," he said.

Chapter Nine

Like someone whose radar had picked up a signal that something was up, Lily's sister called as she was trying to get the girls ready for bed.

Lily rolled her eyes when she picked up the phone and saw who it was, then told herself not to be such a coward. How could Marcy possibly know anything?

Answer: Because she was Marcy, and Marcy just seemed to know Lily's every secret.

"So, still hiding from that gorgeous thing next door?" Marcy asked, once she'd finished complaining about what a jerk Richard was for not coming to take the girls.

"No. I talked to him today, actually."

"Oh. Good." Marcy could purr when she wanted. "And what did he have to say?"

"He couldn't really talk. He had something going on with Jake, who has a thing for Audrey Graham's daughter. And he's such a sweet kid. I'm afraid any offspring of Audrey's could eat him for lunch. Poor Jake."

"What's wrong with Jake?" Brittany said, coming out of the bathroom after brushing her teeth and getting ready for bed.

"Nothing," Lily said. "Jake's fine. Promise."

"I like Jake," Brittany said. "And he likes me."

"I know he does, honey."

"He's gonna teach me to ride his skateboard," Brittany said, her face lighting up.

"No, he's not," Lily said.

"Huh? Why not?"

"Brittany. You remember what we talked about, when Mommy's on the phone?" Lily said.

"Yes."

"Well," Lily held up the phone, so her daughter couldn't miss it, "Mommy's on the phone."

Brittany pouted, but got into her bed. "I need to know how to skateboard."

"Not tonight, you don't. We'll talk about it tomorrow." Lily kissed her daughter on the forehead and walked out, leaving the bedroom door cracked open. "Sorry," she told Marcy.

"It's okay."

"We should be good to talk now. Ginny's already in bed, reading. She probably won't move for hours."

"Good. And I don't really care about poor Jake's love life. I care about yours and your lack of any kind of life at all. What's going on with you and the gorgeous one?"

"He wants to talk," Lily admitted.

"Okay. When?"

"Tonight. Outside in the backyard."

"In the dark?" Marcy's grin came through the phone as easily as her words.

"Yes, it's getting dark," Lily admitted.

"Okay, just please, please, please, think about this before

you turn the man down flat. Because I know you like him, and I know he's gorgeous—and also nice—not an easy combination to find in a man. And he wants you. So what if it's just sex? I mean, the man can even do home repairs—"

"I can do most any home repair," Lily said, hardly able to believe she was having this particular conversation. "You're not really going to tell me I should sleep with a man to get a leaky faucet fixed, are you?"

"No, I'm saying you should sleep with him because the last man you slept with was your jerk of a husband who left you feeling lousy about yourself and men in general. And that you've been alone a long time, and I understand that you're scared to get involved with someone again and to trust anyone. Really, I do. But that doesn't mean you have to be all alone right now."

"I'm fine with being alone," Lily insisted, walking into her own bedroom and shutting the door, so the girls wouldn't hear any of this conversation.

"Of course, you are. I didn't say you had to have a man," Marcy reasoned. "I was just saying…why not let yourself have this man. Just because… Well, just because. Why not?"

"Maybe because my life is complicated enough—"

"Complicated? Your life is lonely. Your life is full of kids and your house and me. You can have more than that. I am here to tell you that you deserve more than that," Marcy said.

"But I'm not ready to get involved with anybody. It's way too soon."

"Perfect. The man doesn't want to start anything serious. He just wants to have sex, and I'm just guessing here, but I bet he's really good at it."

"Oh, just by looking at him, you figured that out?"

"No, by watching him build that tree house. He's careful and strong and so sure of himself. He's patient and kind. I heard the way he talked to the girls and was letting them help, and you said he's so good with his nephew—"

"That's how you judge how a man will be in bed? By how he is with kids?" Lily was highly skeptical.

"That's how you judge how a man is at his core. If he's that way in real life, he'll be that way in bed."

Okay, Lily had to admit, there was probably something to Marcy's reasoning. She'd certainly imagined herself that he'd be kind and considerate and patient and...thorough. Lily imagined him being very thorough. *With her.*

"The question to ask yourself, honey, is why not? Why would you not simply enjoy what this beautiful man has to offer? He's already said you two can keep it quiet and private, so no one needs to know. It'll be your little secret. And mine, of course."

Lily rolled her eyes. Of course, her sister would want all the details.

"Think of it as part of the reclaiming-yourself-as-a-woman, post-divorce-recovery effort," Marcy suggested.

"We're making a recovery effort now? That makes me sound like a disaster area, and believe me, I've felt like one, but I didn't imagine someone making a formal declaration. My life as a disaster area."

"You need to know that not all men are jerks, and that you are a young, sexy, desirable woman, and that you will have a life again, and this man is ready to remind you of all that."

Lily frowned.

Marcy made it sound so easy.

And so appealing.

"I guess... I'm just afraid," she said.

"Of course you are. You got flattened by life, by a man you trusted who was supposed to be with you forever. But you're not dead, honey, and it's time to start remembering that," Marcy said. "Are the girls down for the night?"

"I think so."

"Then go call that man."

* * *

Nick was literally pacing back and forth in the living room, willing Lily to call, when Jake came downstairs and found him.

"Is something wrong?" Jake asked.

"No," Nick lied.

"Because, you look like something's wrong."

Nick took a breath and wondered how much to tell the kid. "Just waiting for a phone call."

"Oh."

Jake hesitated, looking unsure of himself. "Did something happen?"

"No," Nick said. "Why?"

Jake shrugged, looking really young and maybe even scared. "Just…wondering."

"Nothing bad happened, Jake," he said, because Jake seemed to be waiting for the next bad thing to hit, something Nick forgot at times. "Sorry I worried you."

Jake shrugged. "I'm gonna warm up some spaghetti from last night. Want some?"

"No, I'm good," Nick said, then figured he really should talk to the kid about the girl and his bedroom being off-limits.

He followed Jake into the kitchen and tried to remember how his father would have handled something like this. He probably would have just barked out an order. *No girls in your bedroom!* And Nick would have said, *Yes, sir,* and left it at that.

Not that he hadn't managed to sneak a few in.

Something he really liked thinking about now that he was the parent, at least temporarily, and was supposed to keep that from happening.

"Jake, about you and Mrs. Graham's daughter…" he began.

"Yeah?" He'd been inspecting the contents of the refrigerator and didn't even lift his head.

"She's…uh… She looks a lot older than you are."

"Only a year and a half," Jake admitted, pulling out a plastic container of spaghetti leftovers.

"She's…are you two… I didn't know you were seeing anyone."

Jake laughed. "I'm not. She just…she's having some trouble with some stuff and needed to talk. That's all."

"Oh." That was a relief.

"Of course, I would love to do much more than talk to her. I mean…. She's hot. Don't you think?"

"I think a man my age could practically get arrested for even thinking that, so I'm going to pass on that question," Nick said.

"You don't think she's hot?" Jake was incredulous.

Nick thought she was enough to scare the parents of a teenage boy half to death, to blank out all reason in the adolescent mind, which was already not that high in the ability-to-reason area, especially when anything female was within reach.

"I think you really don't need to be entertaining girls in your bedroom, okay?"

"Entertaining?" Jake laughed. "We were talking."

"Fine. Talk in the living room. Or the kitchen. Or outside. Not upstairs," Nick told him, because a door cracked open and Nick pacing back and forth outside just didn't seem safe enough.

"Okay," Jake said. "No girls in my bedroom."

"Okay. Good," Nick said.

That settled that.

No argument. No harsh words. No big deal.

Good.

So why did Nick still felt like he was standing in a minefield, Jake and all these girls, all the possibilities for trouble.

Parenting, he decided, was terrifying.

Lily finally worked up her nerve and made the call, then realized it had started to rain while she'd been worrying and talking to Marcy.

Darn.

The backyard, while offering enough privacy to get into trouble, still seemed much safer than having him in her house.

Which was silly, Lily knew, but…she was looking for any sense of safety she could find, and she was pretty sure the man wouldn't seduce her in the Adirondack chairs in her backyard.

Her kitchen was another thing all together.

Nick answered the phone, that deep, smooth tone of his enough to make her want him, despite how uneasy she was with the whole idea of letting another man into either her life or her bed.

"It's raining," she said.

"I know. Is that a problem?"

"Well, I don't know."

"Are you scared to let me in your house, Lily?"

He didn't say it in a teasing, flirty way, just completely matter-of-factly.

"No. I just… I don't know how to do this," she confessed. "I've been alone a long time. I feel like I've been alone forever, and at the same time, I feel like I've been married forever, and I don't even remember how all this works."

"I know," he said, softly as could be, a world of understanding there.

Marcy was right. He was patient and kind and gorgeous, and Lily would bet money all that came into play in making him great in bed.

"And I'm tempted. Very tempted—"

"I'm glad to hear it," he said, chuckling.

"But it's just not as simple as that. Not for me."

"Okay. I think I knew that all along, Lily, but you can't blame a guy for hoping. So, what do you want to do? Pretend this never happened? Because if that's what you want, I'll do it."

"What if I don't really know what I want?" she asked.

"Well, that could lead to all sorts of things," he said, sounding much more pleased with himself or her or maybe just the moment. "It could lead to me giving you some time to figure out what you want. Me trying to convince you that you want the same thing I do, which I am perfectly willing to do. In fact, I think that could be a lot of fun. Let me try to talk you into it—"

"Talk me into it? Because I didn't think you were talking about a conversation."

"Talking would be part of it," he insisted, sounding like he planned on doing very little talking.

And the other part?

Lily had a feeling she'd really like the other part.

She stood at the window, looking out through the darkness and the rain, trying to see past it all to him.

He was grinning. She could hear it in his voice, and he was so cute when he grinned. It took all that toughness out of his face and made him look instead like a big, sweet, sexy man.

"I think you should let me come over and kiss you good-night," he said. "To give you something to think about."

Lily shook her head. "I have plenty to think about, and I'm not sure you coming over here is a good idea."

"It's a great idea. We'll stay in the kitchen. How much trouble could we get into in your kitchen, with your girls upstairs and Jake over here, used to waltzing in and out of your house all the time? Besides, it's just a kiss, Lily."

Oh, but she'd been kissed by him before.

"Hang up the phone," he said. "I'll be there in a second."

The phone clicked, connection broken, before she could protest.

She'd hardly had a chance to take a breath when he was there, opening the back door and letting himself in.

The rain must have picked up, because it was dripping off his dark, thick hair, had left wet splotches on his shirt, and the look in his eyes when he watched her was enough to make her sizzle.

His charm was a potent thing.

"Let me dry you off," she said, reaching for a clean dish towel from the drawer beside her.

She reached up to press the cloth against the side of his face first and then his forehead, his other cheek, his lips, the touch somehow becoming more of a caress than anything else.

Lily caught her breath, not thinking until then that to take care of him in this way, she had to get very, very close to him. His hands came up to hold her loosely against him, the warmth of his big palms soaking into her back, making her want to do nothing but lean in even closer to him.

She tried to concentrate on the task she'd set for herself, moving onto his hair and then somehow it was her hands, not the towel, brushing the water from the dark strands.

"I've never had anyone dry me off before." He grinned wickedly, not pulling her closer, but making no move to step back. "You're making me wish I'd stayed out in the rain a while longer. If I'd known I was going to get this kind of treatment, I would have."

Lily dropped the towel on the floor, embarrassed by what she'd done, not sure if it was a way to stall what he'd come here to do or just an excuse to touch him, which she found herself wanting very badly to do.

And now, he was here, her in his arms, her with nothing at all to say and nowhere else she wanted to be.

He went still and quiet, his body all but surrounding hers, until he seemed to take over her senses. She could feel the heat coming off of his big body, feel both the patience and the urgency inside of him, and the self-control. She could smell his slightly minty aftershave and hear his slow, even breaths, could feel his chest rise and fall with each one, could swear she felt him staring down at her.

Ever so slowly, he bent his head down to hers, doing nothing more than laying the side of his face against hers.

Lily closed her eyes. Her hands latched on to his arms and held him there almost against her, but not quite.

Don't go.

Don't come any closer.

She wanted both things very much.

His breath warmed her ear for a second before he whispered, "You can have as much time as you need to get used to this, Lily."

"I don't think I could ever get used to anything that feels this good," she admitted.

He laughed against her ear, and then he kissed the side of her face, her jaw, her neck, like a man who had an eternity to do nothing but tease her.

She shivered at each touch. Her nipples bunched into hard peaks, her breasts trembling and seeming to know they were inches away from being nestled against his chest, and she could hardly breathe.

He was grinning. She could tell as his mouth closed against the point where her neck smoothed out into her shoulder, and it was like a jolt went right through her at the contact.

She wrapped her arms tight around him as her whole body sagged and he caught her close, holding her there, letting her feel just how different they were. His body was big and unyielding, even more solid than she'd imagined, made of the kind of muscles that had been tried and tested over a lifetime of what had obviously been very physical work, and she wanted to touch him everywhere.

He was done teasing.

He picked her up easily, as if she weighed next to nothing, and backed her onto the kitchen countertop until she was sitting there, his body nudging her legs apart, sinking in between them.

His lips found hers, and she opened herself up to him, to the heat of his mouth and the delights of his hands running up and down her back.

Lily groaned and wrapped her arms around his broad chest,

thinking this was what a man was supposed to feel like. This was how a woman was supposed to feel in the arms of a man.

Tempted and turned on and all tangled up inside of him and what he was doing to her.

She just opened herself up to him and let him take what he wanted, let him kiss her again and again and again.

He groaned deep in his chest. His hands slid down to cup her bottom, and then he pulled her up against him and leaned into her. If they both hadn't had clothes on, he'd have been inside of her.

As it was, she felt everything he had to offer her, wrapped her legs around his waist and rubbed herself up against him, aching for him, just like that.

He hesitated for the first time, pulling away from her lips just enough to mutter, "Damn, Lily. You're about to make me forget everything I promised you when I came over here tonight."

Which let her know she wasn't the only one who was so turned on she could hardly stand it.

Lily arched herself up against him once more, feeling that big, throbbing hardness against the place in her that ached. He caught her bottom in his hands and held her there and groaned again, his face pressed against hers once more.

"I thought we'd be safe in the kitchen," he said, still holding her there, shaking his head back and forth, breathing hard. "Apparently, I was wrong."

"Apparently."

"Just stay right here and let me enjoy this for a minute before I make myself let you go, okay?"

And it was still there, all the heat, all the longing, all the possibilities, stretched out between them, holding them there like an invisible bond.

It was delicious and thrilling and so tempting.

"You could kiss me again," Lily said shamelessly, lifting her face to his so he could do just that.

"No, I couldn't," he said, easing her back down onto the

countertop and pushing her face down to his chest. "Tell me to go. Tell me to go right now."

But Lily didn't want him to go, especially now that she knew how safe and yet how turned on she felt in his arms.

She eased back and lifted her face to his. "But I don't want you to go."

He shot her a look that told her she was in very dangerous territory. "Don't you do that to me—"

"Do what?"

"Look like you'd give me anything I wanted right now, but you trust me not to take it."

"I do trust you not to do anything else."

"That is so not fair. Not after you caught fire in my arms."

"Okay, it's not fair."

"And you don't look like you're the least bit sorry," he teased.

"I'm not," she said and reached up to kiss him again.

He let her have one kiss, but carefully held his body away from hers.

"I'm leaving," he said. "And if you invite me into this house at any point when the girls aren't here, you'll be naked. I'm just telling you so you know that. Unless it's what you want, we should not be alone here together."

"Okay," she said, thinking that was in all likelihood completely true.

"Think about what you want, Lily. Be sure."

"I will," she promised.

"I have to go."

He kissed her once more, kissed her hard and quite thoroughly, and then he was gone.

Lily lay in her bed that night, unable to go to sleep, and kept running through those moments in the kitchen with him.

Those delicious kisses, the hardness of his body, the gentleness of his touch. It was like she'd been asleep for what felt like decades, and he'd come along and awakened every bit of sexual feeling inside of her, and she wasn't quite sure what to do about that.

Tearing off his clothes came to mind.

But then she had to consider taking off her own clothes, which made her think of her thighs, which she hated most any time she really looked at them.

And then she thought of those last six months or so with Richard, the halfhearted lovemaking that hadn't been love at all on Richard's part, just guilt and obligation and probably trying to keep Lily from getting too suspicious about what he was doing with someone else.

The humiliation she'd felt upon finding out.

The vow she'd taken to never trust another man again.

The fear she felt at the idea of doing just that.

And then she came back to having to take off her clothes in front of another man for the first time.

Complete and total darkness seemed to be a good idea, but then she'd really like to see Nick naked.

Maybe she could be in the dark, and he could be in the light. No, she could undress him in the light and admire him there, and then pull him into the darkness and shed her clothes there.

Yeah. That could work.

Problem solved.

Maybe she could dream of him, have him there in her dreams, find some satisfaction in the fantasy of him without ever really having to trust him enough and take the risk of really letting him into her life, even if it was just sex.

Could she make that work?

Erotic dreams of Nick?

If she was lucky, Lily decided.

If she was very lucky, Nick the Dream-Lover would be enough.

Chapter Ten

She slept fitfully all week and without an appearance by Nick in her dreams.

That Friday, thoroughly disgusted that her dream plan hadn't worked, she concentrated on getting cranky, sleepy girls ready for school and out the door, then what she had to do with her own day.

The girls were anything but cooperative. Brittany couldn't find her favorite red shirt and didn't want to wear anything else. If Ginny weren't only nine, Lily would swear her daughter had PMS and was trying to get on Lily's last nerve by objecting to anything and everything Lily said that morning, even the most normal and reasonable of requests. If this was what lay ahead for Lily, parenting preteen daughters, she was truly frightened.

Richard called to whine about this and that—as if Lily still cared—but it was really to try to explain how he could take the girls on Sunday that week, but not on Saturday and how difficult and stressful and challenging his life was. Lily managed not to reach through the phone and smack him, but just barely.

She needed to go shopping, because she had to make cookies for a party of some kind for one of Brittany's classmates the next day, and Ginny was complaining that her shoes hurt her feet, which meant she'd probably outgrown another pair. One more thing for Lily to take care of.

But first, she had to get some work done in the dining room. The wooden trim had been there, waiting for her to put it up for days, and Lily tried. Honestly, she did. She'd finally decided on some fancy, arts-and-craft wooden trim, actually more like small panels, that she was assembling in the garage. A million little pieces, it looked like at the moment. Impossibly time-consuming, but also ridiculously popular right now.

So she tried.

And got nothing but a huge splinter in her palm, but she persevered beyond that.

It was when she smashed her thumb being careless and distracted with her hammer that she really got mad.

"Ahhh!" She actually yelled, because it hurt and she was so frustrated.

She threw the hammer down in a rather unladylike fit, and it banged against the concrete floor of the garage and maybe bounced off the opposite wall, probably putting a gash into the wall that Lily would have to fix later.

But she didn't care at the moment.

She grabbed her throbbing thumb to try to stop it from hurting and when that didn't work, stuck it in her mouth and sucked on it.

Nick found her like that, sucking her own thumb and near tears. He must have heard her yell or heard the hammer bouncing around in the garage.

He came to an abrupt stop, seeing that she was relatively okay, and stood there, maybe scared to come any closer.

"Don't worry, I won't throw anything at you," she said.

"Promise?" he asked, mouth twitching, like he was trying not to laugh.

"Well, if you start laughing at me, I might!"

And then he did burst out laughing.

Lily, much to her own horror, burst into tears right there in her garage.

Nick looked horrified. "Lily, honey. I'm sorry. I didn't realize you were really hurt."

He rushed to her side and started running his hands over her arms, looking for a broken bone or something.

"I'm not hurt," she said, sniffling furiously. "Just my thumb. I smashed my stupid thumb with the hammer. I'm just..."

"Yes?" he asked, seeming genuinely concerned.

"I'm just mad!" she said, giving up on maintaining any dignity in the situation at all.

He looked flabbergasted and unsure for a moment, maybe afraid of a woman who was all over the place emotionally, then rallied and scooped her up in his arms. "Come on. Let's get you inside and get some ice on that thumb."

Lily gave up and let him carry her, which wasn't any kind of hardship at all, really. She even let her head rest against his chest, took deep, shuddering breaths and tried to stop crying before she really freaked him out.

He got her into her kitchen and sat her on the countertop, then found a dish towel and wrapped ice in it. He came to stand in front of her, as he'd been that night they'd kissed with such abandon, right here in her kitchen, took her hand in his and gently wrapped the towel around her poor thumb, then held it there with his own two hands.

"Better?" he asked very gently.

Lily nodded, still able to feel the tears falling down her cheeks.

"Bad day, Lily?"

"Yes," she whispered.

"Bad week?"

"Yes."

He winked at her. "You're not quite as tough as you look, are you?"

She brought her chin up at that.

"No, don't take it like that. I didn't mean it like that. It's just that…you seem like you can do anything. Like you're Super Woman. Jake thinks you absolutely walk on water. You make all this parenting stuff look effortless. Like you know exactly what to do and how to do it, and you don't need help from anybody. But some of that's just an act, isn't it?"

"It's all an act," she admitted. "I'm never sure of the right thing to do, and I'm tired all the time and mad and…lonely. I'm really lonely sometimes."

There, she'd said the hardest thing.

"Especially since you moved in next door," she added, then immediately felt guilty for it. "Okay, no. That's not right, either. It's been nice having you and Jake there. Really nice. But…it makes me miss things, too."

That looked like it interested him quite a bit.

"What kind of things?" he whispered.

"You know. A man. I miss…having a man in my life, and I didn't before, or maybe I just didn't notice. I don't know. But now, I do."

He nodded, considered, then said, "Sorry."

She frowned. "You are not. You want things from me, and you make me want…all those things, too. And things were much simpler when I didn't want those things. I wish I just didn't want all those things."

He shrugged, as if he just couldn't help himself. "Jake and I could pack up and move, if it helped."

Which made Lily laugh a bit.

She knew she was being foolish, and she knew that he knew it, too.

And he didn't have to be so nice about it or so charming or so close.

"I felt safer when you weren't here," she admitted. "Safer not wanting the things you make me want."

"Could we expand a little on what exactly you want and maybe on why you can't let yourself have it?" he tried.

"Because... Well, I'm not sure why right now. Because I'm scared. The last year was awful, and I'm just starting to feel safe again, and I don't want to get hurt. Again."

"Okay." He nodded. "I can understand that. But...you're lonely, too. You're a beautiful, young, sexy woman, and you're lonely. You're allowed to do something about that, if you want, aren't you?"

"I don't know. It's never really seemed that simple to me. I have the girls and all these things to do, and I'm so busy, and... I really don't like my thighs," she blurted out.

Nick's lips really twitched at that one. "How is that even possible, Lily?"

"No woman really likes her thighs!"

"But I've seen yours. I've seen them in those cute little shorts you wear when it's really hot outside."

"I don't wear little shorts," she insisted.

"I'd be happy if they were even littler, but the ones you have are really nice. Trust me. And I liked what I saw."

Which was nice to hear.

Still... "And...I'd have to take my clothes off if we were to....you know."

Nick considered for a moment. "You want me to say you can keep your clothes on? Because if that's what it takes, honey, I'm willing. I mean, I'd prefer that you take them all off, but if you insist."

"Well...maybe if it was really dark...." Lily conceded.

"Really dark and you keep your clothes on?"

"No. I mean…I don't know! I did think… I was kind of hoping… I really want to see you," she confessed. "All of you."

He laughed out loud then. "Lily, honey. I would do anything I could to make you comfortable with this, and I am absolutely willing to take off every stitch of clothing I have on, and you can keep most of yours on, if you must. But I just don't see how this can work if I'm in the light and you're in absolute darkness."

"I know, I'm being ridiculous! Believe me, I know."

"I mean, we really have to be in the same room, and I don't get how to make half of it light and half of it dark—"

"Stop it!" she cried. "I already feel foolish enough."

He grabbed her and wrapped his arms around her, laughing as he did it, and she reached out and wrapped her arms around him, too, her poor thumb forgotten along with her towel and her ice.

It fell to the floor, the ice clattering and skating along the floor, as Nick leaned down and kissed her, finally, and she forgot how foolish she felt and all her doubts and most of her fears, and she remembered, completely, how wonderful it was to have a big, strong, sexy man in her arms.

At the moment, it seemed impossible that she'd been without one for so long, because suddenly, it was like she couldn't stand to go another minute without this.

She kissed him back with a fury, wrapped her legs around him and pulled him to her.

He groaned and palmed her hips and pressed her against him, and she felt his body's growing response to hers.

It was like going from zero to sixty in seconds flat, and it left her thinking she could just tear his clothes off of him right there in her kitchen.

Which to Lily was nothing more than a fleeting thought, but to her surprise and shock and absolute pleasure, he pulled his shirt over his head and threw it in the direction of the dining room, and then she had a beautifully shirtless man, miles of honey-brown skin and smooth muscles, in her arms.

Lily shuddered and debated the wisdom of exploring all that beautiful skin with her hands and her mouth versus the idea of begging him to carry her upstairs right then or maybe just into the living room and onto the sofa.

It was such a difficult decision to make.

Especially since he was still kissing her like a man literally starving to death and every now and then gently thrusting against her open thighs, a tiny, increasingly frustrating version of what she really wanted him to do.

He finally dragged his mouth back from hers long enough to whisper, "So…exactly where would you like to see me naked, Lily? And when were you thinking of this happening? Please tell me you were thinking right now. Because I think now would be a really good time."

She ran her hands down the smooth, broad plane of his back, enjoying herself all the way, then came to the waist of his jeans, slid down and cupped his hips, pulling him to her.

He groaned, his forehead falling until it rested against hers.

She looked at him, then looked at his gorgeous body, followed that swirl of hair on his chest as it narrowed into a thin line down the center and then disappeared beneath his jeans.

She reached out and kissed one side of his chest and then the other, and one of her palms started slipping down, following that line of dark hair.

His whole body stiffened. He gave her a look that said she was heading into dangerous territory and she'd better know what she was asking for before she did it, but Lily was beyond doubts now.

She let her hand slip down over the waistband of his jeans to find an altogether impressive bulge and cupped him with her palm. She was looking right at him as she did it, so she saw his eyes go even smokier and narrow in on her face like he couldn't see anything but her. He sucked in a breath and stood there and let her explore as she wished, rubbing him and then slipping her hand down inside his jeans.

He sagged against her, his forehead to hers as he half gasped, half laughed, and she thought about how much she wanted him inside of her, right then, big and hot and throbbing.

"Okay," she said. "If you have a condom, I'll get naked."

"Right, front pocket," he whispered.

"You carry a condom around with you?" She was happy, mostly, but surprised.

"Since that last night with you in your kitchen, I do. It seemed like a really good idea," he said, kissing her neck, taking his teeth to it gently, then not so gently as she gasped.

He started to undo her jeans, and she protested, "Someone might see us, Nick."

He turned and looked out her kitchen window. "Only if they're snooping around between the side of my house and the side of yours."

And then he waited, hands on her waist. She closed her eyes and said, "Okay. Let's live dangerously."

He grinned, undid her jeans and then somehow lifted her with one arm and pulled them and her panties off with the other. Lily peeled her T-shirt off while he pushed down his jeans and put on the condom.

He looked back up at her, then the bra, then her again, waiting.

"In my kitchen?" she protested.

He nodded, took her mouth. "Yes, Lily, right here in your kitchen. We'll do it in the dark, behind a locked door in a bedroom next time, I promise."

Which was an image that pleased her almost as much as it shocked her to be naked in her kitchen, but naked she was as she peeled off her bra and threw it in the direction of the sink.

He gave her a purely wicked grin, then hauled her up against him, so her breasts nestled against his chest. She closed her eyes and thought of that day he moved in, all those pretty muscles and the hot skin, standing here in her kitchen practically panting over just the idea of him and how long it had been since she'd even noticed a man in that way and how long it had been since anyone had touched her.

And now, here he was, naked in her arms and as beautiful as ever, even more so, she decided.

He was kissing her relentlessly, like he could devour her whole, and gently rocking against her, giving her a moment to get used to the feel of him and to make sure she was ready for this. Lily already knew she was, embarrassingly so.

He palmed her hips, his big hands hot and insistent, pulling her to him, thrust once easily, then again.

Lily groaned.

"Too fast?" he asked.

"No, not fast enough," she told him, feeling downright greedy for him.

And then he slid all the way inside.

"Ahhh!" Lily nearly yelled, because some things just felt too good. Too impossibly good.

He held her there, firmly but gently, rocking ever so slowly against her, which only multiplied sensation on top of glorious sensation.

The man felt impossibly good there in her arms.

Her breath came in little pants, and she was afraid there were tears seeping out of the corners of her eyes, that her whole body was awash in sensations and emotions of every possible sort, and it was all just overwhelming at the moment.

His hands still cupped her hips, fingers digging into them as he tried to control his movements and hers.

"Lily," he warned, because she couldn't be still, couldn't stand it, or maybe she couldn't move slowly enough, or maybe it was just his way of tormenting her and driving her crazy, and she was messing with his concentration or his self-control or something.

But it turned into a battle of sheer will, his versus hers, to see who could drive each other over the edge first.

She used the muscles in her thighs to thrust herself against him and kissed him hard and ran her hands all over him, very, very glad that he had taken all his clothes off in the light.

"You are so bad," he told her, when she refused to be still and let him set the pace.

She grinned up at him.

He kissed her hard, thrusting and thrusting against her, until everything in Lily's body went impossibly tense and then just stayed there, frozen in time and space with him, before she tumbled over the edge.

Wave after wave of pure satisfaction echoed through her. She cried a bit more and buried her head against his neck, felt him pulsing deep inside of her, shuddering, gasping for breath, gasping her name.

"Lily, Lily, Lily."

They stayed right there, clinging to each other.

Lily was suddenly exhausted, her legs aching, her arms clinging to him even harder, tears still flowing.

He held her tight, so strong and yet so gentle, his chest heaving against hers, making her want to do nothing but burrow closer and wishing they were somewhere in the privacy of a deep, dark place.

But they weren't, and he was trying to figure out what was wrong, trying to see her face, dry her tears.

"Hey," he said. "What is it?"

"Just… I don't know. My eyes are leaking."

"Leaking?"

"Yes, leaking," she insisted.

He gave her a little grin.

"They just do that sometimes," she said. "I'm not upset. I'm not crying. I'm just… My eyes are leaking. Don't you ever get…overwhelmed and find that your eyes are leaking?"

He shook his head.

"Well, mine do," she said, feeling overwhelmed, still, and a bit shy and extremely naked. "Can we go hide in the dark now?"

"Sure. Just give me a second."

He turned away from her, but stayed close enough that she didn't fall off her perch on the countertop, got rid of the condom and pulled up his pants. Then he lifted her into his arms and carried her upstairs to her bedroom.

She snuggled against his chest and closed her eyes, trying not to think of the fact that she'd just had sex with him in her kitchen in broad daylight and that she had few, if any, regrets about it, except for being embarrassed for behaving so shamelessly and not getting her way about doing it in the dark.

Not that being able to see him didn't have its definite advantages.

She directed him to the door on the right, and he got her on the bed, tucked under the covers, then bent over and kissed her.

She wrapped her arms around him when he went to pull away, afraid he might disappear, that this might have all been a dream. Nick, her Dream-Lover. That was easier to believe than them getting naked in her kitchen.

He grinned down at her, letting her hang on to him, but said, "I need to run over to my house and grab something."

"Another condom?"

He nodded.

"Feeling pretty sure of yourself? That you'll be needing it?"

"Hoping. Just hoping. And not wanting to be caught unprepared."

"There's a box of them in my bathroom. Far right drawer, buried in the back," Lily admitted. "My sister gave them to me after she got a look at you."

He grinned and headed for the bathroom. "Remind me to thank your sister the next time she comes to visit."

"That is not funny," Lily yelled after him. "Don't you dare, Nick! Don't you dare!"

* * *

She found he dared most anything.

He walked back into her bedroom like a man who felt very much at home there, closed the blinds tight, asking if that met with her approval and her need for sheer darkness.

"It's better," she said.

Then with the bedside light still on, he watched her as she watched him slowly, matter-of-factly, strip for her once again.

Lily blushed, couldn't help herself.

He was an absolutely beautiful man.

All tanned skin and hard muscles everywhere, a hard stamp of satisfaction in his smoky-dark eyes.

And he wanted her again.

His body left no question about that.

Her breath started coming fast and shallow, and she itched to touch him all over.

"Seen enough?" he asked after a moment.

"No," she said.

"Hey, I'd be happy to leave the light on. I'm just trying to give you what you want, Lily."

She shot him a look of exasperation, because the man knew he'd already given her exactly what she wanted and more, and he was about to do it all over again, and he knew that, too.

Wanting to put him a little off balance, too, if she could, Lily slid over in the bed to his side, reached out to turn off the light herself and then in the darkness, found one, well-muscled thigh with her palm, finding heat and firmness to the touch, a bit of roughness from the dark hairs there.

He let out a breath, but didn't say anything else.

She pressed the tip of her nose against that thigh, running up and down the muscle there, then nibbled a bit, taking in the scent of him and liking it.

"Lily," he groaned.

"What?"

She got up on her knees on the edge of the bed, and wrapped her arms around his waist, her breasts against his thighs, kissing his chest and then letting her head fall back for his kiss.

He lifted her right off the bed and wrapped her legs around him once more, squeezing her hips, rubbing up against her.

"I don't seem to have the patience to do this right today," he said, kneeling with her on the bed, laying her back against it and then following her down, his body hot and hard on top of hers. "Sorry."

"Sorry?" she got out between long, deep, thrusting kisses.

"We'll do better next time," he said, like a promise.

Lily let her thighs fall apart, giving him her body to do with as he pleased, and a moment later, he was inside her once again, and it was even better this time, if that was possible.

She loved having the weight of him on top of her, the sheer volume of the man, those broad shoulders and the tight, sexy hips, all those beautiful muscles flexing and straining, propelling him up and back and then down and in once again.

Lily clung to him as best she could, content to let him set the pace, to let him take what he demanded. She started whimpering when it all got to be too much, clutched at his shoulders, might have sunk her nails into his back in protest when she didn't think she could take it anymore.

And then she gave up, gave up all sense of self-control or pretense or self-protection, and just let herself be with him, be his, be completely free and it was like everything fell away. Like nothing else mattered or even existed, except being there with him, and she was nothing but sheer feeling, sheer pleasure.

He groaned on top of her, gave one more, deep, long thrust, and she felt a pulsing deep inside, first from him and then her own, and then she just didn't care about anything at all, except how good she felt.

* * *

He crushed her to him, breathing hard, lying heavily on top of her, waiting for the sensations to end, trying to hang on to every last second of bliss. Lily would have held him, too, if she'd had the strength. As it was, it was all she could do to lie there, her arms falling to her sides, breathing heavily, limp as could be.

Nick nuzzled the side of her neck, her ear, her cheek, his breath still harsh and heavy.

Ever so carefully, he rolled to his side, waited there for a moment, then rose from the bed and made his way into the bathroom. He was back a moment later, getting in beside her and then pulling her to him, until she rested against his side, his arm thrown casually around her, her face against his chest.

He kissed her forehead and told her to rest, and then the world fell completely away.

Chapter Eleven

Lily woke to a languid warmth and pleasant near-exhaustion that made no sense at all.

She was so relaxed, she thought she might have taken a pill of some sort. A fabulous pill, if it could do this to a woman.

She rolled over in her bed, her skin feeling so good against the soft sheets, feeling tingly and alive, like every pore was happy.

Since when were her pores happy?

"Lily?" She heard a deep, husky voice and felt a slightly raspy cheek press against the side of her face, warm breath on her ear, tickling it. "What time do the girls get home?"

"Girls?"

She had to be dreaming.

She never felt this good awake.

Then she remembered wishing for her Dream-Lover, Nick, thinking she could make do with nothing but the dream, and then remembered the reality of Nick, the lover, insistent and demanding and so maddeningly sure of himself and what he wanted and how to get it.

She remembered her kitchen.

Where he'd gotten it.

She'd left her clothes there, she feared.

"Oh, my God!" Her eyes flew open, searching for the lighted digits of her alarm clock. "Three-ten?"

Lily shrieked, planned to throw back the covers and jump out of her bed, but then realized she was naked.

Nick sat there. "Three-ten is bad?"

Her mouth hung open for a moment, then she waited, fearing the sound of a door opening or footsteps on the stairs. Hearing none, she looked at Nick and demanded, "Go downstairs and get my clothes! Hurry!"

He didn't argue, threw back the covers and went.

Naked.

Really cute, but naked.

Lily whimpered.

He stopped in the doorway, came back and grabbed his jeans off the floor and yanked them on, heading out the door as he fastened them.

Lily grabbed underwear from her top drawer and yesterday's jeans and a T-shirt from the top of the clothes hamper in her bathroom and dragged everything on as fast as she could.

She straightened her bed and then ran down the stairs, worried that Nick might have trouble finding all her things. She had no idea where they'd ended up, just remembered flinging her bra in the direction of the sink.

The door opened just as she got to the bottom of the stairs, the girls blowing into the room like a happy, chatty storm, hardly paying her any attention to her at all, except to call out a greeting.

They dropped backpacks and kicked off shoes into their favorite corner of the room and headed for the kitchen.

"Girls!" Lily called after them, managing to get them to stop and turn around and look at her.

"Mom, are you okay?" Ginny asked, looking at Lily like she was a puzzle Ginny would figure out if she tried hard enough.

"Of course, why?"

"You look funny," Ginny said suspiciously. "Your hair's all messed up."

Lily smoothed down her hair as best she could, wishing she'd taken a moment to look in the mirror, then smiled nervously and claimed, "I was working hard all day."

Then Nick stepped out into the hallway leading to the kitchen, his hair messed up, too, but fully clothed, thank goodness.

He looked like he had no idea what to do, having been caught in her house as the girls came home.

Had he found her underwear, at least?

Lily tried to mouth, "Underwear?" at him.

"What?" Ginny asked, definitely knowing something was up now.

Nick shook his head and frowned at Lily.

Did that mean he hadn't found her underwear, or that he didn't know what she'd tried to ask him?

She didn't know.

And it didn't look like she had time to find out. She just shooed him away as best she could by nodding toward the door behind him, and then giving him a little wave with her hand that she hoped said clearly, "Get out now!"

"Mommy?" Brittany said, coming to hold the hand that Lily was waving, maybe like a woman in the midst of a seizure.

"I'm fine, honey, just…starving. I'm starving," Lily claimed, realizing it was true.

She'd slept through lunch and burned off a bunch of calories in the kitchen and in bed.

How could she have done that in her own kitchen?

She'd never be able to go into that room again and not think of what she and Nick had done there.

And she sure wasn't going into that kitchen now.

"I'm hungry, too," Brittany said.

"Me, too," Ginny added.

"Great. How about we go out for pizza?" Lily suggested.

She could get her girls to forget anything by offering to take them to their favorite pizza place. It was a treat she saved for moments when it was absolutely necessary to distract them from something.

Did that make her a bad mother?

She hoped it didn't, but at the moment she was just grateful to understand so fully how to manipulate her girls.

They scrambled back into their shoes and headed out the door, Lily bringing up the rear.

Whew.

She was safe, for the moment.

Now all she had to do was get the girls upstairs when she got back home and search the kitchen herself.

And try not to think about what she'd been doing all day with Nick.

Lily got through an early dinner with the girls just fine, and then managed to shoo them off upstairs when they got home.

She was frantically searching her kitchen and trying to call Nick a moment later when her back door opened and in walked her sister.

"What is the matter with you today?" Marcy asked as she came barreling into the room, her youngest daughter, Stacy, behind her.

Lily froze, thinking to herself, *What is the matter with you, Lily?*

Years of careful living, gone out the window, lost on the

kitchen countertop, and she still didn't know where her underwear was.

Maybe Nick had found it and taken it with him.

An idea that Lily kind of liked, when she thought about it, then imagined seeing her pretty pink bra in those big, strong hands of his, maybe shoved into his front pocket to remind him of what they had done.

Her face turned bright red, she was sure, and she turned away to try to hide it, went to the sink and turned on the cold water to try to cool herself down, wishing she could immerse more than her hands into the cool spray.

She feared she absolutely reeked of really good sex.

The girls wouldn't know what it was, but Marcy would.

"I...I'm sorry," Lily said. "What did I do?"

"You forgot me, Aunt Lily," Stacy cried, bottom lip trembling visibly when Lily turned around to look.

"Oh, no!" Lily said, not remembering until that very moment. "Oh, honey, I'm so sorry. You were supposed to come here after school today, weren't you?"

Stacy nodded, looking like she'd been orphaned for life, instead of forgotten about for an afternoon playdate while her mom went to the dentist.

"I had to go home with Angelica instead, and I don't like her," Stacy said, laying on the guilt. "And her mother said you were irr...irrreee."

"Irresponsible?" Lily guessed.

Stacy nodded.

"She's right. I am so sorry, Stacy. I just completely forgot. I was working on the wooden trim for the dining room, and then I... I guess I just lost track of time completely, and then the girls and I went out for pizza."

"Pizza?" she said wistfully.

Lily had just made it worse.

"Aunt Lily will find a way to make it up to you later, Stacy," Marcy said. "For now, why don't you go upstairs and play with Brittany?"

"Okay," Stacy said, shooting Lily a look that said she would definitely expect to have this made up to her in spectacular fashion.

Lily had finished with her hands and was drying them, paying extraordinary attention to getting them perfectly dry, and wondering if that slight burn in her cheeks meant she'd been roughed up a bit by Nick's afternoon stubble and if he might have even left a mark on her neck.

Tons of possible things that Marcy could see and then know…

But it seemed Marcy didn't need to see or maybe she already had or maybe she just knew, because Lily's sister looked absolutely delighted.

"Lily, sweetie, what did you do all afternoon?" Marcy asked with a twinkle in her eyes.

"Nothing," Lily insisted. "I mean, I worked. I had a lot of work to do."

"I bet it was more like…somebody worked you over," Marcy said.

Thoroughly, Lily thought, trying so hard not to let it show in her face.

"He finally gotcha, didn't he?" Marcy asked, grinning from ear to ear.

"Marcy, I… Honestly—"

Marcy walked toward her, like she was going to corner her or something. Lily tried to dodge her, thinking to slip past the refrigerator and into the hall. She could run, if she had to.

"I just forgot about Stacy. I'm so sorry. But it's really nothing—"

And then Marcy reached behind Lily and up, above Lily's head, and pulled Lily's favorite pink bra from… Must have been from the top of the refrigerator.

"Been looking for this?" Marcy asked, the pink lace dangling from her hand.

Lily grabbed it and went to put it in her pocket, but she didn't have one, so she settled for hiding it in a drawer behind her.

"He got your bra off in your kitchen?" Marcy asked, laughing.

"He got everything he wanted in this kitchen," Lily said, suddenly deciding to come clean and get it over with. Marcy would probably get it all out of her eventually anyway.

She had the satisfaction of seeing Marcy's look of complete disbelief at first.

Lily glared back at her sister, not backing down one bit from that statement.

"No way," Marcy said.

"Fine. Don't believe me. He didn't get anything."

"No, wait," Marcy insisted. "Wait. I want to know. I won't argue one bit. I just…need to know, okay? I'm your sister, and I've been sleeping with the same man for twenty years, Lily. I need to live vicariously for a moment and I got a look at him, so I can guess that he's really, really good at…everything. So, please, do me this one favor and tell me everything!"

Lily's cheeks flamed as she thought of being here in this room with Nick, how crazy and out of control it had been, how it had been completely unlike anything she'd imagined letting herself do with him.

Marcy groaned, like Lily thought she must have done when Nick sank his teeth into her neck and took a little bite of her.

"That good?" Marcy asked.

Lily nodded, simply having no words.

Marcy sank back against the counter like she'd just been reduced to a puddle, which was how Lily felt, too, every time the man so much as looked at her.

"Well," Marcy said. "If it couldn't be me with that gorgeous hunk of man, I'm glad it was you, honey. You deserve it."

"I have no idea how to handle a relationship like this," Lily said. "I mean, do I even call it a relationship?"

"Beats me," Marcy said.

"What do people call it these days?"

"I have no idea. I could ask my next-door neighbor. She has kids in their twenties. She'd probably know."

"And where do we go from here? What do we do?"

"Anything you two want," Marcy said. "But wait, before we forget, did you ever find your panties? Or should we be looking for them before the girls come downstairs?"

"What did you do today?" Jake asked that night as he and Nick ate take-out Chinese.

Nick tried to look completely innocent and asked, "What do you mean?"

Jake shoved a huge forkful into his mouth and halfway chewed before saying, "You seem...I don't know...happy or something."

"What am I, a grump, normally?"

Jake shrugged. "Not really, I guess. I mean... You just seem awfully happy."

Nick shoveled the last of the kung-pow chicken onto his plate before Jake, the human garbage disposal, could get to it, and lied through his teeth, "I didn't do anything, really. I mean, it was a nice day out. Sunny...and...nice."

Jake looked at him like he didn't believe a word of it.

Nick touched a hand to the outside of his jeans over the pocket where Lily's little pink panties were, for safe keeping until he could return them. He'd shoved her shirt and jeans into the cabinet above her refrigerator, along with her bra, thinking her girls wouldn't be able to reach that spot and would never find them.

But he'd had trouble finding the panties and then the girls had come in, and he didn't think he had any choice, really, but to take them with him.

They were still there, still tucked safely away from sight,

making him a little crazy for her every time he remembered they were there.

Lily, turning into a beautiful, half-wild woman in her own kitchen.

He would never have guessed that.

"See, there," Jake said. "You do look happy."

Nick tried his best to look grumpy and told Jake he needed to take out the garbage and clean up his room. Jake just shrugged, as if he was not fooled at all, and got up and took his plate and glass to the sink to rinse them off, then put them in the dishwasher.

Nick fought the urge to pick up the phone and call Lily, fought an even stronger one to wait until Jake was upstairs for the night and Lily's girls were asleep, to slip across the side yard and into her house and return her panties.

If he was really lucky, to carry her off to bed again.

He didn't think she'd go for that with the girls home, but a guy could give it his best shot and see what he could get before she kicked him out for the night.

His phone rang as Jake was collecting his backpack to go upstairs and do his homework.

Nick grabbed for it with unseemly haste, which also caught Jake's attention, and said, "Hello," probably sounding happy just saying the word, thinking it might be Lily.

"Nick, I finally caught you," a distinctly unhappy voice said.

"Hello, Joan."

Jake made a face. Joan was his father's older sister, the relative who made the most vocal objections to Nick getting custody of the boys and a real pain in the ass.

"If I didn't know better, I'd think you were dodging my calls," she said, in a tone that made it sound like she'd actually said, *You jerk, quit dodging my calls.*

"Jake is just fine," Nick said as pleasantly as he could manage. "In fact, he's right here—"

Jake was shaking his head like a madman, mouthing vile threats toward his uncle if Nick dared give the phone to him.

"I didn't call to talk to Jake. I called to talk to you," Joan said.

Nick mouthed to Jake, *Fine, you're off the hook. Now get upstairs.* Then turned around and tried to find some patience to deal with Joan.

"You're still determined to be responsible for these boys?" Joan asked him.

"Nothing's changed, Joan. We're still here. We're still fine. There's nothing for you to take care of," Nick insisted, wondering how his sister stood having this woman as an in-law.

He knew Joan made her a little crazy, but lately he wondered how they'd never come to blows. Joan was...pushy would be the nicest Nick could imagine. She thought she knew everything, including all there was to know about raising teenage boys successfully.

Jake ran from her when he saw her coming and thought her kids were freakishly perfect on the outside and a complete mess on the inside. Nick thought Jake might be right.

He felt like he could see her glaring at him through the phone.

"Fine. Take your six months, although I doubt it will require that long for you to see what a mistake this is," she said. "I'm calling about Thanksgiving. I think it's very important that the boys be with their family this year, of all times, and I thought I might cook dinner and serve it in their house, so they could have one more Thanksgiving at home."

Nick's first thought was that he'd rather eat in front of the TV, watching a football game, and suspected Jake would be fine with that. Jake's father would have been fine with that, too. Nick had spent Thanksgiving at their house, doing just that, until his sister dragged them all away from the TV long enough to serve dinner in the big dining room.

Joan would have pitched a fit, but his sister had lived in a house full of men and understood. They'd eat, digest awhile in front of more football games on TV, and then move into the backyard for a vicious game of football of their own.

It was relaxed and raucous and just about time being spent together as a family.

"Well?" Joan asked, pushy as ever.

"I'll think about it," Nick said. "And I'll ask the boys what they want to do. We'll get back to you."

He got off the phone as fast as he could, swore long and loud in a way he tried not to do in front of Jake, but when he turned around, Jake was still standing there behind Nick, looking worried.

"She's still trying to get you to give up custody, isn't she?" Jake asked.

"No," Nick said, finding a feeling of satisfaction from seeing that Jake really did want to stay with him. He was never sure how things were going, still wasn't sure he could do this and do it right. "Joan just wants us to spend Thanksgiving with her."

"Ooh! No," Jake said. "She'd have a fit if we wanted to watch a game."

Nick shrugged. "I'll try to be a bit more diplomatic than that when I turn her down."

"You know, I was thinking maybe we could spend it with Lily. You think she'll ask us?"

"I don't know. She may have plans with her family. Her sister's house is only about thirty minutes from here."

"I bet Lily makes a killer Thanksgiving dinner."

Which had Nick picturing her in the kitchen.

Which led to him picturing other things.

Things he shouldn't be picturing with Jake in the room.

"You have work to do," Nick said. "Go."

And Jake went.

* * *

Nick paid some bills, did some paperwork and watched Lily's house as one-by-one the lights went out, then saw her walk into the kitchen.

So, she'd gotten the girls to sleep.

Then he walked across the side yard and knocked on her door.

She stared at him through the glass door for a moment before opening it, looking very pretty and hesitant and a little embarrassed.

"I wasn't sure you were going to let me in," he said.

Her cheeks took on a pink tinge and she looked away, biting her lip not to say anything.

Nick laughed softly, feeling like in this moment his life was as close to blissful as it had ever been. He was surprised he even recognized the feeling.

Digging a hand into his front pocket, he tugged on pink lace until a bit of it showed. "I got everything else in the cabinet above the refrigerator—"

"No, you got my shirt and my jeans in the cabinet. The bra didn't quite make it. It was lying on top of the refrigerator. Mostly on top, I should say. My sister found it."

"Oh." Nick nodded. "Sorry. I thought I got it all in there. I tried. Really, but it all happened so fast."

Was she mad or just embarrassed?

He couldn't quite tell.

"I was going to do my best not to tell Marcy anything, but with the bra as evidence, I didn't stand a chance against her," Lily said. "You've met her. You know what I was up against."

She still wasn't looking at him, and he wasn't going to let her get away with that all night. He took a step closer, planting himself right in front of her, backing her up against that spot on the counter with two hands at her side, holding her loosely, not touching her with anything but his hands, but needing to know.

"Are you mad, Lily?"

"No," she said, staring at the floor.

"Do you think I pushed you into doing something you weren't ready for?"

"No."

"Something you didn't want?"

Her gaze came up to his then. "From what happened here, I don't think there's any room for doubt about me wanting you."

Yes.

He'd needed her to say it.

He knew. No question from the way she'd caught fire in his arms. But he'd needed it spoken out loud between them.

"And what do you want now?" he asked, because just as much, he needed to know where they went from here.

"My girls are upstairs," she said.

"I know. But they won't always be here," he said, watching her breathe in and out, watching the space between them and knowing how easy it would be to erase it completely, wanting to sink into her all over again, thinking she really was the most amazing woman.

All quiet and comfort and gentleness on the outside, as much toughness as she needed to handle whatever life threw her on the inside, and a sweet, innocent, eager sexiness that had blown him away.

He couldn't wait for the girls to leave again.

"No, they won't always be here," she said.

"But I could be. Anytime you'll let me. On any kind of terms you want."

She laughed, sounding a bit nervous. "I just give you a little sign—" She raised a finger and motioned him closer. "And that's it?"

"That's the signal?" He nodded. "Then I'll be here."

"Well, that's handy. A man at my beck and call."

He laughed out loud then.

Lily shushed him with her fingers pressed to his lips. "The girls might still be awake, and I don't want them to know about this."

"Okay. Sorry," he said. "Now kiss me, and I'll give you your panties back."

Lily wrapped her arms around him and pulled him close, into a soft, devastatingly inviting, womanly embrace, opened herself up to him and gave herself to him as sweetly and eagerly as she had that morning.

He pulled away long moments later with a groan, pulled her panties out of his pocket and gave them to her and left, thinking he would sleep deeply, satisfyingly, and dream of her.

Chapter Twelve

Dreaming of her was not enough, Nick discovered.

And the next day was Saturday, and her ex backed out on taking the girls again, that rat. He did take them on Sunday, but Jake just always seemed to be underfoot.

So Nick had to wait until he watched her get the girls off to school Monday morning, watched Jake leave, had some coffee and then waited some more, trying not to seem as desperate for her as he felt.

He made it twenty minutes before he showed up next door to find her painting fancy wooden trim to use on her walls.

She just looked at him, a paintbrush in her hand, a bit of white paint on her nose, and said, "I don't recall giving you the signal."

"Well, I was afraid I might have missed it, being next door," he claimed.

"So you came over just to be sure you hadn't missed it?"

He nodded. "And then…I had an idea."

"Nick, I have to get some work done."

"I know. But I'm not bad with a hammer. I mean, I built that great tree house in the backyard. I was thinking, I could help you with your work. With two of us, we'd get it done in half the time, and that would free up some time in the afternoon for…whatever you want."

"For whatever I want? It's what I want?"

"I was hoping we'd want the same thing," he admitted.

And they did.

He knew it.

"You think I'm going to spend every afternoon in bed with you?" she asked, like it was ridiculous to even think that.

"I can hope, can't I?"

She laughed as he came closer, held him off with her wet paintbrush, and said, "Well, I'm going to have to see how productive you can make these mornings. Because, if you think you're going to come over here and make me forget all about how much I have to do—"

He got her then, grabbed the paintbrush with one hand and her with the other arm, pulling her close, holding her weapon carefully out of reach.

"Nick—"

"Don't make me use this," he threatened, pointing the brush at her.

"I mean it. I have to work." She tried pushing him away, but didn't get very far with that. He had her, and he wasn't letting go just yet. "I have to fix up this house and sell it and make some money, so I can feed my growing girls—"

"Make me a deal, Lily."

"Make you a deal? I have to bargain for—"

"Time, honey. We're negotiating about how we're going to allocate our time to accomplish the things we both want during the day, since we don't have our nights free."

"You make it sound so reasonable," she said.

"I'm a reasonable man," he claimed.

She laughed once again, and he got her close enough to kiss her soundly and then had to remind himself they were in her garage and the garage doors were open, and it was not quite ten o'clock in the morning.

"All right," she said when he got done kissing her for the moment. "We'll make a deal."

"Good. What do you need to get done today?"

She gave him her list, and he said, "Okay. Once we do that, the rest of the day is ours. Deal?"

"Deal."

He'd have her in bed by twelve-thirty, and the girls didn't get home until three. Nick thought this would be the beginning of a thoroughly satisfying way to spend their days.

Lily's life had taken a turn toward decadence.

She spent a few hours a day working on her house with Nick and a few hours most every day in bed with him.

She'd sneaked into the lingerie shop one morning after driving the girls to school and bought a big bag full of new undies. When Nick found out what she'd done, he'd tried to get her to promise to let him go to the store with her next time, so he could help her make her selections. No way she could walk into a lingerie store with him.

Then he started sending her undies in the mail in plain brown paper packages.

She blushed all the way to the mailbox, and all the way back, and was sure her neighbors knew something was going on, watching her the whole time she was retrieving her mail, wondering what she could possibly be getting in those plain, brown paper packages.

He made it a game, to see how quickly he could convince her to abandon her work plans and get her into bed, and they always ended up skipping lunch, so they were starving by the time the girls got home. Lily had taken to making a meal at three o'clock, which puzzled both the girls and Jake, but no one objected to eating it. And then she fed the girls and herself a snack at eight o'clock or so, which, again, they didn't really understand but didn't object to, either.

Richard asked her something about moving mealtimes, and she thought about the look on his face if she confessed, "I've taken a lover, and I just can't get myself out of bed long enough to have lunch, which throws my whole schedule off."

She wished she had the nerve, but evidently, the look on her face said enough.

"Are you seeing someone?" he'd asked, the girls loaded into the car for one of those rare times when he actually kept his scheduled visit with him.

"I see a lot of people," she claimed, then to herself added, *But I'm only having mad, passionate sex with one man, and he is soooo not you.*

She went to the neighborhood association meeting, where different groups planned activities throughout the year and was bombarded with questions about Nick and wild speculation about his love life, and she just smiled and claimed not to know a thing. Except that he was the nicest man, and so was Jake.

And she couldn't walk through the neighborhood grocery store without someone telling her he was surely going at it hot and heavy with Audrey Graham.

Poor Audrey.

Lily honestly felt sorry for her, missing out on the wonder that was Nick Malone.

She didn't think she'd ever had a more delicious secret in her whole life or a more pleasure-filled time. A part of her knew there was no way it could go on being so good for any length of time. She knew he had serious reservations about his abilities to be the parent Jake needed now, and that Jake had an aunt, Joan, who was even more convinced that Nick was not the man to be the boys' guardian. She knew he missed his job in Washington, D.C. She knew that he saw this time as something he owed his sister, to see how things worked out between him and Jake, and that even if he did keep Jake in the end, that didn't mean he'd be here or that he'd be with Lily.

She knew all those things, and yet another part of her was falling hard for him, wanting everything he'd been so careful to never promise her, everything he'd never wanted from a woman.

But she tried hard not to think of that, tried to stay in the moment, especially the ones when they were alone.

Weeks passed.

Halloween came and went. She dressed up as a seventies flower child in some things she picked up at a thrift store, and when Brittany told Nick if he wanted to go trick-or-treating with them, he had to dress up, he pulled out a beautiful dark suit, a pair of dark sunglasses, clipped his shiny shield to his breast pocket and told Brittany he was going as an FBI agent.

Brittany didn't think much of the costume until he pulled a pair of handcuffs out of his pocket.

He managed to convince Lily to let him chain her to her own bed the next day by telling her she didn't have the guts to do it, then took complete advantage of her.

Thanksgiving was fast approaching. The twins were coming home from college. Jake was excited to see his brothers. Nick could not imagine the commotion, the sheer volume of noise that would be made or food consumed in a house with three adolescent boys, and Lily was thinking she'd have to do without having him alone for five whole days, which seemed like an eternity to her now.

How had she ever lived this long without him in her life?

He was nothing like Richard in bed.

Even in the early, heady days with Richard, it hadn't been anything like this.

Nick was demanding, patient when it really counted, impatient at times and that worked, as well, paid such attention to the finest details, took note of everything she liked and exactly how she liked it, and taught her exactly what he wanted from her and when, could be adventurous and fun or exercise the kind of self-control that drove her mad.

She felt sorry for every woman in the world who would never have him as a lover, but she wasn't about to share.

She found herself lying in bed with him one rainy afternoon in November, a chill in the air outside, but toasty and warm, curled up against him, thinking he was the most beautiful man.

He was sprawled out on his stomach in her bed, sleepy and satisfied, and she was curled up against his side, her head on his shoulder. She peeled back the covers a little bit at a time, running her hands over every bit of skin she revealed, her fingers making little patterns on his shoulders, his back, kissing her way down his spine.

He laughed deep in his throat.

"Lily?"

"Hmm?" she said, her hand slipping under the covers to cup that sexy bottom of his.

"I thought you were too tired for this."

"I'm just touching you," she said, thinking about the way he looked in those faded, worn jeans of his, about the play of muscles in his hips when he was on top of her and inside of her, how she liked to have her hands here on his bottom when he was deep inside of her.

She leaned over and kissed the base of his spine, and felt his body slowly come to life, desire streaming through him like a golden light, heat following, breath quickening, heart thudding.

Even knowing what it was like, probably exactly what he was going to do, knowing how it felt, how he smelled, how he tasted, how hard and harsh his voice could get when he was really close to the edge of his self-control, even then, she still couldn't wait to have him, to be in his arms, skin to skin, opening herself up to him, holding nothing back.

She couldn't wait.

And she couldn't seem to get enough.

"You're going to cripple me one of these days," he said, slowly rolling over, grabbing a condom and then pulling her on top of him.

Lily grinned.

She liked it this way, liked it every way, truth be told, but really liked it this way because of the way he watched her. She settled herself on top of him, close, but not taking him inside yet. She leaned down to brush her hair against his chest, brush a kiss against his lips and then her breasts against his chest. And then she rocked against him, still not taking him.

And all the while, he watched her, telling her how it felt when she did this or that, telling her how sexy she was, how pretty, how much of a tease.

After a while, he'd take a handful of her hair and pull her to him, take her hips in his palms and maneuver his way inside of her, and then let her do what she wanted for another period of time, fighting for control, while she tried to tear that control of his to shreds.

And then he'd take her by the hips once again and pull her into the rhythm he wanted, sometimes letting her stay on top, sometimes not.

It didn't matter.

What did, was that she got to be with him, tease him, kiss him, torment him, end up spent and barely able to breathe, weak and boneless, wrapped up in his big, strong arms.

She felt so safe in his arms.

That day, she teased him for as long as she could, felt his hands on her hips as he slowed the rhythm down, until he barely let her move at all, so that the slightest movement at all felt like so much more. She dug her fingernails into his shoulders, tightened every muscle in her body around him, felt his hands dig into the flesh of her bottom, holding her still, right there on the edge.

Until they both just shattered, everything falling away.

She cried out his name, saw that hard, satisfied smile come across his face, and then she collapsed in his arms.

They stayed that way for a long time.

His hand stroked through her hair. He kissed her lips once, then again, then rolled her onto her side and disappeared for a moment, coming back a moment later to pull her back to him, spooning against her, his front to her back, his arms wrapped around her, her cheek pillowed on his arm, his lips kissing her cheek, then toying with her ear.

She was sure she'd never get enough of him.

Jake opened the door one afternoon in November and found Andie's mother standing there, giving him a bright smile that somehow seemed odd.

"Mrs. Graham," he said. "Hi."

Standing in the doorway, teetering on ridiculously high heels, wearing a tight, short black skirt and a low-cut top, she struck a pose that seemed as if she were offering her breasts up for his viewing pleasure. He tried not to look.

"Hi," she said, kind of purring in a way. She brushed past him and into the living room, uninvited. "Do me a favor, honey. Tell Phillip I'm here."

Jake stood there. "Phillip? Who's Phillip?"

She laughed, her voice all throaty and inviting. "You know. Phillip. He isn't expecting me, but he's always glad to see me."

Jake closed the door and then followed her through the downstairs as she called out to someone named Phillip.

"Mrs. Graham, I think you have the wrong house," he said, though honestly, how was that possible?

She'd been here three or four times flirting with his uncle. How she could not remember who Jake was and who his uncle was and that this was their house?

She headed for the stairs, missed the second step and started to fall. Jake caught her and then eased her down to sit on the step. And caught a whiff of her breath in the process.

She'd been drinking.

At four in the afternoon?

He tried to keep her where she was, not wanting her trying the stairs again, but she didn't like that.

"I'm fine," she insisted. "And I'm not leaving until I get to see him."

"Okay," Jake said. "He's not here, but I can call him and maybe he'll come home."

That seemed like the best thing to do.

Except he'd call Andie.

He didn't think her mother would know the difference, at least not until Andie got here.

Jake reached for the phone. He knew Andie's home number because he'd thought about calling it a million times, but chickened out. He thought of the two times she'd been here, looking for her mother, and wondered if this was the problem—that her mother drank and wandered off or got lost or something.

Andie answered on the first ring, sounding anxious as she said, "Hello."

"Andie? It's Jake. Jake Elliott."

"Who?"

"Your neighbor. Two streets over. I go to your school," he said, trying to ignore his own humiliation at being completely invisible to her.

"Oh. Yeah. I can't talk right now. I'm really busy. Sorry," she said, then hung up on him before he could say anything else.

"Great," Jake muttered, disconnecting the call, then hitting redial.

"Look," she said when she answered. "I told you, I have something I have to take care of. I can't talk to you now. Goodbye."

Jake swore and hung up.

Maybe he could get her mother home by himself. If she'd go willingly...

Then he realized he'd lost her.

"Mrs. Graham?" he called out, searching the downstairs for her.

He found her in the kitchen with a bottle of Scotch that his uncle kept in the back corner of the pantry. It tasted absolutely vile. Jake knew because he'd sniffed, then taken a sip and nearly gagged. How could anybody drink that stuff?

Mrs. Graham found a glass and poured herself a drink.

"I don't think you need that right now."

Jake went to get the bottle away from her, but she wouldn't give it up, and in the process, the Scotch in the glass sloshed out and ended up mostly all over Jake's shirt. She dropped the glass, and it shattered all over the floor.

"Oops." She started to giggle, was worse than his stupid friends when they got drunk. More clumsy and argumentative and harder to handle.

He grabbed her hard, afraid she'd step on the glass and fall off those silly high heels and cut herself. "Watch out. You'll cut yourself. How about you sit on the kitchen countertop, and I'll clean up. And then we'll get you home."

"Help me." She held out her arms to him.

He put his hands on her waist and lifted, getting her up there without any problem, and then she grabbed on to him and didn't want to let go.

"You are absolutely adorable," she said, her hand fiddling with his hair.

Jake closed his eyes and reminded himself she was old enough to be his mother, and that she was Andie's mother and very drunk, and tried not to look at her legs, because he was a guy and female legs of almost any kind just seemed to take over his brain at times, and this could not be one of those times.

He had to get her out of here.

"Hey," he said, figuring out how. "I need to call Phillip. Do you have a phone?"

She pulled her phone out of her tight, tight skirt and handed it to him.

He flipped through her contact list to the name Andie and dialed.

Andie answered. "Mom! Where are you? I've been looking everywhere. Are you all right?"

"She's at my house," Jake said.

Complete silence greeted him at first, and then very softly Andie said, "What?"

"It's Jake Elliott. That's what I was trying to tell you before. Your mother's at my house. She seems to think someone named Phillip lives here, and I can't make her understand she's in the wrong place. I think she's been drinking." Jake waited. More silence. Then added, "Sorry. I thought maybe she'd listen to you. I didn't know what else to do."

He heard Andie muttering to herself for a moment, and then she talked into the phone again. "I'll be right there. Just don't let her leave."

"Okay," Jake said.

And then she hung up.

He looked back at Mrs. Graham, who was grinning broadly at him and playing with her blouse. And he thought about how worried Andie sounded when she thought her mother was calling, remembered the times before she'd been looking for her mother here.

Andie had seemed too perfect to him, with her perfect hair, perfect teeth, perfect clothes, perfect body, perfect everything, and now...he wondered if she had an alcoholic for a mother who sometimes left home and couldn't find her way back.

Andie burst into his house a moment later and the look on her face when she saw the mess and her mother—commenting on Jake's nice muscles, then playing with his hair some more—was just awful.

She took her mother by the hand and urged her down. "Come on, Mom. We have to go home right now."

Her mother teetered on her own two feet. "Where is Phillip?"

Andie shot Jake a puzzled look. "I thought, all this time, she was with your uncle."

All this time?

Jake shrugged, didn't know what to say.

"Phillip? It must be…oh, no," Andie said. "Phillip Wrenchler. He lives in the house behind yours. Maybe she's been sneaking through your backyard and into his. Mom, he's married."

Her mother was looking at Jake. She winked at him.

Andie rolled her eyes and swore, then looked at Jake pleadingly. "I don't suppose…if I begged you. Absolutely begged you. You could promise not to tell anyone about this."

"Okay," Jake said.

"Not anyone," Andie said.

"Promise. Want me to help you get her home?"

"No. She'll come with me now. I'm sorry. About the mess and everything."

Jake shrugged. "It's all right. I'll clean it up. No problem. Sorry about…your mom."

Andie looked for a moment like she was about to cry, then took her mother by the hand and led her out of there.

He was still cleaning up the mess when his uncle got home.

Nick caught himself whistling as he walked from Lily's house to his.

Whistling.

Some kind of song…he couldn't remember who sang it or much of the lyrics. Something about an absolutely beautiful day…waiting and waiting and at last experiencing an absolutely perfect day.

The woman did the oddest things to him.

And the absolute best things.

He ran a hand across his jaw, felt the abrasive stubble there and remembered the slightly reddish tint to Lily's cheeks and her pretty lips. If they kept this up, he'd have to start hiding a spare razor somewhere over there, so he didn't scruff her up.

She was so soft.

He didn't want to hurt her in any way.

As it was, it was all he could do to drag himself out of her bed and out the door before her girls got home, and he lay in his bed at night alone waiting for the hours to go by until they could be alone again.

He got to his door, pulled it open, walked into the kitchen, and found that the place reeked of alcohol, and there stood Jake with a broom, trying to clean up broken glass.

Well, hell.

Jake froze, broom and a dustpan full of glass in hand, the garbage can sitting to the side of the kitchen. He'd obviously been at work for a while.

"Hi," he said, looking worried.

"Jake." Nick tried not to bellow. "What's going on here?"

"Okay. It's not what it looks like. I promise."

"Really?"

"Yeah. I can explain." Jake dumped the glass into the garbage and then stood there, looking more worried with every passing minute. "I mean, I would, if I could."

"Oh, you're going to explain," Nick said, taking the broom and the dustpan from his hands, putting them down and pulling Jake along with him, out of the mess and into the living room. "Sit."

Jake didn't. He stood there. "I mean, I kind of promised I wouldn't tell. But…it wasn't me. I wasn't drinking, I swear."

Nick tugged on the kid's shirt, which was wet, sniffed, then rolled his eyes. "You reek of Scotch."

"I know, but I didn't drink any. I was trying to get it away from her—"

"Her? You had a girl over here drinking?" Nick took that like a kick in the gut. The kid was drinking, and he had a girl over, who was also drinking, while Nick wasn't even home? "What the hell else have you been doing while I wasn't here?"

"Nothing. I told you. I didn't do anything except try to stop her—"

"Oh. Okay. You didn't drink anything, you just smell like you did, but you invited a girl over here who was drinking, and you were just trying to stop her? That's your story?"

"No," Jake said.

"Okay, now we're getting somewhere—"

"I didn't invite a girl over. She just showed up."

Nick swore, wanting to grab the kid and scare him into telling Nick the truth. Because the stuff Nick was imagining on his own was pretty bad. The truth could be even worse.

Had Nick missed this completely? That Jake was drinking? That he had a girl? That he had her here, and they were both drinking and doing God-knows-what behind Nick's back?

Had he really missed all that?

"One more time," Nick said, up in the kid's face, letting the fear show and hoping it looked like he was just royally pissed. *Scared straight, Jake. Come on,* Nick thought. "There was a girl here—"

"Well, not really a girl," Jake claimed.

Nick let go of him and backed up, not believing the crap coming out of the kid's mouth. "Not really a girl? What was she, a half girl, half... I don't even want to know what?"

"No, I mean, it wasn't another kid. It wasn't somebody my age."

"You're trying to tell me you're seeing someone old enough to drink?"

"No! You don't get it at all!" Jake yelled, looking like he was about to cry all of a sudden. "I thought you trusted me! I thought we were doing okay. I thought everything was going to be okay!"

"So did I," Nick roared back. "Now tell me, what the hell did you do?"

"I got drunk!" Jake screamed. "That's what you want to believe, fine. I got drunk. I was trying to clean up the mess before you got home, and you caught me. End of story."

Then he stalked off toward the door, like that was it. Like Nick would just let it go with that.

"Oh, no." Nick grabbed him by his arm. No way he was letting the kid leave.

Jake jerked away from him, stronger than Nick expected, and then he had to grab for him again. Next thing he knew they were scuffling, him trying to get some kind of hold on Jake, and Jake squirming and somehow slipping away.

"I swear to God, Jake, if you don't get your ass back here and tell me—

"I already told you," Jake yelled. "It didn't do any good the first time, and I'm sure not going to tell you again. Just let me go."

Nick was trying not to hurt him. He was mad as hell and scared and determined not to let him go, but not to hurt him, either, and it was the Scotch on the floor and the glass that did him in.

Jake got through it, or maybe he got around it, and Nick didn't, skidded on it and lost his footing and went down hard as Jake shot out the door.

Nick laid there and swore some more.

Chapter Thirteen

When he got himself up off the floor, he peeled off his shirt, which smelled as bad as Jake's did and then cleaned up the kitchen, taking the time to try to calm himself down.

Then he grabbed his phone and called Jake's cell, fear shooting through him all over again when it rang and rang and then went to voicemail.

"Jake, get your ass back here. Right now," he said, then could have kicked himself for it.

That was a message sure to make the kid come right home.

He called again, forcing some measure of calm into his voice, he hoped. "Look, we'll talk this out, okay? We'll both be calm, and we'll talk this out. You just…you can't run off like that, Jake. You just can't."

Which was stupid of him to say, because the kid had done just that.

The thing was, Nick had worked Missing Persons for the last year and a half. He'd seen a lot of kids take off after some kind of argument and end up in all kinds of trouble. Or worse, never come back home.

So he was probably overreacting here.

Probably.

But he was scared half to death.

Nick pulled out a sheet of paper with names and phone numbers. He made sure to know who the kid hung out with. He tried the top three kids and all of them swore they hadn't seen Jake and didn't know where he was.

And then, more than anything, Nick just wanted Lily.

Hell, maybe the kid had gone there.

He adored Lily, after all.

Nick went tearing over there and pounded on her back door, obviously scaring her from the look on her face when she flung open the door.

"What's wrong?"

"Jake's gone," he said grimly. "We had a nasty fight, and he's gone. I was hoping he might have come here."

"No. I haven't seen him. What did you fight about?"

"Him drinking. I really screwed up, Lily, didn't have any idea. I must have missed it completely, but I went home and the place reeked of alcohol. So did he, and then he tried to tell me it was all a big misunderstanding and got mad at me for not believing him. Then he took off."

"Okay." She put her hands on his arms, like he might need her to hold him up or something. "Just...take a breath. Teenagers can be really dramatic at times. Believe me, I've heard it all from Marcy. He just probably needs some time to cool down, and then he'll be home, and you two can figure this out."

"What if he doesn't come back?" Nick said, giving voice to his greatest fear.

"Of course, he'll come back. He's not stupid, just mad."

Nick stood there, chest heaving as he fought for breath, fought to calm down. Lily smiled up at him, like he was being ridiculous, and then wrapped her arms around him and just held him.

Which he would have said was silly and completely unnecessary, for him to actually need someone to comfort him. But he all but crushed her to him, afraid he might squeeze the breath right out of her, feeling like he needed her so much right then it terrified him almost as much as the idea that Jake was out there somewhere, alone, and might never make it back in one piece.

"Oh, my God, Lily!"

"It's terrifying, I know. You love your kids so much, like you didn't even know you could love anyone or anything, and then you see that at times you're powerless to keep them safe, and it's absolutely terrifying."

He sagged back against the wall, looking down at her, taking the words in and processing them as fast as he possibly could.

He loved Jake?

Of course he did. Jake was a cool kid, fun to play with when Nick showed up at his sister's house for a weekend here and there. They'd play ball, wrestle sometimes, battle over some silly video game. That was it.

But Lily was saying something different.

Lily was talking *love,* that fierce, you-are-mine, heart-and-soul, and I-would-do-anything-for-you kind of love he'd heard inklings of in the relationship between parent and child, but never thought to experience himself.

Did he love Jake like that?

"Nick, you didn't really think you could do this and not feel that way about Jake in the end, did you?" she asked.

"No. I mean, I didn't really think about it. It all happened so fast, and we were all so shocked that his parents were really gone, and then someone had to be here with them. It's what my sister wanted, so I said we'd try it, and here we are."

Lily nodded, smiled once again, like it all made sense to her. "Welcome to parenthood. It's brutal at times."

"The kid is gone," he said, practically yelling. "He's gone, and I don't know where he is. I don't know what to do—"

Lily put a hand to his mouth, trying to shush him and soothe him at the same time, when all he wanted was to scream.

Did she not understand?

He'd screwed it all up, and the kid was gone!

"I know," Lily said.

"Then tell me what to do now. Tell me how to fix this, because I don't have any idea—"

"Mommy!"

They both heard Ginny at the same time, stopped talking and jerked apart.

Ginny gave them both an odd look, then asked, "Are you guys arguing about Jake?"

"We're not..." Lily stopped, then started again. "We're not arguing. Jake is gone, and his uncle is worried about him. That's all."

"It sounds like you're arguing," Ginny said accusingly.

"Sorry," Nick said. "She's right. I was yelling, and I'm sorry. I'm not mad at your mom. I'm just...scared and sometimes when I get scared, I yell."

Ginny frowned, like she might take him to task for that, but in the end, decided to accept his explanation. "Okay. Just don't do it again. You scared Brittany."

Then she held up the cordless phone and said, "It's Jake."

Nick went to grab it from her, but Ginny put it behind her back and told Nick, "He wants to talk to Mom. He said he can hear you yelling at her, and he wants you to stop right now."

"He can hear me?" Nick asked.

Ginny shook her head, then gave the phone to her mother.

Put in his place by a nine-year-old, Nick stood there, looking out into the darkness. Lily had her kitchen windows open to the night breeze, which meant Jake was either in the house hiding or somewhere in one of their yards.

Which meant, he was safe, wasn't he?

Nick put his hands on the kitchen countertop, bracing himself, and leaned into them, telling himself the kid was safe, crisis averted, and to calm down.

It wasn't working.

He was still terrified.

Lily put down the phone and said, "He's in the tree house. I'm going to go talk to him."

"No. This is my mess. I'll talk to him."

"Nick, trust me on this, okay? You're not ready to fix this, and he doesn't want to talk to you right now. And whatever happened tonight doesn't have to be solved tonight. He's fine. He's safe, and I'll take care of him for now and make sure he doesn't go anywhere except my house or yours, okay?"

"But—"

"I know. You want to charge in there and settle this right now, and I'm telling you that you don't have to. You can let it sit overnight, and you both can calm down and this will all look much better in the morning. I promise."

Nick felt like his entire body was an engine revving at a hundred miles an hour or so, and that charging in to settle things sounded really good to him right now. Essential, even.

And at the same time, he felt like a wet noodle, like there were no bones in his body, no strength, no courage, nothing but a kind of relief that soaked through him and left him weak in its aftermath.

He took a breath, then another, found it just didn't help. He felt like he might fall down at any second.

He'd wanted so much to do this right, for his sister and for Jake, and worried all along that he couldn't, that she'd made a mistake in asking him to, and that he'd end up disappointing her and Jake in the end.

He felt like he'd done all those things tonight.

"Just stay here until I get back, okay?" Lily asked.

"Okay," he finally said, getting out of the way and letting her go.

He watched as she made her way into the backyard and then climbed the ladder into the tree house and disappeared.

He'd imagined the kid hitchhiking to Alaska or someplace like that, and all Jake had done was crawl into the tree house in the backyard next door.

Still, the drinking, the girl, the lying…

How much had he missed? He was afraid to find out.

Nick turned around and found Lily's daughter waiting there staring at him with a mildly disgusted look on her face.

"Grown-ups are so weird," she told him.

"Really?"

Ginny nodded, then took him by the hand. "Come on. You have to talk to Brittany. She liked you so much for building her that stupid tree house, and now you ruined it all by yelling at our mom. You have to say you're sorry and make her think you mean it."

"I do mean it," Nick said.

He had no right to take his temper or his fears out on Lily, and he'd never wanted to scare her girls.

"Just make Brittany believe it," Ginny said, like she might never believe he was sorry, but hoped her sister might.

Jake didn't think he'd ever been so miserable in his entire life, maybe not even the day his parents had their accident.

Because even then, his uncle had called and made it clear that he was on his way, that he would get there as fast as humanly possible, and that he would take care of everything.

And Jake had believed him.

Then he'd found out his parents had made sure that if

anything happened to them, his uncle was to take Jake, and Jake had told himself that it would be hard, but okay, because it was like his parents were still taking care of him, by making sure his uncle was there for Jake.

But now, his parents were gone, and he wasn't going to have his uncle to count on, either.

Which meant, he didn't have anybody who believed him and trusted him and was on his side. Which was the absolute worst feeling in the world.

Then he heard someone climbing the steps to the tree house and thought he might jump off the balcony to keep from having to see his uncle right now, but when he scrambled over to the opening, it was only Lily.

Jake got back in his corner, thankful for the near-darkness, and swiped at tears with the back of his hand and waited in all his misery.

Lily wasn't much like his mom, who said it took a drill sergeant to raise three boys, and she did work hard to keep them in line, tough but fair and lots of fun. Lily was quieter and gentler and really, really sweet.

She climbed into the tree house and sat down beside him, her back to the wall, so she wasn't really looking at him, just there with him, which he liked.

"Sorry he yelled at you," Jake said.

"It's all right. He was just scared."

"He was mad—"

"Yes, but mostly scared," she insisted.

"Well, he didn't have to take it out on you."

"He didn't, Jake. I promise. Now why don't you tell me what happened?"

"He doesn't believe me. That's what happened. I told him the truth, and he doesn't believe it!"

Lily sighed. "Well, you have to admit, it's kind of hard to believe. I mean, he comes into the house. Someone's obviously been drinking. There's alcohol all over the place. It's all over you—"

"You don't believe me, either!" he cried.

"I didn't say that. I'm just saying...try to look at it from his point of view. The situation looks pretty bad."

"He could have believed me," Jake argued. "I don't lie to him. I know he doesn't really want to be here, taking care of me. But we're doing okay. And I've done everything I could to make it easy for him, but then, the first little thing goes wrong, and he just blows up."

"Jake, if he didn't want to be here, he wouldn't be here—"

"Nuh-uh. This wasn't his idea. This was my parents', and they didn't even say anything to him about it ahead of time. They just decided that if anything ever happened to both of them, he'd take me and my brothers. He was as surprised as we were when we found out, and he didn't want to come here and take care of me. But it's what my mother wanted, and it's kind of hard to say no to your dead sister and your dead sister's kid, you know?"

"Okay. Okay." Lily leaned closer to his side and put an arm around his shoulder.

Jake didn't want to want that. He wanted to handle this all by himself because...well, just because.

But he was really glad Lily was there.

"Jake, you have to cut him some slack. Parents don't always know the right thing to do, and with Nick, who's never been a parent before, it's even harder to know what's right when—"

"My mother would have believed me," he insisted.

"Would she really?"

"Yes," he said, then started crying again.

"Oh, Jake. I'm sorry. I'm so sorry."

And then he just gave up and put his head on Lily's shoulder and cried.

* * *

They had something of an armed standoff that night.

Jake refused to go home, and Nick refused to leave without Jake. Lily thought they were two of the most stubborn men she'd ever met, and she finally got tired of trying to broker a deal between them.

She put Brittany to bed in her room, offered Jake Brittany's bed and offered Nick the sofa in the living room.

Ginny thought the whole thing was really funny when Lily explained that Jake wouldn't go home, and Nick wouldn't leave without him, so they were both staying.

Then Ginny said, "Sometimes I don't want to go to Daddy's new house, but you still make me."

And then Lily ended up inviting Ginny to sleep in her bed, too, so they could talk about some daddy things and some divorce things, and when both the girls were finally asleep, and Jake was in Brittany's bed, Lily slipped down the stairs to the living room.

Nick was sitting in the dark, staring at nothing, still as a statue, like a man afraid to move.

Lily curled up in the corner of the couch, just watching him for a moment, aching for him.

"It's kind of scary, being a parent," she said.

"Kind of terrifying, don't you mean?"

She nodded. "Sometimes. But a lot of the time, it's great. And he's fine, Nick. He's upstairs, tucked into a little girl bed with half a dozen stuffed animals watching over him. He's just fine. You both will be fine. You'll see."

"Where would he have gone if you weren't here?" he asked, anguished. "And then what would I have done?"

"It doesn't matter, because I am here and I'm not going anywhere."

"Lily! I don't—"

She was done talking. She put her arms around him and

pulled him to her, leaned back against the big, pillowed end of the couch and stretched out, pulling him down beside her until his head was on her shoulder, his arms wrapped around her. She'd have thought she was asking him to bend steel in his spine, the way he had so much trouble simply accepting that bit of comfort from her.

Was the man so unbending?

"Just close your eyes and tell yourself he's upstairs," she told him. "And he's safe—"

"Your girls—"

"Are asleep in my bed. I'll stay here with you until you fall asleep, and then I'll go up, too."

She leaned down and kissed the top of his head and his forehead and then his lips, just once, then tightened her arms around him and relaxed into the feeling of having a big, strong, for once incredibly vulnerable man in her arms and gave him what comfort she could.

And she tried, she really tried, to tell herself not to fall in love with him. They were just having fun, enjoying each other's company, enjoying being alive.

It wasn't love, but it was enough, Lily told herself.

He didn't even know he loved Jake, when it was so clear to her that he did, and the way Jake told the story, Nick still thought he was only here with Jake out of a sense of duty and obligation. A man like that wouldn't have even given a second thought to loving a woman or maybe even believing he could love her or stay with her.

Lily could have cried herself to sleep, if she'd let herself.

Instead, she'd come down here to comfort him, because for now, he was here and she could have him in her arms and try to make things better for him and Jake.

Tomorrow, she'd try to figure out how to make things better for herself, to protect herself from both of them, if that was even possible anymore.

* * *

Jake stalked back home the next morning, his uncle following behind him. They walked into a kitchen that still smelled like Scotch, and without saying a word, worked together to clean up the mess. Then Jake went upstairs, took a shower and headed off to school.

He wasn't going to say he was sorry for something he didn't do.

He wasn't.

He was halfway to his friend Brian's house to catch a ride to school when a silver BMW stopped beside him. The window came down and there was Andie.

Wow. Never would have believed anything like that would be waiting for him this morning, or that anything could happen that would make him really not care about the mess of the night before.

Life was just full of surprises, and they weren't all bad, he was discovering.

"Want a ride?" she asked.

"Sure," he said, going to the other side and getting in.

She looked like she'd had as tough of a night as he had, and he felt bad about that. Really. "Did you get your mom home okay?" he asked.

She nodded, didn't seem like she wanted to talk about that.

"Nice car," Jake tried. And it really was.

He'd never been in a BMW before, just admired them from afar. The ride was so smooth, and she didn't do anything but barely hit the gas and off it went. The car would probably fly.

Jake couldn't wait to get his permit. Not that his uncle would be eager to let him do that now.

"This is my mom's car," Andie said. "I didn't think she'd be going anywhere today. Or that she should go anywhere today. She probably won't even be awake today until I get home. So I took it."

"I didn't tell anybody about...anything," Jake said. "If that's what you're worried about. And I won't tell anybody. Promise."

She didn't look like she believed him, but he couldn't make her. She'd just have to wait and see, because if he hadn't told his uncle last night, he wasn't going to tell anybody.

"I'm really sorry my mom... I saw the way she was acting with you. She flirts when she drinks too much. It's really disgusting, and sometimes I wish she'd just die and get it over with. I mean... Oh, my God. I'm sorry. I mean... Your parents... I heard... I'm sorry. You must think I'm awful to say that about my mom."

Jake shrugged, trying to play it off.

No big deal.

He had no idea how to handle the topic of his parents' deaths when kids his age brought it up or what to say. It wasn't like there was anything he could really say, after all, to make it better.

"Look, we both have stuff to deal with, and we're dealing, right? I just... You don't have to worry. I'm not going to say anything about your mom. And if you get into a spot again and need somebody to help you with her, you can call me. I won't mind."

Yeah, Jake thought, hoping the next time he helped her out it wouldn't lead to World War III between him and his uncle.

Nick had been watching Jake leave, because he wanted to make sure he was gone before he started searching the house. He figured he had to do that, at least, to see... Well, just to see what else he might have missed.

He'd start in the kitchen and try to remember every drop of liquor he'd brought into the house. The Scotch, he remembered, came from a buddy of his in the marines who lived in town. He'd brought it to Nick's sister's funeral, and they'd had a drink together afterward in his sister's house, and it had ended up in a box of kitchen stuff that Nick had brought here when he and Jake moved in.

So he'd search, find everything that was here and pour it out.

Then he was going to search Jake's room.

He didn't think he had a choice.

He had to know what Jake was doing. He had to keep him safe, as best he could.

Beyond that…

Nick swore long and loud, then glanced out the window and down the street in time to see Jake get into a little silver BMW.

What the hell?

Nick didn't know anybody who drove a car like that.

He didn't think, just reacted. A minute later, he was in his car following them, thinking they could be going anywhere, doing anything, and what would Nick know about it?

A thousand lousy, scary possibilities ran through his head.

But all they did was drive to school.

Jake and a girl, a scarily attractive blonde. It might be the same one who'd been in Jake's room that day.

"Oh, hell," Nick muttered.

No fifteen-year-old boy could think straight around a girl who looked like that.

Nick wondered if she was the one who liked Scotch, if she was the one Jake was covering for, because honestly, he'd probably do anything for a girl like that.

So Nick went home and searched every inch of Jake's room and didn't find much of anything. No drugs. No alcohol. A few condoms and some magazines, but Nick didn't think any fifteen-year-old's room was without those.

He was trying to figure out where to search next when the phone rang.

He grabbed it, hoping in an instant that it was Lily, but all he got was Joan, ready to tell him that he was in no way cut out to be a father to Jake.

Don't I know it, he thought bitterly.

Chapter Fourteen

He did not intend to see Lily that day, thinking it would be best to back off a bit, to think, to make sure he was taking care of things here with Jake, instead of running off to enjoy himself with her.

He was here, after all, to take care of Jake.

Not to fall for a woman.

Not that he'd ever really let himself fall for a woman.

He didn't intend to need her, to depend upon her or to lean on her, and yet he'd done all of those things. And when he sat back and thought about it, it was damned disconcerting to realize how entangled they'd become in each other's lives.

That it had distracted him from seeing obviously troubling things going on with Jake was even worse. He'd never shirked his duty because of a woman. He wouldn't do that now, no matter how much he liked being with her.

Which meant it was better to deal with this now, before they got even more entangled with each other and before he really hurt her. Honestly, he'd never wanted to hurt her.

And it wasn't fair to her, to keep going with this, when…
Well, it just wasn't fair.

Nick leaned into the kitchen doorframe, looking out across their yards, to her kitchen and saw her there, looking back at him.

She knew too much. She saw too much. She wanted more than he wanted to give, and he was sure she knew that, too.

Like anything could ever be simple with a woman like her.

So this was one more thing he'd screwed up and needed to fix.

Grimly, he opened the door and headed for her house. She held her head high and tried to smile, and he felt like a complete jerk, but forced himself to go on, to do this.

"Jake was on the way to school this morning when he got into a car with a girl. A girl with a little silver BMW, looked brand-new. I think it was the same girl who was in our house with him that day. Does Andie Graham have a silver BMW?"

"No," Lily said. "But her mother does."

"Then it was her." *Great.*

"Wait, did they actually go to school?" Lily asked.

"Yeah. I followed them, watched them walk all the way inside. Then I went back to the house and searched his room. I could have taken the place apart without him knowing about it, but then I thought maybe I wanted him to know that I was watching him that closely, so that maybe he wouldn't do anything stupid."

"Did you find anything in his room?"

"No. But that doesn't mean there never was anything there."

"I know, but he seems like a really good kid, Nick. He's almost always at home if he's not at school, and you're almost always there with him. I'm just saying, he doesn't have much of a chance to do anything really bad, does he?"

"Yeah, but if he wanted to find a way, he could. Kids can always find a way, and their parents have no idea what they're really doing or what kind of trouble they're in until it's too late. I've seen it, Lily. I know what the world's like out there."

"No, you know what the worst of it's like. Not what most kids are like," she argued, coming to him, touching him with a hand on his arm, when he'd purposely stayed away, not letting himself touch her. "Maybe you've just seen too many bad things, Nick."

"I know I have," he admitted. "I absolutely know it."

"Look, you should know Jake's convinced you don't really want to be his guardian, that you're going to try it for a few months, but that in the end, you'll go back to your old life and he'll go to someone else. It may have just been that he was upset last night, but that's what he said, and I thought you should know."

Nick nodded, trying to remember exactly what he'd said in front of the kid and what he hadn't. It had just been such a shock. His sister dying. Her husband dying. Them wanting him to take Jake.

He thought in the end, he'd just said, *We'll give it six months and see how it goes.*

Sounded reasonable to him, but he could see now it wouldn't exactly be reassuring to a fifteen-year-old boy who didn't know where he'd go next if things didn't go well between him and Nick.

He tried to remember exactly what he'd offered Lily, too, and didn't remember much more than saying he wanted her, and could he just sneak over here to see her when her girls and Jake weren't around.

Not much to offer a woman, either, and yet that's what he'd done.

"I'm sorry, Lily," he said, kicking himself for hurting her, too.

And he didn't really have to say more than that.

She knew.

"It's last night, isn't it?" she asked.

"Last night, I realized Jake was in trouble, and that I'd missed it. I missed it completely, probably because I'd gotten too caught up in you, and it was nice, Lily. It was really nice between us, but it's not why I came here. I came here to take care of him, and I'm blowing it, and that has to stop."

"Right," she said. "It's not that you got really scared when you realized how much you love him, how you might lose him, too. And it's not that you realized you'd gotten used to having him in your life, when you've never really done that before. And it's not that when you were really scared last night, instead of being alone and having to handle it all on your own, you came to me. You wanted me. You even, for a little while on the couch late last night, let yourself need me, and that's just not something you're willing to let yourself do."

He just stared at her. "I said it was good, okay? It was really good, but you knew it wasn't going to last. It's why you didn't want to get involved with me in the first place, remember?"

She nodded, tears in her eyes but not falling, chin up, still fighting with that quiet, rock-solid strength of hers that he admired so much. "You're just scared, Nick. That's all."

But it was more than that.

It was him, the way he'd always been, the way he always would be.

"I really am sorry," he said again.

She nodded. "Fine."

"Lily—"

"But I hope you know, it's not going to be this easy for you to walk away from Jake as it is for you to walk away from me."

To which Nick said nothing.

He felt sick just thinking about it and what he'd already done.

Jake came home and found that his room had been searched. Thoroughly. Fuming, he went downstairs to find his uncle, who was in the garage doing something under the hood of his car.

"Find what you were looking for?" Jake growled.

"You know I didn't," his uncle said, standing up to face him.

Jake would have slugged him right there if he hadn't known he'd get his ass kicked. Still, it was tempting.

"So, are you satisfied that I'm not doing anything? Or is this the way it's going to be from now on?" Jake thought about what he'd said, then felt even worse, even more furious. "No, not from now on. Until you leave?"

"Jake—"

"Is this what it's going to be like? I just want to know. It's my life, after all."

"Tell me what really happened yesterday." His uncle tried.

"I did. And you didn't believe me. You still don't believe me, even though you searched my room and didn't find anything. So just…believe whatever you want. I don't care anymore."

And then he stalked off to his room and slammed the door behind him.

Lily worked like a fiend the next few days, lonelier than she'd ever been, heartsick really.

Damned, stubborn man.

Mr. I-Don't-Need-Anybody-and-I-Never-Will.

She ripped old carpet out of Brittany's room, pulling and tearing and generally making a huge mess, taking out at least some of her frustrations through her work. Brittany would not be happy, and neither would Ginny, because they'd be rooming together for a while, as Lily redid the wooden floors in their rooms and painted, maybe installed new light fixtures.

Basically ripping out everything she could, just for the satisfaction of it.

"Stupid man!" she muttered, kicking a rolled up strip of carpet downstairs, watching it land with a satisfying thud at the bottom, then heading back to the bedroom for more. "Stupid, stupid man!"

The next time she kicked a piece of carpet down the stairs, she almost hit Jake, who was standing in her living room.

"Was that aimed at me?" he asked.

"No. Sorry. I didn't know you were there."

"I knocked, but…I think you were yelling and didn't hear me," he said, looking really unsure of his welcome.

"I'm taking my frustrations out on carpet. Want to help?"

"Sure," he said, climbing over the mess she'd made and heading up the stairs.

Lily put him on the other end of the room gave him a hammer, to get up the strips of tacks holding the carpet in place, then thought of something. "Shouldn't you be in school right now?"

"Yeah," he admitted, shrugging like he didn't have a good explanation, just hoped she'd understand.

"Your uncle won't like this," she warned.

"So?"

Lily gave him a look that she hoped said his attitude was completely unproductive and didn't show how much she sympathized with him in having to deal with his stubborn uncle.

"Everybody makes mistakes, Jake. You can't just give up on him," she reasoned, because no matter what went on with her and Nick, Jake was his and Jake needed him.

"Why not? He gave up on me and you both."

So, he knew. Lily had worried that he did and wondered what he'd think of that. "Well, I haven't given up on either one of you," she claimed.

She was hurt. She was lonely, and she was good and mad, and maybe she was a fool, too, but she hadn't given up.

She still thought the man would come to his senses and realize he could have a life here, a really good life.

Whether it was the life he wanted… That was another story.

"Do you think he was really happy before? When it was just him and that job of his?" Lily asked, tugging with all her might on another piece of carpet.

"I don't know. I never really thought about it," Jake admitted.

"I mean, he kept doing it. Why would he keep doing it, if he didn't like it?"

"Because…he didn't know what else to do? Because he didn't know his life could be different, and that he could find another life that he liked better than the one he had."

A woman had to hope, didn't she?

He'd certainly seemed…content, at least, with her.

Of course, he could have just liked having someone next door for regular, no-strings sex and a home-cooked meal every now and then, while he was biding his time here with Jake for another couple of months.

Was he really like that?

Had Lily completely misread him?

She didn't think so.

But she was scared and sad and so lonely she ached.

"I thought this would have to be really boring compared to what he's always done," Jake said. "I mean, he's been all over the world. He used to send me and my brothers and my mother the coolest presents, and the postmarks were from some of the wildest places. I always thought he was the greatest."

Still, he could have been lonely, Lily told herself.

He could be sick of it all, if he'd just let himself admit it.

Was that too much to ask of the man?

"Grab that roll of carpet, and I'll take your scraps, and we'll load up my car and throw it away later," Lily said, and off they went downstairs and into the open garage.

"I'm sorry he was such a jerk to you," Jake said, stuffing the carpet into the back of her SUV while Lily held the back end open. "I'd beat him up for you, if I could, but—"

Lily laughed and gave him a quick hug when he was done. "My hero. That's sweet."

Jake blushed, rolled his eyes and then looked as lost and sad as Lily felt.

"I was thinking," Jake said. "Once my uncle's gone, that…

I might be able to stay here? I could help you out with the house, and I could stay with the girls if you needed to go out. I wouldn't be any trouble, I swear—"

"Oh, Jake," Lily said, ruffling his hair.

"No?" He looked panicked at that.

"No. I mean, I'm not saying no. I'm saying…it's complicated. Your parents named your uncle as your guardian, and you can't just pick someone else and move in with them. It doesn't work like that," she tried to explain.

"But he doesn't want me—"

"You don't know that. You just had a fight, that's all. Teenagers and their parents and their guardians fight. It happens. Surely you had fights with your mom and dad?"

"Yeah, but they would have never given up on me," he said, then got all choked up. "Of course, I didn't think they'd ever leave me, either."

"Oh, Jake." Lily wrapped her arms around him and held on while he sobbed.

Poor baby.

She looked up and saw Nick standing by the front door of his house, watching them, his expression looking as hard as something carved out of rock, like it might crack if he showed the least bit of emotion.

Damned, stubborn, stupid man!

"Jake, we will figure this out. I promise. And you are always going to have someone who loves you and will take care of you. That's the most important thing you have to know. You will never be all alone in this world."

But he sobbed like a kid who was facing just that.

Being absolutely all alone in the world.

Jake felt like such a baby, crying in front of Lily, asking if he could come live with her. *God!* Even worse was thinking she might have taken him in that way. He'd thought she really cared about him, that he could count on her, even if neither one of them could count on his uncle.

Stalking back toward the house, he thought if he had to one day, he could go to his brothers' at college. They'd put him up for a while. And then…he just didn't know.

His Aunt Joan's wouldn't kill him, he supposed. He could make her leave him alone, if he really tried. Or at least, push her away. He could be really good at that, it seemed.

Jake walked in the kitchen door, and there was his uncle, on the phone, saying, "I can't make him talk to you, Joan."

Because Jake had been avoiding her very successfully for the past few weeks. Disgusted with them all, Jake held out his hand for the phone.

"You don't have to," his uncle mouthed to him.

Jake grabbed the receiver and took it, liked how it pissed his uncle off, this newfound need to test him physically. Maybe he wasn't all that much stronger than Jake.

"Aunt Joan," he said, "how are you?"

And all the time he was talking to her, he was glaring at his uncle, knowing he couldn't make any kind of fuss about the way Jake had snatched the phone from his hand while he was talking to his aunt.

Jake listened to her for a few minutes, then finally escaped by saying he had homework to do.

He laid the phone down, intending to disappear into his room for hours, but his uncle stopped him by grabbing him by one arm and turning him around.

"Does everything have to be a battle now, Jake?" his uncle asked, right up in his face, seeming massive and just over-whelming.

He'd been an absolute bear ever since he'd broken off with Lily.

Jake shrugged, a little intimidated, but still mad. "Doesn't matter to me."

"Well, I really don't like it. Could we just stop? Couldn't

things go back to the way they were? We were doing okay, weren't we?"

"Back when I thought you trusted me. When I thought you were staying," Jake shot back at him.

"Hey, I'm right here," Nick said. "I haven't gone anywhere."

"You just walked away from Lily. You just turned your back and walked away. How could you do that to her? She's beautiful, and she's really special. I mean, I know I don't know a lot about women, but Lily…" To Jake, that said it all. That his uncle could leave Lily. Jake rolled his eyes and swore. "Do you really think there's anything out there in the world that could be better for you than her? Anyone who'd be better to you? I mean, you almost seemed human these last few weeks. And you almost seemed happy. But if you can't even stay here for her, there's no way you'll stay for me."

"Jake, we're talking about you and me. Not me and Lily—"

"We're talking about your life," Jake yelled back at him. "What do you do out there in the world that's so damned great? Are you always looking for something that's going to be better? Something more exciting, more dangerous, just something… I don't know. More? I mean, what do you think there is, waiting for you out there that you haven't already seen or tried or had?"

"You and me, Jake. Let's talk about you and me—"

"It's one thing not to want to be saddled with a teenager you never wanted, but you could have her. You could have a life here. Her girls are still little. They still need a father, and they're silly and they giggle a lot and they talk way too much. But they're fun to be around, and it's really easy to make them happy. They liked you a lot until you yelled at their mom that night we had a fight. You could have all of that, and you're just going to walk away. I'll never understand that, but honestly, I wish you'd just go ahead and do it. And we can get on with our lives without you."

"That's what you want?" Nick asked him. "You want me to go?"

"I never thought you'd stay," Jake admitted.

He'd hoped he was wrong, but deep down, he'd never really believed it.

He'd been waiting for this day to come.

Nick looked like somebody had kicked him in the gut, like he just hurt.

"We're not done," he called out as Jake stalked out of the room. "Jake!"

But Jake just kept on going.

He went to his room and slammed the door, emptied his backpack of all his school books, just dumping everything on the floor, and started stuffing some clothes into it. Another pair of jeans, a handful of T-shirts, some underwear, some socks.

He wasn't sure where he was going, but he was going.

He'd wait until it got dark, until his uncle went to bed, and then he'd go.

Jake had fallen asleep waiting for it to get dark when his phone woke him. He grabbed it and groggily said, "Hello."

"Jake? It's Andie."

He sat up, wondering if he was dreaming, hoping he wasn't. "Hi. What's up?"

"I'm really sorry about this," she said, and she was crying. Crying really hard. "I just didn't know who to else call."

"What's wrong?" he asked.

"I need help. I really need your help. Can you come and get me?"

Chapter Fifteen

Nick wasn't sure what woke him.

A sound, a feeling, instincts honed over the years.

Something wasn't right.

The clock read 2:43 a.m.

He waited, giving his eyes time to adjust to the dim light, then reached for the locked box he kept under the bed and keyed in the code to open it.

Gun in hand, he heard what sounded like a car door closing, then an engine.

His first thought was that Jake had snuck out and was now coming back home. Jesus, had he missed that, too?

Drinking and sneaking out?

Nick moved silently to the window, pushed open the blinds and saw a car driving away.

No? Saw his own car drive away?

That couldn't be right.

He took off downstairs, pulling on his jeans as he went, out the door and into the street, watching it go.

Somebody had stolen his car out of his own damned driveway?

Then he had an even worse thought.

Back inside, up the stairs, storming into Jake's room...

It was empty.

Drawers were open, clothes spilling out, the drawers seeming half-empty.

Jake had dumped his schoolbooks on the floor, but his backpack wasn't there.

Neither was Jake.

Minutes later, he'd locked the gun back up, had shoes and a shirt on, had grabbed his phone, tried Jake's cell three times and gotten no answer. He'd looked, but found that the set of keys he used daily was missing.

Then he was standing outside Lily's back door.

He knew Jake wasn't there. He'd watched his car go down the street, after all, but he still had to hope somehow Jake wasn't in it. That he'd gone to Lily's again.

That it could all be this simple.

He dialed her number, heard her soft, sleepy voice say, "Hello?"

"Lily, it's me. Jake's gone again."

"What?"

"Wake up for me, Lily. Jake ran away. He doesn't have a key to your house, does he?"

"No," she said, still sleepy. "He's not in the tree house?"

"I'm going to check. I didn't want to scare you by doing that and having you wake up and see someone in your backyard. Will you check your house? To make sure he didn't sneak in somehow?"

"Okay. Yeah. I will."

He thought again of Jake's accusations.

You just walked away from Lily. How could you do that to her?

Do you really think there's anything out there in the world that could be better for you than her?

And the worst: *I never thought you'd stay.*

Nick climbed up into the tree house.

Nothing.

Dammit!

He went back to Lily's and a moment later, she opened the back door.

Her hair was a tousled mess, and she wasn't wearing anything but a little cotton camisole and her pajama bottoms, and he had to look away, she looked so soft and good and inviting.

"He's not here," she said.

"Do you mind if I look anyway. Just in case?"

"No. Go ahead," she said, stepping back to let him in. "What happened? Did you two have another fight?"

"Yeah." He took off through the house, opening closet doors, checking all the dark corners, hoping against hope.

Lily followed him. "About what?"

"Me walking away from you and him," Nick said, disgusted with himself and the whole world right then.

And terrified.

The kid terrified him.

The idea of Jake getting hurt, doing something stupid, being all alone out there somewhere, left Nick terrified.

"I didn't say anything to him about us," Lily told him.

"I didn't think you did, but the kid's got eyes, Lily. And he really cares about you. He just knew."

They headed upstairs, checking the girls' rooms quietly and then even Lily's.

Nothing.

"What are you going to do now?" Lily asked.

"Wake up his friends and his friends' parents. Or maybe drive by their houses. I need to borrow your car. I'm pretty sure Jake took mine."

"What?"

"I woke up and heard someone pulling out of my driveway. I'm afraid it was Jake."

"Nick, you came to search my house, but you knew Jake took your car?"

He knew how ridiculous that was.

Yeah, he knew.

He'd done it anyway, had kept hoping however irrational it was that Jake would be here.

"I was pretty sure he was the one who took my car. I was hoping I was wrong," he admitted. "I mean…he doesn't even know how to drive. At least, I don't think he does. I didn't teach him. I don't know if anybody taught him. But I'm sorry I woke you up."

"It's all right. Don't worry about that."

"I'm sorry about everything, Lily. Honest to God, I am. I have no idea what I've been doing these last few months. I screwed it all up."

"Hey." She reached for him, pulling him close for a moment, all softness and understanding and a comfort he'd never understand that came in her arms. "You don't need to do that. Not right now. Just concentrate on finding Jake, and call me when you do, because I'm going to worry about him now. I doubt I'll be able to sleep, so I'll watch for him, in case he comes back home."

Nick dropped his head to her shoulder for a moment, trembling and completely unable to hide it, thinking he really didn't deserve this woman or her kindness or understanding, and yet here it was, and he needed it desperately.

He gave her a quick kiss, then backed away. "I have to go."

"Here. Keys." She grabbed them off a hook by the back door and handed them to him. "Go. I'll call you if he shows up here."

Lily couldn't go back to sleep, so she made a pot of hot tea and sat by the window, where she could see if Jake came home.

He didn't.

She finally called her sister at five forty-five—Marcy got up at that insane hour to do aerobics—and asked her to come over so Lily could help Nick look for Jake.

Marcy was there by six-thirty when an exhausted, worried Nick returned with no Jake in sight.

Lily made a pot of coffee for him, a ferociously strong brew that she knew he favored, and made him sit down and drink a cup.

Marcy was glaring at him—she'd guessed what had happened between them and was furious, even if Lily was only supposed to be enjoying herself with him—but fortunately Marcy kept her mouth shut that morning.

"You checked with all of his friends?" Lily asked.

"Everyone I know of. I pulled his last cell phone bill and woke up a lot of people. Called the twins. He hasn't had time to show up at their school yet, but they'll call if he does or if he calls them. I called a friend of a friend with the local police department and asked them to look out for the car. Called a friend of a friend at the FBI office in Richmond. He's not at any of the hospitals within fifty miles, and he hasn't been arrested." Nick sat here shaking his head. "I don't know what else to do. I find missing people for a living, and I can't even find my own nephew."

"What about his old house?" Lily tried. "That makes sense. If he was upset, wouldn't he go there?"

"One of the first places I checked. He wasn't there."

"How long ago?"

"A couple of hours, why?"

"Let's go back," Lily said. "It's his home. It's a place where he was happy, and he felt safe. I mean... Where do you go when you feel absolutely lost?"

Nick shot her a look she couldn't begin to decipher, like she'd torn something open deep inside of him. "For just about all of my adult life, I'd have gone there."

"Come on. I'll go with you. Marcy's going to stay here and get the girls off to school."

"Thank you," he told Marcy.

"You don't deserve it—"

"Marcy, not now!"

"But I like Jake," Marcy told him. "A lot. So go find him."

He drove fast, just shy of recklessness, incredibly focused and controlled. Lily sat beside him, her hand on his knee, not saying anything and trying not to make a sound as he got a little too close to a car or took a turn a little too fast.

"Sorry," he said, when he realized he was scaring her.

"I'm okay."

"Lily, I'm really glad you came with me. Marcy's right, I don't deserve it, but I'm glad you're here," he said without taking his eyes off the road.

"I love Jake. And I'm afraid I helped push him away. He asked me yesterday if he could come live with me and the girls, once you left, and...I didn't tell him no, but I didn't say yes, either. I tried to explain that it wasn't up to me and him. That you were his guardian, and if he wasn't with you... I should have just said yes. I didn't know he was this close to running away. I mean, he was upset, but I didn't think it was this bad. What happened?"

"Nothing. I can't come up with anything that I thought would lead to this. I can't believe I would have missed things so completely, but he's gone and he took some clothes with him, so I must have done something."

"We'll find him," she said, wishing she could make him believe it.

Nick shook his head, took a turn that had the tires screeching. "A lot of kids aren't ever found."

"And don't you do that. Don't start thinking of every bad thing that could happen. I know you know all of those things.

I know you've seen awful things, but you get the worst of it, Nick. You work on the absolute worst cases, so you have no perspective here. You have to know that."

"If he's not home by noon, we'll have an FBI team. I called in some favors," he told her.

"It's not going to come to that."

They swung past another car, missing its bumper by sheer force of will—Nick's—and Lily couldn't look anymore. She closed her eyes until the car finally stopped.

She expected to be in the driveway, but they were at a traffic light instead.

"You're not going to run it?" Because he had done that more than once already.

"Not this one," he said grimly. "It's the one where my sister and her husband died. Their house is right there, on that corner up on the hill."

Lily turned and looked.

The house was in one of those old neighborhoods of stately, soaring bricks with ivy crawling up the walls, entangling the house and seeming to anchor it to its surroundings even more strongly. Houses that looked like they'd been there forever and always would be. So solid, so strong, so sure.

Lily thought Jake must have felt perfectly secure there and everything about the boy he was now told her he'd been well-loved, too. It made her ache to think of him here and how happy he must have been, how much he'd lost.

"Jake's room is the first window on the corner on the second floor. He had a perfect view of that spot," Nick told her. "You can get here without going through that intersection, but everybody goes through it to town, to Jake's school, to his best friend's houses. And all of his friends are starting to drive now. Even if Jake never drove himself through that intersection, he'd get in a car with friends and they'd all go through it. He'd sit there and take it, rather than tell them how much he hated it."

"You did the right thing, to get him away from that," Lily said.

The light changed. Nick drove up the hill and pulled into the driveway.

Lily hoped to see his car there, but it wasn't.

Nick led her to the side entrance by the garage, and when he went to unlock the door, he stopped and looked at her. "It's not locked. It wasn't even pulled shut all the way."

"Is there an alarm?"

Nick nodded, stepped cautiously inside, keeping her behind him, and went to the alarm panel. "It hasn't been tampered with. It's just not set."

"So...he must have been here, right?"

"If he was, why would he leave the door unlocked and not set the alarm?" He kept Lily behind him and called out, "Jake?"

No answer.

He kept her behind him in the cool, dark house, going room-to-room downstairs, finding no sign of a break-in, but no sign of Jake, either, until they got to the family room.

"Feel that? It's warmer than the rest of the house." He went to the fireplace and stuck out a hand. "Gas logs. They're still on."

Lily saw a pile of afghans on the couch and a chair, throw pillows pulled into place like people had been sleeping there.

Did that mean Jake wasn't alone?

"If he had some kind of party here, I'll kill him myself for scaring us this way," Nick said, his voice absolutely calm for once.

"I'd help you," Lily agreed. "But if that's all it was, why not just tell you he's spending the night with a friend and have you drive him or have one of his friends come pick him up? Much less chance of getting caught that way. For him to steal your car in the middle of the night...something had to happen."

"I'm going to search the upstairs. I'll be right back."

Lily wandered around the downstairs, feeling like an intruder into these people's lives. Like Jake's parents should be walking in the door at any moment.

Because everything was still in place, like they might just walk back in.

So much loss, she thought. So much life, just gone.

Nick came back, obviously having found nothing. "I don't know what else to do."

She took his hand and tugged, leading him back to the family room where it was warmer. Nick sank down into a big, comfy chair next to the fire, looking like a man with the weight of the world on his shoulders.

Lily walked over to stand behind the chair he was sitting in, wanting to comfort him and not knowing what to do, what he'd allow or accept from her.

"It seems like this was such a happy place," she tried.

"It was," he agreed. "And I can't believe the family's just gone. I mean, the boys are still here, but everything's changed. You think those things should be forever, that someone should get forever and get it right and be happy and safe, and I always thought if anybody could have that, it was them. But if they don't even get that kind of happiness…it makes me think nobody ever really does."

Lily put her hand on his shoulder, wanting to do more.

He leaned his head against the back of the chair, and she leaned over the back of his chair and cupped her hand against one side of his face, her cheek against the other. His hand came up and tangled in her hair, holding her there, her tears falling from her face and onto his.

"You should have had this, too," he said. "This kind of happiness…it should have been yours, Lily."

"But not yours?" she asked, her face buried against his shoulder, as he turned his head and kissed her softly on the cheek.

"No. I just never saw that for me. I never believed it could really happen."

"And now you think you were right? That this proves you right?"

"Come here," he said, drawing her around the side of the chair and pulling her onto his lap, wrapping his arms around her and taking a long, shuddering breath.

Lily fought against it, because she had a point to make and intended to make it. "It doesn't prove you were right. Not at all."

"Fine. Tell me everything I'm wrong about, just let me hold you while you do it."

She sank against him, because that's what she really wanted anyway, and because she was cold and tired and so scared, and he was… She sighed, pressing her face to his chest, draped over him like a blanket, thinking this was where she should have been all night, this close to him, facing this together. That they could have gone through this with each other, trusting, knowing, drawing strength from each other.

This was the way life was supposed to be, having someone beside you when things got really rough.

Which was much more than she could try to tell him right now, not when they still didn't know where Jake was.

"You're going to find Jake," she said. "And he's going to be fine, and he's still going to need a home. He wants that home to be with you."

"Not anymore."

"No. This is just a blip. This is regular teenage stuff. You wait. He'll have some explanation that will drive you crazy, but you'll be so relieved that he's home and safe that you won't know whether to yell at him or just collapse right where you are and try to breathe for the first time in hours. And he'll say something and give you one of those goofy grins of his, and you'll think, He's just a kid. A big, overgrown boy who doesn't have half the sense he needs yet to survive in the world, but he's great, and he's yours. He's a great kid."

He sighed. "Lily, this great kid asked if he could come live with you instead of me, not twelve hours ago."

"The only reason he wanted me was because he was afraid

he didn't have you anymore. But he does, and you're going to tell him that as soon as we find him. Now think. Where else can we look? Who can we call? Someone has to know something."

He put his hand in her hair and nuzzled his face against hers and started running through a list of people he'd already called when Lily's phone rang in the distance.

"It's mine." She was praying it was Jake, but it turned out to be Marcy.

"Any news?" Marcy asked.

"No." Lily wanted to scream. She'd thought this was it, that they'd found him.

"Well, I don't know if this has anything to do with Jake, but you've had three phone calls this morning from neighbors asking if you've heard the latest about Audrey Graham. Something about her getting into a fight last night at a party with another woman from the neighborhood for sleeping with the woman's husband. I wouldn't have mentioned it, but someone said her poor daughter saw the whole thing, and didn't you tell me Jake had a thing for Audrey's daughter?"

"Yes, he does," Lily said.

Could Jake be caught up in something with Andie Graham? Lily turned to Nick. "Did you try to call Andie Graham last night?"

"Yeah. No answer. I even drove by the house. It didn't look like anyone was home. Why?"

Lily shook her head. "Something about Audrey getting in a fight at a party last night and sleeping with one of our married neighbors. Just…wait a minute. Marcy? Which party? The fund-raiser for the heart association?"

"Yes, that was it. Phoenix Rising? Something like that?"

"The Phoenix Club. Okay. Thanks. We'll check it out." She clicked off the phone, then turned to Nick. "Andie's mother went to the heart association ball last night and got into a fight with a woman whose husband Audrey was apparently sleeping with, and it was this big, huge scene, and Andie was there to see it. Do you think, if Andie had a problem, she might call Jake for help?"

"I don't know. He's only fifteen. Why would she call him? Someone who'd have to steal a car to go pick her up?"

"Maybe she didn't know he'd have to steal it. Or that he wasn't licensed to drive it. I don't know. It's something, and it's better than thinking he ran away."

"You know where they live?"

"Yes. Let's go."

They headed out the door and found a police car pulling into the driveway behind them.

Lily felt all the breath go out of her at his stern expression, felt Nick tense beside her as they stopped where they were.

The officer got out of his patrol car, walked up to them and asked, "Everything all right here, folks?"

Nick explained who he was, even pulled out his FBI shield. He told the officer what they were doing, then explained that he was the one who'd asked the local police to keep an eye on the house that morning. "That is why you're here, isn't it?"

"No. Actually, I was following up on a 911 call."

Lily gasped, grabbed for Nick, finding his arm. It was rigid.

"What 911 call?" he asked.

"Possible alcohol poisoning, someone having trouble breathing, maybe needing an ambulance. The operator was trying to get all the information she needed, but the connection wasn't good and before she could get it straight, the caller said not to bother with the ambulance, that they'd transport the victim themselves. We try to follow up on those calls, to make sure we don't have someone in trouble who can't call for help."

"When did the call come in?" Nick asked.

"About forty minutes ago. I would have been here sooner, but I got redirected on a burglary call five blocks away. So, no one's in the house?"

"No," Nick said. "Who made the call?"

The officer flipped through his notes. "Didn't give a name, but it was a female. Gave her phone number as 555-6685. You think the call was about your nephew?"

Nick nodded. "We think he was here. What hospital were they taken to?"

"Get in. We'll use my siren," the officer offered. "I don't think you need to be driving right now."

They sat in the back, side-by-side, his hand clamped down on hers, not saying anything until they came upon a traffic accident being cleared from the road beside them, a familiar-looking black sedan with its side resting against a telephone pole.

Nick went absolutely white. "I think that's my car."

The officer met their eyes in the mirror, reaching for his radio. "Hang on." He asked for information on the accident they'd just passed and relayed it to them. "Black Ford registered to...Nicholas Malone, D.C. plates."

Nick nodded.

The officer went back to the radio to get the condition of the passengers. "The kids seemed good," the officer said. "Conscious, oriented to time and place. The woman was really out of it, though."

"Woman?" Lily asked.

"You have names?" the officer spoke into his radio. "Jacob Elliott, Andie Graham and Audrey Graham."

"Okay. That's them. Thank you," Lily said, squeezing Nick's arm. "We found them."

Chapter Sixteen

Nick had made this ride before, as the agent who helped find the missing.

And by the time he took parents to their missing child, he almost always had some details on the child's condition to relay to the parents. But no matter how reassuring the information was, the parents never really relaxed until they had that child in their arms.

Nick understood that exactly at the moment.

He wouldn't believe Jake was safe until he could see Jake with his own two eyes. He knew he was on his way to Jake and that Lily was beside him, keeping him sane, but nothing else really registered for him. It was like someone had blocked out the world.

He needed this kid like he needed air to breathe, and he needed the woman beside him to stay beside him, to hang on to him, to believe in him, to forgive him, to trust him and more than anything to love him.

"Breathe," Lily told him, hanging on tight.

And maybe to tell him to breathe, too.

The world moved in a surreal kind of drunken fast-forward then, confusing, noisy, crowded. He couldn't make sense of it, but then he was walking down a corridor, and then into a room with cubicles curtained off into tiny spaces for each patient, and then, there was Jake.

Lying on a bed, blood and a nasty looking bump on his forehead, bruised cheek, split lip, looking like he had no idea what kind of reception he was about to receive.

"I kind of messed up your car," he said.

Lily started crying.

Nick just grabbed him and hung on tight.

"So, this was all about a girl?" Nick asked incredulously, finally able to get some answers once the doctor had retrieved the CAT scan results and confirmed that Jake's head injury wasn't serious.

"Not just a girl. Andie," Jake claimed, as if that made all the difference.

Nick turned to Lily, who was still by his side, his eyes pleading, *Help me here.*

Lily fought a grin, knowing how horrifying the night had been. "Jake, what happened with Andie?"

"We've kind of…gotten to be friends. And I like her. A lot. You know?"

"I got that part," Nick told him.

"Well, she's been having trouble, and I've been trying to help her." He looked right at Nick. "You said a man watches out for a woman—"

"You are not a man. You are fifteen—"

"You said we'd watch out for Lily. That we weren't going to stand by and let anybody mess with her—"

"Okay. Yes, I did. Go on," Nick said, thinking a vow of silence might be necessary at the moment.

"Well, that's it, really. I was just trying to help her. Some stuff happened. Some really hard stuff—"

"With her mom?" Lily tried.

Jake clammed up. "I promised her I wouldn't tell."

"Okay." Vow of silence was done. "You're in the hospital. You sneaked out of the house in the middle of the night, stole my car, drove it without a license and wrecked it, with two other people in the car. We're beyond any kind of I-promised-I-wouldn't-tell crap. Spill it."

Lily put her hand over his. He could almost feel her telling him to breathe.

"Jake," she said. "This morning I got three phone calls asking me if I'd heard about Andie's mom getting into a scene at a party last night with Phillip Wrenchler's wife, because Audrey's been having an affair with the woman's husband. So if that's part of the secret you're keeping for Andie, it's out."

"Oh," he said.

"Now," Nick ordered once again, though why, he didn't know. The kid didn't follow orders.

"It's not just this Phillip guy," he finally admitted. "Since Andie's parents' divorce became final a few months ago, Andie's mom started drinking. A lot. And sometimes she disappears, and Andie doesn't know where to find her, and she gets scared. I mean, it's pretty scary when someone you love just disappears."

"Yeah, we got that part," Nick said rolling his eyes.

Jake clearly didn't make the connection.

"Go on."

"So, Andie kept showing up at our house, saying she was looking for her mom, and I knew her mom wasn't seeing you. At least, I didn't think she was. I thought you and Lily were... I mean, I was pretty sure you and Lily were—"

"Yeah, me and Lily. Go on."

"Turns out, Andie's mom was seeing a guy who lives in the

house right behind us. She'd walk down our street and then cut through our backyard, so his neighbors wouldn't see. She got confused one day.... Okay, she got really drunk one day on her way to see him and walked into our house instead, looking for the guy. Next thing I knew, she'd poured herself a drink and when I tried to get it away from her, I spilled it all over the kitchen."

Nick turned around and swore at the pale green curtain, rather than Jake, then faced the kid again. "You mean, that whole mess between us was because of Andie's mom? You couldn't just tell me it was Andie's mom?"

"Andie was so embarrassed. I had to call her to come and get her mom, and her mom was like...flirting with me in front of her own daughter and stuff...." Poor Jake turned red, just telling them about it.

Nick still couldn't believe it.

All this worry and upheaval and outright terror?

Over a girl?

"Go on," he said.

"Well, that was it, really. Andie and I just talk sometimes. None of her other friends know how bad it is. But since her father moved out, her mother's been drinking, staying out all night, chasing after men. Andie didn't want people to know, but I'm like a stranger, practically, and we don't hang out with the same people at all. I promised I wouldn't tell anybody what was going on. So she talks to me, and she's just so...awesome."

He was beaming by the end.

The kid probably couldn't even breathe around her, much less think.

Nick turned back to Lily, pleading with a look.

"She's a beautiful girl, Jake," Lily told him. "And I'm glad she had you to help her. But this is really the kind of problems two teenagers can't solve. You could have told us. We'd have tried to help her."

"She didn't want anybody to know," he said again, sounding

so sincere, like that made perfect sense. That he'd do the same thing all over again.

It was all Nick could do not to scream. He was still scared half to death. His heart rate hadn't yet settled down, and his muscles had turned to mush. It was a miracle he was still standing.

He made a face and leaned his head back to stare at the ceiling, like there might be answers for him somewhere up there.

Lily squeezed his hand once again, urging him to hang on.

"Tell us what happened last night, Jake?" she asked.

"Andie called. Her mom was at that stupid party, and she got really drunk and then she got into a fight with Phillip's wife. Andie went to try to get her mom out of there, but then her mom couldn't remember where she parked her car or find her keys. Andie was crying and said she just had to get them both out of there. So she asked me to come and get them."

"And you didn't think to mention to her that you don't drive?"

"I can drive," he claimed.

"Not legally," Nick yelled.

Jake winced, looked hurt and sad and very young.

"Okay, fine. I'm sorry," Nick said. "I'm just still a little bit... God, Jake, were you trying to scare me to death?"

"We thought you'd run away," Lily told him in her softest, most soothing, understanding, motherly voice.

"I wouldn't do that," he claimed, like it wasn't even a possibility.

"You packed a bag of clothes," Nick reminded him.

"Oh, yeah."

Oh, yeah! Nick groaned.

"Okay, I was thinking about it, and I threw some clothes in my backpack, but I wouldn't have really done it," Jake claimed.

"Well, we didn't know that," Nick practically roared. "And when you took off in the middle of the night without saying anything and wouldn't answer your phone—"

"Jake, he heard you leave the house eight hours ago. We've been looking for you ever since, imagining all kinds of awful things."

"Oh. Well, all I did was go pick them up and take them to our old house for a while, to hide," Jake said. "Andie's mom was still a mess, and Andie just wanted to hide from everybody to think about what to do next. And I knew you'd be mad, but I was mad, too, that you didn't trust me about anything. And I couldn't figure out what to say to you, so...I just didn't pick up the phone. That's all."

"That's all?" Nick said, nodding and trying to breathe. "And the 911 call? Because we heard about that, too."

"When Andie and I woke up this morning, she went to try to wake up her mom, but she couldn't. It was like she was barely breathing, and then we got scared and called 911. But they said it was going to be about ten minutes before the ambulance could get there, and we didn't think we could wait that long. So I was going to drive her to the hospital."

"Because you didn't wreck the first time you drove them that night. So why not do it again?" Nick said, admittedly a little too heavy on the sarcasm. He closed his eyes, so he couldn't glare at Jake. "Then what?"

"I'm not really sure. One minute, we were fine, and then I kind of hit the curb and tried to get back in my lane. But I guess I went too far back the other way, and we slid into the telephone poll. Am I in a lot of trouble for that?"

Nick's eyes popped open and he just stared at the kid, dumbfounded.

Am I in a lot of trouble for that?

"Lily," he said again.

She leaned over and gave Jake a big hug, making him look even more like a silly, little kid in serious need of mothering and fathering. "We were just so worried about you."

She soothed him, which Nick supposed the kid needed, while he thought, *Do kids just have no sense at fifteen?*

Could it even be possible, that their reasoning and judgment could be so lacking at this age?

He knew Jake wasn't stupid. He'd seen the kid's report card. Which just meant...

Fifteen?

Could it be this bad? This scary for a parent?

Then he thought about Joan.

Joan would love it when she heard about this. This was the kind of ammunition she'd been waiting for to use against Nick and his guardianship of Jake. She'd be thrilled.

"Excuse me?" a girl's voice asked.

Nick turned, and there she was, Jake's most wondrous girl in the world. Andie Graham, in all her adolescent, leggy, blond glory, plus a few bumps and bruises, but otherwise whole.

Nick wanted to beg her to never come near Jake again, and to explain to Jake just how dangerous women could be.

Look how much trouble this one had caused them both already.

"I just wanted to make sure Jake was okay," she said.

Jake practically glowed with happiness from his hospital gurney, might have even winced a bit as he grinned, whether as a complete play for sympathy or because his head hurt, Nick had no idea.

"I'm fine," Jake said. "Are you okay?"

She nodded, then waited there on the edge of Jake's little space.

"How's your mom, Andie?" Lily asked.

Andie bit her lip for a moment, looking embarrassed, then said, "The doctors say she'll be fine."

"Good." Lily leaned over and gave Jake a hug. "We'll be outside for a few minutes."

Nick didn't intend to go anywhere. He didn't trust this girl alone with Jake for a moment, but Lily took him by the hand

and led him out of the room. They went down the corridor and around the corner until they'd found a relatively quiet spot.

"You think that was a good idea? Leaving him alone with her?"

Lily laughed. "What are you going to do? Lock him in his room for the next six years until he's twenty-one?"

"Can I do that, as his legal guardian? Because it doesn't sound like a bad idea."

Lily laughed some more and wrapped her arms around him and just held on tight. Nick couldn't get her close enough. He sagged against the wall at his back, and then it was like Lily and the wall were all that kept him on his feet.

Relief washed over him like he'd never felt before, leaving him weak and exhausted and still terrified somehow.

"Oh, my God, Lily!" he said, his face buried in her hair. "He wrapped the car around a telephone pole, swerved all over the road. I don't know how all those other cars missed him. He could have killed that girl and her mother while he was trying to save them. He could have killed himself—"

"I know. But he didn't. And he's fine—"

"And stupid! How can he be this stupid? A few surging hormones and adolescent dreams, a pair of long legs on a pretty girl, and he just turns stupid? Is that the way it works?"

"You never did anything stupid over a girl?" she asked.

"Not like..." He couldn't say that, because it wasn't true.

Nick took a breath and then another one, just couldn't seem to get enough air in his body to make his head stop spinning. Then he looked down at her, trying to make it sink in. That the night was over, and Jake was safe, and they'd all lived through it, somehow, and Lily was here by his side.

"I was going to say I never had," he told her, a hand tangling in her hair. "But I had my own pretty, long-legged blonde, and I thought I could just walk away from her somehow."

She gave him a pretty smile through her tears.

"Tell me you knew all along how stupid that was of me, to think I could really walk away from you. Because I'd hate to think you believed I could and that I'd hurt you that much, Lily."

"I was hoping you couldn't."

"You were right," he told her. "Are you going to forgive me? For ever thinking I could live without you?"

"I don't know," she said, still smiling, a twinkle in her pretty blue eyes. "I mean, how do we know you've really learned your lesson?"

"I cannot raise this kid without you," he said. "I don't want to. I don't want to do anything without you, Lily."

She gave him a kiss, then another.

He pulled back, taking her face in both his hands, all teasing aside. "I think I knew all along, right from the first moment I saw you. I knew you'd be trouble, and I should stay away—"

"Me? Trouble?" She feigned outrage.

He nodded. "But I just couldn't resist. Especially after you helped me get rid of Audrey that day in your kitchen. I could not stop thinking about you. And your neck."

"You're the one who caused all the trouble—"

He laughed, kissed her again. "But when I really knew there was no going back, was when you wanted to go to Jake's house, to look for him again, and you asked me where I would go when I was really scared and sad and feeling all alone in the world. And I realize, the answer is easy for me now. I'd go to you."

She took a breath, started to cry then.

"And everything would start to get better, because you'd be by my side. I need you to always be by my side, Lily. I love you, you know? And I've never said that to another woman in my life, and I promise you, I never will."

"I love you, too," she said, kissing him quickly, urgently, her tears falling fast.

"You can have as much time as you need to be sure and for your girls to get used to me and the idea of us being together, but I want you to promise me now that you'll marry me."

"I will," she promised.

"Just think, we'll actually get to sleep in the same bed all night," he said.

"If you let me sleep." She grinned. "And you have to let me work sometimes, Nick. We have to get some work done."

"We will. Although, afternoons in bed... You have to admit, it's a really nice way to live, as often as we can get away with it."

"You should be warned," she told him. "I've heard teenage girls are so much scarier to raise than teenage boys."

He groaned. "You're kidding."

Lily shook her head. "Too late to back out now."

Lily woke the next morning stretched out on her side, the front of her body chilled, the back all toasty and warm.

Leaning back into that luxurious heat, she felt it give beneath her weight, until she rolled over and found Nick propped up on his side, bare everywhere she could see and most likely where she could not, judging by the feel of his strong, solid length pressed to hers.

He leaned over and kissed her softly, then brushed her hair back from her face, giving her a beautiful smile.

"It's about time I got to wake up with you," he said. "And have you in my bed. I've wanted that for a long time."

Lily smiled back at him, the crazy, scary night they'd spent searching frantically for Jake and the exhaustion of the next day finally over. Marcy had offered to take the girls for the night, and the hospital had kept Jake overnight. Jake, who'd looked highly insulted at the idea that Nick hadn't wanted to leave him alone so soon after fearing Jake had been lost to him for good.

So Nick had brought Lily back to his house, too worn-out

to do anything that night but refuse to part with her. They'd climbed into his bed and slept like the dead, for how many hours she didn't know.

He'd stroked and kissed her awake at some point deep in the night, made love to her urgently, fiercely at first, and then hauled her into his arms and held on to her like she was his only hope of surviving until morning.

That was the last thing she remembered.

Him holding her so tight she could barely breathe, trembling again, her trying to reassure this big, strong, brave man, loving him so much her heart ached with it.

He touched his thumb to her bottom lip, brushing across it, then kissed her again, sweetly, quickly.

"We found Jake," he said, as if he needed to hear it once again.

"Yes, we did."

"And he's safe."

Lily nodded.

His gaze went dark and smoky and serious. "And you've forgiven me for being such an idiot as to think I could ever live without you. As if I'd ever want to."

"Yes," she whispered.

"And you love me?"

"I do. I love you," she promised, reaching up to pull his head down to hers so she could kiss him.

By the time they were done, he'd settled himself on top of her, nudging her thighs apart, his weight on his elbows, back bowed, sliding ever so easily inside her body, still soft and yielding from the last time he'd made love to her, sometime in the night.

She gasped, then gave herself up to what he wanted, needing that connection to him in every way possible, the feelings so intense, still so new. So much had changed so quickly. It was hard to believe any of it was real.

He closed his eyes and groaned, leaning his head down until his forehead touched hers, then started rocking back and forth just a bit, the sensations all the more intense for the slowness with which he moved, the deliberateness, the concentration.

Nick.

She arched into him, trying to make him move faster, harder, deeper.

He kissed the side of her neck, whispered, "Say you're going to marry me. Say it for me now."

As if she'd ever denied him anything.

Lily was trembling. It was as if he'd brought every nerve ending in her body to alert in seconds.

That was what he did to her heart and what he did to her body, and together they were almost too much for any woman to bear. So much more than she'd ever found in any man. A connection she hadn't even known she was missing.

Until she met him.

"Say it," he whispered.

But the words were a pure demand.

"Yes." She gave in. "I will. I'll marry you."

And then the passion he'd held in check, simmering in those exquisitely slow movements of his hips, burst open, in him and in her. She held on tight, felt him surging inside of her, and moments later collapsing in her arms.

When he finally lifted his head and slid to one side to take the bulk of his weight off of her, he looked as vulnerable as she'd ever seen him.

"Tell me you'll never scare me the way Jake did two nights ago. That we can love each other and live together and raise our children together without that kind of terror."

"Oh, Nick. I can't tell you that. No one could."

He nodded, little lines of tension still in his face, put there by the night they'd spent looking for Jake. "I was afraid you'd say that."

"But I can promise that no matter what, I'll be right here beside you, helping you through it."

He kissed her gently, reverently. "I've never had anything in my life that I couldn't stand to lose before. And now…there's just so much. So much I couldn't live without. I love you, Lily. I want to wake up every morning just like this, with you beside me. I want to hold you in my arms every night. I want to give you everything you've ever wanted."

"There's nothing left for you to give," she told him. "Nothing else I need. I've got it all right here, right now."

* * * * *

MILLS & BOON®
By Request

RELIVE THE ROMANCE WITH THE BEST OF THE BEST

A sneak peek at next month's titles...

In stores from 13th July 2017:

- **The Billionaire's Conquest** – Elizabeth Bevarly, Olivia Gates & Emilie Rose

- **One Tiny Miracle** – Stella Bagwell, Jennifer Greene & Ami Weaver

In stores from 27th July 2017:

- **The Bad Boy's Redemption** – Joss Wood, Marie Donovan & Tina Beckett

- **Chasing Summer** – Helen Lacey, Christine Rimmer & Abigail Gordon

Just can't wait?
Buy our books online before they hit the shops!
www.millsandboon.co.uk

Also available as eBooks.

17/05

MILLS & BOON®

Why shop at millsandboon.co.uk?

Each year, thousands of romance readers
find their perfect read at millsandboon.co.uk.
That's because we're passionate about
bringing you the very best romantic fiction.
Here are some of the advantages of
shopping at www.millsandboon.co.uk:

* **Get new books first**—you'll be able to buy
  your favourite books one month before they
  hit the shops

* **Get exclusive discounts**—you'll also be
  able to buy our specially created monthly
  collections, with up to 50% off the RRP

* **Find your favourite authors**—latest news,
  interviews and new releases for all your
  favourite authors and series on our website,
  plus ideas for what to try next

* **Join in**—once you've bought your favourite
  books, don't forget to register with us to rate,
  review and join in the discussions

Visit **www.millsandboon.co.uk**
for all this and more today!